MW00778498

CLASSROOM
OF THE ELITE YEAR 2

NOVEL 5

The first things that caught my eye were the unexpectedly vibrant colors.

"This is…"

"Welcome to Maid Café Maimai!"

Three girls greeted us in unison, each of them dressed in unique costumes.

"*Why... Why... Why... Why?!*"

Kushida came up next to me and grabbed me by the collar, glaring at me intensely. She was furious, but I simply proceeded to talk to her in a matter-of-fact manner.

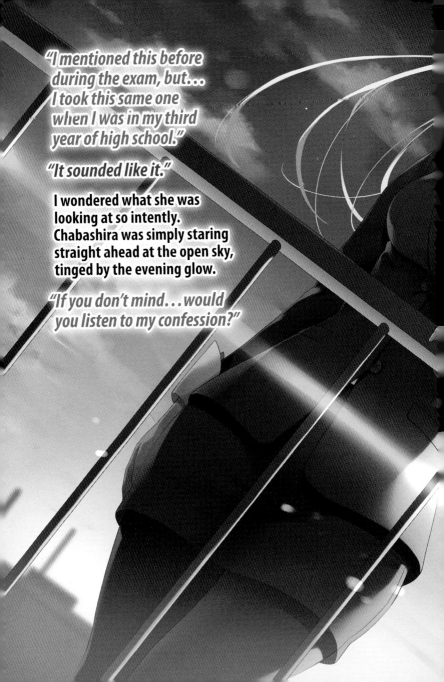

"I mentioned this before during the exam, but... I took this same one when I was in my third year of high school."

"It sounded like it."

I wondered what she was looking at so intently. Chabashira was simply staring straight ahead at the open sky, tinged by the evening glow.

"If you don't mind... would you listen to my confession?"

5

WELCOME TO THE CLASSROOM OF THE ELITE YEAR 2

CLASSROOM OF THE ELITE YEAR 2

NOVEL 5

STORY BY

Syougo Kinugasa

ART BY

Tomoseshunsaku

Airship

Seven Seas Entertainment

YOUKOSO JITSURYOKUSHIJOUSHUGI NO KYOUSHITSU E 2NENSEIHEN
VOL.5
©Syougo Kinugasa 2021
First published in Japan in 2021 by KADOKAWA CORPORATION, Tokyo.
English translation rights arranged with KADOKAWA CORPORATION, Tokyo.

Seven Seas press and purchase enquiries can be sent to
Marketing Manager Lianne Sentar at press@gomanga.com.
Information regarding the distribution and purchase of
digital editions is available from Digital Manager CK Russell
at digital@gomanga.com.

Seven Seas and the Seven Seas logo are trademarks of
Seven Seas Entertainment. All rights reserved.

Follow Seven Seas Entertainment online at
sevenseasentertainment.com.

TRANSLATION: Timothy MacKenzie
ADAPTATION: Harry Catlin
COVER DESIGN: Nicky Lim
INTERIOR LAYOUT & DESIGN: Clay Gardner
COPY EDITOR: Meg van Huygen
PROOFREADER: Stephanie Cohen
LIGHT NOVEL EDITOR: T. Burke
PREPRESS TECHNICIAN: Melanie Ujimori, Jules Valera
PRODUCTION MANAGER: Lissa Pattillo
EDITOR-IN-CHIEF: Julie Davis
ASSOCIATE PUBLISHER: Adam Arnold
PUBLISHER: Jason DeAngelis

ISBN: 978-1-68579-653-2
Printed in Canada
First Printing: July 2023
10 9 8 7 6 5 4 3 2 1

CLASSROOM OF THE ELITE YEAR 2 ⑤

CONTENTS

1 CHABASHIRA SAE'S SOLILOQUY

SINCE I'VE BECOME a teacher, I— ...Well, actually, no, since *before* I became a teacher, I've carried this distressing anguish that I cannot share with anyone. A recurring nightmare. The events of a day that I can never, ever forget are repeated in my dreams. The nightmare unfolds in a different way every time. Sometimes I see it from my own point of view, and sometimes it's from someone else's. At times, the words said and the course of events differ. But there's one thing that each iteration has in common, one thing which always stays the same.

No matter how many times I have this nightmare, the conclusion is always the same.

At that time, there was nothing that those of us in Class B feared. Our momentum overwhelmed the other classes, and we'd gotten so close to Class A that they were within our reach, if we just gave a little push. Of course, it wasn't like getting there had been smooth sailing the whole way. By the time we became third-year students, six of our classmates were gone.

Nevertheless, no one had been expelled that year by that point in our third year, and we were steadily accumulating Class Points. I believed that we could graduate from Class A without losing anyone else. Until that day, that is. Until that very moment.

The end of the third semester. The time when our graduation examinations, our last chance to turn things around, were approaching. Our homeroom instructor appeared before us with a grim expression and told us about a new special exam. At first, we felt like there was nothing to fear whatsoever about it. The rules were plain and simple, and we had no doubt that we'd be able to pass without any difficulties. Looking straight ahead, we sincerely believed that.

We were in such high spirits until we were presented with a certain issue.

Then, the scene changes in the dream, and I'm screaming in class. Chie, my best friend, rushes toward me with an angry look on her face. She grabs me by the collar. Total pandemonium. Our class, which had been united, falls apart in an instant.

"It's fine," he mutters in resignation, a look of understanding on his face. But I can't decide. There was no way I could've been prepared for this. He had been with me through three years of joys and sorrows, and his presence was by no means insignificant to me. An irreplaceable classmate, an irreplaceable friend.

An irreplaceable...special someone, of the opposite sex. He could get a little carried away too easily, but he was honest, kind, and more dependable than anyone else. He showed me an expression that he had never shown me before. That time when he reached out his hand to me under the evening sky, somewhat shyly. I said just one thing to him as I held back the tears that were about to start spilling.

"Thank you..."

Our relationship's beginning and end came at the exact same time.

CLASSROOM OF
THE ELITE

2 SIGNS OF AN APPROACHING STORM

NOW THAT OUR SUMMER BREAK had passed, the second semester of our second year was beginning today. Looking at it more broadly, this meant that our three years spent at this school would soon be over. I fastened my tie and slipped my arms through the sleeves of my shirt. While checking myself out in the mirror, I made sure that my hair was all right and that there weren't any issues with my appearance. After confirming everything was fine, I headed toward the front entrance of the dormitory. On the way, I was joined by Sudou. He let out a loud yawn, and then we exchanged pleasantries as we walked along side by side, heading outdoors.

"Suzune threatened me with the chance that they might hit us with a written exam early in the second semester, so I pulled an all-nighter," he groaned. "An all-nighter, man."

"So you were studying even on the final day of summer vacation, huh?"

"Thankfully, she came up with a curriculum for me that'll keep me pretty busy for a while yet. But man, I'd like to get my Academic Ability rating in OAA up to at least a B though."

Getting to a B or better in Academic Ability would be a big jump, but I didn't think Sudou was just talking big. After all, if he studied hard over the summer vacation, it wouldn't be surprising if he managed to improve his Academic Ability even further than he already had. Sudou had become a genuinely well-rounded man, being an athlete and a scholar. He also had a dramatic decrease in things like tardiness, absences, and other such minor behavioral issues. He still had a bit of a temper that could flare up if the situation called for it, but I supposed that was one of Sudou's defining characteristics.

"Hey, I got a kinda weird question to ask you," he said. "You think that, like, Kanji's kissed Shinohara and stuff yet?"

"Huh?" I blinked.

"I mean, I'm happy for 'im, that he's got himself a girl-friend. But the fact he's ahead of me is pretty frustratin'. I dunno, it's just been botherin' me a bunch lately."

"Wouldn't it be better to just ask him that directly?" I said. "Knowing Ike, I have a feeling he'd tell you if you did."

"Like hell I can ask him that... If he says somethin' like they ain't even held hands yet, or I hear that he's actually gone further than that, like, you-know-what, then... Well, my fists might start doin' the talkin' for the first time in a long time," explained Sudou.

I see. That would be a slight problem. It definitely would be troubling if he started communicating with his fists.

"Considering Ike's personality, I get the feeling that he'd probably go around telling everyone indiscriminately if he was happy about something. So, if we're not hearing anything from him, that likely means things haven't developed too far, right?" I reasoned.

"That's true, you got a point there. But maybe it's different when it comes to love. I haven't experienced it, so I dunno," he sighed. "Hey, Ayanokouji, have you ever had a girlfriend...? What's it like?"

The conversation's topic unexpectedly shifted from Ike to me. I couldn't help but feel Sudou's passionate (I certainly believed it) gaze fixated on me, as if he were asking me, *"Come on, what's it like?"*

"There's no use lying to you, so I'll tell you. I got together with my first girlfriend a little while ago," I told him.

"...Seriously? Like, seriously, for real?"

I could have misled him into thinking otherwise, but since Kei was going to start telling people before long anyway, it wouldn't have been a good idea to even try. After I gave him an honest answer though, Sudou held his head in his hands and let out a sigh. Immediately afterward, he reached over and hurriedly clasped onto both of my shoulders.

"W-w-w-w-w-w-wait a sec, don't tell me it's...?!" he wailed.

"Relax. It's not who you're thinking."

"Seriously?! You mean it really ain't Suzune?"

"Right. It's not her," I replied.

"O-oh, okay. Well, that's good..." Sudou let out a sigh. "Heh, for a minute there, I thought my heart was gonna stop or somethin'..."

He must have broken out in a sweat because he brought his left hand up to his forehead and clumsily wiped it away with his palm. Then, he showed me his damp palm, as if to illustrate just how flustered he was.

"Well, who is it then?" he asked.

"That's—" I began, but I was interrupted.

"Ah! Found you!"

Just as Sudou regained his composure, the sound of running footsteps came from behind us. And when the hurried person caught up with us and matched pace, she looked up at me with a slightly angry expression on her face.

"I was thinking we should go to school together, but you didn't tell me that you weren't in your room!" grumbled Kei. She puffed out her cheeks in dissatisfaction.

"You never told me anything about us going together though," I replied.

"That's... Well, I was feeling nervous about it until the very last minute, so I hesitated, and..." Kei trailed off.

Sudou eyed us suspiciously as Kei and I had this odd back-and-forth conversation out of nowhere.

"Hey, what the heck didja just come and interrupt us for, Karuizawa?" complained Sudou. "We were having an important bro conversation, don't butt in."

Apparently, Sudou hadn't noticed anything strange about the conversation I was having with Kei. He didn't seem to have put two and two together just from her showing up here. Come to think of it, Kei and Sudou had barely ever interacted with one another before at all. As for the question of whether they got along or didn't... Well, all I could say was that they didn't have a particularly good relationship.

"Are you planning on telling people about us today, Kei?" I asked.

"Huh? Y-yeah, I am," she said. "But picking the right

time's a little tough... I mean, making an announcement as soon as we get to school in the morning kind of feels wrong, you know...? It's difficult to just announce it. I mean, it's not the same as just going up to someone and being like, 'Hey, listen to this!' or something."

"It seemed like you were pretty quick to make an announcement back with Yousuke, though," I pointed out.

"W-well, yeah, I suppose. But the circumstances now are completely different."

"Hey, hey, what's...this..." Sudou stammered. "Are you... Huh?"

This had been a great demonstration of just how thickheaded Sudou could be. But now, after hearing me address Kei by her given name and listening to what we were talking about, he stopped moving. He stood there with a completely dumbstruck look on his face, as if he had finally started to realize something was going on.

"Wait a minute... What? H-hey, what's goin' on, Ayanokouji?"

It seemed like he was unable to connect the dots and see what we were together, though...or maybe he just didn't feel like he could be totally certain from what he was seeing.

I supposed that he might be a good pick to be the first classmate to tell. "We're dating," I replied. "Me and her."

Grinning, Kei jabbed me in the arm with her elbow

three times. She might have simply been happy that I had been the one to say it.

"H... Huh-whaaaaaaat?! F-for real?!"

Sudou must have been totally flabbergasted by what he heard, because he shouted in an exaggeratedly loud voice, far louder than I expected. Coincidentally, none of our other classmates were around, but other students still turned their heads toward us, wondering what was going on.

"That was WAY too loud," huffed Kei.

"S-sorry. But wait, hold on, WHAT?! W-why are you datin' Karuizawa?"

"What's *that* supposed to mean?" she retorted. "Is there something wrong with me?"

"No, that's what I mean, it's just... Well, actually, I guess I can't say it's like there's nothin' wrong with it, I guess, but... Umm...?"

Sudou stammered and seemed like he was somewhat taken aback. He was perplexed by the whole thing. He arched his neck a bit, showing that he couldn't quite grasp what he heard.

"What, you wanted me to go out with Horikita?" I teased.

"No way in hell, man! ...Wait, that's not what I meant... It's just...hold up," said Sudou.

He grabbed me tightly by the shoulders, brought his lips close to my ear, and then whispered to me in a low voice.

"'Scuse me for sayin' this, but, uh... You know Karuizawa was, well, datin' Hirata before, and who knows what kinda crazy relationships she had in junior high, yeah? That seriously doesn't, like, gross you out or nothin'? Don't you think she's kinda too much for you as your first girlfriend?"

Well, I supposed that was just the image that our classmates had of Karuizawa Kei. In fact, until I had learned about her past myself, I had thought of her as that kind of girl too.

"What're you whispering about all sneakily?" asked Kei.

"N-nothin'," mumbled Sudou.

After Kei shot him a glare, dejectedly Sudou moved away. I supposed he must have felt sorry for saying something that was so close to bad-mouthing her.

"Ayanokouji and Karuizawa, goin' out... It's no use, no matter how many times I say it in my head, I just can't wrap my mind around it. What a shock. Feels like crazy stuff is happenin' right away at the start of our second semester..."

Though Sudou was quietly muttering to himself, I most definitely heard everything he said.

2.1

WE ARRIVED at school at last. While we were walking over there from the dorms, we occasionally passed by third-year students going in our same direction. They kept shooting me glances just like they did on the boat, but there was no indication that Sudou noticed at all. This was the same odd situation that had unfolded every time I went out during our summer vacation. I didn't think I'd ever get used to it, in the truest sense of the words. Being watched gave one an intense feeling of oppression and entrapment. It was simply going to continue until those gazes stopped.

Kei quickly gathered up a group of girls to talk about things that had happened over the summer vacation, and Sudou started chatting with his good friends Ike and Hondou. I was also casually talking to my own friends in the Ayanokouji Group as I waited for the bell.

Eventually, Chabashira came into the room and opened her mouth to speak, the very same way she did in our first semester.

"There are several major events awaiting you all in the second semester this year," she announced. "First will be the sports festival, which was held last year as well. This event will be held in October. It's meant to evaluate students' physical abilities. Though some of the rules differ from the way things worked last year, there aren't any major differences in the abilities required."

Physical ability was very necessary in this battle that was shortly to come, just as Chabashira herself said moments ago. That might worry students who were only good at their studies. As expected, my close friends Keisei and Airi, who weren't good at athletics, were listening to Chabashira with grim expressions on their faces. The fact that the rules were different this year was also a point of concern.

"Following that, the Advanced Nurturing High School will hold its first-ever cultural festival in November," Chabashira went on. "As with the sports festival, we will provide you with detailed information about the event shortly. But know that we are going to be taking time starting in September to prepare for both of these events, in parallel."

That meant, most likely, that September would mostly be spent preparing for the sports festival, probably in the form of a few more hours spent in physical education classes each week. There would also be about an hour or so per week spent on discussions for the cultural festival. After the sports festival was over in October, the students could begin preparations for November's scheduled cultural festival in earnest. Aside from that, we knew there was also a school trip coming up, but it was unclear whether it would be related to a special exam or not.

"In addition, of course, you will have a mid-term test and a final test in between these events," added Chabashira.

At any rate, there didn't seem to be any doubt that the second semester was going to be a busy one.

"I will provide a more detailed explanation about the sports festival at a later date, but first, I'll talk a bit about the cultural festival today."

Though the sports festival was scheduled to happen first, Chabashira provided us with details about the cultural festival now.

"The cultural festival is going to be a big affair; you'll be seeing a lot of visitors on campus. You will be competing with all of the other classes and grade levels at this school in terms of total sales. You may apply for as many activities and programs as you wish, but your budget is limited. For further details, please look at your tablets."

CULTURAL FESTIVAL OVERVIEW

Each second-year class will be given 5,000 Private Points per student to be used solely for festival preparations. Students will be allowed to spend those available points freely. First-year students will be provided with 5,500 points each for start-up costs, and third-year students will be provided 4,500 points.

Additional funding may be provided for community service activities such as student council activities, contributions via club activities, and so on. Further details will be announced to each class after rules have been finalized.

Start-up funds and additional funds will not be reflected in final sales totals. Any funds that are not used must be returned in the end.

100 Class Points will be awarded to classes in first through fourth place. 50 Class Points will be awarded to classes in fifth through eighth place. No Class Points will be awarded to classes placing in ninth through twelfth place.

Looking at the rewards, we had a chance to get a decent number of Class Points for placing high, and there weren't any penalties for ranking low. As long as we were somewhere in the top eight, we'd get something. As for the rules, they were easy to understand, and it didn't seem like there'd be any confusion. The fact that this was shared with us before we received any details on the sports festival also made sense just by listening to what was said. After all, we couldn't start making preparations for the cultural festival until we had been provided with the rules. By contrast, we could already start getting ready for the sports festival to some extent just by improving our physical abilities in preparation.

"H-huh, it kind of sounds like a typical school cultural festival," commented Shinohara.

It wasn't like she felt like this was a disappointment, of course, but I could understand why Shinohara couldn't help saying that. I couldn't see that there was a risk of losing Class Points, or of anyone getting expelled. However, I supposed the fact that I was starting to suspect there was something more to this event was proof that the inner workings of this school had deeply influenced me.

"It will also be important for you to determine which location you would like and secure a spot on the campus," Chabashira continued. "For example, if you wish to set up a stall in a place where visitors are sure to pass through, like near the main gate, you'll have to pay the school to use that location."

The students, myelf included, looked down at our tablets to see additional information that had just been sent to us. The title of the file was "List of Possible Stall Locations on Campus" and included a campus map. It listed all of the locations that stalls would be available on campus, each with a location name and number. For example, the location closest to the main gate that Chabashira just mentioned was listed as "Main Gate 1," and the cost to reserve that location was 10,000 points.

There seemed to be places that were free as well, but these were located far from the main gate. That would make them difficult for visitors to reach.

Not counting any additional funds, we would have a budget of about 200,000 points. With that in mind, a cost of 10,000 points was by no means cheap. However, there was no doubt that it was a prime location and likely to attract a large number of visitors.

"It is entirely possible that there could be conflicts with other classes and grade levels over stall locations, but only one class is allowed to use a space in each location," Chabashira explained. "In that case, there will be a bidding process, and the class with the higher bid will earn the right to use that stall space."

Meaning that if we were forced to use more of our points thanks to a bidding war over securing the rights to a prime location, the budget we could allocate toward the actual program or goods for our stall would be greatly reduced. We had approximately the next two months to spend coming up with ways to compete with the other classes and grades efficiently, and within a limited budget.

"The school will neither publicly disclose what each class will be doing nor where their stalls will be located. School officials will not leak information, but do be aware that you can't stop other students from over-hearing you. If word about what your class is doing gets out, it would be best to assume that other students will come up with merciless countermeasures against you," our teacher said.

So even if we came up with the perfect plan for our class's stall, there was a risk that other classes would copy it or devise ways to undermine our efforts.

"You may also find that there are additional things you'll need, from time to time. If something is not available here on campus, it can be brought from outside as long as you apply for and are granted permission. You are free to use your budget however you wish, as long as it's within the scope of the rules."

It seemed like I was going to need to look into that matter more closely, as well as into other aspects.

"That's all for the cultural festival and its rules," Chabashira said. "Major preparations and the set-up period will come after the sports festival concludes, but starting today, please begin to discuss what you'll be doing and how you'll allocate your budget on your own time."

The more time that we devoted to the cultural festival, the more prepared we'd be.

2.2

AFTER CLASSES ENDED for the day, many of my classmates remained in the classroom, except for those who left for their club activities. Why? It was because we were having our first discussion for the cultural festival which was going to be held in November, of course. I found it likely that a number of students here had experienced a cultural festival before in their junior high days. Since I didn't have any information in particular about it, I decided to just be a listener, as usual.

Yousuke had gotten permission to use the monitor in the classroom. "First, let's start by making a brief list of options that come to mind easily," he said, typing on his tablet.

"When people think of cultural festivals, the things they typically expect to see are food stalls and haunted houses, that sort of thing," said Horikita.

Yousuke started adding these most obvious examples to a list, one by one: food-related options, a haunted house, a maze, a café, live music, a play, and so on.

"The event will be held from ten o'clock in the morning to three o'clock in the afternoon," he said. "As for food and beverages, adults will be coming as well, so we're anticipating that we'll have to be prepared for that. However, if we do so, we might see more competition in that regard..."

"The rest is just a matter of budgeting things well," said Horikita. "Compared to a haunted house or a maze where we can keep costs down after we've simply constructed what we need, the cost of offering food will inevitably be higher."

Some items, such as music equipment, could be rented for a fee. We could use those for whatever we decided to do, like if we did a live musical performance. However, they were limited in number, so they were first come, first served. There was also the question of how many students were even skilled enough to actually turn a profit.

"We have thirty-nine people in our class," Yousuke continued. "Meaning, our budget as it stands now would be 195,000 points. To be perfectly honest, that's not enough. With that kind of money, even if we said we were going to make food, I don't feel we can simply snap our fingers and decide that."

"I have a suggestion. May I?" said Horikita.

"Of course. Your opinion is welcome, Horikita-san," replied Yousuke.

"As you've said, Hirata-kun, our budget for the cultural festival is limited. However, no matter how much we argue about the options listed, there are many things that we still don't know. If we decided to cook takoyaki at a food stall, we would need answers to a lot of questions, like what ingredients to use, how good our classmates are at cooking, and so on. In that case, I think that the first thing we should do is repeatedly present our ideas to the class and test them, even if we have to use our own Private Points to do so."

Many students nodded in agreement with Horikita's suggestion. It was honestly important that we tested things out no matter what we decided to do, whether it was a food stall or something else. That was certainly true. Of course, there was a risk that we'd end up having to pay out of our own pockets to do that, but it was simple to just dismiss that as a necessary upfront investment.

"But... Well, I'm not trying to say that I think it's a bad proposal," Matsushita started, "but don't you think some people might be reluctant to try anything if they're going to have to pay themselves?"

Matsushita feared that in that case, some students might just decide to leave the planning to the rest of the class and not help with the cultural festival.

"That's fine," said Horikita. "I don't want to waste my time with just any random idea. But that being said, we mustn't disregard anyone trying their best to contribute. If anyone thinks of an idea that sounds like it could be the right one, they should actively try and present it. What if we pay out a reward to whoever proposes an idea that we end up using?"

"Yeah, that's a great idea," agreed Matsushita. "There's nothing wrong with rewarding people for their hard work and giving something back."

"We can work out the specifics of the rewards later, but to give an example, if we're awarded 100 Class Points via the cultural festival, that would mean our entire class will get 390,000 Private Points per month. We can divide that by the number of people who proposed an idea and give it out later. That way, there shouldn't be any complaints."

Hypothetically, if we had five activities or events, that would mean 78,000 points per person. If the number of people who proposed ideas and the number of collaborators was too large for it to be profitable for us to divide the total amount between them, I figured it would still be acceptable even if the total amount was spread out over two or three months. That way, students who had actively contributed to the cultural festival would gain something, and those who cut corners would get some benefit later on too. Ultimately, if our Class Points were going to be increased, there was no reason to object.

"Also, we need to be very thorough in withholding information so that no one steals our ideas," added Horikita. "Be very careful about what you say, wherever you say it, whether you're in school, in the dorms, or at Keyaki Mall."

Strict confidentiality. Over these next two months of preparations, that would be of the utmost importance. From here onward, these discussions would continue, and the class's first step would be for people to present their ideas to either Horikita or Yousuke. If there was a possibility that the ideas presented could be adopted, we could proceed to the next steps.

2.3

FOR THE FOLLOWING two weeks or so, our lives at school carried on as usual. We spent every day working hard in class while preparing for both the cultural festival and sports festival in parallel. It was a precious time when we could say that we were just going through normal, routine, everyday lives at an ordinary high school. Surprisingly enough, news about my relationship with Kei didn't spread past Sudou, and there weren't any signs that anyone else had found out about us.

Then, in mid-September, on the Wednesday of the third week of the month, something happened after class. As I was sitting in the back of the room, someone came into view. It was unusual for this certain someone to reach out to Horikita, but that's exactly what was happening. She came up to her as she sat in the middle of the front row.

"Um, excuse me, Horikita-san?" Satou called to her, sounding a little shy and reserved. "If you don't mind, could I have a minute of your time after class?"

Satou was one of the girls who had *never* interacted with Horikita.

"I need to go to the student council in about an hour to take care of some business," Horikita replied, "but as long it doesn't conflict with that, I don't mind. What is it?"

She seemed puzzled, but she also had never been approached by Satou before. After Horikita's slightly perplexed response, Satou spoke up once more, somewhat meekly.

"Well, about ideas for the cultural festival, we've been thinking a lot about it, and um... Well, you said before, um, that you wanted us to come talk to you if we came up with anything, right?"

"Yes. I did say that we're open to presentations..."

"Yes, that, exactly, let me make a presentation," said Satou. "I've come up with an idea that can seriously win us this cultural festival."

Satou's confidence was showing, but Horikita wasn't going to be so easily impressed. It was little wonder why, though; over the past ten days or so, more than a few students had brought their ideas to Horikita. Both guys and girls had made proposals to her because of the rewards they would receive if their ideas were adopted. The ideas presented were varied and ran the gamut from the mundane to the bizarre, but what they all shared in common was one thing: Horikita wasn't going to take anything you said seriously if you just randomly threw out the name of an idea and nothing more.

On the day that Horikita made a statement about offering rewards to anyone whose idea was accepted, Hondou immediately proposed that we sell karaage fried chicken because it was delicious. However, Horikita turned him away, telling him to go write up a detailed proposal first. She was unwilling to accept a vague idea thrown at her with no additional information. Though Hondou was discouraged after being told off, he submitted a detailed proposal document the next day. Unfortunately, all it contained was a recipe he probably just pulled from the internet and an impassioned statement about how much it would sell and how delicious it would be.

Upon seeing Hondou's low-level proposal, Horikita reiterated the importance of the documentation. For example, if we were going to operate a karaage fried chicken stand, how much would it cost? What location should we use? How many people would be needed to run it? How much would we sell the chicken for, how many customers could we expect, and what was the basis for those estimations? Horikita also rather bluntly declared that she would only listen to those who had gotten their ideas in proper order.

After that, it felt like the number of people who approached Horikita casually with hasty proposals ought to have decreased dramatically, but surprisingly enough, the number of students who came to her with proposal documents actually *increased* day by day. Several ideas had actually made their way onto Horikita's list of things to consider for the festival. However, none of the proposals thus far had been particularly decisive, so nothing had been officially adopted yet.

"Well then, let's see your proposal," said Horikita.

"Oh, um, yes. I do have a presentation prepared, but... I can't quite show you here," Satou said. "If possible, could I have a bit of your time, just a little while from now?"

"Is that so? Well, all right. Where do you want me to go?"

"Oh, um, right... There's an empty classroom in the special building, please be there in thirty minutes. I got permission from the teacher in advance," said Satou.

"An empty classroom?"

Though Horikita sounded perplexed, Satou simply said, "That's right, see you there!" before she turned and walked away. Then, Satou met my gaze as I was watching this happen, and she walked over to approach me as well.

"Hey, um, Ayanokouji-kun, do you have some free time today?" she asked.

"Me? I don't have any plans in particular, no," I replied.

"You heard what I was talking about with Horikita-san earlier, right? I was wondering if you could come with her. Thirty minutes from now."

"Why me, though?"

"That's a secret for now. If you come, you'll understand."

Just like when she was speaking to Horikita earlier, Satou's confidence was visible on her face.

"Okay, I'll be waiting!" she said to me. Then, after checking the time on her phone, Satou hurried out of the classroom.

"What is up with her, I wonder? She certainly seemed pretty confident," said Horikita.

"Maybe that just means she's come up with something special?" I mused.

"Even so, I'm not sure why we're going through all this hassle."

I wasn't sure what it was all supposed to mean either, but we would find out in another thirty minutes. Horikita and I decided to kill some time in the classroom before heading over to the special building.

2.4

$\bullet \bullet$

SINCE HORIKITA AND I were heading to the same place, we walked over to the special building together. When we arrived outside the classroom that Satou had told us to go to, Maezono was there for some reason.

"Ah, I'm standing watch," she said. "We didn't think that anyone would come here after class, but still, figured we'd do this just in case...you know."

"Standing watch...?" Horikita repeated. "This is far more elaborate than I thought."

Horikita seemed surprised that they had gone so far as adopting security measures, even though that was something of a prerequisite if we wanted to keep our ideas hidden until the day of the festival. People wanted to keep others from finding out what classes from which grades were doing what. I was surprised too, though.

Not only had they asked the teacher to borrow a room in the special building, but they even assigned someone to stand watch to prevent interference from third parties. Moreover, they had even gone as far as sealing up the windows, albeit somewhat simply. You could not see into the room from outside.

"Well then, let's hurry on inside and have a look," said Horikita.

"Oh, please wait a minute," said Maezono. "From here onward, it's going to be a trial run, as if it were really operating. That way, you can experience it for yourselves as if you were customers, Horikita-san, Ayanokouji-kun."

"So that's what's going on," said Horikita. "All right. I suppose this is much easier to understand than reading through some hastily-thrown-together proposals."

After seeing how elaborate this whole production was so far, Horikita's expectations had undeniably been raised, whether she liked it or not. Whether she would end up adopting this idea for the cultural festival was another matter, but at this point, it was clear that they were putting in a serious effort to win this. I was sure that must have made Horikita happy.

After the two of us once again made sure that there wasn't anyone else in the vicinity, we slowly opened the door.

The first things that caught my eye were the unexpectedly vibrant colors inside. The decorations that they had put up were so bright and colorful that it made it hard to believe this was just another sterile, nondescript classroom.

"Th-this is..." stammered Horikita.

"Welcome to Maid Café Maimai!"

Three girls greeted us in unison, each of them in a unique costume. Satou, the one who had called us here, and Matsushita, standing next to her, were both dressed in maid costumes. Mii-chan, though, averted her eyes from us shyly and was dressed in a cheongsam.

Although monitors were typically installed in the classrooms, it seemed like the classrooms in the rarely used special building still came equipped with whiteboards. It seemed like they had put it to good use and the name of their café was written out adorably in marker. We were shown to our seats and handed a menu of homemade items.

"What would you care to order, Master? Mistress?" asked Satou.

"Please hold on a minute. May I ask you something before we order?" asked Horikita.

"Huh? What is it?"

"Surely it must have taken quite a bit of time and money for you to put this all together?"

It certainly looked like it would've been difficult to arrange all this in just a day if you had to, that was for sure. Even if they worked hard to get all the decorations up, what about their costumes?

Satou turned to Matsushita. "How long did it take us again, Matsushita-san?"

"About four days of preparation time," Matsushita replied. "I think the costs were surprisingly reasonable, actually. All in all, we spent about 13,200 Private Points. The four of us planned it together—us three here and Maezono-san outside. We divided the costs amongst the four of us, so it was roughly 3,300 points per person. As for what specifically we spent those points on, it was our three rental outfits, and then the items we used to put together the decorations, like origami paper and markers. We picked those up from the general store. All of the tableware here actually comes from our own personal belongings, so there was no cost for that."

Interesting. I supposed that was the reason why there was a lack of unifying cohesiveness to the tableware. Of course, since we were only in the planning stages now, that wasn't a negative factor. In fact, I was genuinely impressed by how well they had prepared for the event while keeping their costs to a minimum.

"The impact was perfect. Better than any other proposal I've seen thus far. But..." Horikita trailed off.

She offered high praise for how thoroughly they had prepared for this, seeing as they had generally prepared everything. However, Horikita wasn't so simple as to decide just from that.

"The main question I have is, have you prepared an overall budget for this? I'd like to see what specific processes you have in mind," said Horikita sharply.

Satou didn't panic in the slightest, however, and turned to look at Mii-chan.

"Um, well, we've tried to put as much as we possibly could into our proposal documentation," Mii-chan said, taking a clear file folder from her bag and handing it over to Horikita.

I wondered if Mii-chan had been the one to write it out. There were three pages in the folder, packed with details written in beautiful handwriting. Matsushita had mentioned that the costumes they had were rented, but it looked like they received quotes from three different companies and rented one outfit from each. There were comparisons in price, quality, and selection. The proposal also contained the costs for tableware that they would use during the cultural festival, including lower and higher cost options. There were also details on the approximate number of guests expected as a criterion, differences between that number and maximum guest capacity, and so on.

"This is far and away more complete than any other proposal I've seen so far," said Horikita. "Well done."

Hearing Horikita's genuine compliments, Satou and Matsushita turned to Mii-chan, poking her in the side and telling her that she was being praised. Mii-chan, though looking as embarrassed as she'd likely be on the day of the festival, gently made a grateful bow to Horikita. You could say that this proposal from Satou and the other girls had earned a perfect score. However...

"It certainly is an interesting idea," Horikita said. "Though you could hardly say such things are uncommon, I feel that it has potential, especially if the experience is well put together. However, there are some downsides. The costume rental fee is 4,000 points per outfit. If we follow your proposal, it will cost 40,000 points for ten outfits. Aside from that, the estimated cost of preparing beverages and snacks comes to 50,000 points. That's a total of 90,000... And then there's the decorations put up in the room, which come to 5,000 points, and then there's the location cost on top of that, which means... This is by no means an inexpensive plan."

Even if we could afford to implement everything without difficulty, especially since we wouldn't need to pay wages to the people working the café, we'd *still* be spending half of our current budget on one single idea.

"Y-yes, that's true...b-but I think that we could raise the costs of the items we offer. To compensate!" said Satou.

As an example, I saw that on the menu that Satou and the other girls put together, one cup of tea cost 800 points. That was more expensive than getting a drink at the café in Keyaki Mall. Of course, it was conceivable that they could reduce their prices significantly depending on adjustments they made in the future, but it still seemed fair to judge that what they offered had a good chance of selling. Horikita looked quite serious as she reread the three-page proposal documentation. With Satou and the other girls standing around her dressed like something out of a fairy tale, something struck me as strangely out of place or unrealistic about the whole situation.

Horikita finally looked up, having perhaps reached a conclusion.

"Just double-checking, but...no one else has seen this presentation yet, have they?" she asked.

"Of course," replied Matsushita with a nod, her confidence showing. "We haven't let anything slip."

Satou and Mii-chan followed suit, nodding as well.

"...Very well. I will be taking serious steps to help ensure that this maid café proposal passes then. Would you be willing to further scrutinize your proposal, including a thorough cost-reduction?"

"Really?! Yay!" shouted Satou.

The three girls gleefully exchanged high fives, each of them overjoyed.

"It's too early to celebrate. Don't forget that we're only taking it under positive consideration for now," warned Horikita.

Though that's what Horikita said, the fact the girls had gotten Horikita to pledge that she'd take care of things to help get the idea approved was a huge gain for them. Once Horikita and I stepped back out into the hallway, Maezono was still there standing watch and waved to us happily. I was sure she was looking so pleased because she had heard the commotion from inside the room.

"You sure seem to have a high opinion of what you just saw," I said to Horikita. "I never expected you to come out and say that you'd take care of things for them."

"I wouldn't just casually accept something if I thought we had no chance of winning with it," she replied. "To tell you the truth, the majority of proposals that had been brought to me were rejected right on the spot, or simply put on hold at best. The fact I said what I did is just a reflection of how strong their idea is."

I figured that the idea of a maid café in itself was likely not that unusual. However, it seemed that Horikita was willing to cooperate with them because she saw the potential to fully demonstrate the strengths of our class and to do something that would impress visitors.

"Supposing for the sake of argument that another class were to run a maid café," I began, "do you think we'd still be able to win?"

"Yes, I do. You don't think so?"

"Well, I don't know."

If we just thoughtlessly opened up a food stand, we'd likely have several rivals. On the other hand, if we ran a maid café, even if we had one or two competitors, it was possible we could outdo them by using the assets we had at our disposal. Aside from those three girls back there wearing sample outfits, there might very well be some other hidden talents lying dormant in our class.

"What are you talking about? I'm going to need your help too in order to make sure their idea becomes a solid success," said Horikita.

"My help?" I blinked. "Wait, you're not asking *me* to dress up too, are you?"

"What kind of stupid nonsense is that? If I'm doing this, then I'm going to make sure we give it our all. So, in that case, we need to have the best people for the job, right? So, with that in mind, I think that you, a guy, should be the one to help in that regard."

"Wait, that's... Well, I don't really understand what that's supposed to mean exactly, but...I would think there are others who are better qualified for this."

"I suppose you have a point. People like Ike-kun and Hondou-kun might be connoisseurs, of a sort, when it comes to this sort of thing. But I fear that if we told them about this idea, that could lead to information getting leaked. They seem to have loose lips."

"I...can't deny that," I admitted.

They were the kind of people who might very well end up carelessly revealing information by mistake.

"I don't want to recklessly increase the number of students in the know here," Horikita said. "Understand?"

"Yeah, I do."

Maybe it was just sheer bad luck that Satou had asked me to come along. Or maybe things were just destined to turn out this way.

"That being said, I'll be leaving the matter of choosing people to you first," she went on. "You can tell anyone that you want to bring about this project, of course, but please remember to keep this strictly confidential. If things go wrong, this proposal will be off the table."

That was just how important it was that we kept this a secret.

"Actually, come to think of it... Yes. With that in mind, I'd like to keep information sharing to the absolute minimum. Can I leave this matter entirely to you? We'll settle on a formal budget at a later date, but I'll need you to scout for people, handle all preparations, and manage things."

"Wait, wait, hold on," I protested. "This is a huge jump all of a sudden. You're *really* planning on having me handle all of this, alone?"

"No one is saying that we're just going to have just one thing for this cultural festival," she pointed out. "We will definitely have more than one offering, considering our balance of human resources, both men and women. Figuring out a way to increase our profits on a low budget is going to take a lot of work, so *I'd* like to focus on that aspect."

Sure, I wanted to let her concentrate on doing that part of the job, I understood that. But I also had to wonder, why *me*?

"I trust this means you're accepting my formal offer?" said Horikita.

I didn't remember showing any suggestion at all of having accepted any offer, but the decision had apparently been made for me.

"Fine, I'll do it..." I huffed.

I wondered if it was even possible for me to operate the ideal maid café. I wasn't very confident. Considering Satou, Matsushita, and Mii-chan were already confirmed to be involved... How many more waitresses did we need? Though the cultural festival was still a way off, it was looking likely that I was going to need to get people together soon.

"I'm going to head over to the student council office," Horikita announced. "See you later."

"Y-yeah..."

Having been made to accept a job that made me want to hold my head in my hands in defeat. As I went to leave the building, I happened to cross paths with Chabashira. Considering the location, it seemed unlikely that she was there through sheer coincidence.

"You went to see Satou and the others?" she asked. "I heard about their proposal and what they're thinking of doing. Not a bad idea."

"Yes, I did, and I agree. I figured they needed to make sure their application to be here was approved before they could have even started preparing for a showcase for us, after all."

It wouldn't have been a laughing matter if they had gone through such thorough preparations without knowing whether they had permission to use the building.

"I was curious about how it was shaping up myself so I thought I'd come over personally to take a look," said Chabashira. "How was it?"

"Good," I replied. "Horikita is positive about it too. She must have thought we have a chance of winning with it. She's working out the details now."

"I see. Well then, I suppose that means I don't need to go out of my way to go see it," said Chabashira.

"I kind of got dragged into this whole thing myself." I sighed. "It's turned into a bit of a bother."

"Meaning?"

"Horikita's instructions were that I was to supervise this project."

"You, Ayanokouji? Wow, that's..." Chabashira trailed off. Then, she smirked at me like she found this whole thing comical. But at the same time, she was giving me a look that seemed to both sympathetic and pitying. "That's great," she finished her thought. "Horikita has some rather interesting ideas herself."

"I think that people like Ike and the Professor would be far, far better suited for this kind of work though," I said.

Even though I had heard of maid cafés, I didn't know a single thing about what they were supposed to be like.

"When it comes to understanding otaku culture, then sure, you might be right about that," Chabashira said. "However, what's important at the cultural festival is sales. Those two might be capable of improving the quality of the attraction, but they likely wouldn't be good at finer calculations and turning a profit. That is exactly why it makes sense for you to supervise it instead. It's a problem that can be solved by asking them for their opinions, if necessary."

That was easy for her to say. For your opinions to have meaning, you needed to have at least a bare minimum amount of knowledge about the topic at hand. If you just listened to people's advice while you were in total ignorance on a subject, there was no guarantee that you'd arrive at the correct answer. At the same time, it would be difficult for you to point out anything that might be wrong.

"Just brace yourself and think of it as an opportunity to learn about something outside of typical academic fields, Mr. Maid Café Manager," Chabashira teased.

"I suppose..."

Just as I was leaving, Chabashira called out to me once more from behind.

"Ayanokouji, could I...ask for a moment of your time again soon?"

"Soon? When?" I asked.

"I'll send you a message before long. Would that be all right?"

"I guess, sure. I don't mind. If I'm busy then, I'll try to make some time."

I could have refused, but I decided to accept. The woman had a serious look on her face.

3 TWO TEACHERS AND A FATED SPECIAL EXAM

THE NEXT MORNING, I was assigned to be the manager (?) of the maid café.

But then, when we saw Chabashira's grim expression as she strode into our classroom, many students immediately noticed that something was off. However, this time, unlike the usual for situations like this, the words "special exam" weren't the first to spring to mind for most of us. That was because they probably assumed the next exam would be the sports festival itself. Furthermore, the cultural festival was coming up right after that.

"Before the sports festival in October, you'll be taking a new special exam," announced Chabashira.

Her statement caused a bit of an uproar amongst the students. There hadn't been any special exams around this time last year, not while we were getting ready for the sports festival. But it sounded like this year was going to be different.

"Ugh, come on, are you kidding me?" Ike groaned. "We *just* got through that brutal uninhabited island exam, and now we have to take another one...?"

Though it had already become customary for him to complain about these things, I heard Ike mutter discontented grumblings before anyone else did. I supposed that for Ike, a new special exam was a grim prospect. He had just managed to overcome the uninhabited island when his back was against the wall and expulsion seemed imminent. On top of that, he had just officially become Shinohara Satsuki's boyfriend as well. No matter how much Ike and Shinohara deepened their relationship and grew closer, suddenly finding themselves expelled from school now was most certainly possible, depending on the type of special exam. There was no doubt that students with particularly low levels of overall ability felt a sense of urgency.

"Hey, bring it on." Sudou, who had absolute confidence in his athletic prowess, smacked his fists together. "I say we clear this special exam quickly before we completely dominate the sports festival."

"Don't get carried away," snapped Horikita.

"...Sorry."

Horikita's immediate warning made Sudou feel a little dejected. He went silent. *What a wonderful master slave relationship they've... Er, well, I suppose I could say that they're nurturing a friendship.*

"If I'm being honest here, there have been very few instances of special exams being given at this time of year in the past," Chabashira told us. "In fact, a special exam will not be held for the first-year and third-year students."

Satou had been leaning against the back of her chair before, but now she pitched forward. "You mean that our grade is the only one getting a special exam before the sports festival?" she asked.

Chabashira didn't deny it at all. She simply nodded.

"Because you second-years have been so exceptional, the school is giving you an appropriate level of recognition for your worth," she replied.

"Huh?" said Satou. "Wait, a special exam because they recognize our worth...? Isn't that a little strange?"

"It is certainly true that special exams come with a level of risk you ought to be wary of," said Chabashira. "Class Points or Private Points could be lost. Some students could even be expelled from school. However, on the other hand, it could be said that these give you even more opportunities to lead a more fulfilling life here at school.

The more special exams that are held, the better your chances are for being promoted to Class A. And that is considered to be the most important thing of all."

It was true that if you wanted to earn a large number of Class Points, it was extremely difficult to do so through ordinary, everyday activities. If anything, the periods of time when there weren't any special exams were largely about keeping our Class Points from falling any lower. Whether it was the uninhabited island special exam or any other, opportunities to move up to higher-level classes only came when a special exam was being held.

"Happiness and unhappiness are two sides of the same coin. So, there are benefits to those risks, right?" said Horikita, having calmly accepted the news and taken a position close to Chabashira's.

"Exactly," said Chabashira.

"That being the case, there's nothing for us to fear," Horikita declared. "We are most definitely closing in on Class A now. There's a chance we can break out of the three-way tie between B, C, and D. This just means that our chance is already here."

The more opportunities we had, the better. That was the commonly held belief for everyone aiming for the top.

"That's true, you're right about that... And it's not like complaining about it will make special exams go away or anything," replied Satou.

Horikita's words seemed to have convinced even Satou and our other lower-level classmates, judging from their expressions. Though you could say it was still a work in progress, Horikita's growth as a pillar of support seemed to be having a clear, positive effect on her classmates. I suspected that Chabashira was probably inwardly pleased by this as well, even if she didn't let it show on her face at all. She wasn't the sort of teacher to show her sweet side in the first place, but lately, I felt like it was coming through a bit more than usual.

"You will be taking what is referred to as the 'Unanimous Special Exam' this time."

The monitor lit up and Chabashira began explaining the exam. It was accompanied with various visual aids that had become customary at this point.

"This special exam is exceedingly simple. Hence, I will be accepting questions at any time if there is anything you are curious about. This exam will be administered tomorrow, and as you can probably surmise from the name, it consists of a series of multiple-choice questions which you will answer repeatedly until the entire class comes to a unanimous decision."

"Tomorrow?" repeated Horikita. "That's...rather sudden."

We certainly weren't being provided with adequate prep time for this. Of course, there weren't any advantages or disadvantages because it was essentially a fair contest, but our class that had just settled down was now beginning to stir once again.

"As I just said, this special exam is simple," Chabashira replied. "The school believes that there will not be any problems in going ahead with the exam tomorrow. There isn't a need to spend time discussing things in advance."

We would vote over and over again in class until we came to a unanimous decision. Just from hearing about that part alone, I certainly couldn't see anything particularly complex about this exam.

"That means we're not fighting against another class this time then, right?" asked Yousuke, immediately hoping for an answer on that point, considering it more important than anything else.

"That's right," said Chabashira. "Since this special exam only takes place within your class, you will not be competing against any rivals. On the day of the exam, the school will give you five 'issues' to complete. These issues are the same for all classes, with no differences between them."

If the issues were different, that would mean the

difficulty level would be different from class to class. I supposed that made sense.

"This might seem sudden, but I'm going to jump right into it. I will provide you with an example to help you understand."

EXAMPLE ISSUE: Lose 5 Class Points, but all classmates gain 10,000 Private Points.

CHOICES: For, Against

The sample issue was shown on the monitor. Just like Chabashira had said, it was simple and easy to understand.

"Hm? Wait, what's this?" said Shinohara. "Um... We'd go down by five Class Points, but in exchange, we can get 10,000 Private Points... This is an issue? Would that be a gain or a loss?" She counted on her fingers, trying to calculate the actual gains and losses in her head.

It wasn't surprising that many unexpected questions would come to mind for people. Still, even though this was only an example, I had expected there to have been more choices to agonize over. We earned 100 Private Points each month for every Class Point. That meant that five Class Points were worth 500 Private Points. If you thought about the issue presented to us, the latter option was worth more in terms of Private Points, and by an overwhelming amount.

However, Class Points would continue to hold value. In one month, five Class Points was worth nothing more than 500 Private Points. However, if you calculated their worth over a longer time span, like say, over a year, then those mere five Class Points would be worth 6,000 Private Points. Considering the time we had remaining until graduation, we had eighteen opportunities left to receive Private Points, meaning from October of our second year to the March of our third year. In other words, we could consider the value of those Class Points to be worth 9,000 Private Points.

But things weren't actually so simple. Supposing the loss of five Class Points here in this exam carried through, and in the end we missed on reaching Class A by that same margin, we would look back on this decision as the worst possible choice we could have made. Of course, the probability that five points would make all the difference between winning and losing probably wasn't that high. In that case, it was quite possible that there could be cases in which it'd be more beneficial for us to gain the 10,000 Private Points.

Whichever point of view we took, there were advantages and disadvantages in the end.

"All thirty-nine of you will vote anonymously on each issue presented, choosing from the options presented to you," Chabashira explained. "You'll probably understand how this works the quickest by simply trying it for yourself, so let's do just that right now. I'm sure that many of you have quite a lot of questions, but I'd like you to try and enter your votes without any time for discussion. Please enter your vote, for or against, on your tablets."

After Chabashira tapped some things on the device in hand, all of the students' tablets' screens, mine included, now displayed something new. Our tablets displayed the issue, and we could either select *For* or *Against* on the screen. This truly was an unusual special exam unlike any we'd seen before.

I decided to consider this issue seriously for a moment.

Private Points had no direct effect on our Class Points. The fact that all of our classmates would get 10,000 Private Points by voting in favor was a simple benefit. And, by voting in favor, we were losing only five Class Points. But still, five Class Points was five Class Points. In that case, I supposed I needed to consider how someone would think about this, in terms of human nature.

It wasn't a question of whether gaining 10,000 Private Points or not losing five Class Points was the better option. The real question was actually the opposite: could we make either of these choices without regretting it later? I decided to press *For*, which was likely going to be the less popular option, to see what the results would be. I figured it wasn't the best idea to be unanimous the first time around. The tallying must have been complete shortly afterward because Chabashira looked up from the tablet in her hands.

"All right. Now that you've all finished voting, I'd like to go ahead and show you the results immediately."

And with that, the tally was displayed up on the monitor.

Round 1 Voting Results: FOR: 3 Votes, AGAINST: 36 Votes

I knew that there would be more votes against, but it was an even wider margin than I had expected.

"H-hey, um? Wouldn't we get more going with the 10,000 Private Points than we'd get from five Class Points?" said Ike, puzzled. He looked around at his classmates. "We'd only get a few Private Points from those, right? Or did I mess up my math? Why'd so many people vote against?"

Judging from that comment, I could assume that Ike had also voted in favor.

"If we're only talking about the number of Private Points we're getting, then yes, it's true that we'd get more Private Points by going with the 10,000 option," said Horikita. "But Class Points are essential if we're going to aim for Class A. If it's only a difference of a thousand points, then why would we deliberately reduce our precious Class Points? There'd be no need to do that."

She must have voted against, and she offered a theoretical explanation for her choice.

"In the unlikely event that those five Class Points end up spelling the difference between winning and losing, then I certainly couldn't help but regret our choice if we gave them up," she added.

Just as I thought, many students were naturally worried about the risks in the unlikely event something happened. I also couldn't forget that the other three classes were also going to be voting on these same issues. If the other three classes voted unanimously to keep the Class Points and we didn't, then that meant this class would be the only one falling a step behind. I supposed it would be a different story if we could make effective use of the 10,000 Private Points gained, though.

"I'm sure that you all have your own thoughts on how this went, but please, listen," Chabashira told us. "We will be doing the vote over again because while there were overwhelmingly more votes opposed, the result was not unanimous. In the actual special exam, there will be a fixed ten-minute interval before the next vote. During that time, you are allowed to converse freely, and at times, you could even be permitted to get up from your seats and exchange opinions. But for the time being, we're going to skip that part. Let's commence the voting once again."

The purpose of the test was to come to a unanimous decision. If we didn't reach one, then the results of the vote would be invalidated, and there would be a mandatory ten-minute interval before the next vote. Even if we came to a consensus quickly, that would still be a significant amount of lost time. It was safe to assume that there was probably some kind of time limit somewhere, considering the structure of this special exam. It was possible we could run out of time if we continuously failed to reach a unanimous decision...

So, for our second vote, what we should do is vote *Against* without thinking too deeply on the issue. If we voted that way, we could steer things toward unanimity. That was precisely why I decided to vote *For* again this time, for the second vote. I thought that by doing so, my classmates would gain a better understanding of this special exam.

Round 2 Voting Results: FOR: 2 Votes, AGAINST: 37 Votes

"H-hey, what?" shouted Sudou. "Some of you seriously voted *For* even after what we just talked about?!"

"I'm sorry," said Horikita. "I'm one of the people who voted *For*, Sudou-kun. I deliberately chose to avoid letting it get to a unanimous decision. Apparently, there was someone else here who had the same idea I did... Hm."

Though she didn't turn to look at me, she might have been referring to me when she said that.

"And here we have the results of the second round of voting," Chabashira said. "Almost everyone voted *Against*, but there were still two votes *For*. In this instance, there would normally be another ten-minute interval before voting resumed. This exam is designed so that voting periods and break intervals are repeated over and over until you finally reach a unanimous decision, either with thirty-nine votes *For* or thirty-nine votes *Against*. Of course, whatever choice you make in these issues will actually be passed. In this particular case, if there were thirty-nine votes *For*, you would all receive 10,000 Private Points, but you would lose five Class Points. Conversely, if all thirty-nine of you voted *Against*, then the issue would be rendered null and void. Nothing would happen."

Meaning, in other words, that no one would gain or lose any points, and this issue would be over.

"Although you didn't reach a unanimous decision, in the interest of saving time, I'm going to have you move onto the next example issue."

EXAMPLE ISSUE: Grant 1 million Private Points to one person in class.

(If the vote is unanimously in favor of the issue, a student will be selected to receive the points, and another vote will be held on that issue.)

CHOICES: For, Against

"I'm sure you must have some thoughts about this example, but during the actual exam, you will be forbidden from whispering amongst yourselves before the first round of voting," explained Chabashira. "Meaning that, first, you must genuinely tackle this issue head-on and vote."

So it wasn't until the second round of voting that we'd be able to discuss what we thought about the issue after reading it.

Round 1 Voting Results: FOR: 39 Votes, AGAINST: 0 Votes

The results were displayed on the screen. It was an obvious outcome. Even if only one person out of thirty-nine would be receiving those Private Points, there was virtually no reason to choose the latter option. Even if you were disappointed that you didn't receive anything yourself, it'd be difficult to get the class to vote unanimously against it.

"If you're presented with an issue like this in the actual exam where a specific individual will need to be selected, the first step would be to reach a unanimous decision either *For* or *Against*, like you did just now in this example issue. If you voted *Against*, then the issue would be considered closed at that point. But if you voted unanimously *For*, the issue proceeds to the next step. During the break interval, you can discuss who you would like to recommend. The names of everyone in your class, yourself excluded, will be displayed on your respective tablets."

The information displayed on our tablet screens had changed on their own, and sure enough, everyone's names except my own were listed. However, the names weren't listed in alphabetical order. They were listed irregularly with no rhyme or reason, not even with separation by gender.

Chabashira offered additional insight on this. "To ensure complete anonymity in voting, the positions of students' names are changed each time there is a vote. This is also the case for options such as *For* and *Against*, which are also randomly switched. The reason for this is to prevent students from spying on their neighbors and guessing how they voted based on the position of their fingers."

She was telling us we would absolutely not be able to guess how other students voted.

"Once discussion is underway, you may each vote at whatever time of your choosing," she went on. "Simply tap on the name of the student you wish to recommend. During that period of time, you're allowed to change your vote for another student as many times as you like by just tapping on the screen again. At the end of that ten-minute period, the majority... Well, in the case of this class, the student that has twenty votes will be designated. Let's say, for the sake of argument, that Ike had the most nominations and was selected."

"Huh, me?! Yeah, dude!" he exclaimed happily.

"Now, Ike will temporarily lose the ability to vote, and the other thirty-eight of you will vote on the issue," Chabashira explained.

To select a student, a simple majority was enough to pass to the next stage. I guessed that was how the whole nomination process worked. At any rate, the issue proceeded to the next step and a new round of voting had begun. We cast our votes.

EXAMPLE ISSUE: Grant 1 million Private Points to Ike Kanji.

CHOICES: For, Against

Round 2 Voting Results: FOR: 0 Votes, AGAINST: 38 Votes

"Say whaaaa?! H-hey, why'd nobody vote for me?!" Ike exclaimed.

"Well, 'cause ain't no way anybody would give you a million points," said Sudou. That was what the entire class was probably thinking. "Just common sense, dude."

"Now, because everyone had voted against Ike in this particular issue and came to a unanimous decision, that would mean Ike would not be granted those points," Chabashira said. "Which, therefore, would mean those one million points would be left up in the air, and Ike would be removed from the list of candidates. The vote then would continue with the remaining thirty-eight students. However, please note that if you are unable to reach a final unanimous decision before the time limit, you fail, and the one million points wouldn't be awarded to anyone."

"Huh?!" said Ike. "Wait, so that means my chances of getting anything would just go down to zero?!"

"That's exactly what it means. However, your name wouldn't have been crossed off the list if just one student had voted in favor of you. Also, please note that self-nominations are accepted. If a student steps forward as a candidate during the discussion interval, they can be accepted as self-nomination on a first-come, first-served basis. However, only one candidacy per student per issue is allowed."

"What would happen if no student got the majority vote within those ten minutes, or if no one steps forward as a candidate?" asked Horikita. "I would imagine such instances would be quite possible."

"In those cases, a student would be selected at random from the class, and the vote would be held regardless," Chabashira replied.

Apparently, the vote wouldn't wait because we were indecisive. We would be forced to vote for someone.

"If we're asked to choose an individual, we might very well end up wasting our time," Horikita observed.

She was exactly right. If that happened, it would be like having as many things to vote for as people in our class. That said, I couldn't imagine it would be that simple to just make a decision with a randomly selected student.

"Let's stay on our toes, everyone," Horikita said. "This special exam might be more difficult than we thought..."

Not all issues could be resolved through discussion. There was a good chance that we would be faced with a choice that we would never be able to reach a compromise on. I mean, if that sort of thing *didn't* happen, then this wouldn't make any sense as a special exam.

"Let me give you one last example issue," said Chabashira. "This time, I'll have you vote on something that would represent an actual physical change."

EXAMPLE ISSUE: An additional facility will be built within Keyaki Mall. Which of the following would you prefer?

(Whichever receives the most votes, based on the collective results of all four classes, will be selected.)

CHOICES: Restaurant – General Store – Recreational Facility – Medical Facility

Unlike the previous example issues, which only allowed us to vote for or against, this time we had four available options to choose from. I assumed we were only going to be voting in favor of or opposed to things, but apparently that wasn't the case. From what Chabashira had said, whatever choice we went with would be implemented. If this wasn't an example issue, did that mean that they would actually go through with building whatever was chosen?

"When an issue is passed, for example if you vote in favor of something, that means the issue in question will actually be implemented," Chabashira said. "However, issues that affect the entire school are processed in a unique way. When these types of issues are presented, your particular class's unanimous vote on the subject counts simply as one vote overall toward the decision. So, if this class were to vote unanimously in favor of the restaurant, but the three other classes voted unanimously for a recreational facility, the decision would be made to add a recreational facility as that would have received three votes."

Everyone in class probably understood what Chabashira meant. Basically, there were two types of issues: those that were immediately actionable after we finished voting on them, and those where our class's position collectively counted as one vote overall. In any case, it seemed like we were expected to guide the class to unanimity with careful, discreet discussion. Whispering amongst ourselves was prohibited before the first vote, and that meant that students would make their initial choices based on their hunches.

Round 1 Voting Results: RESTAURANT: 20 Votes, GENERAL STORE: 4 Votes, RECREATIONAL FACILITY: 15 Votes, MEDICAL FACILITY: 0 Votes

"Now, because you didn't reach a unanimous decision, there will be a ten-minute interval," said Chabashira.

Now, we were experiencing a ten-minute discussion interval for the first time. A countdown timer started ticking on the monitor behind the podium. That timer would continue to count down until the next mandatory round of voting began. Students were free to leave their seats, and they were allowed to share their opinions however they wished, whether they wanted to talk in a loud voice for all to hear or if they wanted to whisper quietly to someone in particular. I observed my surroundings and waited for the timer to count down. Ten minutes passed without anyone giving any instructions in particular. Everyone just chatted away as they pleased.

"Please return to your seats just before the end of the break interval and prepare for the next round of voting," Chabashira told us. "You'll have a maximum of sixty seconds to vote. If everyone puts in their votes quickly, we'll move on to announcing the results right away, without waiting for the time limit to be reached."

From what she was saying, unlike the mandatory ten-minute interval between votes, the actual voting process could be shortened somewhat with a little ingenuity.

"Students who do not finish voting on an issue within those sixty seconds will be penalized without mercy for going over time. Individuals will have a maximum of ninety seconds of penalty time throughout the exam. Students who exceed that penalty allowance before finishing voting on all five issues will run out of time and be expelled."

This was the school's way of regulating us and ensuring that we absolutely would vote. Hypothetically, if a student didn't want to vote and they sulked about it, they would quickly find themselves expelled from school thanks to this system. It was unlikely that a student would bother to do something like deliberately stall and delay each of their votes, because they would lose valuable time if they didn't enter their votes within fifty-eight or fifty-nine seconds.

We had our second round of voting and got the following results.

Round 2 Voting Results: RESTAURANT: 23 Votes, GENERAL STORE: 2 Votes, RECREATIONAL FACILITY: 14 Votes, MEDICAL FACILITY: 0 Votes

Since we didn't discuss the issue so we could come to a consensus, the results were roughly the same as the first round. It wasn't going to be easy to steer things toward a unanimous decision on the first vote unless the issue was something completely obvious, but it didn't seem to be that difficult to get thirty-nine votes for a particular option after coming to a unified opinion. However, that was only if the tasks were all within the realm of our expectations. Depending on the actual content of these issues, some of them could end up requiring considerable discussion.

"I'm going to finish the example issues there, but you should be able to understand how things work by now,"

Chabashira said. "For you to pass this special exam, you need to come to a unanimous decision on five issues within five hours. If you fail to complete all of the issues within that time frame, you will suffer an extremely significant penalty. To be precise, the penalty is 300 Class Points."

"Th-three hundred?!" exclaimed Ike.

As it turned out, this was a special exam that we absolutely *had* to finish.

"However, if you do finish in time, you will be awarded fifty Class Points."

The rewards and penalties seemed unbalanced, but when you considered the exam's difficulty level, I supposed it was reasonable.

"There's no need to panic, everyone," Yousuke chimed in. "We don't have to fight against anybody this time, we just have to come to a consensus. We can vote over and over as many times as we want, as long as time permits, with the interval periods taken into account."

"I'm sure that you have a general idea of what this special exam is going to be like from these examples," said Chabashira. "I'm now going to show you a summary of the rules. Those of you who feel that you want to hold onto them should take a screenshot on your devices."

Unanimous Special Exam Summary

EXPLANATION OF THE RULES

All students in the class will vote from the choices provided on each issue presented by the school. There will be a total of 5 issues with a maximum of 4 choices each.

An issue will be voted on repeatedly until students have reached a unanimous decision on one of the choices.

If students run out of time on an issue, that issue will not pass, regardless of progress made on the vote.

If a unanimous decision is reached on a particular issue, that issue will pass, regardless of whether the class passes or fails the special exam overall.

If students finish voting on all issues, their class will be awarded 50 Class Points.

If students fail to finish voting on all issues within five hours, their class will lose 300 Class Points.

SPECIAL EXAM FLOW

An issue will be presented, and the first round of voting will be held within 60 seconds.

If a unanimous decision is reached, proceed to step 1 for the next issue to be voted on. If not, then proceed to step 3.

10-minute interval: During this time, students are free to move around and discuss the issue within their own classroom.

60-second voting period: Students cannot talk during this time and can only cast their vote. Students who do not finish voting within 60 seconds will accrue cumulative penalty time. If a student's cumulative penalty time exceeds 90 seconds, that student will immediately be expelled.

Voting results are announced. If a unanimous decision has been reached, proceed to step 1 for the next issue. If not, return to step 3.

We would repeat this process over and over and finish the special exam after going through all five issues. If by some chance we failed, we'd be penalized. Losing 300 Class Points here would essentially mean losing our ticket to Class A. That was not an exaggeration. If we lost and the other three classes completed the exam, that would increase the gap between us and them by 350 Class Points.

We could discuss these issues as much as we wanted, but in the end, the problem was that the voting was completely anonymous. You couldn't be sure who voted for what. Someone could claim that they voted against something when they actually voted in favor of it.

"Not even we teachers have any knowledge about what kinds of issues you'll be presented with," Chabashira added. "Some of you may be taking an optimistic view of this, but let me give you a word of caution: do not let your guard down, not by any means. Also, you are strictly forbidden from making any sort of contract or other agreements with other students to force them into voting for a specific option in this exam. You are not allowed to engage in monetary transactions with another student or anything similar that would put them in a binding agreement for a particular choice either. Please note that this doesn't just apply to your own class, but to the other classes as well."

So, forcing someone into voting a specific way via an agreement made beforehand wasn't allowed. Even though we were allowed to consolidate to a certain extent and come to a consensus on an issue, we weren't allowed to back things up with contracts and guarantees. If someone signed a contract that said they could only vote for option number one, there was a risk that the exam would no longer be viable. That would be true even if only one person in a class had signed that agreement. Something like that would make it possible to deliver a vicious blow to another class.

"School officials will be monitoring you closely and enforcing these rules," Chabashira said. "If it is discovered that a third party, someone outside of the class, is somehow involved in something like forcing another student to vote in a specific way, the person or persons involved may be expelled without delay. That is a possibility, so do be prepared for that. Also, if any one of you is approached and asked to engage in illicit activities, please report it to the school immediately. We will do everything in our power to resolve the matter."

If a class ran out of time in this special exam, school officials would most definitely investigate since finishing in time was a prerequisite. Since you were likely going to be faced with a strict penalty simply for talking about doing something against the rules, not even someone like Ryuuen would be doing anything blatantly obvious. Until the special exam started, it seemed like it'd be best to refrain from getting carelessly involved with students from other classes.

"Also, please note that Protect Points will temporarily be rendered ineffective for this special exam," added Chabashira. "The reason being is that it is impossible to conduct a fair special exam if there is only one student who is protected. This means that if it's decided that a student with a Protect Point is going to be expelled in any way, shape, or form, they will be unable to cancel that decision with the Protect Point in their possession.

However, expulsion can still be avoided if either an individual or the entire class collectively pays 20 million
Private Points. That is the only allowable method to
counter an expulsion."

Any student who was going to be expelled was done
for: it would be definite. Did this mean that the school
would sometimes nullify Protect Points since they could
cancel out an expulsion? If we were dealing with a special
exam where we were going up against another class, then
temporarily invalidating Protect Points in those cases
could lead to students feeling unsatisfied. However, in
this case, this was nothing more than an in-class problem.
In that sense, I supposed it wasn't unreasonable for the
school to apply this special rule here. It was inevitable
that people would grumble about it, but even Kouenji
didn't seem to be bothered in the slightest.

"Please understand that during the special exam, all
communication devices, such as your cell phones, will be
collected. This is because the school deemed it possible
that students could use them to contact people outside
of their class. In the unlikely event that a student is found
to have a concealed device, then... Well, I'm sure I don't
even need to spell it out for you at this point."

She meant that expulsion was to follow, just like the
other rules that we needed to observe here.

3.1

. . . .

WHEN OUR LUNCH HOUR CAME, Yousuke imme-diately got up out of his seat and headed over to the podium.

"So, hey, I was thinking I'd like to hear everyone's opin-ions before we have lunch, if that's okay," he addressed us. "What do you all think?"

Kushida raised her hand to answer first. "Um, aren't there going to be conflicts because people will be divided on the options in this special exam?"

"She's right about that," said Horikita. "If we could come to a consensus on matters without fighting over any-thing, then there wouldn't be any reason to go through the trouble of holding this special exam in the first place."

"In that case, wouldn't it be a good idea to decide upon a leader in advance, in case there are times when we can't come to a consensus about something?" Kushida said. "I think that if we follow the decisions that such a leader would make, then we'd be able to get through this special exam without any problems."

"That's true. I agree with your opinion on that, Kushida-san. That means that the leader would have a serious responsibility, though," noted Yousuke.

The more options and conflicting opinions there were, the more criticism that leader would face from students who supported choices that didn't get picked. Whoever it was, it would need to be the sort of leader who could rally people together well.

"Actually, if you wouldn't mind... Would you be able to do it, Horikita-san?" asked Kushida.

"Me?" asked Horikita.

"Yes. You've acted as the leader many times before, and more importantly, I think that you would keep everyone in line well enough that there won't be any unfairness. Of course, it would be a serious responsibility, just like Hirata-kun said. So, if you'd be okay with it, Horikita-san, then... Well?"

"...You're right," said Horikita. "I suppose that it's possible other classes will implement similar strategies, and it'd be a necessary measure to have in place when opinions are divided. If there's anyone who feels hesitant to follow my orders when the time calls for it, please tell me now. This is the time."

Students weren't likely going to make a bid for the position themselves or make negative comments now after hearing what a huge responsibility it would be. Kushida's proposal was swiftly approved, and everyone agreed that Horikita would lead the group in case of emergency. For a while after that, various opinions were exchanged back and forth, but no other major conclusions were reached. In the end, it was simply time for lunch, albeit somewhat later than usual.

"Think it's time to get some food. Yukimuu, Miyacchi, you're coming too, right?" said Haruka, turning back to look at them.

The two guys agreed, as usual, and got up from their seats. These were all members of the Ayanokouji Group. It was a small group of five, including me. Just as we were all getting together though, another student came running up to me. As soon as our eyes met, she called out my name.

"Kiyotaka, let's go get lunch."

She said it without pausing, but she appeared somewhat nervous as she looked me in the eyes. No one had been paying close attention to Kei as she came toward me, nor were they intentionally listening in on what she said. However, now, every student in our class besides Kouenji, all thirty-six of them, turned to look at us in unison.

"Sorry, guys, but I'm going to eat with Kei today," I told them.

Before the people around us could understand what was happening, I pushed my chair back and stood up.

"...I wanna go to the café," said Kei. "Is that okay?"

"Hey... Wha...? H-hold up," said Haruka. "Karuizawa-san, why are you suddenly just butting in?"

"It's not like there's any rule against joining a conversation, is there?" Kei replied. "Didn't you just hear what Kiyotaka said?"

"Y-yeah, I heard it, but... What's going on? I thought you promised you'd come with us already though? ...Also, hold up, 'Kei'?" Haruka asked, rambling.

After a slight delay, Haruka started to understand why Kei and I were calling each other by our given names. Well, no, I supposed she might not have been able to completely understand what was happening here.

"Sorry, but I'm his girlfriend, so I'm his top priority. Okay?" said Kei.

Haruka paused for a moment. "Huh?"

"Girl...friend...?" whispered Airi.

The two muttered their respective comments at the exact same time, though their reactions were completely different.

"Anyway, as you can guess, Kiyotaka might have fewer chances to hang out with you guys as a group from now on," added Kei.

She proceeded to tug me by the arm, leading me out of the classroom. "Come on, let's go," Kei urged. She must have been feeling quite embarrassed, judging from the fact that her face was starting to turn bright red. As for me, I hadn't imagined that we were going to announce our relationship in this way at all...

Haruka, Airi, and the other students were dumbfounded, seemingly unable to follow after us.

3.2

THANKS TO KEI'S BOLD ACTIONS, our relationship that until that point had only been known to a select few had immediately become public knowledge to our entire class. Words would likely spread through our whole grade by the end of the day. Actually, though, I was skeptical about how many students would really be interested in my relationship with her. The fact that Ike and Shinohara had gotten together during the summer vacation had made fewer waves than I had expected as a hot topic. If anything, it was more like people had already assumed that they would have gotten together.

Some of the guys in class seemed to be trying to put up a tough front, like they didn't care about Ike and Shinohara being together. And, some of Ike's friends honestly seemed a little jealous. However, it made no difference. That was because in the end, the fact they became a couple was celebrated by many. Ike and Shinohara nurtured their romantic relationship well, though it was gradual. I was also seeing them together more often lately. They walked back to the dorms from class together, they went on dates, and so on and so forth. What was at first a novel sight soon became the norm. I thought it was going to be the same with Kei and me, though I figured we might end up causing more commotion than Ike and Shinohara and for a longer period of time.

At any rate, we had now reached the end of the school day, and the entire class had come to know about my relationship. I sensed that from the time our afternoon classes started earlier, there was a certain girl in class who hadn't looked at me once since lunch.

That girl was none other than Haruka, Airi's best friend and her cheerleader, someone who understood her well. She approached me after class and called out to me.

"Hey, Kiyopon! If ya don't mind, would you walk back to the dorms with me?"

I was expecting that Kei would suggest we walk back after class together, but when I had shot her a glance earlier, she was surrounded by girls bombarding her with questions.

"Are you sure that's okay?" I asked her.

I had expected that Haruka would have definitely been offering her support to Airi right now, watching over her. Instead, Airi was slowly and silently getting ready to head back to the dorms.

"I know, I know, but there's nothing I can say to her right now," Haruka sighed. "Yeah? But, well, I guess if you tell me there are reasons you can't walk back alone with me though, Kiyopon, that'd be a different story."

Her expression hardened for just a moment.

"All right," I replied.

Now that the fact Kei and I were going out was public knowledge, the number of opportunities that I'd have to get together with the Ayanokouji Group would inevitably decrease. Considering that, I figured it would be a good idea for me to hear everything that Haruka had to say, without restraint. Haruka and I each grabbed our things and headed to the front entrance of the building, walking all the way there from the rear exit. Haruka simply walked on ahead of me without uttering a single word as we moved along, seemingly unconcerned.

I occasionally stole glances to look at her from the side, and I saw that she had what appeared to be a look of anger and sadness on her face. Around the time that we put on our shoes and left the school building, she finally turned to look at me properly.

"There's no point in me trying to ask this in a round-about way, so I'm just going to come straight out with it... Is it really true that you and Karuizawa-san started dating? I still can't believe it."

"As you saw for yourself, yes, it's true," I replied.

After I told her that, Haruka pouted her lips and immediately nodded.

"Yeah... I guess it was plain to see, huh? Sorry, but it's just...I was so shocked. Listen, of course you're free to date whoever you want, Kiyopon. I just never imagined that you'd be seeing Karuizawa-san of all people. Y'know?"

For those who didn't know her, Karuizawa Kei's reputation was by no means clean. Most people had the impression that she was a selfish girl who quickly got together with the popular Yousuke and dumped him for her own self-serving reasons.

"I guess this is what you were talking about before, when we were by the pool. What you said about a little emotional shock. Except, you *do* realize that there wasn't anything little about it at all, right? Airi was desperately trying her hardest to keep it together in the classroom, but she was crying all through lunch."

"I see."

"No, this is not just an 'I see' type of thing... Anyway,

is it true that you guys started going out around spring break? Like, for real?"

"I'm sorry I didn't say anything. But I had a lot going on."

"A lot, huh? Well, I guess there are lots of rumors going around about Karuizawa-san so I can kind of understand what you mean, but..." Haruka's voice drifted off there.

I supposed it was understandable that people might have that perception of Kei since she had been dating Yousuke right around the time we started school here. She also likely fabricated details about her own past.

"So, like, it's *really* true then?" Haruka asked again. "This isn't a joke or anything?"

"It's true," I answered.

She sighed loudly. "I see. Well, it is what it is, I guess. I dunno, it's just like, I'm still so confused by it... Well, sure, I had imagined you could be dating somebody, Kiyopon, or that you were in love with someone other than Airi, but... It's just, I couldn't imagine it being Karuizawa-san, no way." Haruka was deeply perplexed. Apparently, all of her predictions had been way off the mark.

"I talked with Yukimuu and Miyacchi a little too, and they feel the same as me. And I didn't hear Airi say anything about it directly, but I'm sure she must be more shocked than we are."

I was sure she was right about that. Even I could imagine that quite easily.

"I mean, like, what's the story behind it? I can't even imagine that you would have had that many chances to hang out with her, or things in common, or anything."

It didn't surprise me that she wouldn't be able to figure out when exactly Kei and I came to like one another.

"I was in Kei's same group when we had that special exam on the ship last year," I explained. "Ever since then, we started having chances to talk to each other a little more here and there. Then, when Yousuke and Kei decided to break up, that's when our relationship started to take off."

Some of the students had heard about the fact that Kei and Yousuke's relationship ended in February of this year.

"So, you two have been hanging out for a pretty long time then? It didn't look like you've been talking on a regular basis."

"We mostly chatted on our phones," I explained.

"This is going to sound really nosy, but I've got to ask. Which one of you asked the other out?"

It sounded like Haruka wanted to know more, as Airi's protector and her spokesperson.

"I asked her," I replied.

Haruka paused at that. "Okay. I had thought maybe Airi would still have a chance if Karuizawa-san had been the one to ask you out, but wow, I never thought it would've been you who did... I guess that's that, then."

She lightly slapped her forehead, and then proceeded to raise both of her arms up in the air in a gesture of giving up. Just as we neared the convenience store, Haruka spoke up once more, proposing that we stop.

"Hey, time-out for a sec. There's just way too much information to process, and I feel like I'm losing track. Sorry, but can I swing through the store?"

"Sure. I'll wait outside."

Haruka gave me a brief apology for asking and quickly ran inside the convenience store, disappearing from my view. While she was inside, I took out my phone. It had vibrated in my pocket quite a few times as we were walking.

"I'll be waiting for you at Keyaki Mall after this. They've been asking me question after question—it's so exhausting!"

A message from my girlfriend and an invitation to come see her.

"Got it. I'll contact you before I head over."

After I confirmed that my message had been read, I put my phone back in my pocket. After another short minute or so, Haruka returned with a croquette in hand.

"I was so busy talking with Airi during lunch today that I didn't get to eat at all," she explained.

"That must've been a bother," I replied.

"It wasn't like it was a problem or anything, really..."

"I'm not sure if this is the best time for me to ask you for something, but to tell you the truth, there is something I'd like your help with, and Airi's too, if possible," I told her.

"*Our* help?" repeated Haruka.

"This hasn't been officially announced yet, but we decided on one of our acts for the cultural festival."

"Whoa, really?"

"Only me, Horikita, and the people involved in planning it know, so we could make sure that information doesn't get out," I explained. "We're planning to host a maid café for the cultural festival."

"M...maid café? That's, uh, kind of... Well, I'm not, like, *shocked*, but it is a little surprising. I can't exactly picture Horikita-san approving that."

"I think that she's pretty neutral on everything, no matter what's proposed to her. I think that she gave permission to go ahead with the idea because she simply thought that we could win this thing with the maid café idea. She wasn't prejudiced against the concept."

"I see. So...why are you talking to me about it then?" asked Haruka.

"Truth is, after finding out about this project, it turns out that I'm going to be the one managing lots of aspects of it," I replied.

When I said that, Haruka nodded as though she understood. "Still, considering the situation, I got to hand it to Horikita-san for entrusting you with this, Kiyopon," she said.

"I was wondering if I could ask you to help staff it," I told her. "And Airi too."

Haruka listened to my request with a look on her face that I couldn't quite describe. She didn't exactly appear surprised. Well, I supposed that I could more or less guess what she was thinking, from the way she was talking.

"If it hadn't been for this whole thing with Karuizawa-san, I might have agreed to help right on the spot, even though I have some reservations about it," she said. "I really, really don't like stuff like dressing up in cosplay in front of lots of people, but I don't think I could have refused an offer if it was coming from a part of our close friend group. But...gosh, your timing couldn't have been worse."

I guessed that meant it was out of the question for me to make a request like this right now, on the very day her close friend suffered a broken heart from unrequited love.

"It's just well, the problem is I can't really blame you for any of it, Kiyopon. I basically said as much earlier, but you're free to date whoever. And I do understand that you have your reasons for not being able to say anything, I get that. Airi is free to have a crush on you, Kiyopon, and you're free to reject her..."

Haruka clearly accepted it in theory, but her heart couldn't accept it.

"I can't make any promises," she said. "But I'll try talking to Airi when things calm down a little."

"You sure that's okay?" I asked.

"She's going to have to face reality sooner or later. And, well, I don't know how you feel about everything, Kiyopon, but if Karuizawa-san is Airi's rival in love, then Airi might not even have to give up. I mean, even if you're devoted to her, Kiyopon, there's still a chance she might break up with you, right?"

"Yeah, I suppose you're right," I agreed. "I think there is a strong possibility that Kei could fall out of love with me."

"If that time comes, then that just means Airi will get another chance. She doesn't stand out at all right now, but she's a diamond in the rough... And besides, your feelings may change too, Kiyopon."

It was certainly true that if Airi put on one of those costumes and really gave it her all, she'd be just as good as those three other girls. Actually, no, if we took Airi's physical features into account, then she might be without peer. Furthermore, although we weren't talking about visitors who would be coming to our café, even the school officials might be shocked by Airi's appearance. If Airi did work at the maid café, talk would immediately circulate around the school, and it was conceivable that even visitors would hear about it.

"Well, sure, that's true," I said. "But I wonder if Airi's feelings might change after what happened?"

If the person you fell in love with already had a special someone, then it was natural that you'd go looking for your next love. I thought that by mentioning that I was only stating the obvious, but Haruka showed me the angriest look on her face that I had seen on her all day.

"Listen. Don't you think that you're taking Airi's feelings too lightly? I've been watching her for a long, long time, so I really understand how she feels. What she feels for you isn't so casual that it would just change because of something like this happening, Kiyopon."

She strongly rejected what I'd said. That was wholly unexpected.

"I'm sure that you'll be going out on more dates and stuff with Karuizawa-san and stuff, but make sure you actually come hang out with us too, okay?" she said.

"I would hate for us to drift apart over something like this."

"I see," I replied. "I understand. This group we have right now is a part of my life here at this school too."

I figured it would be disadvantageous for me to lose the group because of an incident like this.

Haruka quickly finished her croquette and put her trash in her bag. "All right," she said. "I feel a little better now. I'm gonna head back to school."

She didn't say much about her plans, but it was clear that she was going to go see Airi.

"See you tomorrow," she said.

"Yeah, see you tomorrow," I replied.

I watched Haruka's back as she ran back the way we came. Then, I turned and changed course myself, heading not toward the dormitory but instead to Keyaki Mall.

3.3

· ·

THE EXCITEMENT IN THE AIR still hadn't died down even after class that day. I returned to the dormitory from Keyaki Mall with Kei, the two of us chatting as we walked. When we reached the dorm lobby, we found Horikita sitting on the sofa, seemingly waiting for someone, and who she was waiting for would soon become clear.

The elevator was stopped on the first floor, above us. I pressed the button indicating that I wanted to head up. Once the doors opened, Kei and I got on, and so did Horikita.

"Ayanokouji-kun, may I have a word with you?" she asked.

The elevator stopped on the fourth floor, where my room was located.

"Well, later, Kiyotaka," said Kei.

Kei was the type who got easily jealous, but she was also very good at reading situations. Kei also knew that I didn't even view Horikita as a member of the opposite sex to begin with, and since we just heard about an upcoming special exam, she probably didn't have to give it much thought to determine that it would be better for her not to interfere.

"Okay. I'll talk to you later," I told her.

A year ago, I probably wouldn't have believed that Kei and I would have become lovers and be spending time together like this.

I got off the elevator and Horikita followed suit. Kei stayed put, and when I turned around, I saw her smiling and waving to me from inside the elevator as the doors began to close. Soon, the doors were shut, and the elevator continued on to the upper floors.

"How long have you been seeing her?" asked Horikita.

"Not sure, exactly. Who can say?"

"Rumor has it you started going out over spring vacation, but in truth, didn't this relationship of yours start progressing much earlier in the year?" Horikita turned to me with a look in her eyes that made it seem like she was implying something.

"I wonder," I replied.

Whether or not there was any basis for what Horikita was saying, I was neither interested nor willing to touch on it.

"Enough about that," I said. "You said you wanted to talk to me?"

"Yes... It's about the special exam. There's something I wanted to ask you about it. Is that okay?"

"Sure. I don't mind."

"Huh? Oh...okay."

"What's with that reaction?" I asked.

"Well, it's just, knowing you, I was expecting you to say no," she said. "I was more prepared for that. You did look disgruntled when I had asked you to handle the maid café yesterday. Weren't you?"

Apparently, Horikita was shocked by how readily I had accepted her request for a consultation.

"Not here," I told her. "Step into my room."

Anyone could be listening if we stood around in the hallway, after all. I unlocked the door to my room, room 401, and we went inside.

"You're not going to ask me to help with something again, are you?" I asked.

"Well... I'm not sure. In any case, if you're willing to hear me out, we'll just start there."

Perhaps Horikita was concerned that if she provoked

me too much I would refuse her, because she decided to just start saying what she wanted to say.

"To ensure we make it through this special exam, I was considering holding a semi-compulsory meeting of our own beforehand," she said. "But even if we try to prepare for this special exam, it would be totally absurd for us to attempt to have the class come to a consensus on things when we don't even know what the issues are going to be in the first place, wouldn't it?"

"Depending on the situation, we will inevitably have to go with different options," I agreed.

Even if there were only two choices for an issue, such as for or against, it would be nothing short of reckless to decide on voting only one way before we even knew what the situations were.

"You've probably thought of your own way of making it through this special exam, haven't you, Horikita?" I asked.

"I think that the most efficient way to be certain we can pass this special exam is for someone to have the final say in decisions," said Horikita. "No matter how many options there are, and no matter how the votes are split, we'll have people promise to follow the leader's judgment in advance and act in accordance with the leader's wishes."

That was what Kushida had proposed during our lunch break. With that strategy, we wouldn't consider whether or not any individual would be dissatisfied with the choices. It was certainly true that this arrangement would be the simplest possible solution if we could make it a reality.

"I hope that we're really able to bring everyone together that way," I said.

"Yes, me too... There will definitely be some students who won't be satisfied with some of the issues though... I suppose if this was a dictatorship like Ryuuen's class, then this whole discussion would go more quickly."

Horikita and I wished that we had the type of coercive force to make students do what we wanted, but Ryuuen could exercise that force without mercy. Still, whether or not something like that would actually work in reality was another matter.

"The fact that all voting is done anonymously means that students who are dissatisfied with Ryuuen can vote for the opposite opinion as him," I pointed out. "There's no guarantee that merely issuing an order will mean he can get things to pass."

"If students are dissatisfied with Ryuuen's methods, I suppose there's nothing they can do but rebel against him," Horikita agreed. "But it's also a fact that there is nothing for them to gain by doing so. After all, if the vote is split and time runs out, the whole class will suffer for it, correct? In the end, I'm sure they'll come together, even if Ryuuen leaves them be."

"I understand what you're trying to say, but you're actually contradicting yourself by bringing this up," I said. "No one wants to fail a special exam. In the end, people will definitely come to a consensus and vote accordingly. If that basic premise is true, then you don't even need a strategy in the first place, do you?"

"That's—"

"No student would want to let time run out to the detriment of the class," I added. "But I think it's still best that we don't assume we can finish voting on all five issues if we leave things be. There'd be no reason for the school to even call this a special exam if that was the case."

"Yes...you're exactly right about that," conceded Horikita.

"All you can do right now is make up your mind to be flexible. For example, let's say we're faced with an issue where thirty-eight voted for, and one person voted against. What would you do?"

"I would do everything in my power to get that one person who voted against to change their vote, of course," said Horikita.

"Right. But what if that one person who voted against absolutely, positively wouldn't give in?"

"Well..."

"You may not necessarily always win by going with the thirty-eight in favor. While you're trying to persuade that lone student, some of the thirty-eight students who voted in favor might even end up changing their opinions," I added.

"Even if that one person's ideas are detrimental to the majority of the class?" asked Horikita.

"It all depends on the context, really."

I wouldn't be surprised if an issue like that was waiting for us: something that someone absolutely would not bend on.

"Somehow, this feels a little bit unsettling," Horikita said.

"How so?"

"Because you gave me advice without any hesitation. I...didn't imagine that it has anything to do with the fact that you're dating Karuizawa-san now, but what's your angle here?"

"What I told you could hardly even count as advice," I said. "I'm sure that, in the back of your mind, you've already considered the possibility of something like that happening."

"Yes, you're right... All right, then, I'll come out and tell you about my main purpose for coming to talk to you. I have a proposal regarding tomorrow's special exam. I could ask someone else to do this, but I wanted to ask someone who I knew would understand."

"Meaning you want me to always pick a different option from you in the first round of voting?"

"Could you please not preempt my thoughts?" she snapped.

I moved a little further away from Horikita once I saw that she was irritated.

"It's just that it was something I was already thinking of doing, in the event that no one suggested it," I said. "I didn't imagine we'd have the same idea."

"...Really?"

Apparently, the random excuse I came up with had worked, and Horikita was somewhat convinced. I could see that her anger had dissipated. Well, it was true that I had that idea already anyway, to do at least that much. I guess the excuse I gave wasn't totally bunk. It would be better to avoid the risk of making an unexpected choice as the result of biases caused by the heat of the moment.

"If we came to a unanimous decision through sheer coincidence, that would be a little scary. Even if it was an issue that 99 percent of the class was in favor of or against, or if it was in a situation where both options had advantages and disadvantages," said Horikita.

"That's true. If an issue passes as a result of an entirely random happenstance, we won't be able to take it back. Still, planning to make use of that interval period every time isn't necessarily a good idea. You should keep that in mind. There's a risk that we might encounter an issue that we would've come to a unanimous decision on if we just stuck with the momentum we had from the start, only to find that things are split further when the time comes for discussion. We could end up not being able to reach a consensus. You have to factor that into your calculations."

"Yes, you're right. You're absolutely right," said Horikita.

To delve into the argument was to plunge your hand into the deep. And if you drew an unexpected darkness out as a result, it could end up costing us a lot of time.

"Under the rules of this special exam, there's no way to determine with certainty who voted for what, no matter how much we discuss it," I went on. "Even if people make pledges, it might not be 100 percent true."

"You're saying that people will lie to me?" asked Horikita.

"Depending on the situation, sure," I replied. "It's tough to say right now that the class is really united as one."

Now that I said that, I was sure several people came to Horikita's mind.

"You're referring to Kushida-san and Kouenji-kun, right?" she said.

"Kushida would probably lie without batting an eyelash, but as for Kouenji, there's a chance that he might deliberately choose something different than his classmates. His contrarian nature could rear its head. That's what I mean."

"Hey...why are you telling me all of this in such detail? It really is strange. You've never given me advice quite like this before."

Horikita was naturally, intuitively sensing that there was a change in me.

"Because I judged that as you are now, Horikita, you would be able to genuinely listen to what I had to say. You also have the kind of adaptability to understand it."

"Can I...take that to be a compliment?" she asked.

"In a manner of speaking, sure."

"Yeah... This is kind of unsett—"

Just then, I briefly heard the sound of a cell phone vibrating.

"Excuse me for a minute," said Horikita.

With that, Horikita took out her phone, and our conversation was put on hold. She stared down at the screen and began tapping on it.

"Let me send her a message," she said. "There's a chance I might not see that she's read it for a while if I'm careless about it."

I didn't have any intention of stopping Horikita, of course, but who did she mean by "she"? I couldn't help but wonder about that. Though I was a little curious, I decided to just wait quietly until Horikita finished composing her rather long message. She took about two minutes to do it, but eventually, she sent her message and put her phone away in her pocket.

"At any rate, I've said what I've wanted to say to you," she told me. "I'll be counting on you during tomorrow's special exam."

She must not have intended to stay very long in the first place because she immediately left my room after that.

3.4

I T WAS A LITTLE BEFORE six o'clock in the evening—
the time when the sun would soon set and night would
fall. Though today was supposed to have been an ordinary day, a special exam was announced to us. It ended up
being a very trying day with an unusually large amount of
information I needed to process.

It would have been much easier if I could just let
things be and wait for the day to come to an end, but that
wasn't going to happen. The Unanimous Special Exam,
which had been announced to us on rather short notice,
was being held tomorrow.

"Hey there."

Yousuke was the first to show up as I waited in my
room.

"Come on in," I said.

Thinking about it, this was the first time I had invited Yousuke to come into my room like this, wasn't it?

"Hello~!"

Shortly afterward, Kei arrived as well.

"You know, it's kind of unusual, but it's interesting, isn't it?" she said. "The three of us getting together like this."

"You might be right about that," I agreed.

I hadn't told them the reason why I asked them both to come here, but I figured that Yousuke might have already guessed.

"I thought we should come up with some counter-measures for the special exam tomorrow," I said.

"Countermeasures?" echoed Kei. "But it's just an exam where we just have to come to a unanimous decision on stuff, right?"

"From what we've heard, I certainly don't think it'll be that difficult of an exam," replied Yousuke. "The special exams we've had in the past have been much more diffi-cult, in terms of their rules."

Yousuke gestured as though he were giving the matter some thought. Then, he continued speaking, explaining the situation to Kei.

"However, I think that maybe this one won't exactly be that straightforward either, like those difficult special exams we've had in the past. If you think about it, if we were following along with the rules, then this would be an exam where we'd gain Class Points simply by coming to a unanimous decision. Our class coming to a consensus in itself isn't *that* difficult."

"Yeah, I think so too," Kei said.

"So, in other words, if this exam isn't going to be that easy, that means it's highly likely that there are going to be issues that people will be divided on," Yousuke concluded.

His thinking was right on the mark. Although individual students in class might have their own ways of thinking, they would be willing to be flexible to a certain extent to align their votes if it was in the best interest of the class. It might have been a different story if this exam occurred back when we were first-year students and new at this school, but now that we were second-years, the bonds between us as friends had deepened considerably. Moreover, even if we couldn't reach a unanimous decision at first, there wasn't a penalty for that. We could repeatedly set aside time for discussion and work things out. So, it was understandable that an exam like this, with such relief measures in place, would seem lax from Kei's perspective.

"But, like, what kinds of issues would it be difficult for us to reach a unanimous decision on anyway?" she asked.

"Well, I can't really come up with anything right on the spot," Yousuke replied, "but...I think there would definitely be those kinds of issues..."

What kinds of questions would my classmates agonize over? It seemed like Yousuke wasn't able to come up with any ideas right away. I thought I'd speak up with one easy-to-understand issue.

"Until we graduate, we can only eat either rice or bread starting now. Choose," I told them.

"Huh? What's with those choices?" said Kei.

"Choosing between rice and bread is something that kind of makes me want to chuckle at its simplicity, but it's actually a hard choice," said Yousuke.

"I'd definitely go with bread, myself," Kei decided. "Going without having *any* kind of bread until graduation? Absolutely not, no way."

"In my case, I'd probably go with rice... I've been fine having bread like once a week or so, anyway," said Yousuke.

"If I had to choose, I suppose I'd pick rice too," I said. "And, well, as you can see, we three have our own opinions on this, right? If we were to have the entire class vote on this, it wouldn't be easy. If there were thirty people who were in favor of rice, would you be able to go along with them?"

"No way! I mean, not being able to have any at all until graduation? I'd still vote for bread," said Kei.

There were going to be some students who would resist, like Kei, who wouldn't be easily swayed by the majority and wouldn't back down. That would lead to problems.

"Now, if we were to consider a more realistic comparison, relatively speaking: all future special exams will either be based solely on academic ability or physical ability. What if we faced an issue like that?" I asked.

When I posed that problem, Yousuke and Kei exchanged looks.

"For an athletic student like Sudou, he would absolutely choose physical ability," I went on. "But a student who wasn't so athletically gifted, like Keisei, would have to do anything and everything he could to steer the vote toward a unanimous decision in favor of academic ability."

Of course, it was possible that Sudou could back down and vote the other way, especially since he had been pouring a lot of effort into his studies lately. Even so, he would do much better if he were evaluated based on his physical abilities. And even if Sudou could be swayed, a different student who wasn't academically inclined at all wouldn't be able to compromise on the decision at all.

"If an issue is passed unanimously, that means it's enforced, correct?" I said. "Meaning, in other words, depending on how the situation plays out, would we need to be prepared to lose 300 Class Points as a penalty if we can't choose an option?"

"I don't know... Difficult choices will obviously have to be made, but losing 300 Class Points would mean giving up our ticket to Class A," said Yousuke. "Our first priority should be clearing this exam."

Kei sighed, "I'm starting to think that this is going to be really tough..."

"Is that why you called us here?" asked Yousuke.

"Yeah," I replied. "This next special exam is going to require a strong sense of unity amongst our classmates. The class breaking into complete disagreement once or twice is fine, but if it goes on for a long time, fights could start to break out. When that time comes, you two will be needed to conduct yourselves skillfully and sway the votes. You are the central figures of the class."

"You're right," said Yousuke. "But in that case, shouldn't Horikita-san be included in this discussion we're having now too? She took on the role of class leader for this exam, after all."

Yousuke's point was obvious. It *would* be best if Horikita led these two and controlled the class instead of me taking the initiative here. However, at this stage, I couldn't withdraw my support quite yet.

"This time, we will be supporting Horikita from the shadows," I told them. "What we're discussing here is strictly confidential."

"Why, though?" asked Kei. "I mean, personally, I don't like the idea of following Horikita-san's orders anyway..."

"Kei, Yousuke, you two have the ability to read the room much better than the average student. However, starting now, I want you two to be able to respond to things with even more flexibility than you do now. If you can intuitively sense what Horikita is thinking and what she wants to do, the class will become much, much stronger."

"Why don't you do it though, Kiyotaka? That would solve the problem," said Kei.

"You can't always count on me to be able to act," I said. "You should be prepared for unforeseen situations."

"Unforeseen situations?" she repeated.

"I could suddenly fall ill, or I could unexpectedly get expelled. That's conceivable, isn't it?"

"That's... Well, I... Well, expulsion, like, no way! I can't picture that happening," she replied. "But it is true you could suddenly get sick, that might happen."

I couldn't back them up at any given time forever. If they couldn't act in anticipation of situations like that, they couldn't expect to see the class make a great leap forward.

"Anyway, I understand," Yousuke said. "We just need to follow Horikita's lead well and make sure that the special exam proceeds smoothly, right?"

"Right. Kei, Yousuke, let me give you some instructions and some signals in advance—things that no one other than you two will understand."

Since we were allowed to freely discuss and move about during the interval periods, the act of whispering into someone's ear wouldn't be problematic in itself. However, depending on how the situation played out, it might become necessary to send instructions to Kei and Yousuke without letting anyone else know that we were communicating. Even in situations where whispering amongst ourselves was prohibited, it was still possible to exchange signals, like by coughing, lightly tapping on our desks, and so on. I had both Kei and Yousuke generally memorize multiple patterns of signs and signals.

Then, I looked over at Yousuke.

"Yousuke, one last thing, a warning. This won't be necessary if we manage to get through all five issues smoothly, but if we have fewer than two hours remaining, and it doesn't look like we'll be able to finish the special exam in time, desperate measures may need to be taken."

I decided to tell Yousuke that now so he could prepare himself. So he wouldn't go out of control if that time came.

3.5

● ●

THE DAY BEFORE the special exam had been quite hectic in a lot of ways and it was just about to come to an end. It was now after ten o'clock at night. I was in bed looking at my phone when I received a call. Although I didn't have the caller registered in my contacts, I recognized the eleven-digit number.

"Hello," I said, answering the phone.

"I sincerely apologize for calling you so late at night. Might I have a moment of your time?"

"It's all right," I replied. "It certainly has been quite some time since we last spoke, Chairman Sakayanagi, sir."

That's right—the phone number belonged to none other than the current chairman of the Advanced Nurturing High School.

"I realize that I have made you worry quite a bit, but I'm all right now."

"I'm just glad that you seem to be well."

"It seems that things have been quite trying for you as well. But I must admit, I cannot hide my surprise that you managed to remain safe and sound here at this school without incident. You were in the midst of an extremely disadvantageous battle."

"Only through happenstance, really," I said. "I'm sure that if *he* were serious about it, I wouldn't be here right now."

It wasn't necessary for me to mention any names out loud. I knew that Chairman Sakayanagi understood that I was referring to Tsukishiro, who had filled in for his position while he was away.

"Once I saw that everything was over, I certainly had a few questions of my own about his actions...but let's not talk about that today. I'm going to support you closely from now on. I thought I'd let you know about it as soon as I possibly could."

After a pause, he continued speaking.

"I'm sure you've heard about the upcoming cultural festival, which is a first for our institution. And yes, government officials and their families have been invited to attend. Now that things have been set in motion, I can't stop it myself."

If the parties involved have already been notified, then it would understandably be difficult for him to withdraw invitations now.

"There's nothing for you to apologize for, sir. I'm sure that the students are looking forward to it."

Although the nature of the festival was a bit like a special exam, it was within the range of things a student could enjoy. Whether it actually ended up being nothing more than a simple cultural festival for *me*, though, was another story.

"On that note... I would like to tell you about something that hasn't been announced yet. I would like to share this information with you first, and you alone."

"What is it?" I asked.

"It's about the sports festival to be held in October, which is something of a prelude to the cultural festival. The sports festival is similar to the cultural festival in some respects. First of all, it has suddenly been decided that we will be welcoming some visitors on campus."

"Visitors?" That was something I hadn't expected to hear.

"If you trace the history of the event back to its origins, you'll find that sports festivals are something that students' parents come to watch. In that sense, the idea of welcoming guests is not in itself dissimilar to that original concept of the event..."

"I see." It was true that when I saw them on TV, there were families with cameras and packed lunches at events like athletic meets and sports festivals.

"Suddenly allowing guests to freely come visit for the cultural festival poses some security concerns because it is a rather unprecedented event."

In a sense, it would be kind of like a test for the school. They were preparing to welcome a larger number of guests in full force later on.

"Guest selection rests entirely on the higher-ups, so I can't deny the possibility that Ayan—I mean, that your father might make an appearance. Therefore, in consideration of the danger you face in this, I would like to assign a few people to watch over you."

"I sincerely appreciate the sentiment, but I'm nothing more than a student at this school, the same as any other," I told him. "I don't want that kind of special treatment."

"In that case, how do you plan to handle the situation should you run into anyone sent by your father?"

"I understand that it's a difficult problem."

Obviously, it was unlikely I'd be able to get through such a situation using force. That went without saying. It would be easier for me if he tried to target me in a secluded area. If he sent people to the campus posing as school officials and they instructed me to come along with them while I had friends and acquaintances around, I would have no way of refusing. I couldn't even ask questions like, "You're all a bunch of frauds, aren't you? Agents sent by him?" or anything.

"I think that I already understood that you are that sort of person, I suppose. But if you were to be expelled from school in some way... I'm sure that I would regret it. I would like to avoid feeling regret over not doing whatever I could have done to prevent something like that."

"Even if I were to follow your instructions, sir, it would look unnatural to have a guard watching over me," I pointed out.

"In that case, I would like to ask you to be absent from the sports festival."

"You want me...to not participate?" That certainly hadn't been within my range of expectations.

"I'm sure you yourself understand that sometimes, with events such as these, people fall ill and have to be absent on the day of the exam."

"Yes. Although the class would be put at a disadvantage with me gone, there aren't any mandatory attendance rules that would result in me getting expelled for being absent."

Students were responsible for maintaining their own health, but even so, it was inevitable that people would fall ill sometimes. If it were a small-scale special exam, the school might adopt emergency measures like waiting until all students from each grade were present before going ahead. But for a school-wide event like the sports festival, that wouldn't be possible.

"We will have you confined to your room with everyone operating under the assumption you already underwent a medical check-up. Then, I can go ahead and place a trusted observer outside the dormitory to keep watch."

If I were ordered to rest in my room and be absent due to illness, my classmates would have to agree that I had no other choice. If there was someone loitering around the dormitory building and standing watch, other students would only see that person as just another security guard.

"That might very well keep me out of his reach, if we did that," I conceded.

"There are other risks, of course. As you said earlier, there's no avoiding the fact that the other children enrolled in your same class will be put at a disadvantage. They'd have to face the challenges while one of their fellow classmates is absent."

The fact that Chancellor Sakayanagi was offering to allow me to be absent by faking illness made it clear how generous and kind his support was. It was also gratifying to see that he wanted to keep things low-key, without showing me any excessive favoritism. Still, although it was a very kind offer, my first thought when I heard his proposal was that I would refuse. However, another idea was coming to mind.

"Would you please give me some time to consider?" I asked.

"Of course. I cannot force you, after all, so I will leave the final decision to you. However—"

"I understand. I am seriously considering accepting the idea of being absent."

"All right. Please give me a response one week before the sports festival. There are preparations I need to make on my end, as well."

He needed to arrange personnel and such for this plan, so that length of time was quite practical.

After I ended the call, I thought about the sports festival and how it might end up going on without me. Of course, it was entirely possible that students from other classes and in other grade levels could call in sick on that day too. It wasn't easy to get the entire student body together for every single exam and event, after all.

"No," I muttered aloud to myself, "I need to concentrate on the special exam in front of me first."

This upcoming special exam... It could very well be more painful than any other special exam that had come before. One way or another, we were able to prepare for every other special exam we faced so far. But this time, there was no surefire strategy. We had to believe in our classmates and work together as one.

And after that, a sports festival, and a cultural festival. Though there were new things to worry about this year that we didn't have to deal with last year, before everything else, we simply had to get through tomorrow's special exam.

3.6

SEVERAL HOURS PRIOR.

"Hello, Kushida-senpai."

After class ended for the day, Kushida visited Yagami Takuya in the first-year dormitory. The evening sun was shining faintly through a slight gap in the almost fully closed curtains. Kushida gazed at the steam rising from the freshly brewed tea sitting on the table. She didn't reach for it.

"I didn't poison it or slip any drugs into it, you know," said Yagami.

"I don't care about the tea," replied Kushida, making no attempt to hide her irritation. She pulled out her cell phone and held it out with a grim look on her face. "Can we please just hurry up and get on with it already?"

"Ah, please excuse my rudeness," Yagami said. "Very well then, let's have a listen."

Yagami pressed the play button on Kushida's phone. From her device, he heard Chabashira's voice providing a summary of the Unanimous Special Exam that had been announced to the second-year students. The recording seemed to start somewhere in the middle of her explanation. After silently listening to everything that was on the recording, including the example issues that were given to Kushida's class, Yagami returned Kushida's phone to her.

"You wish to crush Horikita Suzune and Ayanokouji Kiyotaka, Kushida-senpai. That's what this is supposed to be about, right?" asked Yagami.

Kushida, as if to say that she didn't even need to answer that, remained silent.

"I was briefed about this special exam by some upperclassmen beforehand, but I have to say, it certainly is an exceedingly straightforward exam," he went on. "You simply choose an option from the multiple choices available and repeat the voting process over and over again until you reach a unanimous decision. There are five issues in total, and you have five hours to get through them all. What were your thoughts when you heard about it?"

"That it's simple," said Kushida, after a pause.

"Yes, certainly," Yagami agreed. "For something that is being billed as a special exam, it is extremely elementary. However, the punishment for running out of time is quite severe. No doubt that must be because the school created this exam on the assumption that it would be passed. You have to take into consideration the fact that a class would inevitably move toward a unanimous decision once time is close to running out. Anyone would want to avoid a heavy penalty, after all, even if it meant voting for an option that they didn't like."

Yagami reached for the steaming cup of tea that sat in front of Kushida, taking it into his hands.

"Now then, onto the heart of the matter," he said. "You are already in the middle of your second year. However, while you do want those two expelled, you still haven't had the perfect opportunity fall into your lap yet."

"As far as I'm concerned, you're a little bit responsible for that yourself," snapped Kushida. "But whatever, it doesn't matter." She held herself back from going further, understanding that there wasn't anything to be gained by lashing out at Yagami right here and now.

"Have you told Horikita-senpai?" asked Yagami.

"Oh... You mean about being the leader? Yes, more or less. I think she would've gone ahead and done it on her own anyway, though, even if I didn't say anything."

"No, no, it isn't good to leave things in a state of ambiguity. It is important for you to make sure that Horikita-senpai is entrusted with the role and to get her to make a firm declaration that she would handle it, Kushida-senpai."

"So, what now? Do you think I can get her expelled in this upcoming special exam?"

At that question, Yagami let out a little chuckle before taking a sip of tea from his cup.

"Yes, certainly," he said. "I listened to your recording to make sure that there was nothing I missed hearing or misinterpreted, just in case. After hearing what you've provided, things have been made clear. It is...quite possible that you could do that in this upcoming special exam."

"...How could you possibly know that?" Kushida snorted. "The only instance where expulsion is given as a penalty is if someone runs over time. Do you think that Horikita would make a mistake like that? No, not just Horikita; *no one* would make that kind of mistake."

"Certainly not. It's unlikely anyone would be stupid enough to allow themselves to run over time and be expelled for it. But from what I can tell, I think that there are other ways someone could be expelled."

Kushida blinked. "Huh?"

"Expel Horikita-senpai, or, depending on the situation, expel Ayanokouji-senpai. There might be a possibility that you can crush the people you wish to crush. When that time comes, you shouldn't hesitate to guide the conversation toward targeting both of them."

Yagami then proceeded to elaborate on what he meant by using an example: an issue that was expected to be given in this upcoming special exam.

"Is that really true...?" asked Kushida.

"Well, I don't think it'll necessarily be exactly the same, not word for word," Yagami said. "However. I do think there is a significant possibility that there will be an issue on the exam like the one I just told you about."

Yagami hadn't actually been told about this special exam by Tsukishiro, but after listening to the teacher's explanation, he figured that issues like the one he had mentioned would be on the exam.

"So, when an issue like that does appear, there is only one course of action for you to take, Kushida-senpai."

Yagami went on to explain precisely how she could drive Horikita and Ayanokouji into a corner, should that issue come up.

"So, what do you think?" he said. "Doesn't this make the possibility of getting them expelled look much more attainable? Of course, you'll be reducing your entire class to tears by doing this, but that would be a small matter for you, wouldn't it?"

"Do you... Do you really think I could do something like that?" Kushida asked.

"In my view, you certainly have the capability. Or am I wrong in my assessment of you?"

"You certainly seem to have a high opinion of me."

"Well, I had to test my senpai when we first met, to see if you were someone I could use."

"...What do you mean by that?"

"Do you remember when I approached you that time? 'It's me. Do you not recognize me?'" asked Yagami.

"I was flustered," she said. "What about it?"

"What about it? Well, normally, anyone would have had their doubts in a situation like that. After all, we were complete strangers then, Kushida-senpai. We hadn't met before, not even once. Despite that, you immediately navigated the conversation, deftly managing to make your way through by improvising. That was exactly how I came to understand that you, senpai, are someone capable."

"But what if I had said, 'Who are you?' back then, when we met?" said Kushida. "I might have simply forgotten if we met before."

"I don't think you would have. Because if you didn't know where we met before, it could have turned out that we went to the same junior high. If that was the case, there'd be a possibility that I knew about your past. I'm sure it would've been a big problem for you in the unlikely event I were to say something like, 'I know about *that* incident' to you."

Yagami was implying that in order to reject the possibility of something like that happening, Kushida immediately improvised back then to go along with the flow of conversation.

"If I wasn't someone who attended your junior high, I could, for example, have gone to the same cram school. Or I could have been someone younger than you who just happened to live in your neighborhood. If you found out that it was one of those things later, then the risk of me being someone who knew about your past would be greatly reduced and you could laugh things off as a simple misunderstanding. Your first priority with any new person is to make sure they didn't go to your junior high school, right? That way, even if someone were to bring up a topic even only tangentially related to your past, it would be easier for you to divert the conversation away from it."

Having finished his explanation, Yagami drank about a quarter of the tea in the cup and set it down on the table.

"Who even are you, anyway?" asked Kushida quizzically. "How do you know about my past if we didn't even go to the same school...?"

"I understand why you are so guarded, but please, just consider me a guest in a rather unique position," Yagami said. "Yes, just so. My purpose is to play with Ayanokouji-senpai."

"Huh? To play with him?"

"Yes, well, I don't think he knows about me at all. Right now, what I'm most preoccupied with is testing out various things without Ayanokouji-senpai noticing."

"What if I got upset back then, when we first met? If I didn't give you the answers you wanted?" asked Kushida, curious about what Yagami would have said at the time.

"I would've found it interesting," he replied. "I am sure that Ayanokouji-senpai would have noticed your discomfort, saw that something was off, and he would have eyed me with suspicion. I probably could have *greeted* him at a much earlier stage, I suppose."

"...Did you and Ayanokouji go to the same junior high, by any chance?"

"Well, who can say? Anyway, that's of little concern to you, Kushida-senpai. Let's turn our attention to the special exam for now, shall we?" said Yagami, redirecting the conversation.

"I know. If that issue that you're hoping for does come up, then...at that time, I'll try to make a move."

"You will *try* to make a move? That's not good enough."

"Not good enough?" Kushida spat back. "What the heck do you mean, not good enough?"

Yagami got up and moved in close to Kushida, grabbing her by the shoulders. The young woman reflexively tried to flee.

"Hey! What are you doing?!"

Kushida tried to break free from his grasp, but Yagami was stronger than she imagined he'd be despite his slender build. She was utterly unable to move.

"Please listen very carefully," he told her. "You are in far more dire straits than you think you are, Kushida-senpai. Not only do you have people near you like Ayanokouji-senpai and Horikita-senpai to worry about, but you have other causes for concern as well. There are others whose very presence continues to pose a threat to your safe daily life, such as myself and Amasawa-san... Isn't that right?"

"That's...true..."

As Yagami looked straight into her eyes, Kushida glared directly back at him without an ounce of fear.

"It goes without saying, but it's no easy feat to get one of your classmates kicked out of this school," he went on.

"It's also quite a challenge to drive someone toward expulsion in the course of ordinary daily routine. If you have the chance to expel them through a special exam like this one, then, without a doubt, a golden opportunity has fallen into your lap,."

"I understand that," Kushida said. "But if I push too far, I'll be putting myself in danger too."

"That means you just need to be prepared for that," Yagami said. "Either you remove them, or you'll be removed yourself."

He was putting Kushida under great pressure. It was essentially kill or be killed.

"Of course, the decision is yours to make, Kushida-senpai. Anyway, if I were to say something like, 'If you don't want everybody to find out about the way you caused your old class to fall apart, then get either Horikita-senpai or Ayanokouji-senpai expelled...' Well, that would be nothing short of a threat, and thus a violation of the rules of the exam."

"I'd say what you just said right now sounds like a threat," muttered Kushida.

"Please pardon my rudeness," said Yagami. "I didn't intend to threaten you. I just think the truth is that you're not prepared enough for this, Kushida-senpai. Be prepared to eliminate them no matter the sacrifice. If you can't do at least that much, you will never, ever be able to drive them to expulsion."

Then, removing his hands from her shoulders, Yagami stepped away and sat back down.

"Let me ask you once more," he said. "You wish to have those two expelled. Is that right?"

When he looked into Kushida's eyes once again, she looked back at him with a mixture of anger and frustration. She didn't even have to speak her answer aloud. She had been wishing for that every single day for the past year and a half, almost like she were trying to place a curse on them.

"Yes," she replied at last. "I want to have Horikita and Ayanokouji expelled. I *will* definitely get them expelled...!"

"Wonderful. I can feel it," said Yagami. "I'm finally able to confirm that your convictions are indeed genuine, Kushida-senpai."

Kushida had made up her mind: in order to prevent her wound from opening up any further, she needed to have Horikita and Ayanokouji expelled from school as soon as possible. And as for Yagami, who had been running his mouth freely...she would have to get him expelled as well.

4 DARK CLOUDS

BRRRR-ING!

The same alarm clock I've had for the last ten years was ringing in my ears. I quickly and silently reached for it, and violently slammed the button to stop the alarm without a single care. The excess force caused the alarm clock to fall off the nightstand, letting out one final *ping!*

My alarm clock wasn't so weak a partner that this level of abuse would break it though, not after all the training it had been through at my hands.

"It's already six o'clock...?" I muttered.

Ultimately, I had only gotten about two hours of sleep before morning came. I took off my pajamas, wondering why I'd even bothered putting them on in the first place, and walked over to the washbasin in my underwear with heavy, plodding steps. As I crossed the room, I picked up my alarm clock off the floor and realized the cover had come off. Specifically, the latch that kept the cover in place had popped out. It had broken before and I had patched up with tape. On top of that, one of its batteries was loose on the floor.

"Looks like I was a little too rough with you," I said to my alarm clock. "I'll be more careful tomorrow, so forgive me, okay?"

I walked over to the mirror.

"Ugh, I look awful..."

I supposed it wasn't *too* bad, but there was no way I could show my face to my students the way I looked right now. The dark circles under my eyes were even more pronounced because I'd been having a particularly hard time sleeping the past few nights. After carefully washing my face, I lined up my cosmetics, which I typically didn't use at all.

I really am a mess...

Well, I supposed it was just because I didn't want my students to know how stressed out I was.

I reached for the container of lotion and took it in my hands, but I suddenly caught sight of myself in the mirror.

"I certainly look terrible."

Without really thinking, I reached up and touched my cheek. The feel of my skin under my fingertips probably couldn't begin to compare to what it was like during my school days.

"I guess I'm getting old too," I muttered.

You could say it's only been a little over ten years since then, but still, *ten years*. Just feeling my face was enough to remind me that so much time had passed whether I liked it or not.

"Well, I guess that's probably a trivial problem now..."

It wasn't as though this was the first time I was confronted with the passage of time. I always had a firm grasp on the concept. I resumed my previously halted movements, opened the lid, and silently began applying lotion to my skin.

I knew this would be coming someday. I knew it from the moment I decided to become a teacher. But even so...I wasn't really prepared for it. I couldn't be.

"Calm down," I told myself. "This is not my fight. The situation now is different from the way it was then too. The way the class is now, I bet they'll make it through without incident. Yes, they should be able to do just that. There's no point in me being nervous."

As I felt my heart beating faster and faster, I tried to tell myself that this was essentially not my problem. Such shallow thinking was useless though, and my heart started to pound in my chest. At this rate, I wouldn't be able to keep myself together before the special exam ended, I was worried about the future.

I pressed both of my palms against the mirror and glared at my reflection.

"You have to be prepared..."

4.1

MORNINGS WERE SURPRISINGLY busy for teachers. We were already at our place of work without commuting since we lived in the dormitories on campus, close to the school building. Even so, there was a mountain of things for us to do: preparing for our classes, checking for new messages, sometimes checking the water quality of the pool, and so on. However, the start of our actual workday was when homeroom started, so essentially, taking care of those things amounted to unpaid overtime. They were things we had to take care of on our own.

After our respective morning preparations were finished, we teachers had a meeting as well for morning assembly. The rush of activity in the mornings was twice or even three times as intense on days like today when special exams were being administered. Any mistake on the school's part would be absolutely unforgivable as it would affect some of the students' lives.

"The most important thing for you to keep in mind during this special exam is that as instructors, you are not to intervene," warned Ikari-sensei. He wore a stern look on his face. "Please make absolutely certain that you avoid any kind of situation where you inadvertently offer help to your students because you want to protect your class."

Ikari-sensei was in charge of we four homeroom instructors, and he was also responsible for proctoring this particular special exam.

"Um, excuse me," said Chie, "I know it might be too late for me to speak up now, but may I ask a question?"

"What is it, Hoshinomiya-sensei?" he answered.

"The last time this... Eleven years ago, when this exam was last administered, the school implemented a rule to shuffle the classes around for this exam, so each class wasn't led by its usual homeroom instructor, correct? So, why is it that this time, we're watching over our usual classes for this exam? I would think that, for the sake of fairness, this aspect should be changed."

It was clear from the school's warning to the teachers that the administration wished to prevent teachers from intervening in the exam. However, shuffling the classes so that teachers would be overseeing different students would certainly be a much more reliable method. It was unlikely any of the teachers would go so far as to take on such risks themselves for the sake of helping a rival class.

"Isn't it simply because the school believes that fairness will be upheld in any case?" Sakagami-sensei said this calmly, having come to that conclusion after listening to the conversation thus far.

"Is that really so?" remarked Chie.

"...I cannot provide you with any reasoning for it," Ikari-sensei replied. "I can only state that things are the way they are because it's been decided that way."

"Meaning it's a decision that came from the top?" asked Chie.

There was not a single thing we teachers could decide ourselves for any of the special exams. Everything was decided upon by the higher-ups, meaning Chancellor Sakayanagi and those involved in the administration and management of this institution. All we could do was follow the rules and enforce them accordingly. However, something about this decision didn't seem to add up, and Chie made no attempt to hide her dissatisfaction.

Seeing this, Ikari-sensei spoke once more, in a low, strained voice.

"This is only my own personal opinion here, but I believe this exam could potentially offer insight into the hidden workings of the students' minds," he said. "There is, essentially, a great deal of information to be learned. I suspect the school administrators felt that allowing teachers from other classes to access that information could impact subsequent special exams."

"That sounds like they don't have faith in the teachers then," said Chie.

"There's nothing that can be done about it," said Ikari-sensei. "Besides, three of the homeroom instructors present here have experienced something similar to this special exam in the past, and... Well, perhaps it has something to do with the fact that each of you were assigned to your usual classes during last year's In-Class Voting special exam as well?"

"I suppose that's true," said Chie. She sounded convinced at that, as though this was something she'd understood from the beginning.

"Hoshinomiya-sensei... May I continue now?" asked Ikari-sensei.

"Yes, yes, please do! I understand, so please go on ahead!" she replied.

Though Ikari-sensei was clearly annoyed, he resumed his explanation, sounding like he had given up on trying to argue.

"If the person on monitoring duty deems it necessary,

you will be issued a warning," he said. "If there are re-peated attempts to intervene, pay cuts will be involved. While we aren't worried about you doing this, please keep in mind that, in the worst-case scenario, if it is found that any teacher intervenes in an underhanded manner and intentionally tries to coax their students into making a certain choice, that teacher will be demoted."

The Unanimous Special Exam was all about choice. If a teacher were to try anything that guided their students toward a particular choice the teacher favored, it would naturally undermine the very purpose of the special exam itself. Of course, neither myself nor any of the teachers from the other classes had any intention of doing that. As usual, I wouldn't let myself get too emotionally involved with my students—I would simply press on ahead silently. That was all. Even if this special exam was full of bitter memories for me, I wasn't going to do things any differently.

"That is all. Now then, I wish you all the best of luck in today's special exam," said Ikari-sensei.

After the morning meeting ended, I simply tried to get through my morning classes the way I usually would. Well, I was probably the only one who felt like I was being my usual self; in reality, I might have seemed different.

I felt like I had no sense of time and before I knew it, it was already time for lunch. I sat in the faculty office with my lunch on the desk in front of me. After I had gotten about a third of the food down my throat, my chopsticks just suddenly stopped moving altogether. Not wanting myself to be seen like this, I decided to put my remaining lunch into a bag and put it away.

Then came the sound that signaled the start of afternoon classes. As I left the faculty office with my eyes on the ground, I heard the sound of footsteps approaching from behind me.

"Guess it's finally time. Huh, Sae-chan," said Chie.

"...Chie?" I replied.

"You've been like this since this morning," she said. "I take it you couldn't sleep last night because you were thinking about the special exam?"

I dismissed her obvious and cheap provocation, letting it wash over me like water off a duck's back. Actually, it would probably be more correct to say that I simply couldn't muster an answer to it.

"My current class has nothing to do with me," I told her. "It doesn't matter if my students pass this exam easily or not."

"Hm? It doesn't look like you really believe that yourself though."

I started to walk away. As I turned my back to her, Chie said something else. She made no effort to hide the resentment in her voice.

"Well, whatever. Don't forget that you don't *deserve* to aim for Class A, Sae-chan."

Throughout that whole exchange, I was unable to lift my face at all.

4.2

· ·

I T WAS SEPTEMBER 17, shortly after our lunch break.
Less than three weeks after our summer vacation ended,
the next special exam was here. When I came back to the
classroom roughly five minutes before the exam was due
to start, there was already an adult standing by, quietly
watching the students from the back of the room. I was a
little surprised to find that I wasn't assigned to my usual
seat. I had been placed in another seat just for the dura-
tion of this specific exam. Perhaps that was to ensure even
stricter adherence to the rules.

Interestingly enough, I was seated by the window at
the very back of the classroom, where I used to sit in
my first year here. As for the rest of the students, they...
appeared to be spread about randomly, with no relation
to where they were seated this year or last. I guess that

meant it was only a coincidence that I was assigned in the same spot I used to sit in. When I looked over at Horikita, already in her seat, I saw that she was still placed in the front row. She was only one seat over from her usual spot.

Satou was seated to my right, and Onizuka was seated in front of me. The students then began to arrive, one after another.

Starting now, we would be undertaking the "Unanimous Special Exam." We would simply choose from the options available for the five issues presented to us and repeat the voting process over and over until we reached a unanimous decision on each issue. Nothing more and nothing less. Simple. While there was little of anything of note for this particular special exam, it was also true that there was little we *could* do in order to prepare for it.

There were only a few preparations we could make. We promised to split our votes in the first round regardless of the contents of the issues we were voting on, because communication wasn't allowed prior to the first round of voting. We would also pay careful attention to the time limit when it was time to vote. Thirdly, we decided in advance whom we would follow in the event that a dispute arose over the choices and votes were split. That was about it for us, and about all that any class could do to manage the situation. That was probably the reason that there wasn't really any kind of heavy, oppressive air hanging over our class.

On top of that, this was an exam all participants could manage quite easily. All we had to do was make a choice and press a button for whatever we wanted to vote for. As a result, the class was more relaxed. Of course, there were still some feelings of nervousness over this particular special exam...

Our tablets were covered with a protective film to prevent any prying eyes from getting a look at what was on the screen. Even if a person in a neighboring seat did try to sneak a peek, they wouldn't be able to spy on you. We weren't allowed to get up from our seats during voting either, so it was impossible for us to figure out exactly who was voting for what based on sight.

Even if you could see someone else's voting results through some other means, or even just by accident, whether anyone would actually believe you if you tried to say anything was another matter entirely. It was impossible to make a fuss about who voted for what since we were forbidden from stealing glances in the first place. We had no other choice but to take this special exam as it was, head-on. It also looked like the tablets placed on our desks had been turned off, and we were forbidden from turning them on without permission.

"Heya!" Ike called to Shinohara. "So, like, if we pass this entire thing in an hour or two, let's head over to Keyaki Mall."

"Well, sure, I'd like to go," she said, "but we're supposed to be doing self-study in the dorms after, right? So, how about we go in the evening?"

Ike and Shinohara, now dating and much closer with each other than they were before, were talking about what they were going to do after class. Would we really be able to pass this special exam so easily? Maybe. I wondered, though, just how many of the students here right now understood that there was a chance this exam could become fraught with difficulties, depending on the conditions.

The issue was that voting was anonymous. It was impossible to know who voted for what during the exam. Or ever, actually. Complete anonymity. In this particular exam, everything came down to how big an impact that factor would have. At any rate, the time limit for this special exam was a long five hours, from one o'clock to six o'clock in the afternoon. Put simply, that meant we could spend no more than one hour on each issue. It wouldn't be surprising if we completed this special exam in one or two hours then, like Ike had said earlier.

If we managed to finish within the time limit, we would get a quick and easy fifty Class Points. On the other hand, in the event that we failed to pass the exam within those five hours, we would be penalized by 300 Class Points. That meant coming to a unanimous decision on all five issues was an absolute necessity. Still, in light of the mechanics of this exam, you could say that the scant rewards and heavy penalties were acceptable.

As I sat in my spot in the corner of the classroom, I noticed that about half of the seats were filled now. Chabashira, the facilitator of this special exam, stood over by the podium, while the teacher assigned to monitor both us and her was stationed in the back of the classroom.

"As you have already been informed, we are now going to collect all communication devices," announced Chabashira.

There were restrictions on the bags that we could bring into the room, and the school had arranged to monitor us from both the front and the back of the classroom in order to prevent anyone from stealing glances at other students' tablets. They were being much more thorough than was strictly necessary. To me, that was proof positive of how much they were trying to prevent people from finding out who had voted for what.

It might have seemed harsh, but it was the right call for them to make.

In order to ensure that the students' true, genuine feelings were being reflected in the voting, total anonymity had to be assured. If there were opportunities for students to get a look at what others were doing, then the chance that they would succumb to peer pressure would increase.

For example, let's say everyone went with option alpha. Even though you really wanted to go with option beta, maybe you voted for option alpha, because that's what everyone else did. That's what the school wanted to avoid happening.

They were placing a lot of importance on students' respective wills, which was the purpose of this special exam. But still, from the perspective of the students, we wanted the vote to come to a unanimous decision anyway, whether it was coming from peer pressure or not. In that sense, the measures the school was taking weren't to our advantage.

In any case, there wasn't any room for fraud. Whatever issues we were going to face, we had to come to a unanimous decision on it.

"Come on, Airi. You decided that you were going to say something, didn't you?"

Hm? When I drew my gaze back from the window

to see what was happening inside the classroom, I saw Haruka pushing Airi from behind.

"U-um, excuse me, Kiyotaka-kun...!" Airi stammered. "I... If you don't mind, would you... Would you mind, um, give me a minute, after school today? Maybe?"

Haruka, standing beside her, nodded several times. She then looked at me with an appeal in her eyes, as if to say, "*You understand that you've gotta respond to her efforts, right?*"

"Um, I wanted to...to talk to you a bit. About the cultural festival," added Airi.

"Oh, that's what this is about," I said. "I figured I'd need to speak to you about that in person anyway, so I don't mind. Sure."

"Th-thank you!" she squeaked. "W-well, okay then, later!"

Airi quickly shot away from me like she was trying to run away. She proceeded to take her seat, far away from mine, with her back facing me.

"She managed to get a grip on things, somehow," said Haruka. "She's still not over her heartbreak yet, but she is trying her best to face forward."

I didn't mention it when Airi was standing in front of me earlier, but she was really struggling to make eye contact with me.

"Still, now we'll have to see if she really wants to go for the idea. It's all going to come down to how much effort you put in, Kiyopon."

"I'll negotiate with her to the best of my ability," I said.

"All right. Well then, see ya after school, 'kay?"

It seemed to be that Haruka had been taking very good care of Airi. Or more like, the two of them had been together a lot lately.

Just two minutes before the start of the exam, Chabashira, the one overseeing us, started explaining how things were going to work.

"Well then...it's about time we begin," she announced. "The special exam will start now. Please note that due to the length of today's exam, you will be granted a maximum of four total bathroom breaks. You will only be allowed to take breaks after you've come to a unanimous decision on an issue and before the class moves on to the next one. During the course of the exam, you cannot take breaks at any point while you are engaged with an issue and haven't yet come to a unanimous decision. Also, please note that you will be granted a maximum of ten minutes for each break. However, the exam time will continue to count down during that time. It would be wise for you to skip taking a break if you deem it unnecessary to have one."

Everyone in class had already used the restroom anyway, so that likely wasn't going to be a problem for a while. No one in class seemed to be having any issues that would warrant an unplanned bathroom break either, like a stomachache or anything similar.

Well, it's finally time for the special exam to begin, eh? Or that's what I thought, but Chabashira simply looked around at the students without actually doing anything to start the proceedings. She stood there in a daze, like her mind wasn't actually here right then. The students initially didn't notice anything, but now they were starting to exchange glances with each other. The other teacher standing at the back of the classroom also seemed to notice that something wasn't right.

"Chabashira-sensei," said the instructor. "It's time."

"O-oh, yes," Chabashira said. "My apologies. Now then, we will begin the Unanimous Special Exam. Starting now, we will proceed in accordance with the rules. Do note that we will be observing you very carefully, so we caution you not to get up from your seats outside the prescribed intervals, and to not talk amongst yourselves during the times you are prohibited from doing so. Please bear that in mind."

A timer was now displayed up on the monitor, beginning its countdown from the twenty-six-second mark.

The slight delay in the start of the countdown was probably due to the delay in Chabashira giving us the sign to go
ahead, but it wasn't going to hinder the students. When
the countdown finally reached zero, text appeared on the
screen, showing us the first issue.

> **ISSUE #1:** Choose which class you will face in the year-end final
> exam to be held at the end of the third semester. Your choice will
> still be in effect even if there is a change in the class rankings.

*Note: The numbers in parentheses ( ) represent the additional
Class Points you will earn if you win in the chosen matchup.

CHOICES: Class A (100), Class B (50), Class D (0)

"Your choice here is to determine who you will be
facing in the year-end special exam, which will be held
at the end of your third semester of your second year,"
Chabashira explained. "As indicated in the issue description, if you make a unanimous decision to choose
Class A at this point in time but the current Class A is
demoted to B before the end of the school year, you will
be going up against the class that was ranked as A at the
time of this vote. Furthermore, you will still earn those
additional Class Points as indicated. In the event that
you do not come to a unanimous decision on a desired
opponent, then the school will decide for you at random."

So, if we were to put it in simpler terms, the class's choices were to fight against Sakayanagi, Ichinose, or Ryuuen. And no matter who was selected here, our opponent wouldn't change.

"It is important for you to discern which class you can win against if you go up against them," Chabashira went on. "Of course, you may not necessarily...get to fight against the class that you wish."

If Horikita and her class nominated Sakayanagi's Class A and Ichinose *also* nominated Sakayanagi's class, did that mean that the decision of whether to compete against Horikita or Ichinose would rest with Sakayanagi? And then if Sakayanagi's class didn't choose Horikita *or* Ichinose and instead picked Ryuuen's class to be their opponent, then that would confirm their choice to go up against Ryuuen. But then if Ryuuen's class was avoiding Sakayanagi's class, in the end, no one's choices would go into effect and the matchups would be decided randomly.

Normally, it would make the most sense to choose a class with a lower level of strength. However, as one could see from the choices in the poll, lower-level classes were treated differently from the high-level classes. If you were able to defeat a high-level class, you would be rewarded with additional Class Points. On the other hand, we wouldn't get any additional rewards for going up against a lower-level class. In ordinary circumstances, you wouldn't want to go up against Class A, but if there was merit in doing so, then the issue was worth considering.

"We will now begin the first round of voting," Chabashira told us. "You have sixty seconds."

If we didn't enter our votes within the sixty-second time limit, we would enter penalty time. Of course, our classmates were going to simply go ahead and pick their favored option as Horikita had instructed them to do in advance so we could avoid any trouble in the first round. As for me, I had already talked things over with Horikita and informed her that I was planning to choose the first option right away, so I went ahead and chose Class A without hesitation. Horikita was going to choose the second option, Class B. At this point, it was not going to be a unanimous decision. But the other thirty-seven votes in class would give an indication of which class everyone genuinely wanted to fight against.

"Now that everyone has finished entering their votes, I will announce the results," said Chabashira.

Round 1 Voting Results: CLASS A: 5 Votes, CLASS B: 21 Votes, CLASS D: 13 Votes

The votes were concentrated on Ichinose's Class B, rather than on Class D, the lowest-ranked class.

"Because you haven't come to a unanimous decision, there will now be a break interval."

For the next ten minutes, students were freely allowed to get up out of their seats, talk to others, and engage in conversation. It didn't matter whether you spoke up a little more loudly or if you just quietly whispered into the ear of one particular student. Horikita, seated directly in front of Chabashira, raised her hand, stood up, and turned around.

"Please allow me to go ahead and make a suggestion right away, so that we don't waste any time on this first issue," she announced.

Since Horikita was in the position of leader for this special exam as well, she was taking initiative to demonstrate that she had an idea.

"As the votes seem to be scattered, I'm sure that means you each have your own thoughts on the matter," she said. "I'm sure you must have doubts, so I don't mind if you ask me as many questions as you like. Feel free to voice your opinions out loud to the entire class."

Then, Horikita took a deep breath, and began to explain what her preferred choice was.

"My ideal opponent to go up against at the end of the year would be Class B. In other words, Ichinose-san. I have three reasons for this. The first is that, unlike

Sakayanagi-san and Ryuuen-kun, Ichinose is far more likely to fight fair. A match-up between us would be a pure contest between our respective potentials. Even if it were some kind of irregular special exam, I have little worry that we'd be outmaneuvered by an underhanded scheme. Next is that they are currently ranked as Class B. We would be able to earn Class Points in addition to the regular rewards, which would give us an advantage in building a lead over the other classes. Now, the third and final reason is because the title of Class B is nothing more than pretense. We're in Class C already, and our two classes, as well as Ryuuen-kun's Class D, are all basically neck-and-neck with each other. At this point in time, we're separated by only a few Class Points, but Ichinose-san's class is now on a downward slope. In my opinion, they would be an ideal opponent."

I got the impression that she was concerned about the time because she spoke somewhat quickly. Despite that, she conveyed her reasons clearly, and what she said resonated with many of the students in class.

"If there is anyone here who has any objections, I would like for you to offer your opinions right here and now," she said. "On the other hand, if you don't mind choosing Class B, this discussion would be over quickly if we all simply went ahead and voted for them as soon as possible."

Horikita had wanted to come to a unanimous decision in the second round of voting on this particular issue. She had conveyed those intentions loud and clear.

As if in response to that, Yousuke stood up. "I agree with what you're proposing, Horikita-san," he said. "Though we would receive greater rewards for defeating Sakayanagi-san's Class A, there's little doubt that they're far more formidable enemies. Of course, we can't drop our guard against Ichinose-san and her classmates either. They have strong bonds and a tried-and-true fighting style, but I also think that they'd be the best opponents for us to face."

After Horikita and Yousuke both endorsed the choice of Class B, our classmates were starting to look in that direction. Then, as if to take hold of the momentum and push it forward even more, another person spoke up to offer her opinion from her seat.

"I'm all for this idea too," said Kei. "We don't get any additional rewards for fighting against Ryuuen-kun anyway, and I kinda don't like to say this, but it wouldn't be a laughing matter if we lost to Sakayanagi-san, y'know?"

Before anyone could voice any dissent, Yousuke and Kei quickly solidified public opinion toward voting for Class B. It was possible that they were simply supporting Horikita and following through as we had planned, but it was probably safe to assume that they legitimately wanted to choose Class B too. It was easy to see that was where this was trending, and Class B received the most votes in the first round anyway.

We still had close to six minutes left in the discussion period, but no dissenting opinions came forward in the end. Then, while checking the time, Chabashira resumed the voting once again.

"All right," she said. "We will move onto the second round of voting now that the break interval is over. As soon as the information is displayed on your tablet screens, you'll have sixty seconds to vote, just as I explained to you before. After sixty seconds have passed, any time that you go over will accumulate and count toward your penalty. Remember that."

Such words of warning were unnecessary, though, as everyone had got their votes in for the second round in under ten seconds. The results were tallied and immediately displayed upon the monitor.

Round 2 Voting Results: CLASS A: 0 Votes, CLASS B: 39 Votes, CLASS D: 0 Votes

It seemed like Kouenji hadn't screwed around and decided to vote for another class. We succeeded in coming to a unanimous decision for the first time, without any slip-ups.

"The decision is unanimous. You have all selected Class B for the first issue," Chabashira told us. "We will inform you which class you will be competing against in the year-end final exam as soon as the decision is finalized. That will likely be some time tomorrow or later."

So, in just a little over ten minutes, we managed to clear one of the five total issues. W successfully managed to guide the vote toward Class B, which was Horikita's and the other students' preference. Speaking personally, I would've chosen Ichinose's class too, if I had to pick someone to face. Horikita had already stated all of the reasons why and I had nothing else to add. Aside from that, we had to hope that Sakayanagi and Ryuuen would be matched up against each other, but since Ichinose's class would be the easier target, we might have three classes competing over the same choice if we got unlucky. Hopefully, Ichinose's class would choose to fight against Horikita and there wouldn't be any hassle.

"I don't think that anyone here needs a bathroom break, but I'm asking anyway, just in case," Chabashira said. "Does anyone here mind if we go ahead and move onto the next issue?"

None of the students in class objected to that, of course, and we immediately went onto the second issue.

"All right then, we'll continue. Here is the second issue."

ISSUE #2: Choose a destination for the school field trip scheduled for late November.

CHOICES: Hokkaido, Kyoto, Okinawa

I heard some students in class mutter things like, "What the heck?" Since we were forbidden from talking amongst ourselves though, they immediately went silent after Chabashira shot them glares. But it was an undeniable fact that many students did indeed mumble their surprise. Still, we couldn't talk about the issue at all before voting first. They just had to think for themselves about which option they genuinely wanted to choose and vote accordingly.

"This vote is similar to the previous one, however. Your votes alone won't finalize the decision. The outcome may change depending on what the other three classes vote for. We ask that you please understand that."

Round 1 Voting Results: HOKKAIDO: 17 Votes, KYOTO: 3 Votes, OKINAWA: 19 Votes

Putting Kyoto aside, judging from the tallied votes, the vote this time seemed to be a much closer contest than the previous one.

"Since you didn't come to a unanimous decision, there will now be a break," announced Chabashira.

"Man, can you even really call this a special exam?," said Hondou with a laugh. He almost sounded disappointed. "This is way too easy, dude. It's practically a no-brainer."

It was certainly true that the first and second issues hardly warranted preparing such an ostentatious set-up as this. We could've resolved these issues in a regular homeroom session. However, we were still only on the second issue. But, similarly, you could say we were *already* on the second one. When we finished voting on this one, two-fifths of the special exam would be over.

This special exam really did feel far too easy. Many students were probably starting to relax now instead of feeling nervous. What was interesting, however, was that there were some students who actually were even more anxious when situations like this arose. In particular, those were cautious and particularly thoughtful students like Horikita and Yousuke. While everyone else in the room was laughing and talking about where they'd like to go, those two were seriously examining the issue at hand.

Well, that was just as well. It was absurd to imagine that we'd have easy issues like this one all the way until the end. If anything, it felt like the easier the first part of this exam was, the more pressure we'd be under in the latter half. As I mulled over that premonition, I quietly watched everyone during the interval.

"I'm sure that everyone has their opinions about the exam overall, but let's focus on this issue first, okay?" said Yousuke. He was wary of everyone getting distracted and wanted to get the class back on track.

I had voted for the first option as I promised, just like I did the last time. That meant I put my vote in for Hokkaido. Still, I wondered, what was going to happen? The issue was the same for every class, so whichever option got at least two of the four classes' votes would be where we'd be going. Each individual vote was important, then, in determining where the school trip would be.

"Horikita-san, it seems like opinions are split here," said Kushida. Perhaps she was worried about the fact that Horikita hadn't spoken up immediately like before. "Do you perhaps have any words of advice?"

Horikita, however, didn't immediately respond to Kushida's question. She was completely silent.

"Horikita-san?" asked Kushida, sounding a little worried.

That second time though, Horikita answered in a hurry. "I'm sorry. I was just a little lost in thought... It's not a complicated issue or anything, but I was thinking that it might actually be difficult to come to a unanimous decision on this. A school trip is an important event for students, after all, and I can't make everyone settle on a decision with just a few words."

Everyone in class had promised to follow her decisions as leader if the time came when it was necessary, but that didn't mean Horikita was allowed to decide on the destination for our school trip all by herself or anything. It was a tough choice then, considering that it wasn't a matter of advantages and disadvantages. It was just a matter of personal preference.

"At any rate, I'll guess I'll start by opening the floor. Would anyone like to share their input on where they'd like to go for the trip?" said Horikita.

Sudou raised his hand, as if he had been waiting for his moment.

"Welp, guess I'll go then," he said. "I put my vote in for Okinawa. I mean, when people think of school trips, they think of the beach, right? And Okinawa's a classic choice! 'Sides, it's got the most votes already, so I think it's pretty much a done deal, don't you?"

"Wait, wait, just hold on a second," said Maezono. "Okay, I'll admit that yes, Okinawa is one of the go-to choices, but so is Hokkaido. And on top of that, it was a really close vote. Doesn't everyone want to go skiing?"

"I wanna go with Okinawa too," exclaimed Onodera. "I want to go snorkeling!"

Another student cut in. "I've already been to Okinawa a bunch of times, so I think Hokkaido's..."

Students began to clash, arguing over the two destinations that had the most votes. It wasn't surprising that students were critical of the choice that they didn't want since each side felt that the choice they made was better than the other.

"I mean, Hokkaido is all about snow in the first place, right? That's totally *boring*!"

"Okay, but if you turn that around, Okinawa's all just ocean, right?"

Students argued back and forth for a few minutes without seeming like they were anywhere near a resolution. Finally, unable to just sit by and watch, Yousuke intervened.

"Yes, both Hokkaido and Okinawa are equally popular destinations for a school trip, so it is understandable that we might fight over it, but... I think we should maybe be a little more considerate of other peoples' opinions, okay?" he said. He pleaded with his classmates to refrain from making comments that came close to being insults.

At first, the students had just been saying how wonderful their choice of destination was. But as time went on, then the discussion devolved into students hurling comments that denigrated the other side's choice at each other.

"Hirata-kun, you voted for Hokkaido, right?" asked Maczono.

"Hey, Hirata! You chose Okinawa, didn't ya?" said Sudou.

"Huh? Um..." stammered Yousuke.

Yousuke looked visibly flustered to find himself sandwiched between both sides.

"Well, I guess it's...kind of...a secret?" he squeaked out.

Under these circumstances, it would be hard for him to answer either way. In a sense, this was the kind of moment when anonymity really came into play.

"Okinawa's the only place where you can swim in November, y'know?" said Sudou. "Don't you want to go down to the beach?"

"I've had enough of the beach myself," said Maezono. "We already got enough of that on the uninhabited island special exam. I'm all for Hokkaido, for sure!"

Yousuke had managed to put the brakes on the arguing for a moment, but things immediately started to heat back up. The exchange between Sudou and Maezono could probably be seen as a microcosm of the opinions of the entire class as a whole.

"Wh-what do we do, Horikita-san?" Kushida had a troubled look on her face as she appealed to Horikita for help.

"Yes, this is a tricky issue after all," said Horikita.

Unanimity was difficult. Maybe this was an issue that was going to be troublesome for us to decide on after all, and it had come up rather quickly in the exam. There was no simple way for us to wrap up discussion on the subject, and the ten-minute interval had already come to an end.

Incidentally, I was planning on voting for Kyoto in the second round. Kyoto has a rich history, and I had a strong desire to go through it and take in the sights.

"Very well, then," said Chabashira. "Now that all of the votes have been cast for the second round, I'll show you the results."

Round 2 Voting Results: HOKKAIDO: 18 Votes, KYOTO: 4 Votes, OKINAWA: 17 Votes

"Oh, hey, Hokkaido came in from behind and took the win!" Maezono cheered. "Yay!"

"Agh, damn it!" grumbled Sudou. "Who the hell changed their votes from Okinawa to Hokkaido?!"

Although Hokkaido had slightly more votes than Okinawa, it was still pretty much an even split. Both the Hokkaido camp and the Okinawa camp immediately started arguing over the direction of the votes again. Even if we tried to settle the issue, at this rate, we wouldn't come to a consensus no matter how many times we redid the vote.

Still, it was just kind of sad that Kyoto wasn't being talked about at all. Well, it had gotten my vote now and the tally went up a little, but...

I supposed that it was possible that Horikita might not have changed her vote between rounds, voting for the second option again like she did in the first. Of course, it was impossible to say for sure since she might've voted for Hokkaido or Okinawa and someone else could have voted for Kyoto. At any rate, it was *possible* for Horikita to just force a decision here and have us select whatever option had gotten the most votes...but doing so meant some people were bound to hold a grudge over it. After all, Hokkaido had gotten the most votes in the second round, but Okinawa had gotten the most votes the first time.

"Looks like we don't have any other choice," Horikita declared. "Now that we've gotten here, we're just going to have to decide with a contest. Let's have three people who want Hokkaido and three people who want Okinawa come forward to represent each side and play rock-paper-scissors. Each side will determine in what order their members participate. We will do this tournament-style, winner takes all. However, Kyoto has the fewest votes, so they will only get one person on their team. It'll be a difficult battle for them, but this way, we'll be keeping things as fair as possible."

That was true; it wouldn't be fair at all if Kyoto could compete on equal terms with the other two while having the smallest minority of the vote. If Horikita was going to bring this issue to a resolution without coercing anyone or spending a lot of time on it, this was the method we should go with. There was no avoiding some degree of dissatisfaction, but since we set a rule to follow Horikita's orders in advance, we had no choice but to obey.

There was a little bit of squabbling over who exactly would play rock-paper-scissors for each team, but everyone soon decided on the contestants.

Team Hokkaido was an all-girl team made up of Maezono as player one, Ishikura as player two, and Shinohara as player three.

Team Okinawa was a mixed guy-girl team consisting of Onodera as player one, Hondou as player two, and Sudou as player three.

"All we need now is someone who voted for Kyoto," said Horikita. "Will someone step forward to play for Team Kyoto?"

One of the guys in class raised his hand high and spoke up for the Kyoto camp, as if he had been biding his time for this very opportunity.

"If no one else is going to, then I'll volunteer. I will definitely be bringing the whole class to Kyoto," declared

Keisei, expressing his strong resolve as he entered the difficult battle.

Kyoto was also my preferred destination for the school trip. *Well, I'll leave this matter to you, Keisei. I'm sure it'll be a grueling battle, but I hope that you'll pull it off, somehow...*

They immediately got started playing rock-paper-scissors so we could get to the third round of voting quickly. First, Onodera threw scissors while Maezono and Keisei both threw paper. Team Okinawa had achieved victory in no time at all. Team Kyoto's dreams were shattered in an instant, and Keisei left the battlefield with a broken heart. Keisei's time spent in battle was fleeting; he was eliminated not even ten seconds after he stepped forward.

I also happened to witness the moment when Horikita placed her hand against her forehead and let out a sigh. That must have been proof that she was yet another person who had actually wanted to go to Kyoto. But the contest continued on, as if the team who wished for Kyoto never even existed in the first place. Onodera, who had defeated both Maezono and Keisei right away in the first round, also defeated Ishikura in the second with a consecutive win, putting her team in the lead. However, Onodera ended up being defeated by Shinohara, the final player on Team Hokkaido. And then, in an unexpected twist, Shinohara went on to defeat Hondou right afterward.

In the end, it was a showdown between the final players on each team. Both sides stared each other down.

"We're definitely going to Okinawa! Okinawan soba! Okinawan lion dog statues! Fishing!"

"We're definitely going to Hokkaido! Crab! Hot springs! Skiing!"

Sudou and Shinohara clenched their fists tightly as they shouted things at each other that I didn't quite understand. Then, the two of them raised their fists overhead before thrusting them back down.

They each threw paper. A tie.

Perhaps they felt like they'd get another tie right away, because even though they clearly wanted to go again, both parties paused for a slight break before throwing again. This tournament was only to decide where we were going for our class trip, but the situation was unusually tense.

"Rock, paper, scissors... Shoot!"

The combatants then clashed once more. Sudou threw down a powerful rock. Shinohara, on the other hand, threw out a magnificent paper for the second time in a row.

"I did it! Hokkaido wins!" exclaimed Shinohara happily.

All of Team Hokkaido let out cheers of triumph.

"What the hell, Sudou?!" shouted Hondou.

"D-damn...!" huffed Sudou.

I didn't intend to rain on their parade or anything, but this only meant that there was one vote for Hokkaido overall, meaning the one from our class. If multiple other classes voted for Okinawa or Kyoto, we could still end up going to one of those places. Horikita must have understood that this wasn't the kind of situation where you could say those things out loud though as she only had a look of exasperation on her face. Everyone went ahead and cast their votes for the third round, entering their votes on their tablets all at once.

Round 3 Voting Results: HOKKAIDO: 39 Votes, KYOTO: 0 Votes, OKINAWA: 0 Votes

"Having come to a decision in the third round of voting, you've now cleared the second issue," said Chabashira.

About half of the class was dissatisfied with the result, but the fact remained that we had successfully managed to come to a unanimous decision in the third round of voting. It happened in a brilliant fashion with students engaging in a fair fight that conformed to the established rules. Although Kyoto, my heart's desire, had not been chosen in the end, I was still very much looking forward to seeing Hokkaido for what it was. And besides, depending on what the other classes voted for, it was entirely possible that we could still be going to Kyoto or Okinawa anyway. At any rate, no matter where we ended up going, this issue made me excited for the school trip.

"Now then, let's move on to the third issue."

Although Chabashira didn't look any different now than she did at the start of the exam, I could tell that there was a slight change in the tone of her voice. I figured that after the easy issues we had faced so far, we might be about to face something that would change the flow of the exam.

ISSUE #3: Select one of these options. Regardless of which option is chosen, Private Points will be affected for six continuous months.

OPTION ONE: Three random students in the class will be awarded Protect Points in exchange for the entire class being awarded zero Private Points each month.

OPTION TWO: One student, chosen at will, shall be awarded a Protect Point in exchange for all students receiving half of the Private Points they would normally be awarded for your Class Points.

OPTION THREE: If neither Option 1 nor Option 2 pass, then the five students who score the lowest in the next written exam will receive zero Private Points for six months.

Unlike the previous two issues, this issue presented serious advantages and disadvantages for our class. The first option offered the greatest return due to the large number of Private Points we'd be losing. However, we couldn't overlook the fact that the Protect Points were going to be given out to randomly selected students. Protect Points were exceptionally powerful, but if you thought about it, there were some students who would become unnecessary over the course of our time at this school. It was possible that the Protect Points could be completely wasted if they were assigned to students like that.

Option Two wasn't exactly a cheap price to pay either. We'd be losing half of the Private Points deposited into our accounts for all those months. And on top of that, only one student would get a Protect Point. However, the fact that we could choose who would be getting it was an important factor.

Then, Option Three minimized the loss of Private Points as much as possible. That would likely be the option to choose if you decided that Protect Points were too expensive or that you didn't need them in the first place. Still, you couldn't ignore the fact that even though only five students would be affected, those five would suffer a setback. It would be necessary to consider not only the gains versus the losses, but the class's overall situation in class and so on. I figured that some students might have a lot to say about this, but we had no other choice but to vote on it first.

"Before we have you all vote," Chabashira started, "I'd like to mention what will happen if you unanimously choose the second option—namely, the option to grant a Protect Point to a specific student. If you unanimously choose for the second option, you won't be moving on from issue three yet. Instead, you'll go on to select the particular student who will get the point. You remember the examples I gave you before, yes?"

One person would be chosen during the interval, and we would vote for or against granting the Protect Point to that student. If we voted unanimously in favor of that student, they should receive it. If we voted unanimously against, that student would no longer have any chance of being considered for the issue. Then the remaining thirty-eight students would discuss it again and another person would be nominated. We would repeat the vote over and over with the pool of available candidates getting smaller and smaller each round as we voted for or against.

"All right then. With that in mind, I'll now show you the results for the first round of voting."

Round 1 Voting Results: OPTION ONE: Grant to three random students: 12 Votes; OPTION TWO: Grant to one specific student: 5 Votes; OPTION THREE: Do not grant any Protect Points: 22 Votes

The results of the first round seemed to indicate that most of the students in class were willing to turn a blind eye to the slight inconvenience some students would face and give up on the Protect Points. That was just as well, I supposed, since it was already a given who the bottom five scoring students would be on a written exam, and they'd be the ones to lose Private Points. For students who didn't fall into that category, it was essentially a risk-free move. On the other hand, I was sure some students felt that since they weren't going to be getting Private Points for six months anyway, it would be better to get the Protect Points.

Ike and Satou were the very first to speak up: two students with some of the lowest grades in class.

"H-hey, hold up a second! I don't really get what's goin' on!"

"Me either! So, like, this means we don't get any Protect Points, and only five people lose out on Private Points?"

"Well, come on, it ain't like it's a surprise," said Sudou, trying to persuade Ike. "I mean, not getting any Private Points at all for half a year is tough, and... On top of that, people get selected at random for the Protect Points. I feel like I probably wouldn't get one because of the low chances... So, come on, take one for the team here, Kanji."

I supposed that was because, in terms of academic ability, Sudou had gotten himself out of the bottom five students in our class.

"That's not fair, though!" argued Ike. "I need Private Points too right now, y'know, for all sorts of stuff!"

"You're not going to say you're using your points to pay for dates with Shinohara and stuff, are you?" replied Sudou.

"Huh? Huh? Wait, seriously? How in the heck did I get found out? Aw, man..." Ike didn't seem to be too bothered by the fact people had found out what he was using his points for, but he was acting like getting those points was a life-or-death problem.

"All right, so that settles it," said Sudou. "It's unanimous. We're gonna decide to keep our Private Points and forget the Protect Points."

"That'd be bad for me, though!" wailed Ike.

"In that case, study," Sudou told him. "That'll fix the problem, won't it?"

"Grr... I don't know, it's like, the fact that *you're* the one saying that makes me feel like I can't accept it, Ken!"

It was important for Ike to study and get out of the bottom of the rankings, but no matter how many points

Ike specifically would get after breaking out of the bottom five, the fact remained that five people would still be getting nothing.

"I understand what you're trying to say, but it's far too early to be pessimistic," said Horikita. "We should minimize the number of Private Points that will be lost, and all of us, the entire class, should shoulder that burden to make up for it. Those five students who wouldn't be getting any Private Points deposited into their accounts each month could be given a number of points based on averaging the number of points the remaining thirty-four students get. We would spread points out to those people. That way, we won't just be making specific students feel dissatisfied with the decision, right?"

For simplicity's sake, if one student earned 50,000 points per month on average, then to make up losses for those five students, we'd have to pay out a total of 250,000 points per month. So, if the thirty-four students in our class received 1.7 million points in a month, and if we divided that number by thirty-nine and rounded to the nearest whole number, that would come to 43,590 points. Losses were unavoidable, but that meant we'd only be losing about 6,500 points per student. Even if that situation were to continue for six months, the stress placed on each individual student would be kept to a minimum that way.

"W-well, I guess if we did that, then it'd be fine..." said Ike.

"I'm fine with sharin' what I get, I don't really mind," said Sudou. "I mean, ain't like we got a choice."

Sudou seemed to have some grumbles about it still, but nevertheless, he sounded like he was willing to help Ike out. Since many students preferred the option of foregoing Protect Points, opinions naturally began to coalesce around the idea of going with Option Three.

But then, Yousuke chimed in with a question. "Horikita-san, do you think it's best that we choose the option of no Protect Points?"

"It's difficult to say," she replied. "To be completely honest, it's a rather distressing choice to make. Protect Points are an extremely powerful tool that can prevent expulsion. However, the same could be said for Private Points. Do you have a different opinion on the matter, Hirata-kun?"

"This is only my personal opinion, but I think that we should go for the Protect Points with this issue. For three, of course."

"Not being able to get any Private Points for half a year would be a tough pill to swallow," Horikita said. "Not only would it put a great deal of stress upon us in our daily lives, but depending on the situation, it could even have an effect on our special exams."

There was no denying the possibility that Private Points could very well spell the difference between winning and losing.

"We can protect three students with those points, though, in the event some unforeseen situation comes our way," argued Yousuke. "There are very limited opportunities for us to get Protect Points, and besides, they're so valuable that we can't even put a price on them."

It was easy to understand Yousuke's somewhat passionate point. Protect Points, which were capable of preventing a student from getting expelled, were effectively worth 20 million Private Points each. And like he said, we didn't have many opportunities to get three of them. Especially for someone like Yousuke who cared for his friends, they truly had more value than money.

This was a very different issue from the matter of deciding where to go for the school trip, but it was also something it would be hard to come to a consensus on. It was difficult to influence the class's decision on where to go for the class trip, sure, but this matter of Protect Points was a problem for the class as a whole. Getting them might mean saving people in the future.

Keisei stood up then, indicating that he had something to say. "Excuse me, but I'd like to share my opinion," he said. "We are intending to increase our Class Points over the next six months, aren't we?"

"Of course," said Horikita. "We don't have time to stagnate if we're aiming to move up in the class hierarchy."

"Let's say we get fifty Class Points for this special exam, and 100 for placing high in the cultural festival," Keisei said. "And, assuming a similar increase in points with the sports festival... By the end of our second semester, we could end up getting 200 Class Points, or maybe even 300, depending on how things play out. Is it safe for us to assume that?"

"Yes, I would think so," replied Horikita.

If we managed to get 300 Class Points before the end of the year, then we could expect to reach a total of around 1,000 Class Points. If that happened, the total amount of Private Points that would be paid out to us over the next six months would be increased by about 50 percent over the amount we would get as of now, coming to around 2 million points. If we considered all of that, then the maximum value of just one Protect Point would be equivalent to about half a year's income for the class. It made for a clean figure, almost as if it had been calculated that way.

However, if we chose to go for the three Protect Points here, it would come to about 7 million Private

Points per every one Protect Points. There was a very fine line. The option of choosing one specific person to give a Protect Points, the least likely option to be chosen, looked like it had a good combination of advantages and disadvantages. At the same time, it was the least cost-effective choice and the most difficult option to pick. However, the fact that it was the only option that has the benefit of allowing us to choose a specific student was important. Still, if we did elect to give a Protect Point to one specific student, then of course we'd need to come to a unanimous decision on whom. If we carelessly jumped headfirst into the decision of granting the point to just one student, there was a possibility that fights could break out over who to give it to.

"So, are you saying that prioritizing Private Points would be an offensive strategy, whereas prioritizing Protect Points would be a defensive strategy?" asked Kushida. It seemed that she was trying to sort out the situation.

The three standing students, Keisei, Horikita, and Yousuke, all nodded at almost exactly the same time.

"But there's also the risk of those Protect Points essentially becoming an expensive waste of points if we end up not using them, right?" Kushida pointed out. "I'd be fine with it, even in spite of that, but..."

It was inevitable that this point was going to be brought up in order to make sure that everyone in class understood that fact ahead of time.

"Yes, you're right," said Horikita. "If we don't use those points, in the end, they'll be worthless. Of course, there *is* the sense of security and relief that comes with holding onto Protect Points, but..."

"Whether they have value or not is a different discussion," said Keisei. "Even if they end up no longer being necessary for their intended use, we could still use those points to employ strategies that require intentionally spending Protect Points, like launching a surprise attack or self-destructing on purpose. They might not simply be something we can use for protection. We might be able to use them for offensive purposes."

It was easy to understand from Keisei's explanation that there were various ways to utilize Protect Points. Being able to fight in a somewhat underhanded way and turning the idea of having the ability to prevent expulsion on its head was a significant advantage. We wouldn't know what future special exams would be like until later though, not until all of the details were made available to us. There was no guarantee that we would ever get the opportunity to put those points to good use in the future.

Still, this issue, or rather, this special exam as a whole, was unexpectedly deep. Even though the same issues were presented to all of the classes, things were different for each group depending on each class's respective rank and situation. If you were in a situation where your class had zero Class Points, your class would unanimously decide to choose the option of getting three Protect Points, and there wouldn't be any complaints about it at all. It could be a chance to catch up to the other classes.

On the other hand, though, for Class A, which was in first place by a huge margin, that option would be much more costly than it would for the other classes. Though the meaning of each individual on its own may seem less significant, the gap between classes could most definitely be narrowed. If we were to look at this from another perspective, you could interpret the first and third options in this issue to be slightly inconvenient for Class A.

"So then, Yukimura-kun, in that case, are you saying that we ought to grant Protect Points to three students?" asked Horikita. She was trying to get a definitive statement from Keisei so she could get a final confirmation and narrow down the choices.

"No... The second option is the one that I'd suggest choosing," said Keisei. "The option that allows us to grant a Protect Point to a specific person."

Horikita was surprised to hear that Keisei was hoping to go with Option Two, which seemed to be the most unlikely one.

"So then, are you insinuating that we should grant it to you?" asked Horikita.

"Well, I would be honestly flattered if you did," Keisei chuckled. "But no, that wouldn't be realistic. I think that, basically, everyone in class would want to have it, after all."

Even if we were to ask for a simple show of hands, it wouldn't be a shock if everyone in class raised their hands and said that they'd like the point.

"It's difficult to choose a particular person," he added. "Still, no matter how good of a deal the three Protect Points would be, I don't know how well giving them out to three random people is going to work."

"You seem like you have a clear idea of who to give the point to," said Horikita. "Who might you have in mind?"

"Well, if we're trying to make a strategic decision here... there's no one else I can think of other than you, Horikita," Keisei replied clearly and definitively. He looked directly at Horikita as she stood opposite him.

"...Me?" said Horikita.

"Yes. Right now, you're demonstrating your capability as the leader of this class. I have no complaints about your abilities in OAA either. You could say that being the leader is the most dangerous role there is since you'll be competing against the likes of Sakayanagi and Ryuuen in the days to come. It wouldn't be too surprising if those two targeted you and tried to get you expelled without mercy. In that case, you would be able to come up with strategies and fight against strong opponents from other classes without fear, as long as you're holding onto a Protect Point. That's the kind of scenario I'm imagining," explained Keisei.

Normally, there might have been animosity over this, but our classmates were listening closely. That was because Keisei had solid reasoning for his proposal—he didn't just randomly throw it out there.

"And those aren't the only reasons," he added. "Ordinarily, if someone has a Protect Point, there's a chance they might let their guard down. They might become less serious about things since they'd be the only one who feels protected, but I feel like...you're probably not that sort of person."

Keisei was saying that instead of simply giving a Protect Point to someone capable, we ought to give it to someone who, after being given the point, would be inclined to demonstrate their abilities for the sake of the class even more. And, according to Keisei, that person was Horikita.

"I understand what you're sayin' and all," said Hondou, "but...we're talking a lot of points here, aren't we?"

If you weren't the person being granted the Protect Point, this arrangement simply meant you'd be getting your Private Points cut in half for six months. It was no wonder that there were students like Hondou who felt that way.

"I'm sure that some people will feel like this is a loss because they're thinking only about the Private Points we'll be losing," Keisei said. "But this is an investment. By going with this option, Horikita will turn this into more Class Points, more than what we're paying here. If you think about it that way, the choice becomes easier, doesn't it?"

"I don't know, you might be overselling this a bit... It's possible we could run into financial problems, right?" asked Hondou.

"I don't think we can beat Class A without taking risks," Keisei replied. "I understand that now, because I've been fighting here at this school for a year and a half."

"*Fu fu fu*. Well then, that settles it, no? I agree with your proposal, Glasses-kun." Kouenji, who had not once thought he would get involved with this special exam, voiced his support. "We can have Horikita Girl work desperately harder than everyone else, then, for a value commensurate with the Protect Point given to her."

"You have a Protect Point, but you don't seem to be working hard yourself," snapped Sudou.

"Because working hard is what commoners do, you see," replied Kouenji.

Despite Sudou's barbs, Kouenji didn't seem to care in the slightest. At any rate, getting approval from Kouenji seemed likely to be the biggest hurdle, so this was a big deal. I had been expecting the class to go with the first or third option, but I could agree with Keisei's presentation. More importantly though, if anyone was going to voice their dissent at this late a stage, people would be looking for a good reason why. Simply saying that you didn't like the idea of not getting Private Points was hardly something you could say was for the class's sake.

As the class was still mulling over what Keisei had proposed, the next round of voting arrived before we knew it.

Round 2 Voting Results: OPTION ONE: Grant to three random students: 0 Votes; OPTION TWO: Grant to one specific student: 39 Votes; OPTION THREE: Do not grant any Protect Points: 0 Votes

Keisei had brilliantly brought the class together and his proposal had been adopted. However, the only thing that was somewhat of a bother was the fact that there was an interval period between now and when we'd vote for who to give the point to. Since no student had stepped forward to object to granting Horikita the Protect Point, students used the interval period to speak freely and just pass the time. It had already been decided that Horikita would be the one we'd give the point to, so there wasn't any need to nominate anyone else to run.

There were no further disturbances for this issue. The decision was unanimous, and all thirty-nine votes were in favor of Horikita. I had expected this to be stressful, so the fact that the class had gotten through it unexpectedly smoothly was significant.

"And so, that concludes the third issue," said Chabashira. "For the next six months, starting now, everyone's Private Point deposits will be cut by half equally, and Horikita will be granted a Protect Point now."

Horikita, the acting leader, wasn't going to be able to make use of it in this special exam of course, but the class had succeeded in giving her valuable protection. It was by no means an inexpensive transaction, but it wasn't too expensive either.

ISSUE #4: One of the following adjustments will be made to the written exam being held at the end of the second semester.

CHOICES: Increased Difficulty, Increased Penalties, Decreased Rewards

What incredibly mean-spirited choices. No matter which one we chose, there were nothing but drawbacks for the class. If talking was allowed, I'm sure a lot of grumbling would be going on right now.

Round 1 Voting Results: INCREASED DIFFICULTY: 6 Votes, INCREASED PENALTIES: 18 Votes, DECREASED REWARDS: 15 Votes

Essentially, none of the options were things that anyone *wanted* to choose, so the vote was split. The issue was expected to drag on for quite some time as there was a heated debate between students who were confident that they could handle the next written exam and those who were not.

But in the second round, the class ended up unanimously voting for *Increased Penalties.* Horikita's highly persuasive assertion that students could avoid the penalties as long as they worked diligently seemed to have paid off.

4.3

THOUGH WE HAD a five-hour time limit for the exam, we were only about an hour into it. We had gotten to the last issue almost too quickly. A few students must have been thinking that clearing the exam was a certainty now, given how smoothly things had been going. Once we finished the next and final issue, the special exam would be over, and we would be awarded fifty Class Points.

However, if there was one cause for concern for everyone right now, it was probably the look on our homeroom teacher's face.

"Well then...that brings us to the final issue," Chabashira said slowly.

It was clear to see that as we tackled each issue, the color drained from Chabashira's face more and more.

It was obvious to the students that she had finally reached her peak, as she had now turned deathly pale.

"Sensei, are you all right?" asked Yousuke.

Even though the issue still hadn't actually been read to us yet, talking amongst ourselves wasn't exactly encouraged. Yousuke couldn't overlook the situation and decided to speak up anyway.

"...What do you mean?" she asked.

"Well, it's just... You're clearly looking unwell, that's all," said Yousuke.

Chabashira paused. "You think so? I'm fine."

It didn't sound like she was putting on a brave face. In other words, it seemed as if she herself didn't realize that there was anything wrong with her. Or perhaps you should say it was like she wasn't conscious of it at all. At any rate, Yousuke had no other choice but to back down since Chabashira told him nothing was wrong. The other teacher watching in the back of the room wasn't making a move either, so at this rate, the final issue was about to be announced.

However, one thing was certain. Namely, it was that we should've assumed the next issue had a lot to do with Chabashira's condition.

"Now then, I'll show you the final issue. Get ready to vote."

With that, Chabashira started tapping on her tablet that she held in her hands. At the same time, the woman was trying to get her breathing under control.

Then, the final issue was displayed.

ISSUE #5: In exchange for expelling one of your classmates, gain 100 Class Points.

(In the event the class is unanimously in favor, a vote will be held to choose the student to be expelled.)

CHOICES: For, Against

This final issue had the fewest choices of any issue we had voted on so far as there were only two options. At first glance, it was easy for one to think that given the fewer the choices, the easier it would be to come to a consensus. But in reality, the number of choices didn't actually have that much of an effect on that. If the vote was being held with a large gathering of total strangers, or if it wasn't possible to have any discussion, then having a large number of options was a disadvantage. In this situation, our class was able to hold repeated discussions.

What was important for us was how much time we had and the substance of the issue. We either expelled someone, or we would give up Class Points. Right now, we were being presented with one of the worst possible issues that I could have envisioned. Students were still forbidden from speaking amongst themselves, but I was sure that after reading this issue, they were quite shaken inside.

If we voted in favor of this issue, then that would mean one of our classmates would be expelled.

Under normal circumstances, the entire class should vote against an issue like this without hesitation. The prospect of 100 Class Points was certainly no small amount, but the majority of the class would likely prefer not to have one of their classmates expelled in exchange for those points. If this issue were decided by a simple majority vote, then the most likely outcome would be that the majority of the class would vote against in the first round of voting, and that would be the end of it. However, as the previous four issues had proven, things weren't quite so simple. This was the simple yet difficult problem of unanimity.

"I'll be starting the sixty-second countdown now... Everyone, begin putting in your votes," said Chabashira.

We weren't given any extra time. The sixty-second voting period had already begun. If the class voted unanimously in favor of the issue, we would immediately begin the process of selecting who would be expelled. I'm repeating myself here, but there was hardly anyone who wanted that, of course. This issue was for 100 Class Points—not so great a sum that we had to do anything it took to acquire them.

However, if this was the third semester of our third year of high school with only one or two more special exams left to go before graduation, then we likely wouldn't be in the same state of mind. Those 100 points would jump in value at a time like that, when the competition between classes was so close that even a single point would make a difference. A battle where we'd have to make the ultimate choice between two options might very well be waiting for us when that time came.

But the circumstances *now* were different. We weren't in the kind of situation where nearly everyone in class would hesitate to vote *Against* in this issue. Still, it was true that there were some causes for concern, and one of those was Kouenji. That was exactly why I was slowly thinking things through as I held my hand over my tablet. As Horikita and I agreed, I would vote for the first option in the first round of voting, no matter what the issue was. That was my role. However, if all thirty-eight other students in class, Horikita included, voted against the issue, then it might be better for me to simply go ahead and vote against as well, so that we'd get all thirty-nine votes in and not have to waste time with the interval period.

I decided that this was an issue that we should finish quickly and without spending any extra time. Besides, there was no guarantee that students might not get swayed by the 100 points once we were thrust into discussion. I determined that, in regard to this issue alone, an interval was unnecessary.

After nearly sixty seconds had passed, a notification was displayed indicating that all votes were in.

"...Since all votes are now in, I'll show you your results," said Chabashira.

Despite the fact there was obviously something off, Chabashira maintained her composure and continued with the exam.

Round 1 Voting Results: FOR: 2 Votes, AGAINST: 37 Votes

So, it's not unanimous, huh. I removed my finger from the button and quietly stared at the results.

The entire room was silent.

Chabashira should have been reading the results aloud and continuing the exam process, but she remained motionless. She simply stared at the monitor without a word, like the students were. These results were surprising... The split was unlike anything that we had seen before. There was no guarantee that we would've come to a unanimous decision on the issue immediately without an interval period. In that case, maybe this was the issue that Chabashira was concerned about.

Though it had only been a few seconds, Chabashira had remained completely still. Her inaction prompted the teacher in the back of the class to urge her to move on with the exam.

"Chabashira-sensei," said the observing teacher. "Please continue."

"Uh... Please excuse me," she said. "Um... That's two votes for, and thirty-seven votes against. Because you didn't come to a unanimous decision, we'll have an interval period now."

Two votes in favor.

"Hey, who the hell voted in favor of this?!" yelled Sudou. "Are you kidding me?!"

Though he was questioning who voted that way, Sudou shot a fierce glare directly in Kouenji's direction. Kouenji had made some comments regarding the Protect Point issue earlier, but he hadn't stood out much during this exam. Still, he was probably the only person who came to mind when you considered the issue and who might vote that way. Sudou had simply made a snap decision on his own that it might have been Kouenji, but I was sure that many other students shared his opinion.

"Which did you vote for, Kouenji?" asked Sudou.

"I don't need to answer that, do I?" replied Kouenji.

"If you can't answer the question, that means you voted *For*, didn't ya?" snapped Sudou.

"I don't think it's a good idea for you to be so judgmental, Red Hair-kun," Kouenji said. "Besides, according to Horikita Girl, we should be allowed to make whatever choice we wish in the first round of voting anyway. In that case, I don't think you have any right to complain about how I vote, do you?"

Sudou wore an overtly disgruntled expression in the face of Kouenji's solid argument.

"Still, if we figure that one of those votes was Kouenji, that means there's still one other person who voted in favor, right?" said Ike, focusing on the other voter.

"Yeah, that's definitely a problem too. Seriously, who the hell was it?!" roared Sudou. He was frustrated, most likely because he was unable to figure out who the other voter was.

"Don't panic," said Horikita. "Ayanokouji-kun was one of the people who voted in favor," replied Horikita.

"Huh? A-Ayanokouji voted in favor?" asked Sudou. "How can you say that for sure, Suzune?"

"I've been keeping this secret until now, but before this special exam began, he and I came to an agreement about the voting. I did it to make sure that regardless of what issue we were presented with, we wouldn't have a unanimous decision in the first round. And that is because I made sure that we adjusted things accordingly in advance."

Now that we had gotten to the final issue, Horikita began to explain the details of the arrangement that she and I had made ahead of time. It was certainly true that there wasn't any advantage in keeping it a secret any longer now that we had gotten to this stage. It would obviously be a waste of time and effort trying to figure out who the other person who voted in favor was.

"And you did that to avoid a situation where we unexpectedly came to a unanimous decision on something, right?" Yousuke chimed in with a few words to make things clearer for the students who still didn't fully understand yet.

"Yes," replied Horikita.

"Huh... So that's how it is," said Sudou. "In that case, you should've just told us a lot earlier."

"I couldn't. Things wouldn't have worked out that way," Horikita replied. "In the first round of voting, we aren't allowed to talk. That round is a valuable opportunity for us to find out what our classmates' preferred choice is out of the available options. If you all knew of my strategy to avoid coming to a unanimous decision right away, students might have just entered in votes at random. I wanted to avoid that from happening. It was Ayanokouji-kun's job to cast his vote for the first choice every time, and it was mine to vote for the second. So, in truth, there's really only one person here who actually voted *For*."

As she spoke, Horikita surveyed the classroom, as if she was speaking to that certain someone in particular.

"This is a bit of an extreme issue, but individuals are free to decide which choice they'd like to vote for. I don't think that it's wrong to vote in favor of this issue in order to gain Class Points. However, we should come together as a class and vote *Against*. Still, if anyone has any objections, I would sincerely appreciate it if you could speak your mind right now like we've done with previous issues... What do you think?"

Normally, the student who voted in favor of the issue would step forward now. However, no matter how long we waited, no one responded to Horikita's question.

"How long are you gonna stay silent, Kouenji?" snapped Sudou.

"*Fu fu*. Like I mentioned before, I would appreciate it if you didn't assume that I voted *For*," Kouenji replied.

"The hell with that! I know you're just messin' around anyway."

If it wasn't Kouenji, then whoever it was might've had a difficult time announcing themselves. They might have felt apprehensive about Sudou's tendency to rush to anger. If we came to a unanimous decision in favor of the issue, that meant we'd have to vote on who to expel. Somewhere in this room, there was someone who wanted to gain 100 Class Points in exchange for expelling one of their classmates. That would draw attention and make them a target for criticism. Deep down, they didn't want anyone else to know they were thinking that way.

"All right, enough of—"

"Calm down, Sudou-kun," said Horikita. "It's still only the first round of voting. There's no need to be in such a panic."

"B-but! I just can't stand that someone voted in favor of this kinda thing!"

"You are free to interpret the situation however you wish," she told him. "But there's no proof that it was Kouenji-kun. Besides, the way that I see things, the person who voted in favor of the issue must be feeling sorry about it as they aren't coming forward. Since this vote is anonymous, let's not pursue the matter too far. If everyone votes against the issue in the second round, it'll be unanimous, and that will be good enough."

And so, the issue would be settled, and we'd finish it.

From the sound of it, Horikita seemed to have decided that there was no need to spend any extra time on this. Not pursuing the issue was probably one of the best choices we could make right now. I had been thinking the same thing myself.

"There's no need for further discussion on this issue," Horikita said. "Come on, let's get this over and done with the next vote."

Seeing Horikita calm down, Sudou slapped both of his cheeks at once, to center himself. Then, after a little bit of irrelevant chatter in the classroom, it was time to begin the second round of voting.

"We'll now begin the sixty-second voting period," said Chabashira.

The LCD screens of our tablets now displayed buttons labeled *For* and *Against*. Apparently we didn't even need the sixty seconds we had been given, as everyone finished voting in about twenty seconds.

"Now that all votes are in, I'll show you the results for the second round..." said Chabashira.

Round 2 Voting Results: FOR: 2 Votes, AGAINST: 37 Votes

This special exam hadn't caused any especially tense feelings so far, but the moment the second round's results were announced, everyone froze. Once again, two people had voted in favor of expelling someone. That meant the votes didn't change even after what Horikita said earlier. That harsh truth was conveyed to us via the cold, sterile monitor.

"Wait, hold on a moment... What is the meaning of this?" asked Horikita.

As Horikita said those words, her gaze fell upon me, of all people. Her gaze was asking me, *"Why did you vote in favor of the issue in the second round?"*

The students who had come to understand Horikita's strategy after she had explained it to them were looking at me as well, Sudou included.

"Actually, I voted *Against*," I admitted. "Both in the first round of voting and just now in the second round."

"Huh?" said Sudou. "H-hey, what the hell? Ayanokouji, wasn't your job to vote for the first option, though?"

"Yeah, it was. But because of what this issue was, I decided on my own that it would've been better to go ahead and vote against the issue anyway, in the first round. I didn't say anything before because I didn't want to create any unnecessary confusion."

If everyone knew that there were actually *two* people who legitimately voted in favor of the issue in the first round, more people would be upset. It would no longer be possible to just end the conversation by saying, *"Oh well, it's probably just Kouenji messing around."*

Horikita, who had been calm and collected throughout this process so far, now looked somewhat shaken. "I see... That means right now, there are two people who are in favor of the issue," she said.

She brought her hand to her lips and put her mind to work. I was sure that she wanted to stop and think long and hard about things, but the precious time we had in this interval period was ticking by.

"If whomever is voting in favor plans to continue voting that way, I ask if you would be so kind as to provide me with a good reason as to why?" said Horikita. "As you can see from the results, there are two of you voting *For*, and thirty-seven of us are opposed to the issue. If you want everyone else to change their vote to your side, you'll have to present your case accordingly."

Essentially, discussion was essential for changing votes. If more and more people determined that there were greater advantages in being in favor of an issue, then votes would naturally shift in that direction. Conversely, if there was no discussion, then it wouldn't be easy to sway the vote.

Kushida, unable to bear the silence any longer, spoke up and asked Horikita a question. "H-hey, Horikita-san. It's...going to be okay, right? No one's going to be expelled from class, right?"

"My policy, as I've stated before, is to not have anyone expelled," said Horikita, reiterating her stance.

But after Horikita had expressed her determination, there was another period of silence. It was easy to keep asking people to speak up over and over, but...

Yousuke stood up. "I don't know who is voting in favor of this issue. But whoever you are, I want you to listen very carefully." His words were gentle yet forceful. "You should not choose to abandon a classmate to get Class Points. Even if we could gain 500 or 1,000 Class Points, I don't think a choice like that would be worth it. More importantly, though, we would only be able to get 100 points here. We can make up for missing out on that many Class Points quite easily."

It was a natural appeal from a man who hated the idea of sacrificing anyone more than anything. Thirty-seven of the thirty-nine students in class seemed to have some degree of understanding of what Yousuke was saying. He believed that we could forfeit 100 Class Points, but we couldn't allow someone to be expelled. However... it was another matter entirely whether actually getting Class Points were these two voters' true intentions.

Even before the first round of voting had started, the results of the vote, meaning whether people were voting against or in favor of the issue, were largely swayed by silent peer pressure. There were surely some students in class who must have thought that they could never be expelled, so in times like these, it made sense that some of those students might genuinely believe that they didn't care if their fellow classmates were sacrificed.

"*Fu fu fu.* This special exam is getting quite interesting, don't you think? It's kind of *cool*, I would say." Kouenji let out an amused chuckle, and then continued to speak without even the slightest trace of guilt in his voice. "Putting me aside, I thought for certain that the other person was going to vote against the issue in the second round of voting."

"Wait, 'aside' from you, so... I knew it, that means you DID vote for it, Kouenji!" snarled Sudou.

"Kouenji-kun, is that true?" said Horikita. "I would like for you to stop being a lone wolf right now, because it could cause a nasty mess if you don't."

Horikita's first priority was to clarify whether Kouenji was really for or against the issue.

"Rest assured," he said. "I firmly voted in favor of the issue in both the first and second rounds."

"Would you mind telling me the reason why...?" asked Horikita.

"The answer is simple. We'd be increasing our Class Points by a hundred points, yes? Which, in other words, means that we'd inevitably get more Private Points every month as a result. There's no reason to vote against the issue."

"Stop spoutin' crap," said Sudou. "You seriously think Class Points are more important than your friends?!"

"Well now, you've said something rather interesting," said Kouenji. "You didn't seem like that sort of person when we first enrolled in this school. Hm?"

"Screw you!" Sudou shouted.

"I'm voting in favor of the issue, so naturally, I have taken such things into account."

"Seriously, though. Don't you think about your friends...?" Sudou huffed.

"Friends? I have never once thought of you people as my friends."

"Meaning you ain't planning on changing your vote next time?" asked Sudou.

"Of course not. I will continue to vote in favor of the issue *if things remain as they are*. I'm sure that Horikita Girl wishes to avoid letting time run out, no?"

"Fine," snapped Sudou. "Don't think that this is going to go the way you want it, Kouenji. If that's the way he's going to play it, then let's not show 'im any mercy either, Suzune. We can just have everyone vote in favor of the issue, and then get Kouenji expelled!"

I was sure that was a response that Sudou simply came up with in the heat of the moment, but it was also true that what Sudou said could apply to those who were in favor of the issue. The class could come together in solidarity and chase out a villain who went so far as to say that he was fine with getting his classmates expelled.

People unconsciously chose what they wanted to believe and justified the reasons for those choices later. No one wanted to have anyone else expelled, but there were some students in favor of the issue, so they didn't have any choice. A person's brain would start to move toward justifying that there was no other option but to have that person expelled. People would also accept convenient logic, conspiracies, and misinformation without questioning it.

"I wish for nothing more than for everyone to vote in favor of the issue," said Kouenji. "However, it'd be best for you not to assume that you'd get *me* expelled. Isn't that right, Horikita Girl?"

That much was obvious. There was no way that Kouenji wasn't aware that, in normal circumstances, if someone came forward and said that they were one of the people in favor of the issue, it would naturally cause a stir and they'd become a target for expulsion. Kouenji's composure made it clear to everyone that he was absolutely sure there was no way he'd be expelled.

"...He's right," said Horikita. "We can't expel Kouenji-kun."

"Whaddya mean?" asked Sudou.

"I made a promise to Kouenji-kun before the uninhabited island exam began, remember?" Horikita said. "If he took first place in the exam, I said I would protect him from then on, until graduation."

Our classmates should have remembered their conversation back then.

"I hadn't expected him to win first place," she added. "But thanks to him doing just that, our class jumped up in the rankings and we're now neck-and-neck with Class B. That is an immeasurable achievement."

"S-sure, I guess that's true, but... But, if he's tryin' to put our class at risk, then that's a whole 'nother story!" shouted Sudou.

"Putting the class at risk?" said Kouenji. "Unthinkable. I am simply free to make the choices that have been presented to us, nothing more. You can't assume that me voting in favor of the issue is *evil*, now, can you?"

For the sake of argument, let's suppose the issue had said, "You may expel one person from class. Vote for or against." In that case, you could state with certainty that voting in favor of the issue would be seen as bad. However, in this case, we would be getting Class Points in exchange for having someone expelled. While it was difficult to define the specific value of a single student, no one could deny that Kouenji was allowed to calculate that he would gain more by voting in favor of the issue. And, considering Kouenji's solid argument and the promise that Horikita had made to him, there was no way that she could be in favor of Kouenji's expulsion either.

"W-well, fine then," grumbled Sudou. "You'll just have to go back on your word! If Kouenji doesn't think of any of his classmates as friends, then ain't nobody gonna be bothered if he's expelled."

"Not happening. I have no intention of breaking my promise to him," said Horikita.

"There you have it," said Kouenji. "After all, no one would trust a class leader who doesn't keep her promises. In that sense, I trust you more than anyone else right now, Horikita Girl."

Kouenji's nastiness had reared its ugly head. Now that it had come to this, Horikita had to first try to persuade Kouenji, somehow. There were still plenty of opportunities for her to do just that. Even if he fundamentally believed that she wouldn't betray him, that still didn't necessarily mean that Kouenji was 100 percent protected.

He must have been keeping the possibility that Horikita could abandon him in the back of his mind. To put it another way, even Kouenji would change his attitude if he saw the situation start to turn against him.

If Horikita decided to immediately cut Kouenji from the class after he had delivered results, right after Horikita had awakened to her responsibilities as leader, then that choice would likely create major obstacles for her in the future.

"Okay, so if you ain't kickin' Kouenji out, what are you gonna do, Suzune?" asked Sudou.

"Please give me some time to think... But well, that being said, I can't just sit back and be silent right now either, I suppose."

If Kouenji was the only person in favor of the issue, then the situation would've been fine. But the fact that there was *another* person in favor of the idea who hadn't stepped forward was something that couldn't be overlooked.

"I'm wondering if the person besides Kouenji-kun who voted in favor of this issue might be willing to come forward?" said Horikita.

If we didn't know who it was, then we couldn't move this conversation forward. However, the only thing Horikita got in response to her request was a long, stifling silence. After all, that person must have feared that if they stepped forward now, it would lead to intimidation and condescending arguments, like what had happened with Kouenji. If anything, that person might be met with even *more* disapproval than Kouenji.

All that Horikita got was silence. Eventually, time ran out, and it was now time for the third round of voting whether we liked it or not. The silver lining here was that there was no limit to the number of times we could vote. We had a chance to come to a unanimous decision every ten minutes, as long as time permitted it.

Round 3 Voting Results: FOR: 2 Votes, AGAINST: 37 Votes

The results were the same as the previous two rounds. Kouenji and this unseen other both voted in favor of the issue again. Many students were still focusing their attention on Kouenji, but now I had to wonder what was going to happen eventually. It wouldn't be long before they were faced with the perplexing reality that there was another student who hadn't come forward and was continuing to vote in favor of the issue. They were surely keeping a close eye on the situation. We were about to come face-to-face with the true danger of anonymity, which was the thing I had been hoping to avoid the most.

However, dealing with Kouenji was our first priority. There wasn't going to be any resolution until the *For* votes were swayed over to *Against*.

"We cannot ignore whoever is voting in favor of this issue," said Horikita. "Still, it's not as though I'm absolute either. I'm sure that whoever this person is, they have a certain conviction about this issue, considering the fact that they are still stubbornly voting in favor. In that case, I would very much like to hear from both of those who voted *For* at the same time. That includes the person other than Kouenji-kun, who we haven't seen yet."

Without wasting any time, Horikita began gathering her thoughts.

"The thirty-seven of us will continue to vote against this issue. And you two will continue to vote for it. The absolute worst-case scenario that awaits us if we continue to do that will be that we run out of time. As classmates, we lose out on Class Points together, in the same way. Put another way, it might seem like both sides, *For* and *Against*, are going to suffer. But if we, the faction voting *Against*, win, then that means even though we miss out on Class Points, we aren't losing any of our friends. We can make it through this special exam without anyone getting expelled. Now, if the faction voting *For* this issue wins, they will lose quite a lot rather than gaining anything substantial. It's essentially putting the cart before the horse. Am I wrong?"

Horikita specifically explained the concrete losses and gains to be had, and the risks of the exam ending in disagreement. Of course, the person who hadn't come forward wasn't answering, but I couldn't help but wonder about Kouenji.

"Yes, it is most certainly true that if we run out of time, things will happen as you say," replied Kouenji. "That is why you should go ahead and vote in favor." He said that as though it were a matter of course.

"...Yes, I agree that if we unanimously vote for the idea, we'll be able to take a step forward," said Horikita. "But what awaits us afterward is an even bigger hurdle: the question of *which* of our classmates we expel. Surely you don't think we'll be able to come to a unanimous decision on that so easily, do you?"

"It's *your* job to make that work, Horikita Girl," Kouenji said. "Besides, expelling someone isn't such a bad thing, now is it?"

"No, it is a bad thing. We shouldn't expel anyone," replied Yousuke, cutting in before Horikita could give a rebuttal.

"I don't understand this. You all seem to be afraid of expelling anyone, but surely it would be much easier mentally to view this as a positive, no? We can delete an unnecessary student as we wish, and we'll even get Class Points for it. If you simply change your line of thinking on this issue, you can understand what a wonderful option voting *For* is. The other person voting in favor of the issue understands that."

A pointed line of thinking, to be sure, but it was good enough of a reason to vote as he was.

"I think you're wrong about that, Kouenji-kun. Losing someone from class is in no way a positive," said Kushida, backing up Yousuke.

In response to that, the people on the side of voting against the issue who hadn't said much until this point all started voicing their objections at the same time. Kouenji, however, simply smiled broadly, his attitude not budging a bit. He was the person that I wanted to hear the most from, but he didn't respond to any calls for debate after that point.

The time then came for the fourth round of voting.

Round 4 Voting Results: FOR: 2 Votes, AGAINST: 37 Votes

After so much time spent on appeals that didn't have any effect whatsoever on the results, Chabashira signaled that we had now entered the third interval period.

"Seriously, what the hell do we do, man?" huffed Sudou. "Dammit, ain't there a way we can like, punch his lights out and then just vote for him or somethin' once he's out cold?!"

"Of course not," said Horikita. "Let's try thinking about this objectively for a moment... If we do that, even Kouenji-kun might change his mind."

Horikita was essentially forced into trying out other approaches as she wanted to avoid a situation where we never came to a resolution.

"Whaddya mean, 'objectively'?" asked Sudou.

"I mean asking ourselves what the other three classes will choose."

"That's, well... Well, no doubt in my mind that Ryuuen's class is gonna just go ahead and get rid of any rando without a second thought," Sudou immediately replied. He took on a casual stance, crossing his arms and resting them behind the back of his head.

Many of our classmates made comments here and there agreeing with him. Considering the actions and thinking that people in Ryuuen's class had exhibited so far, there was a good chance it would happen that way.

"Yes. His class may be the most highly likely to choose that option," said Horikita.

"On the other hand, there's no way Ichinose-san's class is going to do it," remarked Yousuke. "But as for Sakayanagi-san's class... I'm not sure."

Most of the students in Ryuuen's class were expected to be in favor of the issue. Most of the students in Ichinose's class were expected to be opposed. And it seemed that Sakayanagi's class could go either way. All of our classmates came to the interesting revelation that, coincidentally, all three classes had different trends. In this case, there was almost no argument whatsoever about Ichinose's class, who they expected to vote against the issue. The focus of the discussion then landed on Ryuuen's class, as expected.

"I definitely don't like the idea of Ryuuen overtakin' us," said Sudou. "They got a lotta momentum right now, and if they just get a little bit of a push, they can become Class B, right?"

"Even so, the difference wouldn't be significant," said Horikita. "Supposing even if they were to get a slight lead here, they'd only be getting ahead by 100 Class Points. Just one special exam would be more than enough to make up for that gap."

"I understand what you're trying to say. I'd just like to add one thing, though." The person entering the conversation was Akito. He had been quiet throughout the special exam so far, but he broke that silence now and began to speak up. "The chances are low, but there is still a possibility that missing out on these 100 points might come back to bite us one day, right?"

"The hell, Miyake?" said Sudou. "Does that mean you wanna expel somebody?"

"Don't get me wrong. I am clearly against the idea," said Akito, shooting a look at Sudou that seemed to convey dismay rather than anger. "I think that it's best for us to shoot for Class A without anyone from class getting left out, but that's exactly why we've got to understand the weight of this decision. We should not take these 100 points lightly."

"Whaddya mean?" asked Sudou.

"It means we have to consider a future where this special exam is actually an important turning point as we're approaching graduation, and with that in mind, we all need to express our opposition to this issue."

Akito's opinion was that it would be a mistake for us to simply vote against the issue without truly thinking about what it meant.

"I-I definitely hadn't thought about that..." said Sudou.

We had to vote against the issue, and without hesitation. The students in the classroom were well aware of the looming specter of peer pressure.

"Kouenji, I know you did a lot for us in the uninhabited island exam. I would think that it'd be ridiculous if people in favor of this issue voted to expel you, even if you didn't have that promise with Horikita." Akito was expressing his thoughts not only to Horikita and Sudou, but now to Kouenji as well. "But even so, you can't just keep on making trouble for the class forever, doing as you please. Class Points aren't the only thing that make a relationship work. Do you understand what I'm saying?"

"*Fu fu fu...*" Kouenji closed his eyes and nodded deeply. It wasn't clear if he was thinking about something or just going through the motions. Then, he opened his eyes and glanced over at Akito. "Of course I...don't. Not at all."

"Tch..." tutted Akito.

"Think about the system by which this school operates," said Kouenji. "Everything is ruled by points. It has nothing to do whatsoever with friendship, or affection, or anything of that sort. Class Points determine whether you ascend in the class hierarchy or not, and Private Points function as personal assets. It is a two-sided value system. I do not think there's anything bad about voting in favor of the issue to prioritize points."

"God, you're so up your own ass, just spouting total bull!" yelled Sudou. "You never *ever* contributed to the class in all this time until now! Just 'cause you got first place in the uninhabited island exam doesn't mean you can just mouth off like this all the time, you jerk!"

"I think you'd best look in a mirror, Red Hair-kun. I think if the question is who has contributed more to this class, you or me, the answer is quite clear."

Sudou was getting increased recognition now, but when he started at this school, he was a problem child on par with Kouenji. Well, actually, no—if you factored in the fluctuations in our Class Points, then Sudou was even the worse of the two.

"Still, though. It's not the Class Points that are important to me," said Kouenji.

His stance of being in favor of the idea still seemed entirely outlandish to everyone by this point.

Horikita, however, did not fail to catch what he just said.

"Class Points are not important to you," she repeated. "Meaning that these 100 Class Points aren't so that we can move up to Class A, but for Private Points. That's why you keep voting in favor of the issue, isn't it?"

"Exactly," he replied. "I wish to vote in favor of the issue for Private Points. Because of two issues prior, we chose the option of cutting our monthly deposit of Private Points in half for six months. I accepted it without complaint because I deemed it necessary if you were to protect me. However, I'm afraid, I'm not backing down this time."

Kouenji wanted Class Points to compensate for the Private Points he was going to lose. That was his reasoning for voting in favor of this issue. Some students might take offense at the fact that he was trying to get a student expelled for Private Points. Horikita, on the other hand, saw this as an opportunity.

"I understand, Kouenji-kun," she said after a pause. "Let's make a deal. One that isn't bad for you at all."

"Oh? Intriguing. Sure, I'll listen to your offer." Kouenji wasn't surprised by her words in the slightest. In fact, he seemed to welcome Horikita's proposal with open arms, almost as if he had been waiting for it.

"If you vote against the issue right now, and what follows is that the class is unanimously opposed, then *I* will personally pay you 10,000 yen's worth of Private Points every month from here onwards until graduation. That would be the same as gaining 100 Class Points for you, wouldn't it?"

"S-surely that would make it pointless for Kouenji-kun to vote in favor of the issue then, in that case..." said Kushida.

"Bravo, Horikita Girl. It didn't take you very long to come to that conclusion after all."

"Should I take it to mean that you've been voting in favor of the issue because you were trying to get me to make this proposal to you from the very beginning?" asked Horikita.

"It means that my one vote just has that much value.

Perhaps I could have continued raising the price, but I needed to make you into a reliable ally, Horikita Girl. So, let's commit to the deal then, with those terms."

"There's no need for us to put this in writing, is there?" said Horikita. "Chabashira-sensei is right here too, after all."

"Of course not, it's fine," said Kouenji. "I don't expect you to go back on your word. And with that, the agreement is decided."

And so, Kouenji's vote, which we hadn't expected to be swayed, would change. By striking that deal, Horikita had gotten him to promise that he'd vote against the issue. I guess I should say that it was rather expected of him to deliberately vote in favor of the issue over and over in order to get Horikita to come forward with a proposal like that. And so, we had now gotten to the fifth round of voting.

Kouenji's declaration that he would now be voting *Against* surely must have had an effect on the unseen other. It wouldn't be easy for just one person to continue voting in favor of the issue, standing in opposition to everyone else, even if it was anonymous. In other words, it was possible that whoever it was, they could change their vote now, even without overt attempts to persuade them.

However...

Round 5 Voting Results: FOR: 1 Vote, AGAINST: 38 Votes

Kouenji had switched sides, but there was still one vote in favor of the issue. While some of us might have wanted to feel like there was a weight taken off our minds by one vote having changed, it also felt like the real battle was just about to begin. Someone else was absolutely committed to voting in favor, anonymously. If we were going to push ahead, we would need to uncover who exactly that someone was.

Unfortunately, that was going to be more difficult than anything else. It was basically impossible to get a look at anyone's tablet screen, but if you wanted to try and judge what someone voted for by the position of their fingertips against the screen, you could do that... However, the school had anticipated that, and the order of options on our screens had been randomized from the very beginning. It was also impossible to check via finger movements because the options were arranged differently every time there was a vote. There was no other method for working it out except by repeatedly making use of the interval periods.

"My oh my, it would seem that things won't be so easy after all, hm?" mused Kouenji.

"As I stated before, unless the class is unanimously opposed, the deal we had just made will be null and void," said Horikita.

"I understand," said Kouenji. "If the situation ends with a unanimous decision in favor of the issue or if time runs out, then that means I'll be forced to give up on our deal."

Since it was anonymous, there was no way to prove that Kouenji wasn't still voting in favor of the issue other than the results showing a unanimous decision in opposition. From the way he sounded, Kouenji didn't seem to think he could get those Private Points by making any other choice, after all. If he voted selfishly now, then that tantalizing deal would go up in smoke. More importantly, though, it would be inconvenient for Kouenji to make an enemy out of Horikita. He just wanted to make things easier for himself.

We had about three hours left. Despite our struggles, Horikita showed that she was making clear progress toward a breakthrough with a solid strategy. However, I couldn't just stand on the sidelines and watch forever. I needed to bring the class to a unanimous decision before the time we had left ran out. I simply intended to sit back and quietly watch the battle unfold until the time came for that. I wondered, though, if I could offer some small degree of support.

During the interval period, I coughed a couple of times. Just two light coughs. No one paid any attention to unconscious acts like coughing amidst all of the chatter. Even if someone were aware of it, they would just hear a simple cough.

"Hey, um, Horikita-san?" asked Kei.

"What is it, Karuizawa-san?"

"So, um, this is just a simple hunch on my part, but do you maybe have an idea of who is voting in favor?"

"Huh? Why...? What makes you think that?" Horikita was surprised at Kei's rather unexpected observation.

"Just a feeling, I guess. That's all," Kei replied.

Not long ago, Horikita would've likely interpreted what Kei just said as a thoughtful observation. However, now that the fact that Kei and I were dating was public knowledge, things were beginning to change.

"Yes, I suppose... What you say is true, Karuizawa-san. I think I might have an idea of who keeps voting in favor."

"What?" said Sudou. "In that case, come out and say it. Who the hell is it?"

"I can't," Horikita replied. "This special exam is designed around anonymity. If I say a name just because I *think* I have an idea it might be them, I wouldn't be able to take it back if it turns out I'm wrong."

"But!" wailed Sudou.

"...I understand. Which is why I think I need to be fully prepared to do it. Let's go through the vote a few more times. If we still don't see the votes in favor go down to zero, then... If that happens, then I'll have no choice but to say the name out loud."

"I'd like you to hold off on that, Horikita-san," said Yousuke. "I can't agree to this. As you just said, we have no way of knowing for sure who is voting for which side. However, I don't think it's permissible to come out and name someone just because you have a hunch. Of course, I'm not just throwing this out there because I don't want anyone to be expelled, though. You understand, yes?"

"I agree with Hirata-kun on this," said Kushida anxiously. "I don't think you can say who it is without absolute certainty."

After those two voiced their stances, the class was wrapped up in anxiety. If Horikita were to make some kind of mistake and throw someone's name out there, that person would be criticized. And if the class started shouting at them, asking why they were voting in favor, that person would feel betrayed and forsaken by everyone. Then, if thirty-eight students ended up panicking about time running out and voted in favor despite already being opposed, it would be inevitable that whoever had been named would be brought up in discussion as a target for expulsion.

"I understand that... I understand," said Horikita. "Which is why I haven't mentioned their name yet. But we cannot let time run out, can we?"

"I understand how you feel," said Yousuke. "I am not the same as I used to be either. If I had to make a truly necessary choice, I would feel like I would be prepared to make it. However, I would have to be 100 percent sure."

"Right..." Horikita agreed.

I thought I should try to introduce a few changes into the situation, since things had started to get a bit heavy.

"Aside from Horikita, are there any other students with an idea of who is voting in favor?" I asked.

"Nope," said Sudou. "I mean, if the question's like 'If there's anyone out there other than Kouenji who'd be so stubbornly in favor of the idea,' I've got no clue."

Sudou probably wasn't the only person in class who had those doubts. It would have to be someone who could approve of a situation where someone would be getting expelled.

"If someone here has an idea of who might be voting *For*, even if we can't name any names, then our thinking might still change a little," I said. I wanted to try to give the class a little push. "I'd like anyone who has even the slightest hunch of who it might be to raise their hand."

However, not a single one of them seemed to have any idea of who it was. No one followed up on what Horikita said earlier.

"Yousuke, I know you don't want to suspect anyone, but since you have such a wide circle of friends, both guys and girls, surely there's *someone* who comes to mind, right?" I asked.

"There isn't," he replied after a pause. "That's not a lie. I really can't think of anyone."

"I see... In that case, what about you, Kushida?"

Even though I was suddenly addressing her, Kushida didn't appear out of sorts at all. Rather, Horikita turned to me, somewhat shaken and upset, almost as if she were silently asking me, "*What are you going to say?*"

"Who do you think is voting in favor?" I asked.

"Hmm... I'm sorry, Ayanokouji-kun," she replied. "Like Hirata-kun, there isn't anyone who comes to mind for me either."

"You know the class best out of anyone, Kushida," I told her. "I thought you might know a little about which students are feeling dissatisfied. Everyone knows that you care about the class more than anyone, and you're always there to offer friendly advice. I want you to try and think hard."

After I had said those words, the class's eyes turned to Kushida with looks full of anticipation.

"U-um... I don't think...anyone is really coming to mind," she said. "But if I think of anything, I'll be sure to let you know."

"Thanks. We're counting on you. I have a feeling that people like you and Yousuke are indispensable for this special exam."

Without everyone's combined efforts, it would be difficult to break through the opposition in this issue. However, those discussions proved to be in vain, as the results of the sixth round of voting showed...

Round 6 Voting Results: FOR: 1 Vote, AGAINST: 38 Votes

The results hadn't changed. We discussed it again and again.

Round 7 Voting Results: FOR: 1 Vote, AGAINST: 38 Votes

Round 8 Voting Results: FOR: 1 Vote, AGAINST: 38 Votes

There still wasn't any change in the results. Our conversations were marked by more and more silence. Now, we were about to enter into the eighth interval period. A little over an hour had passed since we started this issue.

CLACK!

With a loud rattling sound, Chabashira suddenly toppled over, losing her balance. She managed to prevent herself from falling over completely by holding her arms out against the podium. In the position she was in, it was like she was bowing before us.

"*Huff... Huff...*" As our discussion continued, Chabashira, who had been standing up at the podium this whole time, started breathing heavily.

"S-Sensei?!" shouted Yousuke, worried.

"I-I'm all right..." she replied, adjusting her posture, as though she were trying to rouse herself.

The students stared at Chabashira with wide, vacant eyes, wondering what she was thinking. Eventually, she exhaled deeply, sounding as though she had finally come to a decision about something.

"We teachers are not allowed to guide students toward any particular choice," she said. "So, naturally, I won't be doing anything of the sort. However, may I tell you an old story? Of course, by doing so, it means I'll be taking away your precious time. But if you don't mind, I'll share it with you."

"Chabashira-sensei," the monitor interjected. "While teachers are not banned from making statements, if you violate the rules, you will not resolve this matter with a simple apology. If it's determined that you are trying to induce a decision, to protect the class, then..."

"Yes, I understand. I am prepared to receive punishment

should the school see what I say as an intentional effort to guide the class into making a certain choice."

Now that Chabashira had said she understood, the monitor had no choice but to fall silent. It was a totally unexpected proposal from Chabashira, someone who never meddled in special exams as a matter of course. This could be seen as a single ray of light being shone upon us while we were stuck in this standstill.

"We are really struggling with this current situation," said Horikita. "As long as what you say doesn't influence what option we'll choose, please share your story with us, Sensei."

Horikita figured that if what Chabashira said could offer some way of breaking through this situation, we should welcome the opportunity. Of course, if I was going to be honest, I would've liked to see momentum driving us to oppose the issue, but while we were under the watchful eyes of the monitor, direct expressions had to be avoided.

"...I also attended the Advanced Nurturing High School," Chabashira told us. "And when I was a student here, I took this same special exam."

Horikita and the rest of her classmates were surprised. This was the first time they had heard about this.

"Sensei, you took the Unanimous Special Exam too...?" asked Yousuke.

"That's right. There were five issues. Some of the issues back then were slightly different from the ones you've voted on, but the final issue, the one you're facing now, is the exact same as the one I experienced. Word for word. Either you can get Class Points in exchange for expelling a student, or you can protect your classmates and not gain any Class Points."

The students all turned their attention to Chabashira's story. They hung onto her words as she told them how she experienced this same special exam.

"There's one thing for certain," she said. "You have to give it your all with no regrets. Whatever choice you decide to make, whether *For* or *Against*, or to let time run out... Seek a way forward that will leave you with no regrets about the outcome. There's still time left."

All of the students listened intently as Chabashira spoke to them with real, genuine feeling for the very first time. She wasn't guiding the students toward a particular option, nor was she presenting us with a concrete solution. It was simply clear advice, just barely within the lines of what she was allowed to give us, as a teacher. The other teacher listening from the back of the classroom didn't announce that Chabashira had violated any rules and simply listened quietly until the end.

I didn't know whether this would change the outcome or not, but those were most definitely words that would help students face this special exam.

Even with the support from Chabashira, though, it wouldn't be a good idea to waste the time we had left in this interval period. Horikita kept struggling to increase her chances, even if only by a single percent.

"The time when we'll need to make up our mind is coming... But before we get to that point, please let me say something to you, just one more time. I am not your enemy... I am on your side," said Horikita, addressing the person who voted in favor.

I was sure that the name of this person had likely crossed Horikita's mind many times over. That person's face, their voice, their eyes, their breathing. Horikita was trying her best to persuade herself into not revealing to everyone else who this specific person was. I was sure she must have been telling herself that over and over.

I personally thought she should just come out with it and say that person's name, but the reason Horikita didn't do that was because she truly, genuinely wanted to be on this person's side. Horikita's appeal was something akin to a tragic, grief-stricken cry.

But in response to that, the ninth round of voting had come. And the results were...

Round 9 Voting Results: FOR: 1 Vote, AGAINST: 38 Votes

That one vote in favor hadn't been swayed after all. It was just one person. One, single student who seemed to be clinging to those 100 points for as long as it took. Well, it was more like...they were clinging to the right to have someone expelled. That was the real truth that only I, or perhaps just Horikita and I, knew.

It was safe to assume that this certain someone was going to continue voting in favor of the issue without exception. At the same time, there was no objective method to confirm whether that person was opposed to what was happening right now or not. Horikita said that if time were to run out, she would have no choice but to give a name. However, in reality, no matter how many times the vote was repeated, Horikita still hadn't said it. She was likely thinking, *"Are you actually against the idea of this?"*

Horikita knew that there wasn't actually any use in asking such a question. Rather, the moment that Horikita uttered that person's name, she would lose everything going forward. Even though we still had a bit of a grace period, the time limit was approaching us. We had about two hours remaining until our deadline to make the choice.

5

ICHINOSE HONAMI'S CHOICE

B EFORE THIS SPECIAL EXAM began, there was one class that every teacher thought was going to pass it for sure, without question. On the other hand, though, while they were expecting this class to make it through the exam without any difficulty, at the same time, they feared that this class might fall behind in the competition to reach Class A in the future.

And that class was Ichinose's Class B.

ISSUE #5: In exchange for expelling one of your classmates, gain 100 Class Points.

(In the event the class is unanimously in favor, a vote will be held to choose the student to be expelled.)

After reaching the final issue in a short amount of time, Ichinose and the other students in her class finished entering their votes and were now waiting for the results. There were no signs of anyone feeling anxious or upset... except for one person.

Kanzaki prayed as he stared at the thirty-nine other people in class who already voted. He strongly hoped that the results of the vote would show that there was a split, even if only slight.

"...Well then, I'll now show you the results," announced Hoshinomiya, sounding somewhat dejected as she tapped on her tablet.

As everyone watched, the results were displayed...

Round 1 Voting Results: FOR: 1 Vote, AGAINST: 39 Votes

After confirming that this was the worst possible outcome, Kanzaki closed his eyes once more. It wasn't a surprise, of course, that the overwhelming majority of students in Class B voted against the issue. They had no doubts that the class would be unanimously against it, believing that was just how it should be. They didn't even suspect anything regarding the fact that someone had entered a vote in favor of it.

"Hey, who the heck voted *For*?" said Shibata. "You pressed the wrong button, dude."

Shibata didn't sense any danger from the results. He simply turned and looked around behind him from his seat.

Exactly—he didn't even consider the possibility that one person could have voted in favor of the issue on purpose.

It wasn't just Shibata, either; everyone in class had the same assumption.

Kanzaki understood this well, and that was why he felt an uncontrollable anger welling up inside of him. Up until now, he had quietly helped his classmates as much as he possibly could, taking their wishes into consideration. However, it wasn't as though he could continue this farce of fighting only to protect his friends, no matter what situation they were in. Because of Kanzaki's position as an adviser of sorts, he felt these concerns more strongly than anyone else.

"Welp, I'm sure we don't need to really discuss anything anyway, so let's just take things as they come in the next vote and..."

There was no sense of urgency. Just a mindset that no student should ever prioritize Class Points over their own classmates. After having seen these attitudes so clearly in his classmates, Kanzaki could no longer continue to be silent.

Kanzaki interrupted Shibata. "Please wait a minute... Sure, we could come to a unanimous decision and oppose this issue. But can we really say with certainty that continuing to choose to protect our classmates is the right thing to do?"

Though Kanzaki continued to speak calmly, he force-fully slammed his hands down on his desk as he stood up.

"I can only assume that every one of you is trapped by normalcy bias if none of you find it unusual that all thirty-nine voted against this issue, without any doubts, without any hesitation at all."

The normalcy bias he referred to was a tendency to not pay attention to unfavorable events, information, and so on and thus not recognizing danger.

"If our class is going to win in the future, we're going to have to make new decisions. We're already on the edge of a cliff here, at a critical juncture. Don't you think that you're all making light of the threat we face and that we're going to fall over that cliff eventually? If we don't chase after Class Points more greedily, then moving up to Class A will simply be a pipe dream."

Kanzaki wanted them to understand those things, but he knew he wasn't very good at making speeches.

The eyes of his classmates were filled with composed indifference as they looked at him.

"What are you talkin' about, Kanzaki?" Shibata turned to him. "Does that mean you're the one who voted in favor of the issue?"

Before, Shibata didn't seem convinced that Kanzaki hadn't simply entered his vote in favor of the issue by mistake. No, it wasn't just Shibata. Hamaguchi, Andou, Kobashi, Amikura, Shiranami too   a lot of people in class were looking at him in the same way.

"That's right," said Kanzaki. "I admit that yes, it is important to protect your classmates. However, our class has been slowly losing points from the time we started here at this school. And if the classes below us prioritize Class Points over their classmates, then this special exam will result in us dropping down to Class D."

The only person who was probably listening to Kanzaki's plea and hanging on his words intently was Hoshinomiya, the instructor in charge of the class. However, being a teacher, she couldn't say anything that would sound sympathetic to his appeal.

"That's true, but... Well, there isn't anyone in class who'd be willing to be expelled," argued Shiranami immediately, signaling to him that there was no room for debate.

"...I understand that. I do," said Kanzaki.

"You say that we're going to fall down to Class D, but I can't imagine expelling somebody for only 100 Class Points," said Shibata. "Well, if we're talkin' 'bout Ryuuen, I'm not so sure. But in this special exam, the condition is we gotta come to a unanimous decision, by way of anonymous vote, with the entire class. I don't think that the rest of the classes would choose to expel someone."

If they anticipated that the other classes would vote unanimously against the issue, then the gap between classes wouldn't widen.

"It's certainly true it wouldn't be easy for any class to make the decision to eliminate one of their fellow classmates. But it's the mechanism here that I'm attaching importance to. Isn't it only natural that, if not half, at least *some* students here would think that they should prioritize their class as a whole over their friends?" asked Kanzaki.

"You mean you wanna argue this issue? Even though it's pretty much a given that we're going to vote unanimously against it?" asked Shibata.

"It's...not a given," Kanzaki said. "There's still room for debate, to settle on a unanimous decision in favor of the issue."

"No, wait, hold up," said Shibata. "That doesn't make any sense. It's *because* we have friends that we want to work hard, to make sure that we don't lose anybody. Right? There's absolutely no reason for us to abandon anybody."

Class Points and classmates. If it were a simple choice between which of those two options was more important, Kanzaki would have no doubts whatsoever. However, the situation had changed dramatically since he first started at this school. He started in Class B, but now, their class and the classes below were all neck and neck in Class Points. In the first semester of their first year, they had a substantial lead over the bottom two classes. If they had only maintained that lead, then he wouldn't be feeling so disgruntled right now as his classmates preached to him about how their friends were so precious.

"Isn't there anyone...anyone at all out there who has an opinion on the issue, past simply voting against it?" asked Kanzaki, looking around at his classmates. He wanted to believe in that possibility, but he was on the verge of giving up.

As it was, not a single student showed any sign that they agreed with him. Supposing even if there were some who agreed with him inwardly, even partly, there wasn't anyone who could put it into words. Everyone believed, no, rather, *expected* that the second round of voting would result in a unanimous decision against the issue.

"I'm sorry, but I... I do not intend to let it come to a unanimous decision of *Against*," muttered Kanzaki. Despite the heavy pressure, he still intended to fight.

Ichinose had been quiet up until that point, but now she spoke up to ask Kanzaki about his true intentions. "Does that mean...you'll be voting in favor in the next round?"

He paused momentarily. "...Yes."

"But Kanzaki-kun, our thinking hasn't changed, you know?" said Ichinose. "Sacrificing our friends to gain Class Points... We would never want our class to turn into something like that."

"Yeah, Kanzaki," Shibata agreed. "No matter how you look at it, this issue is like a challenge from the school. Or like a trap or somethin'. Sacrificing your classmates for Class Points in the short term. If we start thinkin' like that, then we're going to suffer the same kinda pain in the battles to come."

"But if we can gain Class Points, even if it means throwing away our friends, we can get closer to Class A," Kanzaki said. "And if chances like that come again and again, it would be all the better. On the other hand, if we only choose to protect our friends, we will be overtaken by the other classes."

"I don't think it'd be that easy to sacrifice so many people," Shibata argued. "And besides, I don't know how a class like that would even keep winning. Like, seriously? A class where people protect and believe in their friends—*that's* the class that'll win in the end. Don't you think so?"

Almost everyone in class nodded in unison at that.

"Look at the reality we're facing, Shibata," said Kanzaki. "The situation we're in is significantly different from how things were last year. We are in a crisis. We've lost a lot of Private Points because we chose the path of not letting anyone get expelled. On the other hand, the three other classes have all lost classmates and are doing quite well."

"It's not going to last forever," said Shibata.

"What proof do you have, that you can state definitively it won't?"

"Okay, let me turn it around then. What proof do you have that it will?"

"Just look at the current situation. We're in second place now, but we're in danger of falling into fourth," said Kanzaki.

"You're the one who should look at the current situation, Kanzaki. Right now, we're Class B. Whether we've got a lead of one point or a hundred points, the fact remains we're still Class B, right? Besides, even if we do drop a little, we can come back eventually."

In the past, Kanzaki let himself be pushed around by the expectations of those around him. But now, with this issue, he was trying his absolute hardest to stand his ground. He was fighting desperately to make everyone question this line of thinking.

"Kanzaki-kun," said Ichinose. "I understand that you want to have a variety of options to win. However, there are some choices that you should never make. And I feel like this choice, this issue, is one of them. It's not because we'd be getting too few Class Points in exchange for someone's expulsion, either. It's because it's wrong to weigh your friends against Class Points."

Ichinose's statement solidified the resolve of their classmates—or rather, they had already been firm in their determination to prioritize their friends, but now they were even more so. Kanzaki felt deeply disappointed by that. This class had often been the envy of the other classes. They were an ideal group of students: they were kind, cheerful, and fair, and they were well-balanced in both academics and sports. That was an advantage that came from their leader, Ichinose. But on the other hand, it was also a major drawback.

Her presence easily attracted followers and created an environment where people didn't pay attention to messy things. Even if they were told with absolute assurance that if they expelled someone they'd get to Class A, the class would still prioritize friendship. It was an obsession that made them say, "I'd rather be in Class B then abandon my friends."

Once again, Kanzaki was reminded of this fact—of Ichinose's single, but significant, shortcoming.

"Yes... You're probably right. Maybe I am wrong," he said.

In order to bring that shortcoming under control, to surmount it, Kanzaki knew and accepted the risks. He was willing to take drastic measures. Although he knew that he wasn't the one suited for this job, he had no choice but to do it, as no one else was qualified either.

"What if I continue to vote in favor of the issue until the end? One vote has a lot of power in this special exam. I can continue to vote in favor over and over, while ignoring the intentions of the thirty-nine of you."

"Uh, no, you couldn't?" said Shibata. "If you we run outta time and fail, that means we'll get 300 points taken away. And if that happens, then we really won't be able to compete with the other classes, would we?"

There was no way anyone would choose to do something like that, to let time run out. That was common sense.

"It's the same either way," said Kanzaki. "If we don't sacrifice someone here and get those 100 points, I don't think we'll graduate from Class A. So, whether it's 100 or 300 points we're talking about here, it doesn't matter. The number of points lost is a trivial matt—"

"All right, that's time. We'll have to stop discussion there as it's time to begin voting," said Hoshinomiya, interrupting Kanzaki. She then began the sixty-second timer for the voting period.

The display on the students' tablets changed, and now there were buttons labeled *For* and *Against*.

Kanzaki quietly stared at the buttons. The class stopped moving and a hush fell over the room. There was a certain feeling in the air that seemed to tell him that the thirty-nine others in the room finished voting in less than five seconds. In truth, they really had finished voting. Hoshinomiya started moving at the same time that Kanzaki made up his mind and pressed a button.

"All right. Now then, I'll show you the results since everyone finished voting!" said Hoshinomiya.

Round 2 Voting Results: FOR: 1 Vote, AGAINST: 39 Votes

Kanzaki's desperate attempt to persuade his classmates had been in vain. The results were completely unchanged from the first round. Of course, the same was true for the one vote in favor of the issue, which came from Kanzaki.

"You've got to be kidding me..." muttered Shibata.

"Kanzaki-kun, did you really vote in favor?" asked Ichinose.

Kanzaki's classmates, Ichinose included, were more stunned than angry, as evidenced by their responses. However, the carefree vibe in the room was gradually changing bit by bit thanks to Kanzaki's firm will.

"Yes. I voted *For* on purpose, for the second time in a row. I want us to be unanimously in favor of this issue."

Even though the interval period had just started, the class went completely quiet at Kanzaki's response.

"If I keep voting in favor of the issue, after a few hours pass, you'll have no other choice but to unfreeze your stopped thought processes and think. You'll have to debate whether voting against this issue really is the correct thing to do."

He was telling them that he was fully prepared to use the remaining three and half hours they had remaining in this special exam.

"There's only one way for you to break free of this situation, and that's to change your opinion on the matter. You should vote unanimously in favor," declared Kanzaki.

"What are you saying, Kanzaki-kun?" Ichinose said. "That's—"

"'That's not realistic,' right?" he said, interrupting her. "Because, as you have all said, none of you had any intention of sacrificing your classmates from the very beginning. No one did, except for me. Still, that said, I will not budge. I will keep voting in favor." Kanzaki didn't stop his resistance and continued to speak. "In that case, then there's really only one option. You choose to vote in favor of the issue, and then you expel me."

He wanted to change this class, even if it meant sacrificing himself. He expressed his will out loud, for everyone to hear.

"If you don't have the courage to take a step forward in this special exam, then you won't be able to make it to Class A," he went on. "And if that happens, you'll spend the remaining half of your days here at this school in vain, for no reason at all. If that's the case, then I'd rather drop out of school and find another path."

It sounded like a strange plan, but it was also the only way that Kanzaki could actually do anything. There was no way that this class, one that sheltered the weak, could take action that would result in them having to choose someone to expel. That being said, when faced with the serious penalty of expulsion, they wouldn't rely on methods where they'd just leave things to chance.

Kanzaki continued to resist—they repeated the vote three more times, with intervals between them. And then, even after taking the vote five times, the results were still one *For* and thirty-nine *Against*. The same screen showed the same results, over and over again; not a single vote had been swayed.

"All right, we'll have another interval period," announced Hoshinomiya.

Perhaps it was because she was getting fed up with the stalemate, but Hoshinomiya didn't try to hide her annoyance. Even so, the other teacher assigned to monitor the class from the back of the room didn't have any problem with a teacher acting that way. The monitor's assigned role was only to maintain fairness and that was all. It didn't matter if the students were fooling around or if the teacher wasn't motivated—those were all behaviors allowed within the scope of the rules.

More importantly though, another thirty minutes had passed. Meaning, in other words, there had been three further rounds of voting, and the same results came every single time. The unchanging tallies were shown back to the class every time, deadlocked.

"It's already been over an hour, y'know?" said Shibata. "And just for the final issue."

"But there's nothing we can do about it," Ichinose said. "We can only wait until Kanzaki-kun changes his vote."

The thirty-nine who voted *Against* were hoping that Kanzaki would eventually run out of patience and change his vote. At first, the students were accommodating and tried to reason with him in a friendly way. Then, they moved onto admonishing him with a firm tone. They tried so many methods, but Kanzaki simply kept single-mindedly voting the same way over and over without a word.

At last, Hoshinomiya, who had been watching over her class this whole time, opened her mouth to speak.

"Hey, listen, everybody. I'm getting a little bored with this silence, so do you mind if I tell you all a story? Oh, if anyone isn't interested, you can feel free to ignore me, okay?" said Hoshinomiya. "You see, to tell you the truth, I actually went through this same experience when I was a student here too. What do I mean by that, you ask? I mean I *also* took the Unanimous Special Exam. And the issue you're voting on now is the exact same one our class voted on back then."

"It's rather unusual for you to talk about your high school days, Sensei," said Ichinose. "This is the first time you've brought it up with us, isn't it?"

The students in Ichinose's class had a good relationship with Hoshinomiya, and they knew early on that she attended this same school. More than a few students tried asking her about her days as a student after finding that out, but it was safe to say that there hadn't been any opportunities to get into serious conversation about it.

"I remember our class being stuck on this same issue for a long time too, like you are," she said, "although our situation was completely different from yours."

She wore a somewhat pained smile on her face as she recalled those days.

"It was the ultimate decision: would we choose the Class Points, or would we choose our friends? So, we fought, and we fought. Some of the guys in class were even grabbing each other by the collar."

"I-isn't that going a little too far?" said Shiranami, meekly.

The students in this class probably couldn't imagine a situation where they'd be grabbing each other. Shiranami chuckled awkwardly, exchanging looks with the other girls in class.

"Well, we took the exam at a different time in our academic career too," said Hoshinomiya. "In our case, it was the third semester of our third year. At a time like that, you'd go all out for just a single point. Still, if there was talk about a specific person being expelled, even if only a rumor, then their friends would speak up to cover for them as a matter of course. But sometimes...you just have to let go of somebody if you're going to win, right? If you were in a situation where you only needed a hundred more points to get to Class A, would you be as firm in your decision as you are right now?"

Hoshinomiya understood very well what Kanzaki had wanted to ask the class too, and she put it into words, directly.

"We can't expel anyone. We'll just try our hardest to make up for it in the next special exam and—"

"And what if there is no next time? Suppose this special exam is the last one before graduation? Let's say that at that time, you all reached Class A, which you hoped for dearly. But let's also say that the gap between you and Class B is only a few dozen points. If you prioritize protecting your friends in that situation, you'll go back to being Class B. So, what do you do? Of course, the class below you in that situation, the one in B, wouldn't have a next time either, right? They'd take the points, even if they had to get rid of someone."

No matter how many good-natured people were in your class, you would have to give that matter some thought. If you protected your friends in that situation, then falling back down to Class B was almost a complete certainty.

"Would you vote unanimously against the issue, like you are right now?" said Hoshinomiya. "Would you try betting everything on a fairy tale that the class below you in that situation would decide to give up on Class A themselves?"

The students who initially only argued against the idea were now starting to speak less and less.

"I know these are mean-spirited questions," admitted Hoshinomiya. "To tell you the truth, that's not the kind of situation you're in now at all. But still, one thing is for certain—if you want to move up to Class A, a time will come that you'll need to be in favor of an idea like this. Even if it means you have to decide over rock-paper-scissors or some other means. Letting time run out would be absurd."

"Sensei, what... What choice did you make, back then?" asked Shiranami.

"Me? Well... As for me, personally, I choose to abandon unnecessary people. Because in the end, what's important is yourself, even if people are talking about friends or best friends. I'm sure that all of you voting against the issue right now feel similarly, right? Deep down, you're thinking that it'll be fine as long as you yourself are saved."

Everyone was aiming to get to Class A and then graduate. That's what everyone wanted. Still, many people understood, deep down in their heart of hearts, that such thoughts were idealistic. What was more important: friends? Or self-preservation? When the students were asked that, they couldn't find the words to answer.

"We're being closely monitored by the other teacher at the back of the room, so I cannot tell you anything more than that," Hoshinomiya said. "I will respect you all, no matter what option you choose. But you absolutely cannot just make a throwaway, noncommittal decision about this. If you are only friends on the surface, then don't worry about it and prioritize Class Points. You've all known each other for only a little over a year and a half now, you know? They say that the sting of losing friends will heal in time. Think about this: the three other classes have had students get expelled and they've already put it behind them, haven't they? But know that if you can't make it up to Class A in the end, that is going to stick with you for a long, long time. However, if you truly value your friends more than anything else, you must put them first."

Hoshinomiya hadn't advocated for the students to choose either option. She avoided the monitor's glare as she finished saying what she had to say. She merely spoke as a teacher, informing her students that there were advantages and disadvantages to either option.

The next round of voting came just as Hoshinomiya finished her speech.

Everyone started to feel a strange sense of discomfort as they looked at the *For* and *Against* buttons on their tablets. It took some time for the results of the vote to come, but they still showed one in favor and thirty-nine against. Just like every time before it, not a single vote had been swayed. Hoshinomiya in particular wasn't surprised by this. If anything, it was like she had been shown the composition of the class.

"Hey, come on, Kanzaki-kun. Can you just knock it off already?" asked Himeno. She sounded exasperated and spoke up as soon as the voting period ended and the interval period began. "Look, I completely understand what you're trying to say, Kanzaki-kun. And after hearing what Hoshinomiya-sensei had to say too, I understand it even more. But still, it's just, I don't think it's going to end up with everyone else voting in favor of the issue right here and now. That fact's probably not gonna change, even if we run out of time."

The class was going to let time run out if it meant protecting their friends. That was the view that Himeno and most of the other students in class had.

Ichinose then spoke up, sharing her own thoughts on the matter. "I can understand very well what you're saying, Kanzaki-kun, and what Hoshinomiya-sensei told us as well. But still, I'd like to say something about what you were talking about before, when you asked what we'd do if we were put into a situation like that. I understand how everyone's hearts and minds can be swayed, and I don't think that's a bad thing necessarily. But...if I were put in that kind of situation, I wouldn't think there would be any meaning in reaching Class A by expelling my friends. So, what can we do to get to Class A still? I think what will be important then, in order to avoid a situation like that from even happening, would be to get Class A within our grasp while making sure we avoid putting ourselves in a scenario where we have to make such unreasonable choices."

"That's...idealistic," said Kanzaki. "Putting ourselves so far ahead that we'd be an overwhelming Class A with no one being expelled? How many Class Points would we even need to collect to make something like that a reality...?"

"We may not be good enough to pull it off right now," Ichinose replied. "But that's the kind of class I'd like for us to be."

Their classmates listened intently to Ichinose. It was a story that could have only been interpreted as a fairy tale, but they nodded repeatedly after hearing it. Kanzaki's resistance wouldn't have any meaning anymore. As Himeno had said, even if he continued to vote in favor of the issue, they would simply let time run out.

"Let's do our best together, Kanzaki-kun," said Ichinose.

"...I understand," he replied.

The one person standing alone against the rest had been preyed upon and devoured by those who didn't know fear.

"I wanted to change the class, in my own way, even if I had to force it somehow," he said. "But it would seem that

I'm not qualified to do that... No, it seems like I even lack the ability to do it."

Enough time had passed to convince Kanzaki that this class was not going to change. He didn't know if they would be Class B or even Class D in the end, but he knew they'd never reach Class A. There was absolutely no vitality in Kanzaki's facial expression as he decided to change his vote, though it was unlikely anyone would notice. The time for voting came again, as though there had been no disputes or anything since the beginning. And the answer that the forty students had come to was...

Round 10 Voting Results: FOR: 0 Votes, AGAINST: 40 Votes

The class had chosen to throw away the Class Points and protect their classmates instead.

"Well then, now that you've come to a unanimous decision on the final issue, that means that this special exam is now over," announced Hoshinomiya.

"Hey, it's all right, Kanzaki," said Shibata. "We're gonna get fifty points as a reward."

It had taken them roughly three hours to finish. They had to leave the school building and would now have free time.

"By the way, it sounds like Class A already completed their special exam as well," said Hoshinomiya.

"Whoa, for real? Guess that makes sense, being Sakayanagi's class and all," said Shibata.

"I guess that means Ryuuen-kun and Horikita-san's classes are still taking the exam," noted Shiranami.

"All right, everyone. If you're going to chitchat, you'll have to leave the building," said Hoshinomiya. "The other classes are still in the middle of the exam, so please don't disturb them. We'll lead you out now, so please get up from your seats quietly."

While the rest of the class expressed their joy after finishing the special exam, Kanzaki emotionlessly got up from his seat.

CLASSROOM OF
THE ELITE

6

RYUUEN KAKERU'S CHOICE

T HE UNANIMOUS SPECIAL EXAM began at one
o'clock in the afternoon.

Class D was another class of forty students. The classroom was becoming enveloped by a thick, heavy atmosphere, and this was, of course, due to the intense nature
of the final issue they had finally arrived at.

ISSUE #5: In exchange for expelling one of your classmates, gain
100 Class Points.

(In the event the class is unanimously in favor, a vote will be
held to choose the student to be expelled.)

Round 1 Voting Results: FOR: 14 Votes, AGAINST: 26 Votes

This was the moment when their voting results were
revealed. Like in Horikita's and Ichinose's classes, the

majority of voters were opposed to the issue. However, in contrast to those two, there were more than a few students in favor of expelling someone. In other words, it meant that one in every three students felt, at least at first, that they ought to prioritize Class Points, even if they had to expel someone.

"Wh-what do we do, Ryuuen-san?" grumbled Ishizaki.

After seeing the results, the very first person that Ishizaki turned to for guidance was Ryuuen Kakeru, the leader of the class. Ishizaki had done the very same thing after every other issue. Since the probability of coming to a unanimous decision in the first round of voting was low, the class used the first interval period to hear the leader's policy on it, and they aimed for unanimity in the second round of voting and beyond. The sequence of events in this class was similar to that of other classes, but the degree of precision in this class was extremely high.

In the first issue of selecting another class to face off against, the third issue where they voted on the matter of Protect Points, and in the fourth issue where they voted on test conditions, they had come to a unanimous decision on the matter after only one interval period. In those cases, they chose the answer that Ryuuen ordered them to. The only issue where Ryuuen let his classmates vote as they pleased was the second one, regarding where they wanted to go for the school trip.

Ryuuen let his classmates debate for roughly thirty minutes about where they wanted to go, and in the end, they voted unanimously in favor of the destination that had the highest number of votes by that time. It was obvious now to everyone that while the content of the fifth issue was different from that one in essence, it would still work the same way. Every issue that seemed to need direction was settled by just a few words from Ryuuen.

The students were only deeply conscious of how Ryuuen voted on issues. If Ryuuen was in favor, that meant it was an absolute certainty that someone was going to be expelled. His decisions were absolute. That was the peculiarity of this class—students here were held together by a dictatorship.

Ryuuen stood up from his chair and stared at the results with a smile on his face. "Well, it's been boring as hell so far, but guess the school wasn't gonna just let things end on an easy note after all. If they did, things wouldn't be so interesting now, would they?"

Though he muttered those words to himself, he said it loud enough for all of his classmates to hear. He then proceeded to the podium. Sakagami, the teacher in charge of watching over the class, sensed Ryuuen approaching and moved away. He was well aware of the fact that this was where Ryuuen's showboating act was set to begin.

Ryuuen sat atop the podium as if it were a seat specially reserved for him. He leaned forward so that he could look out over all of his classmates. "Raise your hand if you voted in favor."

His order didn't show a hint of consideration for anyone. There was incredible tension in the air for everyone, regardless of how they voted. Ryuuen hadn't directly asked everyone what they voted for in any of the previous issues. After a few seconds of hesitation, scattered hands began to rise. Among them were Nishino and Kaneda, who raised their hands while staring out the window, as if they were somewhat unwilling.

"...Five of you, huh," said Ryuuen. "Well, that ain't bad for the first time."

The truth was that there were nine other students who had voted in favor of the issue who didn't obey Ryuuen's order and weren't coming forward.

Students like Ishizaki and Komiya were surprised to see this.

"Hey, come on now. You know no good's gonna come from tryin' to hide it?" Komiya appealed to his silent classmates. "It's not like people are gonna be mad at you for voting in favor for this one time or anything."

After all, if they spoke up now, there wouldn't be any trouble.

"Besides, it's not like we were ordered to vote one way or another," he added. "We're each free to vote either *For* or *Against*, right?"

This was also Komiya's way of checking with Ryuuen that he had his facts correct though, just in case.

When Ryuuen didn't answer right away, Komiya immediately started feeling nervous. If there was a difference in their interpretation of the situation, it was possible it could lead to a reprimand.

Ishizaki, not liking this change in the air in the classroom, immediately panicked and followed up on what Komiya said. "Come on!" he said, flustered. "Get your hands up in the air before you get us in trouble!"

One more student raised their hand, fearfully and apologetically, bringing the total to six. That meant that the remaining eight students hadn't budged and left their hands down.

"It's all right, Ishizaki," said Ryuuen. "If they don't wanna raise their hands, they don't gotta. For now, at least."

"Huh? R-really?" asked Ishizaki.

"Komiya said it himself. Everyone's free to vote *For* or *Against*. So, first of all, each one of you should think about what you yourself are gonna do. We got a little over eight minutes left. That's plenty of time."

Ryuuen checked the clock leisurely. He didn't relax his posture, and the smile never once left his face. He had only vaguely told the other students to think about it, that was it. He remained completely silent for more than two minutes, not doing anything in that time.

"Listen up now," he said at last. "Don't waste this time. Think about what choice is the right one."

There was another period of silence. Ten seconds. Thirty seconds. Even after another minute passed, he didn't say another word. In all of the issues so far, Ryuuen had forced them to come to a decision after the first interval period. Because of that, the only thought going through the students' minds right now was, "*Why isn't Ryuuen giving us instructions?*"

However, there weren't many students who could just speak up and voice their opinions like that, and the more time that passed, the more their mouths felt like they were sealed. Ishizaki and others like him were among the first you'd expect to say something like, "*Please give us an order!*" However, even they kept their heads down. Their lips were pressed together as if they had been fixed in place with glue.

The seconds ticked by and the more they felt like they were almost losing the desire to speak at all anymore.

Eventually, those who wished to say something would stop speaking up, shifting instead to hoping that someone else would say something on their behalf. And when even more time passed, students began hoping that it would be time to vote again soon, even though they had a lot of time remaining. The first interval felt incredibly long and drawn out, and it ended with the majority of time spent in total silence. Even Sakagami hadn't expected that, and he ended up forgetting to transition to the next round, when they were a few seconds over the scheduled interval time.

"Sakagami," Ryuuen said suddenly as he hopped off the podium and headed back to his seat. "It's time, ain't it?"

"...Yes, you're right," said Sakagami. "We'll now begin the second round of voting. You'll have sixty seconds."

As soon as everyone finished putting in their votes for the second round, the results were displayed up on the monitor.

Round 2 Voting Results: FOR: 10 Votes, AGAINST: 30 Votes

Four of the fourteen votes in favor of the issue in the first round had been swayed to the other side. For the majority of students in the class who didn't want anyone to be expelled, this result was, generally speaking, not a bad one. One or two more sternly worded warnings from

Ryuuen would reduce the number of votes in favor. And, in the not-too-distant future, they would see the class vote unanimously against the issue.

The results of the second round indicated that to those students, but at the same time, Ryuuen didn't seem satisfied.

"Is this the answer you came up with?" he said. "I don't believe it."

"Because of the small reduction in votes *For*, you mean?" asked Kaneda, adjusting the position of his glasses.

Ryuuen immediately denied that supposition.

"So, does that mean...that you're voting in favor of the issue, Ryuuen-kun?" asked Kaneda.

Ryuuen denied that as well, letting out an exasperated but amused snort.

"Wh-what in the heck is up with you Ryuuen-san?" Ishizaki wailed. "I just don't get it!"

"Did the votes in the first and second round really reflect what you truly think?" said Ryuuen. "Your will? This last issue is obviously unique, it's the only one like this. And that's exactly why I wanna know your true *intentions* here. Don't worry about what I voted for. Vote how you honestly feel."

After saying that, Ryuuen got up from his seat once again and slowly walked around the classroom.

"For these next ten minutes, talk about it," he ordered. "Intensely. Whether you want to vote in favor of it or vote against it."

With those instructions, the class was unavoidably forced to debate the issue. The students began talking as much as they pleased, and the classroom was filled with a hurried, panicked commotion. As Ryuuen listened in on what the others had to say, he would occasionally lean in close to a student and whisper something in a quiet voice. He said something to Nishino and Shiina, then Yoshimoto and Nomura—he didn't seem to be especially choosy about which students he talked to. Then, he approached Suzuki, and whispered in a similar manner as he had before.

"You're free to vote for or against. Vote according to whatever you think."

When Ryuuen said those words to Suzuki, however, Tokitou overheard him from two seats away. Although some students wondered why Ryuuen deliberately went out of his way to say things to some students, the discussion continued for as long as time allowed.

Then, it came to be time for the third round of voting.

Round 3 Voting Results: FOR: 9 Votes, AGAINST: 31 Votes

The results on the monitor were hardly any different from those of the second round.

Ryuuen took a seat upon the podium desk again and decided to offer his thoughts during the third interval period.

"Raise your hands if you voted in favor," he ordered.

Once more, after seeing the results, Ryuuen ordered everyone to raise their hands. Only two people raised their hands this time: Nishino and Kaneda. The remaining seven refused to step forward, keeping their presence hidden. Ishizaki was visibly annoyed by these unseen supporters of the issue, but Ryuuen didn't pay them any mind. Instead, he turned his attention to Nishino and Kaneda.

"You two voted in favor three times now," he said. "What's the reason, Kaneda?"

"To win," Kaneda replied. "While it's not good by any means to have students be expelled, I think it's important to get those 100 Class Points."

"Didn't you think that if you raise your hand, you'd be a candidate for expulsion?" asked Ryuuen.

"That's a stupid question, Ryuuen-kun. You would dispose of people you can't use—people who are unnecessary. But you wouldn't dispose of someone you need. At the very least, in this class, 100 points doesn't match my worth." Kaneda had measured his own value and confidently determined that he was in no danger of being thrown aside.

"Well, looks aside, you're a lot of use to me," replied Ryuuen.

"Thank you very much." Kaneda nodded in satisfaction, conveniently paying no attention to the remark about his physical appearance.

"Nishino, you the same as Kaneda?" Ryuuen asked.

"Huh? No way. I'm just voting yes because it's a quick way to get more Class Points, that's all. I raised my hand because I don't like being all sneaky. There's nothing wrong with voting in favor."

Ishizaki was even more nervous than Nishino herself because he knew that Ryuuen was likely to glower at anyone who talked to him like that if they weren't careful.

"All right, I figure it's about time I tell you all what you've been wonderin' about. What *I* voted for," said Ryuuen.

"P-please tell us!" Ishizaki loudly voiced his wishes and pitched forward as he spoke.

Things couldn't officially start until the class heard what Ryuuen's vote was. Or, in other words, what the class's policy would be.

"All right. For this issue...I voted in favor of it. All three times."

As the results currently stood, that meant that three of the nine votes in favor had come from Ryuuen, Nishino, and Kaneda.

"S-so, basically, this means...someone's gonna get expelled from class, right?" Ishizaki asked meekly.

Ryuuen smiled ominously. "Don't jump to conclusions," he said. "I'm just tellin' ya how I voted, that's all. I already decided that in this issue, you all gotta figure out what you want to do yourselves."

"U-us...you mean?" Ishizaki stammered.

"That's right. I voted in favor three times now without hesitation."

If Ryuuen had voted in favor three times, then it was safe to assume that his plan was for one of their classmates to be expelled. However, since Ishizaki didn't approve of this plan of action, he didn't understand what this all meant. He was at a loss for words.

"The reason for voting in favor is simple," Ryuuen told the class. "If we get rid of one person, we get a hundred points. Or, putting it another way, this is a golden opportunity to take out the trash and get Class Points for it. It's the best possible choice. It's one that's gonna help us and not hold us back. But, even after votin' three times now, there're still more votes *Against* than *For*. Meanin' that over half of the class voted against the issue, basically. If that's the case, then I'm gonna respect their wishes, and change my vote to *Against*."

Ryuuen was giving up on the Class Points and setting a plan of action where they'd hold onto their classmates.

Ishizaki looked relieved after hearing this easy-to-understand plan. He appealed to his classmates to follow along. "I-it's settled! Everybody, don't vote in favor! Vote *Against*! Those're Ryuuen-san's orders!"

"Hold on a minute," said Ibuki, sounding dissatisfied. She had looked bored through this entire special exam so far. "This isn't like you."

"What do you mean?" asked Ryuuen.

"You're in favor of the idea, aren't you? In that case, you could just force things ahead and make everybody vote *For* like how you always do. But *now* you're trying to act like the good guy and say something like how you're gonna protect your friends?" Ibuki was implying that Ryuuen would always go for the Class Points in front of him.

"What, so you voted in favor too?" asked Ryuuen.

"I voted *Against*," Ibuki replied. "But my intentions are none of your business."

"If this thing weren't anonymous, then yeah, I might've let it come to a unanimous decision in favor, without a second thought," Ryuuen said. "It would've been quicker if I just drove one of the people who defied my opinions toward expulsion. But unfortunately, this time they're doin' this exam by way of an anonymous vote. As long as I can't be sure who voted for what exactly, it'd just be faster to get everyone to vote *Against* since that's already got over half the votes."

"So, you're saying that you're not confident that you could get a unanimous decision in favor?" asked Ibuki.

"*Ku ku*, you can think whatever you want," said Ryuuen.

"Y-you shouldn't go overboard with what you say, Ibuki," Ishizaki cut in. "Ryuuen-san said to vote *Against*, so isn't that good enough? If we'd be losin' Class Points, that'd be one thing, but we're not. We're just gonna finish the exam."

"Whatever," huffed Ibuki. "It's just that this is all a little out of character for him. I was curious, that's all. Do whatever you want."

Now that a plan had been set in place, a great deal of the interval period was spent in silence. And when the fourth round came, the results were...

Round 4 Voting Results: FOR: 7 Votes, AGAINST: 33 Votes

The students had expected that, if it wasn't a unanimous decision, then almost all the votes would be against the issue. However, there were a surprising number of votes in favor. In fact, there were only two fewer votes than last time.

"Kaneda, Nishino, what did you two vote for?" asked Ryuuen.

"I voted *Against*, as you had instructed, of course, Ryuuen-kun," said Kaneda.

"Well personally, I'm still for the idea, but I voted *Against* because I felt like that would've messed up the harmony we were going for, y'know?" Nishino said.

The two people who had raised their hands before and indicated they were in favor had changed their votes. And considering the fact that Ryuuen had changed his vote as well, there was no way he'd accept these results unless he saw that the number of votes in favor had gone down by at least three. On top of that, he had given the other students an order and told them they weren't free to vote how they wanted. They were now being coerced into voting *Against*. Despite that, though, there were still seven votes in favor. Ryuuen couldn't rule out the possibility that either one person switched their vote to be in favor, or that Kaneda or Nishino was lying to him.

Ryuuen himself had voted 100 percent against the issue, but there was no way for the others around him to confirm that was true either. And so, a new sense of unease gradually began to spread across the room. Ryuuen calmly thought about the results. Instead of simply looking at the number of votes, he decided to try detecting the flow of votes to see through the anonymity.

"Who's still voting in favor?!" screamed Ishizaki.

Ryuuen's orders were to vote against the issue. Ishizaki couldn't calm himself down when he saw that seven students didn't do as they were told, even though they were given clear orders. If Ryuuen changed his mind and voted in favor of the issue, then that meant someone would be expelled.

"*Ku ku*, all right, don't scream your head off, Ishizaki," Ryuuen said. "Actually, things are gettin' more interestin', I'd say. This exam is completely anonymous; there's no way that anyone can find out exactly who voted for what. That means there's more than a few people out there really in favor of the idea and are votin' for it."

"B-but people not followin' your orders is a big problem, Ryuuen-san!" complained Ishizaki.

"Nah, not really. Nothin' wrong with tryin' to get Class Points at the cost of our classmates. Actually, if anythin', this means that there are seven students here greedy enough to shoot for Class A. That right?"

Ryuuen clapped his hands with delight, as though he welcomed this development with open arms.

"But if we're gonna say it's okay for somebody to get expelled, then there's the question of *who*," he added.

"I bet the seven people who voted in favor have a clear idea of who it should be."

"W-wait... You don't mean, like, me, do ya?!" Ishizaki started to panic, wondering if he was going to be a target.

"Well, can't rule out the chance that there're people who think no one needs you," Ryuuen replied. "But is there anybody who has got the guts to come forward and say it? The kind of person who wants *me* of all people expelled, not anybody else?"

Ryuuen issued a challenge to those students, like he was ordering them to come forward. However, the classroom once again was enveloped in a still silence, and, of course, that meant there wasn't anyone ready to speak up.

He sighed. "Well, guess you aren't gonna spill your guts that easy after all, huh. *Ku ku*, then I guess we'll do this nice and slow."

With that, the fourth interval period had come to an end, and it was time for the fifth round of voting. The class had already spent about forty minutes on this issue.

For this round, the results showed...

Round 5 Voting Results: FOR: 8 Votes, AGAINST: 32 Votes

There was now one additional vote in favor of the issue, contrary to Ryuuen's goal of decreasing those votes.

"What are you gonna do, Ryuuen?" said Nishino, sounding depressed. "It's already been almost an hour now, you know?"

"Don't be in such a rush," Ryuuen told her. "We've still got lotsa time, right?"

"But there's still a lot of people going against your wishes and voting for this thing. Isn't that, like, bad?"

The number of votes in favor clearly showed that Ryuuen's dominance wasn't complete. He wasn't able to control everyone.

"Yeah," he said. "And I can't rule out the possibility that you're still voting in favor either."

Nishino was somewhat surprised by Ryuuen's comeback, but she met his gaze and responded with firm intensity.

"...Maybe," she shot back.

"Even if I hound people about it, it's not like I'd get any proof unless the person in question admitted it themselves."

This was an exam where it was difficult to punish those under suspicion.

Having watched the situation unfold up until this point, Yabu Nanami spoke up. "Can I make a suggestion?"

"Speak," replied Ryuuen.

"What if we just vote unanimously in favor of the

idea and then find someone who'd be fine with getting expelled?" said Yabu.

"I take it that means you voted *For*?" asked Ryuuen.

"No. I voted *Against* every time. But I'm starting to think that if the people in favor aren't budging, then maybe it'd be a good idea to just change our plan of action instead. For example...what if we expelled Ibuki-san?" She shot Ibuki an icy glare.

Following Yabu's lead, Morofuji Rika spoke up in agreement. "If Ibuki-san's who we're choosing, then I think I could agree to it too... Oh, but just to be clear, I've been voting *Against* this whole time, okay?"

"Hey, come on you guys," said Ishizaki. "Ryuuen-san said that we're voting *Against*, so that's what we're doing."

"Hold on," Ryuuen said. "I welcome their opinions."

Ishizaki blinked in surprise. "H-huh? Really?"

"From the looks of it, I'd say it's probably true they've been voting *Against* this whole time. If there aren't at least two votes added to the side in favor, then that means there's a contradiction. You two wouldn't slip up like that, would you?"

Both Yabu and Morofuji responded to Ryuuen's question with a resolute nod. Of course, the possibly couldn't be discounted that one of the eight anonymous voters who voted in favor might change their vote in the next round couldn't be discounted, but Ryuuen was well aware that was a separate issue.

"Besides, these two were so prepared to vote in favor that they even offered a name," Ryuuen went on. "Unlike those eight anonymous people. Judging by the looks on their faces, there are probably more people out there aside from Yabu and Morofuji who are on board with this idea."

The group of girls made up of Yabu and her close friends occupied the highest rung of the social ladder in the class. Although Yabu's and Morofuji's opinions were ostensibly their own, what they said could be taken as a sentiment shared by the group as a whole.

"We'd like to know what you think about our suggestion, Ryuuen-kun," Yabu said. "Could you tell us your thoughts?"

"The biggest prerequisite for gettin' a particular person expelled is making sure there wouldn't be any votes in support of that person," said Ryuuen. He addressed the class as a whole. "Who in this class wants to protect Ibuki? Who'd be willing to risk their own expulsion over it?"

No hands were in the air after he asked that question.

"Well, there you have it then, Ibuki. Would you accept being expelled from school?"

Everyone was sure that if Ibuki answered that she accepted it, or if she told Ryuuen to just do whatever he wanted, then Ryuuen would set Ibuki's expulsion in motion without hesitation.

"Sorry, but I don't have any intention of letting myself get expelled," Ibuki responded. She didn't so much as glance at either Yabu or Morofuji, the people who nominated her.

"Oh?" said Yabu. "I thought your stance was that you didn't particularly care if you got expelled, Ibuki-san. Wasn't that right?"

"I don't really care about this school or whatever," she replied. "But there is someone here who I want to get my revenge on in my own way. And besides, do you honestly think I'd accept getting expelled like this? I'm not gonna conveniently let myself be taken advantage of by people I hate."

"You just don't want to be expelled, no matter what the reason is," said Yabu. She smiled, trying to provoke Ibuki further. "You're trying to act tough like it doesn't bother you, but I bet you're scared, aren't you?"

"Hah," Ibuki scoffed. "You've become quite the big shot, huh? Even though you used to be Manabe's flunky, hanging all around her. Does it make you *that* happy to have become the leader of the girls the second that she was gone?"

Hearing Ibuki's comeback, Ryuuen's smile faded, and he glowered at her with intimidating eyes.

"Hey, Ibuki," he warned. "Be aware of your position right now. Yabu has friends who'd be against her getting expelled, but you don't have a single person to cover you. Besides, you never really had any kind of attachment to this school anyway, did you?"

"...So what?" snapped Ibuki.

"I don't hate you, but if this means we can get you to contribute to the class by bowing out gracefully, then I'm afraid that's a different story. It doesn't matter to me what your intentions are, 'cause we're the ones who're gonna feast on your flesh and blood."

"Serves you right, Ibuki-san," sneered Yabu. "You thought you were Ryuuen-kun's one and only favorite, huh?"

"So, do you resent me, Ibuki?" asked Ryuuen.

"Not really. But I never cared one bit about trying to be friends with you in the first place. I know you'd do anything to win, so I'm not surprised. But like I said, I have no intention of getting expelled."

Ibuki repeatedly indicated that she refused to accept the situation.

Ryuuen's tone was growing somewhat scathing in return. "It doesn't matter whether you've got any *intention* or not," he said. "I'm gonna ask you one more time. The stakes here are that we're gonna see what happens if there's a unanimous decision in favor of it. Raise your hand if you're willin' to put yourself on the line for Ibuki. But you gotta decide within one minute."

Ishizaki started trembling slightly in the midst of the tense, stinging atmosphere. It wasn't out of fear of Ryuuen, but it was because the time had come for him to choose, to make a decision.

"Don't do it, Ishizaki."

The person who stopped him was Nishino. She had come up next to Ishizaki and stood beside him without him even noticing she was there.

"Wh-what, Nishino...?" he sputtered.

"We're fighting to win," she said. "Your half-assed idea of friendship is only gonna cause confusion."

"B-but, I mean, Ibuki's, I mean, she's our—"

"...Time's up," said Ryuuen.

A minute had passed, and in the end, not a single student had come forward to say they would protect Ibuki. All sorts of thoughts and feelings ran through the students' minds in that still silence. There were scornful stares of Yabu and her friends, pitying looks from other students, and feelings of relief yet other students had over not being targeted themselves.

"Oh. I see. In that case..."

Half in desperation, Ibuki was about to give her answer. But then, she suddenly stopped, her words sticking in her throat. She understood that she was at a disadvantage in this issue because she didn't have a single true friend. That was exactly why she announced early on that she had voted *Against*. However, now that things had come to this, she had no choice but to try and protect herself.

"In that case, what?" asked Ryuuen.

Ryuuen maintained total silence in the room after asking that, as if he were waiting for what Ibuki was going to say.

"I still have unfinished business at this school," said Ibuki, after a pause.

"Oh?"

"Sorry, but I don't intend to go along with whatever you're hoping to do. Even if the rest of the class votes in favor, I'll vote against it. If we don't come to a unanimous decision, then that means we're gonna fail this special exam."

"H-huh?" said Yabu. "Are you planning on forcing the class's hand for your own sake?"

"That's exactly it." Ibuki had made up her mind, declared her intention to vote against the issue, and was standing her ground.

"Well, it's obvious you would do that," said Ryuuen. "Yabu, your idea of changing to vote in favor wasn't bad, but it was way too early for you to name names. If you really wanted Ibuki gone, you should've waited until after we got a unanimous decision on the issue and *then* brought it up."

"Gr...!"

If someone knew that they were going to be expelled, they would never vote in favor.

"Just settle down and vote *Against*."

Nishino felt like there was something strangely off when Ryuuen gave them those instructions.

"Wait, why did we even have everyone go through that whole charade just now?" she asked. "Wasn't it just a complete waste of time?"

There was no need for Ryuuen to ask for a pointless show of hands. Yabu and Ibuki's arguing could've been stopped much earlier—it was obvious it would've been really difficult to come to a unanimous decision once someone was nominated out loud.

"I was just killin' time," Ryuuen answered. "We got way more time on our hands than we know what to do with anyway."

Despite his claim there was no deeper meaning, there were some students in class who realized Ryuuen had another purpose in doing all of that. They realized that the reason why Ryuuen went along with Yabu's proposal, even though it was never going to pass, was so he could get Ibuki to say that she'd never vote in favor of the issue. By doing this, he was indirectly showing everyone the fact that a unanimous decision in favor would be difficult to obtain. To those students, this seemed like a skillful and composed move on Ryuuen's part...but at the same time, it may have been a desperate measure born out of impatience and not having been able to do anything else in this situation.

In the sixth round of voting, the results showed seven votes *For* and thirty-three *Against*. The seventh round showed six votes *For* and thirty-four *Against*. Little by little, the number of votes in favor was decreasing, but in the eighth round, there were seven votes *For* and thirty-three votes *Against* again. The results had gone back to how they were before.

Eventually, the time came for the ninth round of voting.

Round 9 Voting Results: FOR: 7 Votes, AGAINST: 33 Votes

The votes in favor of the issue remained steady. This figure also seemed to represent Ryuuen's leadership at this current point in time. From the sixth round through the ninth rounds, he simply sat at the podium for ten minutes during each discussion period, not uttering a single word. He just watched everyone before him with an unsettling grin on his face. The situation only changed during the interval before the tenth round of voting began.

Ryuuen had been smiling up until that point, but now, he suddenly called his class out with one short word.

"Hey."

The students who had been engaged more in simple conversation rather than actual discussion on the issue came to attention in a panic.

"You people can't even vote against this thing yourselves without me givin' you an order?" asked Ryuuen.

Every student immediately shut their mouth in response to the clear change in the classroom's atmosphere.

"I'm sure you ain't afraid of how things are gonna go down if everyone votes in favor. But if you think that I'm just watchin' you all vote for no reason at all...you're makin' a big mistake."

SMACK! Ryuuen kicked the podium hard with his heel.

"It might feel like you're just sittin' back, hiding in anonymity, but I can see it from the looks on your faces, y'know," he said. "I've got a rough idea of what's goin' on here. And if you keep screwing around... You *know* what's gonna happen, right?"

Round 10 Voting Results: FOR: 6 Votes, AGAINST: 34 Votes

After Ryuuen's intense statement, one of the votes in favor had changed. However, in truth, Ryuuen's threats hadn't been all that effective, considering that the votes in favor had already once fallen to six before in the seventh round. They thought they had ample time, but now they were using what time they had left like it was going out of style.

"............"

The students noticed that Ryuuen's smile had faded quite some time ago, to be replaced by a stern look.

"Whoever you people are, you're stubborn," he said. "I'm gettin' sick and tired of dealin' with you."

There were about three and a half hours left before the exam's time limit ran out, but they had already been voting on this final issue for an hour and a half.

Round 11 Voting Results: FOR: 7 Votes, AGAINST: 33 Votes

"Seriously, with the way things are going right now, how can we keep on waiting for things to change?" Nishino made no attempt at hiding her annoyance. She asked Ryuuen what his plans were.

"Yeah. Guess it's probably about time to end this, huh," he replied.

"You can do that?" asked Nishino.

"Do you people really think I've been watchin' you all this time for nothin'? You realize that there's been an odd one out, one weird voter that showed up in rounds six to ten, right? I'm talkin' about the colossal dumbass who keeps flip-floppin' between *For* and *Against*. And now I'm gonna tell you exactly who that is."

Tensions were running high. Under normal circumstances, it wouldn't be possible to see through perfect and total anonymity. However...

"It's you, ain't it? Yajima."

The person Ryuuen called out was Yajima Mariko.

"H-huh...?! N-no!" she sputtered. She then shot upright, attempting to deny it, but she was clearly flustered and unable to calm herself down.

"Don't think I'm gonna believe you if you deny it, just because this thing's anonymous," he said. "If I think you're the one who did it, then you're *definitely* the one. You understand what I'm getting at, right?"

"N-no, that's not... I...!" she protested.

"If I say you're the one that did it, then you're the one. And if I say you're not the one, then you're not. Since you're the first person I called out, I'm gonna give you

CLASSROOM OF THE ELITE

one chance. From here out, you ain't got the right to vote in favor of this issue without my permission, got it? If *I* decide you ain't following my rules, you're getting expelled, and that's that."

It was a high-handed threat. Even if whoever it was continued to oppose the class on this issue and waited things out, even until the class failed the exam in the end, Ryuuen was suggesting that they'd eventually be expelled via some brutal, fiendish means in the not-too-distant future.

Yajima didn't need very long to imagine that was what Ryuuen was suggesting at all.

"I've figured out who's votin' in favor of this issue, though not all of 'em yet," he continued. "So, question is, are they so stupid that they can't understand unless they're told directly, like Yajima? We're gonna let the next vote decide."

And so, the twelfth round of voting had come.

Round 12 Voting Results: FOR – 5 VOTES, AGAINST – 35 VOTES

As Yajima was now completely committed to voting *Against*, the votes in favor hadn't increased. But even after the situation had come to this and with Ryuuen having issued his final warning, the votes in favor had still only gone down by two. That left a total of five in favor.

The class was beginning to realize that things like threats were no longer going to work against them.

"Five people, huh..."

After muttering those words, Ryuuen checked the time and got back on his feet.

"Guess I gotta admit it: these people have backbone," he said. "But still, I ain't so happy about this. Look, if you ain't gonna back down here, no matter the cost, then just cut the crap already and come forward. These five anonymous people want me expelled. In that case, we just gotta wait until we reach a unanimous vote *For*. I mean, it'd be boring as hell to just let things end by running out of time, wouldn't it? So, make your move. That way, we can fight on equal terms."

The class wouldn't pass this special exam unless they came to a unanimous decision one way or the other. And until they identified the students who hoped that they'd settle on being in favor, they would just repeat this same process over and over, endlessly.

It seemed like none of those students in favor would show themselves at this point in the situation, but then...

"Okay. Fine, Ryuuen. In that case, I'll come forward... I'm voting in favor."

At long last, one of the anonymous supporters of the issue made up his mind and stood up.

"Tokitou, you ass!" yelled Ishizaki. "Do you know what the hell you're sayin'?!" Ishizaki charged forward, like he was intending to pounce.

Katsuragi grabbed him by the arm and stopped him in his tracks. "Stop, Ishizaki. We're in the middle of a special exam. Do you honestly intend to resort to violence right now? Make one bad move and Sakagami-sensei won't hesitate to call this exam off. Isn't that right, Sensei?"

"Of course," Sakagami replied. "If that were to happen, this exam would end with your disqualification."

"Grr...!"

"Besides," added Katsuragi, "although Tokitou's come forward and announced that he voted in favor, there is no guarantee that it's the truth."

Even if they were 99 percent certain, there was no way they could be 100 percent sure since it was anonymous. They couldn't ignore the possibility that he was pretending to be in favor while actually voting *Against*.

"It's the truth, though," said Tokitou. "Y'know, I always wondered if a special exam like this would ever come up. There's nothin' I could do in a regular special exam, but the instant this issue came up? It was like I got hit by lightning... I knew this was it. This was the only time I could get rid of Ryuuen."

"Why are you coming forward now though, Tokitou...?" asked Katsuragi.

"Because I've locked eyes with Ryuuen a few times now. He probably guessed that I've been voting in favor. I could have come forward earlier, that would've been fine. But the number of votes in favor weren't goin' down, and seein' him get all confused was exciting."

"All right, Tokitou," said Ryuuen. "Your rebellious attitude ain't nothin' new. In fact, I'm honestly glad that you're on the side of those in favor."

"How long can you keep up bein' so full of yourself?" Tokitou said. "You can't afford to."

"I know," Ryuuen agreed. "No matter how many times we do this vote, we're never gonna get the votes in favor to go away. And if we run outta time, our class loses 300 points. We'd seriously be out of the running for Class A."

"Exactly," said Tokitou. "You're the leader of this class. Which means if we fail this special exam, the blame isn't gonna be on me, it'll be on you. Besides, you've been selfish and controllin' all the choices in this special exam from the get-go. You *forced* us to pick Sakayanagi's class to be our opponent without even tryin' to listen to the people who said we should fight Ichinose's class. So, you can take responsibility when we lose, can't you?"

"I get it now," said Ryuuen. "So that's why a rebel like you's been so obedient in all the other issues so far."

"I'm doin' this to teach everybody in class that this is a mistake. I don't wanna make trouble for the class. I just don't want you bein' the leader."

"But along came the opportunity for us to get one person in particular expelled. And you decided to take a chance on it. And?" Ryuuen taunted him. "Come on, show me some real defiance here. What do you want most?"

"If you want me—no, I mean, if you want *us* to vote against the issue, then step down as class leader, right here, right now. If you swear to that right in front of us all, you'll get more votes opposing the issue for sure."

No matter how much Tokitou hated Ryuuen, he also knew how difficult it would be to get a unanimous decision in favor of the issue. That was exactly why he was proposing this compromise.

"Come on, don't be so boring," said Ryuuen. "You aren't confident you can get me expelled?"

"Don't make me laugh. If the decision is unanimously in favor, you'll be the one who gets expelled, Ryuuen."

"May I ask you one question, Tokitou-kun?" Kaneda raised his hand, adjusting his glasses. "It's certainly true that, should we fail the special exam, it's logical that part

of the blame would fall upon the leader. However, if we were to come to a unanimous decision in favor of the issue and initiate the process of selecting who to expel, you would most definitely be the one to be expelled, no? Because in truth, many students have continued to vote against the issue as instructed."

Tokitou wasn't shaken in the slightest in the face of Kaneda's calm and collected explanation of the events that he saw laid out ahead.

"The votes against the issue right now mean nothin'," Tokitou replied. "Don't tell me you actually think all of those votes are people who submit to Ryuuen. Do you? Yeah, there's only a few people who can openly rebel against him, but still. Right now, there are four other votes in favor besides mine. That means even though he stood up there over and over tellin' us to vote *Against*, there are still four people who voted *For*. That just goes to show how many people with strong backbones are here, who want *you* gone!"

"Compared to Yabu and Morofuji, you seem like you got a lot more sense, Tokitou." Ryuuen gave Tokitou a round of applause in admiration and praise. Then, he continued speaking. "In that case, don't hold back. How 'bout you and I have a go, Tokitou? One-on-one."

"What?" he asked.

"I'll force all thirty-five people who have been votin' against the issue this whole time, myself included, to change their votes. And when that happens, we'll start voting on who is gonna get expelled, just like Kaneda said. What'll happen next is simple. You and I are gonna have ourselves a showdown in votes."

If other students weren't going to be eligible targets in the decision of who would be expelled, there was no reason for them to fear a unanimous vote in favor.

"You sure about this?" said Tokitou. "If you eliminate all the *Against* votes right now, that means it's gonna be inevitable. Someone'll get expelled. And there ain't no way you'll be the one to survive, Ryuuen."

Giving Ryuuen the possibility of ending the exam with a unanimous decision of *Against* was Tokitou's way of being merciful.

Ryuuen shrugged. "Everybody wants to avoid runnin' out of time. In that case, we'll settle things with a one-on-one showdown. You against me. That would be way more interesting for all the folks in our class, wouldn't it?"

There was no chance that Ryuuen would accept Tokitou's proposal. Instead, he advocated for a unanimous vote in favor.

"People are selfish, they're gonna look out for number one," Ryuuen went on. "Nobody's gonna be thrilled about comin' forward if there was a risk they could get expelled. They couldn't do it. But if it's just gonna be either you or me who gets expelled? Well, that'll make their eyes light up. They'll be all too happy to vote on it if they're promised a hundred points as a reward."

"You think the people votin' in favor right now are gonna agree to expel *me*?" asked Tokitou.

"Well now, who can say?" said Ryuuen. "But hey, if you've got a bad feelin' about this, you can always vote no. Y'know?"

"To hell with that!" shouted Tokitou. "If anybody's gettin' expelled, it's not gonna be me! You're gonna be the one out of here, Ryuuen!"

"I see. Then let's get on with it and have ourselves our little showdown, one-on-one."

There were the four anonymous voters who continued to support the issue, and there were also students who disliked Ryuuen but continued voting against the issue because they had no choice. Tokitou was confident that if they were voting on whether or not to expel Ryuuen Kakeru, then as more time that passed, the more votes there would be in favor of it.

"Fine." Tokitou said. "If you insist that strongly, then—"

Just as Tokitou was about to go along with Ryuuen's provocations and readily accept his challenge, someone banged on their desk. The sound echoed throughout the room.

"Wait a moment, Ryuuen. Couldn't you give Tokitou just a little time?"

The source of both the sound and the voice that spoke up was none other than Katsuragi. He hurriedly stood up and called out to Ryuuen.

"Huh? What do you think you're doin', Katsuragi?" said Ryuuen. "I don't remember givin' you the right to speak. Do you?"

"I do not intend to be robbed of my right to speak," Katsuragi replied, unwavering. He ignored the order to shut up and then turned to Tokitou.

"It's not wrong for you to think that, because like you said, as long as there's someone who doesn't obey Ryuuen, there's no need for you to worry. However, what Ryuuen says is also true. If we hold a vote on the issue with the condition that we'll be deciding only between you and him, the class's emotions will be greatly shaken during the remaining time we have left. If that happens, then the person who controls the majority, meaning Ryuuen, will have an overwhelming advantage."

"I told you," Tokitou replied. "Don't just assume that he actually has the advantage here, Katsuragi. Truth is, a lot of people in class don't love Ryuuen bein' here.

They're just being held down by force. They're frustrated. If time starts runnin' out, then I'm sure more and more people are gonna stop defendin' him. Even someone like that dog over there, Ishizaki."

"The hell you just say?!" shouted Ishizaki.

"You stood up to Ryuuen once before," Tokitou told him. "Remember your rebellious spirit!"

"Th-that was—"

Last year, there had been an incident: Ayanokouji was called to the roof and there was a fight. In the aftermath, the story was that Ishizaki defeated Ryuuen, and temporarily took control of the class afterward. That was what Tokitou was referring to.

"I don't know what happened back then," Katsuragi said. "But do you think you'll win this in the end?"

"Yes, I do," replied Tokitou.

"Then allow me to ask you another question. If Ryuuen is expelled, who is going to lead the class after he's gone?"

"We can discuss it or whatever, but it's not gonna be an outsider like you, Katsuragi."

"It's certainly true that as an outsider, I might not be an option," Katsuragi conceded. "But it's also true that if a clear leader doesn't appear, we won't be able to make decisive moves going forward. We will not be able to catch up to and overtake Sakayanagi."

Katsuragi took a broad view of the situation, looking at the big picture. He kept trying to explain that to Tokitou, but Tokitou wouldn't budge.

"Give me a break... So what?" he scoffed. "If I wasn't prepared to cross swords with this guy, even if I had to sacrifice myself to deal a blow, I wouldn't have come forward, from the beginning."

"*Ku ku ku*, from the beginning, huh? It looked to me like you took quite a long time just waitin' and watchin'."

"Shut the hell up!" snapped Tokitou.

"Well, guess that makes sense, since you couldn't really do anythin' without havin' a few like-minded people there with you," Ryuuen said.

After all, it was only after Tokitou confirmed there were several voters going against Ryuuen's orders that he had made his move.

"Please, Ryuuen," said Katsuragi. "Give Tokitou a chance."

Ryuuen heard what Katsuragi said and interpreted it to be solely to his advantage.

He snapped his fingers. "All right. Tokitou, I'm gonna give you a chance. Everything's gonna come down to your one vote in the next round. If you vote in favor, then I'm gonna have you expelled."

"Hah... Big talk. You think you can get me expelled?"

"Yeah, I do." Ryuuen said. "In the next round, every other vote except for yours will be against the issue. Which means it'll be one vote *For*, and thirty-nine *Against*. That's the situation. So, if you vote against the issue, it'll be unanimous, and we'll be done here."

"Hey, hold on. When did the four other people who voted in favor besides me disappear?" said Tokitou.

"*Ku ku...* Well, I flipped those four votes during the interval."

"Enough with the lame jokes. There's no way you could've done that."

Aside from the fact that Ryuuen himself had stubbornly been in favor of the idea up until this point, he had spent most of this interval period talking with Tokitou. He hadn't even tried to talk to any others to get them to change their votes.

"Then let's put this to the test," he said. "You vote in favor as you've done all this time. Do that, and you'll find out."

Time continued to tick by during this interval. There was now less than a minute remaining. Although the air-conditioned room was kept at a comfortable temperature, sweat was slowly starting to trickle down Tokitou's back. Ryuuen was merely threatening him; it was just a bluff. It was hard to imagine that anything had actually changed during the interval. But...what if all the other voters in favor really had changed their votes? That would indicate that those four other students were following Ryuuen.

Tokitou could have employed the same defensive measure that Ibuki mentioned—he could vote against the issue when the rest of the class was going to vote in favor before they could come to a unanimous decision. But Tokitou couldn't go that route now. It would be disgraceful. At any rate, a deciding vote between him and Ryuuen was likely inevitable. And if that happened, it was a certainty that Tokitou would be defeated.

"You're prepared for expulsion, aren't you?" said Ryuuen. "Don't hold back. Vote in favor."

"...You don't have to tell me twice," said Tokitou.

Soon, the time would come for them to vote. Tokitou cast his vote in favor of the issue, without looking back.

"Well then, I'll show you the results," announced Sakagami, displaying the voting results on the monitor.

Round 13 Voting Results: FOR: 2 Votes, AGAINST: 38 Votes

"Wha—?!"

When Tokitou saw those results, he was sure his heart was racing more quickly than anyone else's. It was almost just like Ryuuen had said. Nearly all of the other people who were voting in favor had changed their votes. Only one person hadn't.

"Hah. Now that's certainly a shock... But this just means that there's still one other student here who has got a strong will like me! Someone else who didn't give in, no matter how much you threatened 'em!" bellowed Tokitou, as though he were declaring victory.

However, Ryuuen wasn't looking at Tokitou. Instead, he was looking at someone completely different.

"What's the meanin' of this, huh? You voted in favor, didn't you, Katsuragi?"

"What...?" asked Tokitou, shocked to hear Katsuragi's name.

"That's right," Katsuragi replied. "If I had voted *Against*, then it would've been one vote *For* and thirty-nine *Against*, as you declared. That means it would've gone on to a deciding vote. If that happened, it would've been impossible for us to get through this exam without one of the two of you being expelled."

"That's the way it should have gone, yeah," said Ryuuen. "And depending on the explanation you give me right now, you might not get off with just an apology."

"I have one reason. I think that Tokitou is a student this class needs. Well, actually, not just Tokitou. Yes, I am an outsider and came to this class from Class A.

However, that is exactly why I've been able to look at this class with an objective eye. As a result, I can tell quite clearly that there isn't a single student here who isn't needed."

"You're sayin' that Tokitou is a student we need? Somebody who doesn't follow directions?" asked Ryuuen.

"That's right. Actually, I would consider him a valuable asset. He's someone who can disagree with your opinions without hesitation, like I do. No, actually, even more than I can. Of course, that being said, the way he did it in this particular case, in a special exam, was wrong. I wasn't impressed by the fact that he put the class in danger just to take you down, Ryuuen."

Katsuragi wasn't only going to address Ryuuen. He turned to speak to Tokitou.

"If you don't like the fact that Ryuuen is the leader, make your case fairly and honestly in a way that doesn't involve anyone else. If your argument is correct, then I will not hesitate to take your side."

"Katsuragi, you..." huffed Tokitou.

"If you fall for Ryuuen's tricks here, you'll be expelled from school having accomplished nothing. We'd all move forward and Ryuuen won't even remember that a student named Tokitou Hiroya ever existed."

"B-but, what about the four other people who voted—"

He was referring to his invisible reinforcements who had helped push Tokitou to this point. The foundation for his courage.

"There were no such people from the very beginning," Katsuragi told him. "It was an illusion."

"An illusion...?" repeated Tokitou.

"To be precise, I suppose I should say that they were weeded out through repeated voting. Five votes in favor remained after Yajima's was called out. That included you, Tokitou, and..."

Katsuragi paused and slowly turned around, directing his gaze elsewhere. He pointed at other students one by one. "Shiina, Yamada, myself, and...Ryuuen. The four of us."

Katsuragi gave Tokitou an answer that neither he nor any of their other classmates could understand.

"Wh... Wait, what are you talking about? Ryuuen was... voting in favor too?" asked Tokitou.

"When there were only five votes *For*, that meant there was really only one anonymous vote remaining. However, everything came to light when you stepped forward," said Katsuragi.

"So during this entire interval, Ryuuen was just mocking me in his head, huh... That figures," huffed Tokitou, dejected.

"That's not true," said Katsuragi. "While our intention *was* to smoke out whoever was voting in favor, when you came forward, that matter was settled. You could have simply stayed silent and kept voting, not challenging anything. If that happened, the vote would've naturally resulted in a unanimous decision *For*, and the next vote would have ended with an expulsion."

"So you were playing word games just to insult me?!" snapped Tokitou.

"No, we weren't. We were giving you the possibility of *not* being expelled," said Katsuragi.

"Wha...?!"

"However, you pushed on ahead, not noticing that chance. I suppose that was because you didn't think that Ryuuen would give you one, even if it was in a round-about way."

"I-I...!"

"Still, no matter how much I try to convince you, if you won't listen to me, that'll be the end of it. I'm sorry that this has taken up so much time, but please give Tokitou one final chance, Ryuuen," Katsuragi said. "I would like you to give him one more opportunity to vote *Against*, before having everyone else vote in favor of the issue."

"One more chance?" asked Ryuuen. "You think that I'm that nice?"

"You also share some fault here. You were overly argumentative and completely overlooked the idea of saving someone. Now that everything has been revealed, you can finally give Tokitou a choice."

"And if he doesn't cooperate, you ain't gonna object to me expellin' him, will you?"

"No, I won't. You can do whatever you like."

Katsuragi closed his eyes and crossed his arms. Now, the matter of deciding Tokitou's future was in Tokitou's own hands. If he voted in favor of the idea, there was a 100 percent chance he would be expelled. On the other hand, if he voted against the issue, it would be a unanimous decision and he would avoid expulsion. However, voting against the issue would still mean submitting to Ryuuen in some form. It would be a serious blow to Tokitou's pride.

"Now then, we'll begin the sixty-second voting period," announced Sakagami.

At the same time he made that announcement, the countdown began. All thirty-nine students except for Tokitou finished entering their votes within the sixty-second time limit...and the counter continued to run.

Sakagami looked up and glanced over at Tokitou. "As was explained to you in advance, if you exceed sixty seconds, you will accrue penalty time," he said.

Tokitou stared downward, alternating glances at the two words displayed on the tablet: *For* and *Against*.

"Damn it... Damn it!" he groaned.

This should have been the signal fire marking the start of a counterattack, he realized. However, it had turned out that Tokitou had been alone the entire time. He had been dancing solo in the palm of Ryuuen's hand through all of it. He felt frustrated, embarrassed, and pathetic. All sorts of negative emotions took hold of Tokitou's heart and wouldn't let go. For a moment, his pride was clear on his face, like he was saying he was not about to give in to Ryuuen here.

He could go out in a blaze of glory. Or he could intentionally vote yes instead, in order to buy himself some time. If he continued to vote opposite the thirty-nine other students, he might also be able to make the class fail the issue in the end. The exam would end not with his expulsion, but by him making the entire class fail the special exam...

Those thoughts flashed through his mind, but Tokitou quickly shook his head to dispel them.

There was nothing for him to gain, not even if he did those things to try and resist Ryuuen. It would only cause more trouble for his classmates and make them hate him more than they did Ryuuen. That was not what Tokitou wanted.

"God... DAMMIT!!!"

Tokitou lifted his arm up high in an exaggerated motion and slammed his finger down on a button to cast his vote.

"...All votes are now in," said Sakagami. "I'll show you the results now."

The teacher paused to take a breath, fiddled with his tablet, and displayed the results on the monitor.

Round 14 Voting Results: FOR: 0 Votes, AGAINST: 40 Votes

"It's unanimous—the class has voted against the issue. This concludes the special exam."

Everyone had thought that chances were high someone would've been expelled from Ryuuen's class. But the exam ended with all students remaining. Ishizaki turned to look back at Tokitou, about to say something to the downcast Tokitou.

"Tokitou, you—"

"...Don't get the wrong idea here, Ryuuen," Tokitou spoke over him, addressing Ryuuen instead. "I don't approve of the way you do things. If I decide that your way is gonna prevent us from moving up to Class A, I will take you out, no matter how many times I gotta come at you."

"Then come at me any time," Ryuuen replied. "I'll take you on without mercy."

"Hmph..."

It would have been awkward for Tokitou to remain in the classroom any longer, so he left as quickly as he could. After watching him leave, Katsuragi walked over to Ryuuen's side.

"You overstepped, Katsuragi," Ryuuen told him. "I was welcoming the idea of someone gettin' expelled, remember?"

"I'm sure half of you was. But the other half of you was open to exploring other possibilities, yes?"

"The hell are you on about? Do I look that nice to you?"

"I don't know whether you're nice or not," said Katsuragi, "but if your objective is complete control over the vote, it's important to keep the students loyal to you on your side without pushing things too far. However, after the second round of voting, even though you walked around and said things to some other random students as well, you gave your true orders to Shiina. If you go around whispering only to specific students, people will think that you're planning some kind of strategy. Then, through Shiina, you gathered together a group of people to falsely pose as supporters of the issue and vote *For*. I was included among that group. The reason you did so was that you knew I would protect Tokitou, isn't it?"

"You'd protect Tokitou?" Ryuuen repeated. "And where exactly would I have gotten that information?"

"Shiina overheard Tokitou and I talking about you. It wouldn't be surprising if you found out about it from her reports."

"I was just bein' selective in lookin' for people who would vote in favor so he'd be misled by fake votes. And that was so I could get him expelled, of course, so I could get Class Points. Disappointing."

Ryuuen left the classroom sometime later. After that happened, Katsuragi turned to look at the person who was watching him. He was honestly moved to see Shiina smiling warmly at him.

"So, it's possible that it was Shiina's judgment call, one she made on her own, that brought me into it..." he muttered.

In any case, the fact remained that Ryuuen laid the foundation for Tokitou to be saved and gave him a chance. As Katsuragi looked around at the other students, feeling relieved that no one had been expelled, he felt convinced of something. He felt like this class actually had the potential to defeat Sakayanagi and become Class A. And he wanted to pursue that path together with them.

7 SAKAYANAGI ARISU'S CHOICE

A LITTLE OVER AN HOUR had passed since the special exam had started. Though Class A, led by Sakayanagi, had gone through several votes and break periods, things were moving along quite smoothly. And now, they had arrived at the final issue.

> **ISSUE #5:** In exchange for expelling one of your classmates, gain 100 Class Points.

(In the event the class is unanimously in favor, a vote will be held to choose the student to be expelled.)

Seeing the word "expel" startled the students, but they proceeded to cast the first round of votes in silence as they were instructed. In order to avoid any unexpected incidents, Sakayanagi, like Horikita, had given her classmates instructions in advance to ensure that votes were split among the four people closest to her. Because there were two options in this vote, that meant it was a given that there would be two *For* and two *Against*.

As such, the results showed...

Round 1 Voting Results: FOR: 2 Votes, AGAINST: 36 Votes

And that was that. The results showed that, aside from the two controlled votes that Sakayanagi had engineered to be in favor, all the students were against the issue.

"Welp, there you have it. So, what are you gonna do, Princess? Are we all votin' no next round?" Hashimoto immediately looked to Sakayanagi for confirmation once the interval period began.

Hashimoto was given the assigned task of always voting for the first option, so he had voted in favor of the issue.

"What do you think, Hashimoto-kun?" asked Sakayanagi in return.

Hashimoto was a little surprised by that, as he hadn't expected his question would be met with another. He read the issue once again in his mind.

"If we wanna head straight to a conclusion, then we should oppose the issue," he said. "But when I step back and think about it more logically, I feel that going for 100 Class Points is surprisingly not that stupid of an idea."

"Meaning you think we should move to gain those 100 points, even if it means expelling one of our classmates?" asked Sakayanagi.

"Well...I wouldn't say all that, no. I'm just saying I wonder if it's okay to completely disregard those points so casually. That's all."

"If this exam had come toward the end of a competitive school year, then I would've likely had no choice but to adopt a policy of abandoning classmates," Sakayanagi said. "However, as it stands now, our class is by far in the lead. With that in mind, one might say it would be quite nonsensical for us to choose to expel someone here and now to gain 100 Class Points."

"Of course. I was just sayin' that it'd be too bad if we were regrettin' these Class Points later, y'know?"

"A reduction in the number of people also comes with its own disadvantages," Sakayanagi said. "Simply put, the total number of Private Points our class would gain every month would decrease, the class's morale would decline, and there would be feelings of distrust. It's an interesting move to be sure, but we do have the option of deliberately choosing to expel a student now, only to turn around and save them by spending 20 million Private Points. That way, we could gain Class Points without sacrificing anyone. However, doing so would have an adverse effect on our assets, which would in turn affect the upcoming sports and cultural festivals. Even talking about a difference of 100 points, if we take the possibility of unforeseen factors into account, I believe that there isn't much difference in terms of gains or losses no matter how this issue plays out. Or perhaps...is there anyone in this class who would willingly volunteer to be expelled?"

Sakayanagi briefly surveyed the class. Of course there was no way that any of them would voluntarily drop out of Class A because, as Sakayanagi had said earlier, their class was in the lead by a wide margin.

"I'm sure that the other classes must be struggling with this issue, since they're essentially in a three-way contest right now," she added. "Even if one of those classes makes the difficult choice of choosing someone to expel, that class may not necessarily rise in the ranks. Losing a fellow classmate is not such a simple matter, after all."

And with that, Class A's plan of action had been set. Hypothetically, if Class A had chosen to expel someone, they would have come to a unanimous decision on it without delay. And in all likelihood, whatever student Sakayanagi had chosen would be the one to be expelled.

"All of you, my classmates, are different from those we have lost, meaning Katsuragi-kun and Totsuka-kun,"

Sakayanagi said. "I would never do anything to abandon my friends who are working so diligently for me."

What Sakayanagi said was a lie. In the unlikely event that Class A was pushed into a corner, she wouldn't hesitate to make the choice to expel students. However, if she chose to expel students carelessly in a non-critical situation like right now, it would sow the seeds of mistrust. She had simply decided that as things currently stood, she'd have more to lose by putting herself into that situation.

Round 2 Voting Results: FOR: 0 Votes, AGAINST: 38 Votes

They had arrived at a unanimous decision *Against*, just like Ryuuen's class and Ichinose's class. But as those classes arrived there after a great deal of stress, Class A had come to their decision in just the first interval, spending just over half of the interval ensuring that their classmates would vote accordingly.

"Well then, that's everything," said Mashima. "That concludes all the issues in the Unanimous Special Exam. This class has completed the exam with the fastest time. Please note that the other classes are still in the middle of their exams, so please exit the classroom as instructed. The rest of your day will be spent in self-study in the dormitories, as planned."

Although the students were not allowed to leave the dormitories, they essentially had free time.

8

HORIKITA SUZUNE'S CHOICE

"**W**ELL THEN, I'll now show you the results," announced Chabashira.

Round 10 Voting Results: FOR: 1 Vote, AGAINST: 38 Votes

It was a sight I was tired of seeing and it simply kept repeating itself over and over. Even though there were appeals for the person to come forward, the results didn't change. Despite our repeated discussions, they seemed to have no effect. The number of votes in favor hadn't increased, but they hadn't decreased either. Suspicions were running wild, making us wonder if there wasn't actually such a thing as a fair vote after all, and if this was just the same screen being displayed repeatedly.

"Since the decision was not unanimous, we'll now have an interval period," said Chabashira.

We could clearly hear the fatigue in Chabashira's voice as she gave us that standard announcement. Now that she had told us about her past, all she could do as an instructor was watch and see how this issue developed.

"How is this even happening...? Is there really someone here who keeps voting in favor of it?" asked Keisei.

It wasn't any wonder why he would want to voice his doubts. Even if we wanted to continue the conversation at this point, we had already exhausted all possible ways of discussing the issue. Just how many times had Horikita and Yousuke tried to persuade this lone voter now?

"Would everyone who is against the issue...please raise their hands?" asked Yousuke.

Yousuke, seeing that calling for whoever was in favor was futile, requested that the students who were opposed raised their hands. Even though this proposal was a meaningless reversal of the standard question, he remained steadfast in his efforts to make some kind of breakthrough. Students all throughout the room started neatly raising their hands up in the air. I raised mine too, of course. By doing this, we could see that thirty-eight people, Yousuke included, were voting against the issue. The only person who hadn't raised their hand was Kouenji, but...

"I won't be raising my hand. But do not worry—I am voting against the issue," Kouenji said in response to Yousuke's anxiety-filled look.

"Like hell I can believe that, Kouenji," grumbled Sudou. "You're really the one votin' for this thing, ain't you...?"

"How many times have we had this argument now, hm? It seems that you never get tired of bringing it up."

Even for Sudou, there was no other option but to keep going back to Kouenji. It wasn't unreasonable, after all, if the current situation continued. As of now, it was difficult to believe that another person in class was continuing to lie.

Somewhere out there, a student was proudly raising their hand and to say they were voting *Against* but was still voting in favor.

"I don't want to think that there's someone here with their hand raised right now who is lying to us," said Horikita. "So, I'm going to try asking each of you, one by one, looking directly into your eyes. If there is someone here voting in favor, please, tell me... No, I *want* you to vote *Against* in the next round of voting."

Horikita struggled desperately during those ten minutes, making every effort she could. Without sparing any expense, she began confronting each individual student. She must have been as exhausted as anyone else, but she couldn't say that. Everyone answered Horikita's question while looking straight into her eyes. Everyone, including Haruka, Airi, Keisei, and Akito. And then Ike, Sudou, Mii-chan, and Matsushita. Kushida, Onodera, Okiya, and Mori as well. Every one of them said that they were voting *Against*.

Eventually, Horikita came to me, the very last person, seated at the far back of the classroom near the door. There was a mixture of impatience and anxiety in her eyes, but they still held a fiery passion.

"And what about you, Ayanokouji-kun?" she asked.

"I'm voting *Against*, of course," I answered.

"...I see."

That meant we'd once again completed questioning each and every student individually. It was practically an interrogation. There hadn't been any changes in the students' statements. All our classmates claimed to be voting against the issue. The only thing left for us to do would be to appeal to the pangs of conscience remaining in this person's heart and ask that they oppose the issue, but...

"Ten minutes are almost up," said Chabashira. "Return to your seat, Horikita. The vote is about to begin."

Round 11 Voting Results: FOR: 1 Vote, AGAINST: 38 Votes

The results hadn't changed at all. There wasn't anything else to say about it. The same results were being shown to us over, and over, and over.

"Ah, I can't take it anymore!" yelled Sudou, scratching his head wildly. "I feel like I'm losin' my friggin' mind! I don't get what's goin' on here!!!" He slammed his elbows down hard on his desk. "B-but seriously, what are we gonna do? We don't got a lotta time left, do we?"

Up until this point, the students had been operating on the assumption that the person persistently voting in favor would eventually back down. The entire class, Horikita included, must have believed there was no way this person would choose to let time run out. Absolutely. Almost. Surely. Probably. Maybe. Anyway, the person voting *For* would ultimately be afraid of letting time run out. And then, at last, that person would change their mind and vote opposed at the last minute. We'd come to a unanimous decision, and the special exam would be over.

The class was sure that's how things would turn out, and then the class would move on to the sports festival and cultural festival next. However...the person voting in favor wasn't budging. Their answer wasn't changing even after waiting another ten minutes, thirty minutes, an hour...

All that awaited us was the worst possible scenario: running out of time.

We had nine minutes remaining until the next round of voting. But those next nine minutes weren't *just* nine minutes because after that, the deadline would be less than two hours away. Horikita had been fighting hard to overcome this final issue for the past three hours. It wasn't like her strategies were overly optimistic. Even if I was to do everything in my power to bring the issue to a unanimous decision opposed to the issue, it likely would have been impossible for me. Why was that? What was the fundamental reason?

Because persuasion, negotiation, and every other kind of action would have been meaningless. This person supporting the issue was simply fighting to avoid a unanimous decision of *Against*. And what was most frightening of all was that whoever this person was, they didn't see running out of time as the biggest loss. Normally, that would be unthinkable in a special exam like this. When you looked at this issue objectively, you could see that the priorities of the three possible outcomes were fixed.

Against ≥ *For* > Time Out

That was an absolute relationship, which was shared between all students from all four classes. It was precisely because this fixed priority existed that this special exam was built upon it. It was a basic premise.

However...what would happen if there was just one single student who had different priorities?

For > Time Out > *Against*

If someone had such distorted priorities, then this issue wasn't going to be viable. That was precisely why the school was preventing the classes from interfering with each other via strict monitoring and rules. It was to prevent students from signing contracts with the likes of Sakayanagi or Ryuuen, who might invite them to join their class or transfer a substantial number of Private Points in exchange for allowing time to run out in their own class.

This special exam had devolved into chaos because a student who wasn't aligned with the rest of the class was thrown into the mix. If we continued to stubbornly press on ahead, all that awaited us was timing out.

If that was the case, what should we do? There was only one thing that we could do in the two hours that we had remaining.

Unanimous approval.

That was the optimal solution. There was no other way for us to press on ahead except for that. This idea was probably already in Horikita's mind, but she wasn't taking the plunge. It wasn't easy to get rid of a classmate, and it would be infinitely more difficult for our class to select one person to expel than it would be to get a unanimous vote of *Against*. Once we took the first step on that path, there was no turning back. We wouldn't be allowed to say something like, *"Oh, we can't expel someone after all, so let's just go back and all vote* Against.*"*

And yet...I was still hesitating to conduct the plan even after it came time to vote. Why? The ideal route was off the table, and the ideal time for me to execute the plan was already approaching. If we used up extra time now, that would present an obstacle when it came to selecting a person to expel after coming to a unanimous decision of *For*. But even so, I wanted to try to come to a unanimous decision *Against* just one more time, even if it took up precious time.

A rather inconvenient feeling, the likes of which I had never experienced before, started to cloud my mind. *What kind of decision would you make in this situation?* I thought, asking Horikita Manabu that question in my mind. Though there was no way I was going to get anything resembling an answer, I decided to add an amendment to my plan. I bet on this last chance, but without letting the exit strategy change.

"Well then, the results..." croaked Chabashira.

After Chabashira had finished tallying the votes, she stumbled on her words for just a moment.

"...I-I will show you the results."

Round 12 Voting Results: FOR: 2 Votes, AGAINST: 37 Votes

"W-wait, what?" exclaimed Sudou. "No way, why?! The number of votes in favor went *up*?!"

After all this time, one of the thirty-eight people who consistently voted opposed had changed their vote, now voting in favor. This would likely have a sufficient impact to make a fissure in the united opposition.

"It's like I'm having a bad dream..." Horikita muttered.

The person who had cast the additional vote was none other than me. It wasn't like it was *just* one vote, though. It was one powerful vote in favor of the issue, cast by one of the thirty-seven people, other than Kouenji, who had previously been firmly united. Horikita hadn't even considered this option in the slightest before I did this, but now she had her thinking cap back on. She was thinking about what we should do if we couldn't reduce the number of votes in favor to zero.

Horikita quickly understood that this one vote shifted so we could avoid running out of time. No matter what we ended up voting for unanimously, neither of them would be as bad as what would happen if we failed the exam overall. That would be the worst-case scenario. Even if no one were expelled in that situation, we would still lose 300 Class Points. Assuming that all the other classes finished the exam successfully, that would mean there would be a difference of 350 points between us and them. And on top of that, if there was a class that finished the exam with a unanimous decision in favor, then that would mean there'd be a maximum gap of up to 450 points between us and them.

With such a huge gap, it would be impossible to count on being able to catch up to the other classes, even though we had more than a year of school remaining. Actually, no, there was absolutely no way that we could. Even if you avoided expulsion in that scenario, having to give up on reaching Class A was no laughing matter. Once that conclusion became widespread, it was inevitable that students would begin questioning the point of continuing to push for voting *Against*.

They would begin to wonder whether it would be easier to get those voting opposed to swing the other way since there was the possibility of getting everyone to change as a group rather than trying to change the stubborn voters in favor. Even if what awaited us afterwards was the immensely daunting hurdle of choosing who would be expelled, it would mean being able to take at least a half-step forward from the deadlock we were currently in.

"H-hey, so, uh, I guess this means we just have to vote in favor? Right?" asked Ike.

"What are you talkin' 'bout?" snapped Sudou. "You know that if we do that, we're gonna have to expel someone, don't ya?"

"But dude... If we run out of time, that's it. We're finished, y'know?" said Ike.

The united front was starting to gradually erode. People were shifting closer to voting *For*. The first people to change their votes would be the students who thought highly of themselves and felt that there was no way they'd be expelled. On the other hand, students who tended to feel that they might be expelled would continue to vote *Against*. The number of votes in favor would continue to grow internally, secretly.

However, not a single student would come forward and actually say that they were voting in favor. That was to be expected, because after all, if it became known that someone supported the issue, they might be targeted for expulsion.

Round 13 Voting Results: FOR: 5 Votes, AGAINST: 34 Votes

Three more votes in favor. People were still loudly ranting and raving, asking who changed their votes, but that was as far as it went.

Round 14 Voting Results: FOR: 12 Votes, AGAINST: 27 Votes

The steadily increasing stream of votes in favor wasn't slowing down, and the number quickly continued to grow and grow. The number of votes in favor reached double digits for the first time, swelling to nearly one-third of the total vote. It was likely that the number of votes *For* would increase even more in the next round. Now that we had reached this point, we only had about an hour and a half remaining until we reached the overall time limit.

"W-wait, please wait. If you really think that voting in favor is a good idea, you're wrong!" Undeterred by the critical situation, Yousuke attempted to appeal to the students voting *For*. "I understand that we can't let ourselves run out of time, but still... That doesn't mean that a unanimous vote in favor is going to be the resolution we're looking for. Okay?"

"That's right," said Horikita. "If we do this, we will then need to unanimously choose just one person out of all thirty-nine possible students in the class. That will be far more difficult than it would be to unanimously vote opposed now. We only have an hour and a half remaining. Do you understand that?"

In order for us to finish this exam if we were to vote in favor, we would then have to decide who would be expelled.

"It's still not too late," pleaded Yousuke. "We can make it. I think we should vote against."

"I'm of the same opinion," said Horikita. "We can't let ourselves be swayed."

Our classmates continued to struggle emotionally. At this late of a stage, the students were no longer able to make normal, rational judgments about whether it was right to vote *For* or *Against*.

"More importantly, I'm sure that you all know that we shouldn't be voting in favor of this issue," Horikita went on. "Even though twelve of you are, not a single one has come forward. Isn't that true?"

Even if the number of *For* votes continued to increase through repeated rounds of voting, we wouldn't be reaching ideal unanimity unless I intervened in a big way and forced things back on course. Originally, I was intending to steer things toward a unanimous decision in the next round, but I decided to accelerate my plans and put things into action now.

"...Can I offer my opinion?" I asked.

"Huh...?"

Horikita must not have expected this, as she looked somewhat taken aback when I spoke up to offer my advice.

"Horikita, I voted in favor just now, in the fourteenth round," I told her.

That was technically a lie—I actually started voting in favor starting in the twelfth round and just continued to vote that way, but nobody could prove that.

"Ayanokouji-kun, why..."

"Why? Because if we keep stubbornly trying to get everyone to vote opposed, we're going to run out of time," I argued. "If that's how things are going to be, then there's no other option but to vote in favor. I'm sure that everyone already understands that by now."

Someone had to take on this role if we were going to increase the number of votes *For*. Satou, sitting over the chair next to me, anxiously stared at my face. Well, no, it wasn't just her—I was sure that anyone who was worried about this situation was feeling the same way.

"That's still not going to fundamentally solve the problem here," Horikita said. "In the end, we'll be fighting over who to expel."

"That's true," I admitted. "But it's a way for us to break free from this deadlock. Even if we could find out who voted in favor this whole time, I don't see that person changing their vote. In other words, we can't expect a unanimous decision *Against*. However, right now, a unanimous decision *For* is possible. Then, we could put that sole defector on trial, meaning the person who originally voted in favor of it, and have them judged by the thirty-eight other people. It's a heavy-handed move, but we'd get to a unanimous decision."

There was one person who came to both my and Horikita's minds. Of course, there was no guarantee that person was the original *For* voter, but Horikita knew what I meant.

"That's—"

"On trial?" Yousuke interrupted, latching onto the latter part of what I said. "Do you think we really have the right to do that just because they were voting in favor?"

"We do," I replied. "If we can't come to a unanimous decision, we won't be able to move up to Class A. Not a single student in this class would find a person who voted in favor while knowing that fact to be blameless."

"B-but, but that's... I'm sure that once we get even closer to the time limit, they'll definitely change their mind, and—"

"Closer? We only have a few more opportunities to cast votes. Are you going to take all your classmates along for such a slim chance? The more times we go through this, the fewer and fewer opportunities we'll have of even getting out of this situation by voting *For*. Doing that would mean completely cutting off our chances of reaching a unanimous decision at all."

Even if I hadn't deliberately spelled it out, I was sure that Yousuke and the rest of our classmates already understood the situation. That being said though, most of the students still hadn't taken that first step forwards a unanimous decision in favor. They knew the biggest hurdle we had to face would appear after we agreed to the proposal.

"I'm sure it's true that a lot of students would be hesitant to vote in favor," I added. "That's exactly why I'd like for us to identify who voted that way all this time and adjust our course so only that person would be targeted for expulsion. Doing so would, in other words, mean ensuring the safety of students who are still voting against the issue now."

Satou had been listening to me more intently than anyone else as she sat beside me and meekly raised her hand.

"I'm glad to hear that," she started, "but...if we don't know who's been voting *For*, there's no point. I mean, once time starts running out, in the end, we're not going to have any other choice but to just choose someone to expel at random, and ... I'm scared."

"If we can't narrow down the list of candidates of who to expel, we could always choose to let time run out," I said. "But what we need to avoid right now is letting ourselves waste time by refusing to take steps that would allow us a chance to clear this special exam."

I offered further encouragement to help the students who were still hesitating in an attempt to get them to come to a decision.

"Also, as Horikita mentioned earlier, I also have some idea of who had been voting in favor since the beginning."

"In that case, why not just come out and say it right now?" said Miyamoto. "But wait, hold on, Horikita hasn't said that person's name, like, this whole entire time. Doesn't that mean that she actually doesn't have a clue? Maybe she was just thinking like, she could get 'em to vote against by bluffing, or threatening 'em a little?"

His theory was off, but it certainly wasn't unreasonable for him to think that way.

"If you really got some idea who it is, then let's all try talkin' it out with whoever it is, together," he added.

"I can't do that," I replied. "That's why we're doing things this way. The person voting in favor won't be swayed just because their name is brought up. They'd rather stubbornly stick it out until the very end. I want to avoid that happening."

I said that both as a way to induce students to vote in favor, and also, to offer some mercy from me to the person in question, at the very last minute. If that person had heard this much, they must've been keenly aware that I knew they were the one voting *For*. And if that person was afraid of being exposed, they might be the only person voting against the issue in the next round.

"Prepare yourself, Horikita," I said. "Your opponent is laying a trap with the intention of taking you down. There's no other way out of this fight. It's hunt or be hunted."

Horikita remained silent. Then, I turned my attention to another student.

"And Yousuke—I understand your feelings quite well. You don't want anyone from class to be expelled. If you really want that, then you need to make sure we get results before time is up. Understand?"

The day before the special exam, I had repeatedly warned Yousuke about this until I was blue in the face. Even with just a sideways glance, I could tell that he was struggling deeply. I could understand why he wanted to keep resisting.

"But, I—"

"The next vote is going to be a turning point in deciding our fate," I told him.

"...I..."

It was a difficult decision, but even so, Yousuke wasn't the same person he was before. He had grown since last year's uninhabited island exam, and the In-Class Vote, when he was at a standstill.

"Y-yeah, you're right," he conceded. "That's... That's just how I feel, and I can't cause trouble for the rest of the class..."

Though Yousuke hung his head low, he decided to move forward of his own volition.

"I'm going to vote in favor," he said. "Then, just like Ayanokouji-kun said, I think that we should adjust our plans accordingly and expel the person who was voting *For* this whole time."

Yousuke was the backbone of the class. With his decision, the situation would change even more significantly.

"The rest is up to you, Horikita," I said, turning back to her. "It's time for you to make up your mind so that we can avoid running out of time."

The next round of voting was about to begin. The discussion period was almost over.

"Please," she said. "Just one more time. Just give me one more chance to come to a unanimous decision *Against*.

If we don't get a unanimous vote in opposition in the next round of voting, then... I'll have made up my mind."

What she wanted was not going to happen. I already succeeded in creating a new situation. Still, the last possible round for the class to come to a unanimous decision *Against* had begun. It took almost no time at all, and everyone cast their votes in seconds. Still, sometimes things diverged greatly between the ideal and reality.

Round 15 Voting Results: FOR: 1 Vote, AGAINST: 38 Votes

"Damn it!" shouted Sudou. "I friggin' knew it!"

What Horikita did was a dangerous way to try and force the votes back to *Against* again after they had already started swaying to supporting the idea. With the time limit fast approaching, even this last-ditch strategy to bring about a unanimous decision had ended in failure. But now, because of this, everyone understood what was happening: the student who had continued to vote in favor was prepared to run out of time.

"Horikita, Yousuke, any objections?" I asked.

I successfully managed to confirm that I had both of their consent. At any rate, the groundwork for a battle to have a student expelled had been set. With the intentions of Horikita and Yousuke, two main players in class made clear, a large number of votes in favor would follow. Still, it was easy to imagine that students who were worried they might be expelled would still hesitate to vote in support of the issue. Those who were resolved to cast their votes against the issue would need to make up their minds about this.

"If anyone votes *Against* in the next round, we will need them to clearly state the reason why," Horikita said. "We already know all too well how painful it is for us to waste ten minutes on each vote."

It was no surprise that some students might still feel disgruntled about the situation since we still had some time remaining. However, our escape route had been completely cut off now since we only had one hour remaining until time ran out. It was a rough job to essentially force the students who lacked the decisiveness to make a choice on their own to come to a decision.

"Now that things have come to this... We have no choice but to expel someone," said Horikita.

"Wait, for real?" said Sudou. "We're doin' this?"

"Personally, I do not want to lose any of my classmates," Horikita said. "But if we don't expel someone, our class is going to suffer enormously. We must avoid that above all else."

If you looked at the developments in Class Points up

until this point, you could see that the painful outcome of losing nearly 300 Class Points would sting badly.

The interval lasted for ten minutes. The students needed to summon their willpower and suppress the urge to run away and vote against the issue.

Round 16 Voting Results: FOR: 39 Votes, AGAINST: 0 Votes

It was a unanimous decision. When these results were displayed before us, everyone's fears and anxieties were plain to see on their nervous faces.

"Unanimously in favor..." muttered Chabashira, almost as though she had long been prepared for everything that was about to happen.

She continued the proceedings. Now that we had made this choice, the only way forward was to either expel someone or let time run out. The latter, of course, would mean this class would simply be fighting a losing battle until graduation. That meant that of the thirty-nine students here, someone was going to be leaving the school for good in about an hour. Of course, I already had an idea of who that person should be.

"Individuals can be selected either by voluntarily nominating themselves one time or by choosing a student's name on your tablets, to cast your vote recommending them," Chabashira explained. "However, please note that, as was explained previously, if there are no voluntary nominations and no one has a majority of the nominations at the end of the interval, the student being voted on will be chosen randomly."

Naturally, many students were looking to me and Horikita now, as it was finally time to decide who would be expelled. A certain type of pressure washed over each of us in succession, and we could practically hear their voices. *Hurry! Let's hear names now!* This was an interval that was infinitely more important and precious than any of the previous ones. While this period was still ten minutes long, we were now going to be required to choose who to nominate for expulsion.

"So, we've unanimously voted in favor of the issue... I would, at the very least, like to wait one interval period to let the original voter have time to come forward and confess," said Horikita. "That's the policy I'd like to take here. Depending on the circumstances and situation, we can choose to let time run out and help the student."

Of course, there was no way that a proposal like the one Horikita just made would be accepted without criticism. Students weren't about to approve of a choice like that as it would mean losing Class Points. However, Horikita was silent from that point onward and began actively listening to and enduring everyone's complaints.

For my own part, I needed to watch and wait for just the right time so I went along with it, staying quiet. It was a dark, harsh time, and students hurled their grumblings at both of us, trying to discourage us from what we were doing.

Obviously, this meant that we hadn't chosen anyone to be a candidate, and the interval was nearing its end. I was sure that if students saw their names up on the monitor, they would feel like their heart was in a vice grip. It was absurd to expect the class to come to a unanimous decision on who to expel right now, especially because this was the first round of voting.

"Sensei, may I nominate myself?" asked Yousuke.

"Of course," she replied.

"In that case, I would like everyone to vote for me."

And so, Yousuke came forward, nominating himself as a candidate just moments before the interval ended.

HIRATA YOUSUKE WILL BE EXPELLED.

FOR, AGAINST

This vote had a different weight to it than any of the previous votes we had made. If anyone voted in favor this time, it amounted to nothing else but a direct statement on their part that they wanted Yousuke gone, or at least that they didn't care if he disappeared.

Round 17 Voting Results: FOR: 6 Votes, AGAINST: 32 Votes

The silence was so heavy that you could almost hear every student breathing. While Yousuke must have felt relieved that a majority voted against his expulsion, I was also sure he'd be haunted for some time by those invisible six who voted in favor. Still, knowing Yousuke, he might be more greatly relieved that we were able to overcome this first difficult obstacle via his self-nomination.

"Man, what're we gonna do...?" said Sudou. "Are we seriously gonna expel somebody?"

"We don't have any more time." Keisei, unable to wait any longer, pressed us for an answer. "Come on you two, let's hear it. Who has been voting in favor all along?"

"I can name the person I have in mind, of course," I said. "But I know that the circumstances aren't quite that simple."

"Not that simple?" Keisei repeated. "We don't have room to choose anymore. Now that we've decided to expel someone, we need to find out who this person is as soon as possible."

There were still many students who regretted the decision to vote in favor of this issue. They were feeling anxious. Those people would be worn out emotionally and mentally, feeling like we just wasted ten minutes.

They wanted something that would make them believe that voting in favor earlier hadn't been a mistake.

"So, um, if things stay as they are and the clock keeps tickin', people are just gonna get picked at random for the next vote, right...?" said Sudou.

It was easy to understand why Sudou was so restless. Even Yousuke, of all people, had gotten six votes in favor of his expulsion.

"Dude, don't worry, Ken," said Ike. "I'm gonna vote against it, if you're up... S-so, buddy, you gotta protect me too, okay?"

"Course, Kanji. Y-yeah. If we got each other's backs, then we'll definitely be fine... Right?"

Our classmates were losing their composure. Among the many voices, a faint sound of crying could just barely be heard among them.

"*Sniff... Hic...*"

A student was covering their mouth and trying to hide their eyes from sight, but it was clear who was making those sounds.

"Kikyou-chan... A-are you okay?" asked an anxious Mii-chan, who had rushed over in a hurry. She placed a hand on Kushida's back.

"Yes, I'm sorry..." Kushida sniffled. "It's just, when I started wondering how we ended up in this mess, I...

I just couldn't stop feeling so overwhelmed with regret, and..."

"I feel the same way too," said Mii-chan. "But someone has to... Someone has got to be expelled..."

Most of the students in class hadn't come to such a realization, that this was actually happening. They felt like they were being forced to do something kind of unrealistic.

"I'm just, I'm regretting my choice so bad right now," said Kushida. "I should have continued to vote against the issue, no matter what..."

"The same goes for us too," said Keisei. "But we didn't have any choice. If we ran out of time, we'd lose 300 Class Points."

The decision was inevitable, which, in his mind, justified the vote in favor.

"But still... That doesn't make the regret of voting for it go away, no matter how much we justify it...!"

Kushida voiced her regret over the fact we had unanimously voted in favor, and she had played a part in it happening. Those feelings started to appear more strongly in other students who felt the same way, though they weren't expressing it in words.

Sudou and Ike comforted Kushida as well.

"Don't blame yourself, Kushida-chan," said Ike. "After all, everybody's in the same boat... Right?"

"It's so sad... It's just so sad..." said Kushida, tears streaming down her cheeks. As she wiped away her tears, she held herself tight, her body trembling. Then, she looked back up. "We really had a chance to unanimously vote *Against* though, didn't we? If we kept up our efforts to persuade that person, I'm sure that they would've understood eventually, in the end..."

"That's... But the time is..." sputtered Ike.

"I can certainly understand what Horikita-san and Ayanokouji-kun have been saying, though. We absolutely mustn't run out of time. Yes, I do understand that... But still, even if we were going to get penalized for letting time run out, we should have been the kind of class where no one got expelled, right?" said Kushida. She was letting out all the thoughts and feelings that had accumulated in her mind.

"Well, but hold on, it's definitely the person who voted in favor that's at fault here," Ike said. "For sure."

"No one should be expelled," said Kushida. "Whether someone excels or not in academics or in sports, that doesn't matter. It's trivial. That alone isn't enough to decide who should be expelled."

Her real, honest intentions were to protect even the person who originally voted in favor and caused this situation to occur.

"B-but, wait, in that case, how are we gonna decide who?" asked Ike.

"W-well, how about...somethin' like we all draw straws?" asked Sudou.

"That wouldn't work," Kushida said. "If someone were expelled because of that, then... I'm sure that no one would accept it."

After wiping away another smattering of flowing tears with her fingertips, Kushida continued speaking. "I'm going to say something, fully prepared for the criticism I'll face for it."

She put her hand to her chest and made her appeal to her classmates.

"I... I think that Horikita-san, as the leader of this special exam...or perhaps Ayanokouji-kun, who encouraged us all to vote in favor... They should be the ones to take responsibility for this situation."

I had a feeling this was how she was going to play it. Kushida had made her first move. There wouldn't be any benefit for her in a student like Ike or Sudou getting expelled here. Her words were filled with a fervent desire— that of the anonymous voter who had continued to vote in favor this whole time. I was sure of it.

"I feel so disgusted with myself for mentioning their names aloud that it almost makes me hate myself," she said, sniffling. "But we can't let time run out. Someone must take on the heavy burden of saying it... So, I-I'm prepared to take on the role of being hated... *Hic...*"

She was claiming that didn't want anyone to be expelled, but if someone had to be removed, then the selection process was inevitable. Just like those who were being removed from class, the person who advocated for this restructuring would also bear a similar suffering. So, according to Kushida, she had taken on that role herself. Naming names required both a reason and a considerable amount of determination.

Her statements were expertly worded to make us look like targets to our classmates while not making them suspect that she was the anonymous supporter of the issue. Kushida was much, much cleverer than I'd thought. Considering her position, she wouldn't be expelled no matter what, even if she remained completely silent all the way until the end of the exam. There were a number of students who would vote against her expulsion because she had many friends and people had a great deal of trust in her.

However, both Horikita and I had already figured out that Kushida was the anonymous supporter of the issue. In the unlikely event that either Horikita or I raised our hand and started slandering Kushida's reputation, it could lead to an unexpected develop-ment. She reasoned that it would be effective to suffer a non-fatal wound instead, using this situation as a de-fensive tactic. Now that she suggested Horikita and me, even if we tried to say something to discredit her, she could convince people that we were acting in revenge against her having advocated that we be removed from the class.

"You have GOT to be kidding me!"

Neither Horikita nor I were the first to object to Kushida's proposal. It was Kei.

"Why should Kiyotaka be expelled?" she said. "All he said was that we were going to run out of time, and that we should vote in favor even though it's a hard decision. What does he have to take the blame for?"

"...Yes, you're right," said Kushida. "I understand what you're trying to say, Karuizawa-san. I honestly think it's wrong for me to even give his name right here, but... It's just, if I didn't, we wouldn't be able to move forward at all."

"Well, I would never vote for Kiyotaka to be expelled," said Kei. "You do know that he is never, ever gonna get expelled if it comes down to it, right?"

"Wait, hold up, Karuizawa," said Hondou. "That's a little selfish, don'cha think?"

"Huh? Hondou-kun, didn't you just secretly promise Onizuka-kun that you'd vote no if he got targeted? This isn't any different," said Kei.

"Uh... B-but I wasn't the one who said we should vote unanimously in favor though..."

"Gosh, you're sooo self-centered," huffed Kei. "How can I be sure that he won't get expelled if I don't say it? So we can't go to Class A if we run out of time, huh? Well, so what? Kiyotaka is everything to me. Whether we end up in Class B or Class D, whatever, I don't care."

Kei was relentlessly venting her anger, but I needed to make her stop now.

"Kei, stop," I told her. "What Kushida's saying is correct. It's a fair argument."

"B-but!"

I had stopped Kei from going any further, but she continued to glare at Kushida. She made no attempt to hide her dissatisfaction and irritation.

"If you let your emotions get the better of you and you keep arguing, then that would mean the question of who should bear the most responsibility for this situation might get confused," I told her. "Instead of me and Horikita, the people Kushida had said should take the blame, someone else could be targeted instead. You know that much."

Kei deflated. "...Yeah..."

If she had completely lost her composure, I could have reined her in even more aggressively, but that didn't happen. Kei had enough sense to keep herself in check as long as I gave her a firm order. It wasn't a bad thing that our classmates were able to speak about what they were keeping to themselves in the back of their minds as a result though.

"I'm just gonna come out and say it," said Sudou. "I won't ever vote in favor of Suzune gettin' expelled. And all right, sure, we might not've been able to get the ideal unanimous decision here, but that ain't Suzune's fault. It's that jerkoff who kept voting in favor originally, stayin' anonymous and refusin' to come forward at all. *They're* the one at fault. I mean, do you guys really think we can even get to Class A in the future without Suzune? Besides, we all agreed that we can count on her, and we even gave her a Protect Point. Right, Yukimura?"

"...Yes, you're right about that." said Keisei, adjusting his glasses. "We did decide that we should give the Protect Point to Horikita. But, still, if we fail this special exam in the end, then giving her the point will be meaningless. Wouldn't it be the same thing as losing 350 Class Points?"

"But I'm sure that as long as we got Suzune here, she can get us back on track!" roared Sudou.

"This school isn't that simple," Keisei responded. "The 300 points that Kouenji earned from the uninhabited island exam was something of a miracle. Putting that aside, think about it. How long did it take for us to get the number of Class Points we have right now? It's just not very realistic, is what I'm saying. Sure, the loss of Horikita would leave a big hole, but not big enough to warrant losing 350 Class Points."

Would we try to compensate for the 350-point handicap we were in together with Horikita? Or would we fight against the other classes on even ground without her? While it was difficult to express the idea in simple figures, what Keisei was saying was generally correct.

"I can't vote in favor of either Kiyopon or Horikita's expulsion right now," Haruka cut in. It was rather unusual for her to interrupt like that. "I think that first, we should listen to what they each have to say rather than hearing about people's personal relationships and stuff. I mean, it's just like Sudou-kun said, it's the person who voted in favor originally who's at fault here, right?"

Kushida looked up with a start after Haruka suddenly spoke up. Haruka's explanation wasn't that of someone standing up for a friend. Rather, she was just saying it was too early to decide anything.

"Yes, I guess you're right," said Kushida. "I uh, I might've, um, lost my cool a little bit too... But still, if Ayanokouji-kun says who voted in favor all this time and he's wrong about it... Actually no, even if he's *not* wrong and he comes out and says that person's name, I'm sure that whatever relationship Ayanokouji-kun and this other student has is going to be completely destroyed..."

I could feel a kind of pressure from Kushida that seemed to be telling me, "*Don't say my name, not even by mistake.*" At any rate, the baton was passed back to me once again.

"I know we're still in the middle of discussion here, but I think we should call it here," I announced. "Ten minutes will be up soon, and we need to decide who to vote for to be expelled. If we don't, it'll be a random vote."

"...Very well," said Horikita. "We don't have much time left until we need to vote. I have no other choice. Please vote for me."

"H-hey, Suzune, what're—?! Whaddya think you're doing?!" shouted Sudou.

"If we're going to have to take a vote, then I want to make sure of something anyway," Horikita said. "I want to verify just how many students want me gone."

Horikita raised her hand and asked that she be the subject of the vote, as though she were testing herself. If there was a unanimous vote in favor of her expulsion, she would be gone. Conversely, if the class voted unanimously against her expulsion, she would be exempt from being targeted again. But if the class didn't come to a unanimous decision either way, then we'd have to start all over again and someone else to vote on. And Horikita would still be included among the possible candidates.

"Now then, we'll begin the vote for Horikita Suzune," said Chabashira. "You have sixty seconds to vote."

We voted on whether we'd be expelling Horikita from school. How many students would be pushing for her expulsion, I wondered... All the votes seemed to have been cast in about thirty seconds, and Chabashira displayed the results up on the monitor.

Round 18 Voting Results: FOR: 16 Votes, AGAINST: 22 Votes

Was I alone in thinking that these results were rather interesting? Objectively speaking, Sudou was the only person who would unequivocally vote against her expulsion. Next in line would likely be Kouenji, since Horikita was his sole ally. He wouldn't want to let her go. On the flip side, this meant that the other students had voted purely after asking themselves if they were for or against Horikita's removal. Horikita's presence was deemed not that important to the invisible sixteen who voted against her. However, I supposed there might have been some segment of that group that would just be fine with anyone getting expelled, as long as they weren't.

"What the hell, are you all stupid?!" bellowed Sudou. He shot up out of his seat in frustration. "Whoever voted in favor, put your hands up! Imma knock your lights out!" He probably assumed there would've only been a few votes in favor at most.

"Stop, Sudou-kun," said Horikita.

"Like hell I can!" he shot back.

"You making a fuss is only going to waste time," she told him. "Let's have a more constructive conversation."

"Horikita-san's exactly right, Sudou-kun," said Yousuke. "Unanimity is the ironclad rule for this special exam. Even if there are thirty-seven votes in favor, as long as you continue to vote opposed, Horikita-san won't be expelled."

He was right, there was no need for Sudou to get so upset. Just as Yousuke said even if you were dissatisfied with things, it'd be fine as long as you kept just one person on your side. That alone would absolutely prevent you from being expelled.

That was another peculiarity of this exam. Just a single vote... With just one unwavering vote *Against* as your defense, the fate of expulsion could be avoided. On the other hand though, if you lost that one final vote, there'd be nothing you could do to prevent it anymore.

"We really don't have that much time left," said Keisei. "It's about time you tell us the name of the student that originally voted in favor."

"I know," I said. "But before I do, I'd like to make a suggestion."

"A suggestion?"

"Yeah. I will give you a name now, but it's not like I'll be able to just give a statement and that'll be that. If I happen to be wrong about this, I won't be able to just wave it away and say it was just a rumor."

"That's... Well, yes, that's true," said Keisei.

"That's why I'm not going to just casually say it. And on the flip side, if it turns out that I got the wrong person, I will take responsibility for it and drop out myself."

"Wha... Kiyotaka?!" sputtered Kei.

The class exploded into an uproar when they heard me say that.

"A-are you really sure about this?" said Kushida. "Ayanokouji-kun, you... I don't want any of my classmates to be expelled... And that includes you too, Ayanokouji-kun, you know...?"

"Thanks for your concern, Kushida. But I'm okay," I replied.

"Wait, you say that you'll drop out, but Karuizawa-san is going to vote against your expulsion, right, Ayanokouji-kun? So that would mean—"

"I won't let her," I said, cutting Kushida off. "Taking responsibility also means that I'll prevent anyone from voting against me. If the time comes, I will have Kei vote in favor of my expulsion. Okay?"

"...I-I understand. But I still have faith that it's never gonna come to that," said Kei.

"I certainly accept what Kushida said about me, to a certain extent," I added. "I was the one who encouraged the rest of the class to vote in favor of the issue, so I should take part of the blame. However, I'm still of the opinion that the person who stubbornly voted anonymously in favor of the issue the whole time should be the one to take responsibility for this."

"Yeah, that's right!" Kei came to my defense. "I mean, come on, this means there's someone in this class who thought they'd be all sneaky and take advantage of this thing being anonymous to get somebody expelled, right?"

"I-I think so too!" said Airi. "That's the person who... should take responsibility for this."

"Yeah, you got that right," Haruka agreed. "It's the student who voted in favor all this time who is the bad guy here."

Airi and Haruka offered me support. Akito joined in as well, silently coming to my defense.

"So, have you...made up your mind then?" Kushida gave me one final warning with an anxious look.

"If I'm going to be naming names, then I need to have my mind appropriately made up and pay the appropriate price," I replied. "More importantly though, I can speak up and say this, risking my own expulsion, because I'm as close to 100 percent certain as I can possibly be."

"I-I understand," said Kushida. "In that case, I trust you, Ayanokouji-kun."

As Kushida said that, she kept a strong gaze fixed on me. Since I was delaying the timing of my announcement, drawing it out like this further increased the other students' interest. Apart from the one student who had actually voted in favor of the issue this whole time, the rest were anxious and on the edges of their seats. They were waiting impatiently to hear the name of the person who had been voting *For*. They wanted a good reason to attack somebody and were waiting for the time to come, when they would shower shouts of abuse until their throats went hoarse.

"That person is—"

The person I thought should be expelled. The person I had decided to expel. I was going to reveal everything right here and now.

"—Kushida. You."

A silence fell over the classroom. We were now in a world where sound had completely disappeared; you couldn't even hear the ringing in your ears.

I know, Horikita. I understand almost painfully well the reason you concluded that you had no other choice but to vote in favor, and why you still couldn't take the plunge.

However, Kushida hadn't taken any steps to meet Horikita partway. She continued to cast her vote in favor of the issue without a care, determined to get either Horikita or I expelled like this. Whether or not she realized that it had been a bad move on her part was a trivial matter now.

I decided that it was pointless to try and rehabilitate Kushida, but you wanted to face her head-on until the end. You kept yourself from saying her name for so long, even considering sacrificing the class as a possibility. You may not have been able to save Kushida, but there was no need for you to sacrifice her on your own.

I didn't know what Horikita was thinking in this exact moment, but she was looking over at me much more calmly than I had expected. If that was the case, I had no choice but to fight. I'd be the one to carry the burden of defeating this opponent.

"Huh...?"

It wasn't just Kushida who said that. The word just spilled out of nearly every student's mouth in unison. They were unable to understand what was happening.

"M-me?" sputtered Kushida., pointing to herself. She couldn't believe that her name had been called.

Actually, I was sure that she was already expecting me to call her name. That was exactly why she launched that preemptive strike—she was preparing for it. But even so, I guess that Kushida just couldn't believe I would really sell her out like this. Perhaps even more so now that she thought she had a few things over me.

"That's right," I replied. "You were the one who stubbornly voted in favor all this time, even when you were being encouraged to vote *Against*."

Our classmates had been ready to attack whoever the mystery voter was but were at a loss for words.

"M-maybe you're... Maybe you're naming me because I said that you or Horikita-san should take responsibility, Ayanokouji?" said Kushida.

Hondou, seeing Kushida's eyes welling up with sorrowful tears, quickly rushed to her defense. "N-no matter how many times you say it, Ayanokouji...there's no way it could have been Kushida-chan! You're just doing this because you have a grudge."

"That has nothing to do with it," I said. "I was already

thinking that it was her before she even mentioned me. I've been thinking it ever since the first round of voting on this issue."

"W-wait a minute," protested Kushida. "I've been voting *Against* up until the very last minute, you know? So why would..."

"You're suggesting I'm making a false accusation? Well, I suppose it's only natural it would look that way, under the circumstances."

It was clear that anyone would look at what I was doing as a random outburst out of retaliation because I was about to be expelled from school.

"There's no proof that you kept voting against the issue," I went on. "And that's because the voting was anonymous, of course. However, that being said, I'm going to present what grounds I have for saying that you're the person who has been voting in favor all this time. Do you have any objections?"

"That is just so awful... There's nothing I can say to that," said Kushida. "Yes, I was the person who brought up your name and Horikita-san's names first... I was prepared for what was going to come though. Because I decided that even if you slandered me with lies, I was going to sacrifice myself to protect the class."

No matter what Kushida said from here onward, it

was all going to be lies. By putting up that line of defense now, she would be able to keep her supporters from leaving her.

"First, I'll tell you the reason I think that Kushida was the one who continued to vote in favor of the issue. That's because there are people in this class who she desperately wants to have expelled. I'm sure you're not going to believe me on this, of course, but just hear me out. The people she wants gone are the people Kushida herself already mentioned by name, meaning Horikita and myself."

A considerable number of people were just wondering what in the world I was talking about. Kushida should have been more distraught than anyone else right now... Well, I supposed she was keeping up appearances by looking distraught, but this was a debate where you couldn't make even a single mistake.

She calmly spoke up once more, choosing her words very carefully. "So, since I gave your names earlier, that's how this is going to be, huh..." she said sadly.

"No, it's not like that," I said. "More than anyone else, Kushida, you've thought of Horikita as an obstacle ever since she started school here."

Now that it came to this, I was sure that Kushida should understand what was happening, even if she didn't want to. I was about to disclose everything I knew about her right here and now, and she couldn't order me to stop. If she was continuing to play the part of the innocent good little girl, there was no way for her to cut me off.

"Kushida," I said. "You and Horikita have something in common that you don't share with the rest of your classmates. Isn't that right?"

"Huh? S-something in common...?" she asked.

Even though she already knew what I meant, it was necessary for her to act like she was ignorant, at least for the time being. I could have interrupted her act, but I deliberately decided not to. That was because Kushida's instinct to protect herself would cause her to suffer more from here onwards.

"Um... Oh, are you maybe talking about, um...that we went to the same junior high? Or something?" she asked.

It was likely that no one else knew about that. Looks of surprise appeared on our classmates' faces as they heard this for the first time. She had no choice but to reveal that bit of information herself now. It was something she had been desperately trying to keep hidden at all costs up until now, rather than letting me divulge it.

"That's right," I replied. "I'm sure that no other student in this classroom knew about that, did they?"

Horikita, the very person we were talking about, was now staring straight ahead at the podium so I couldn't see the expression on her face. However, I could easily tell that our classmates' gazes were on me.

"W-wait, hold on a moment," Kushida said. "What? It's true that I hadn't told anyone about it, but it was just because I didn't have an opportunity to bring it up specifically. Besides, it was a big school. We were never in the same class, anyway... It even took me a while to make sure that Horikita-san even went to my same school."

Kushida was saying that there was no way she could have even considered wanting to expel Horikita from the beginning based on that.

At this point, students who couldn't just sit by and watch Kushida go through this started to act.

"All right, knock it off, Ayanokouji," said Ike. "You said that you knew whoever voted in favor, so I shut up and listened to you. But come on, this is Kikyou-chan, y'know? There's just no way."

Other voices quickly joined in, one after another.

"Yeah, that's right. Ayanokouji-kun, isn't what you're saying here just absurd?"

"Like, seriously? You were the one who got us all to vote in favor, and in the end you're just taking your anger out on Kushida-san and pointing a finger at her. Come on!"

"Okay, and 'sides, how the heck does going to the same junior high means she wants her expelled in the first place? Wait, or are you trying to say that you went to their same junior high too?"

Our classmates were posing perfectly reasonable questions. Discontent and protests erupted, starting with just one person and growing from there. The troops rallied around her one after another without even being asked. There was no doubt whatsoever that this was a powerful weapon that Kushida Kikyou had in her arsenal.

"And besides, since when were you like this, anyway? Something has been weird with you for a while now, Ayanokouji."

"Y-yeah, that's true. It's actually kind of scary, I mean... He always had this quiet vibe about him, and yet..."

Some of the students weren't just covering for Kushida, they also began to show distrust toward me and my unusual behavior.

"Don't criticize him, everyone..." Kushida said. "I'm sure that Ayanokouji-kun doesn't want to be saying this stuff either. I understand it's tempting to lay the blame on someone in a situation like this..."

She picked up on our classmates' words with exquisite precision, attacking me while pretending to protect me.

"You're way too nice, Kikyou-chan. You can't just let him say whatever he wants."

Kushida's supporters lashed out automatically, nearly stripping me of my right to speak. But I had a weapon of my own to allow me to resist.

"Ayanokouji-kun has the floor right now," said Yousuke, cautioning any student who would try to interfere. "We shouldn't interrupt him while he has more to say."

"Seriously, get real, Hirata. What's even the point of listening to Ayanokouji's lies anymore?"

"We should only offer our criticisms, about whether it's the truth or a lie after he's said his piece," Yousuke said. "Of course, if what he says does turn out to be a lie, I will not allow it either."

"Is it even worth listening to him?"

"Yes, it is," Yousuke insisted. "This isn't just going to affect Kushida-san because she was named. This is going to greatly affect Ayanokouji-kun's own academic career here. Isn't that right?"

I had told Yousuke there was a possibility I'd control the votes if our time remaining was running out. There was no way he could've known in advance what this issue was going to be, and naturally he was incredibly surprised about this whole conversation about Kushida. As a purely neutral person, he would have to judge things so that there wouldn't be any errors in our conclusions.

"This has nothing to do with where they came from," I said. "Or rather, there isn't much significance to the fact that they came from the same school. However, the truth of the matter is that Kushida has a big secret, from back when she was in junior high."

Kushida started to cry right on the spot. "Please, stop it, Ayanokouji-kun... Stop piling on lie after lie..." Tears rolled down her cheeks.

"Hey, come on, Kiyopon," Haruka spoke up. "Look, I'm your friend and all, but... I think I'm with Kyou-chan on this one. What I'm trying to say is, is this *really* a conversation we need to continue?"

Haruka was originally a member of the Ayanokouji Group and would defend me, as I said earlier. Haruka had few friends outside of our group, but I knew she and Kushida got along well. Wouldn't it make sense that she'd try to stop this conflict if she cared about the both of us?

"Haruka," I said. "You were waiting for the identity of the anonymous supporter to be revealed, weren't you? If so, then you need to hear everything I have to say."

"B-but, I mean, Kyou-chan is..."

"'Not like that'? I understand why you'd think so, but Kushida is not who you think she is. I'm sorry, but I'm going to ask that you let me keep going. Her secret lies in her true nature, which she keeps hidden."

"Kyou-chan's...true nature?" Haruka repeated.

"That's right," I replied. "The Kushida you see, on the surface, appears to be a good person in everyone's eyes. She's kind, considerate, and a perfect model student. She's someone who is capable both academically and in sports. But what if she was, in fact, the sort of person who was more jealous than anyone else, and only satisfied being the best? What if, as a result of her true nature being revealed during her junior high days, she drove her class to destruction?"

"Honestly? I'd say it'd be impossible to believe," said Yousuke. "But even if that were true, it just doesn't add up. It's true that in Horikita-san's case, if she went to her same school, then she might know about her past, sure. But how would you know about it, Ayanokouji-kun? I can't imagine Horikita-san would tell you."

"That's because I had the opportunity to see Kushida's true nature shortly after we started school," I answered. "I witnessed Kushida acting differently, venting her negative emotions."

Even after everything I had said so far, Kushida hadn't done so much as glare at me. She continued to play the rule of the kind, innocent, good girl just watching a mean classmate tell lies about her. She thought highly of herself and believed that as long as she kept this up, she'd absolutely be fine. Of course, having someone speak poorly of you is bad, regardless if it was true or false, and it would cast a shadow over the remainder of your school life. But this was also a sign of her strong will—she was willing to make a small sacrifice here if it meant getting either Horikita or I expelled.

"Kushida wants to be thought of as a kind person, so she wants to avoid letting people find out about how she really is," I continued. "That being said, she can't stomach being put in a situation where her weakness is sitting in my and Horikita's palms. That's because she wants to be the person holding the power, standing above others, always."

"...You have about one more minute remaining until the interval ends." Chabashira interrupted our discussion to notify us that time was almost up, just in case.

"Wh-what are we gonna do?" exclaimed Sudou. "It's almost time for the next vote!"

"That's... Well, I guess for the time being, we'll just have to hold a vote for me then," I said. "Won't we?"

With the current situation being what it was, I figured it was obvious I was going to be next in line.

"Stop—!"

However, someone stopped me. It wasn't Kei or even Haruka. It was Kushida.

"That's enough... My heart can't take any more of this..." she said.

"K-Kushida-san?" said Yousuke.

"If I'm speaking from the heart here, my opinion still hasn't changed... I don't want either Horikita-san or Ayanokouji-kun to be expelled," she said. "I even made Ayanokouji-kun go as far as to lie about me because I brought up their names earlier in the discussion... I don't want to go through this stressful, painful argument anymore. That's why... I'll... I'll drop out... If I do that, then everyone can go back to how they were before, right?"

Kushida volunteered as an expulsion candidate herself. According to the special exam's rules for selecting a person to be expelled, a person was allowed to come forward and nominate themselves. That nomination would be accepted without the need for a vote, as demonstrated by Horikita and Yousuke earlier.

"Are you sure about this, Kushida? Once you say you're nominating yourself, you can't take it back," I told her.

"Yes, it's all right, I don't mind... Please, everyone, vote for me to be expelled, okay? Please..."

Now that Kushida's name was entered, a new issue was displayed on our tablets. Kushida's unexpected self-nomination had clearly upset our classmates.

Round 19 Voting Results: FOR: 5 Votes, AGAINST: 33 Votes

Time passed and we voted. The results showed that the class overwhelmingly opposed her proposal.

"E-everyone... Why?" asked Kushida.

"Because there's no way we could ever get you expelled, no matter what, Kushida-chan," said Hondou. "Right?"

The thirty-three students who opposed her expulsion nodded their heads in response, as a strong show of their solidarity.

"Ayanokouji," Hondou added. "I honestly think it's gross that you've been attacking Kushida-chan just so you don't get expelled yourself."

Putting aside my single vote in favor of expelling Kushida, only four other students seemed to agree with me. Well, while I would have liked to have said "only" four, but to be completely honest, I was surprised that there were even five votes against her.

"Ayanokouji-kun's turn next then, right?"

It was true that if things continued as they were, there was going to be a vote for me with my expulsion on the line. If that time came, given the current situation, I could expect the possibility that the class would unanimously vote in favor of my expulsion. However, that was only if they could come to a decision on that within the next ten minutes.

"Ayanokouji-kun, I hear what you're saying, that Kushida-san's true nature is different from how she is normally. It's not like we can just suddenly believe that, though."

"Yeah. Besides, has Kushida-san really even tried doing anything to get Horikita-san expelled before? If she really wanted Horikita-san gone, she would've done something a long, long time ago, wouldn't she?"

I knew that if I waited for just the right opportunity, people would naturally ask me what I had to say.

"Because it's not easy to get a classmate expelled," I replied. "But you know, I've been Kushida's target at least once before too, in an exam structured like this Unanimous Special Exam."

Without saying it out directly, I was able to make my classmates dig deep through their own memories, with their own hands.

"Oh, the class vote thing... If I remember right, at the time, Yamauchi-kun and Kushida-san were..."

That's right. We had a vote in our classes for the first time last year to expel one of our classmates. As a result of that exam, Yamauchi had been expelled. However, Kushida was one of the people that had been guiding him along, trying to use him to get me expelled. The events of that exam were likely still fresh in everyone's minds.

"Do you think it's a coincidence?" I asked. "Both times that we've had this kind of test, I've been targeted for expulsion. And on top of that, Kushida was involved both times. Everything lines up far too neatly for it to be mere coincidence."

If the others remembered what happened at the time, then surely, they must have thought that something was strange about Kushida then.

"It's true that I thought it was just a coincidence. Still, Ayanokouji, if Kikyou-chan were intentionally trying to get you expelled, why would she be carrying out such a plan now after doing that?"

The student was arguing that she would have done this more cleverly then to avoid suspicion in the future, but things weren't so simple.

"It's because Kushida thought that I was on her side. I doubt she had any idea whatsoever that her secrets might be exposed like this." I turned to her. "Isn't that right?"

"...On my side?" she repeated.

"Yeah. Or do I have it wrong, Kushida?"

"...I really don't know what to do here, Ayanokouji-kun... What kind of answer are you looking for from me?"

Basically, Kushida could only either deny what I said or turn around and ask me a question. If she didn't affirm, then that meant the initiative would always sit with me.

"Give us some proof, Ayanokouji." Hondou bullishly came to her defense. "If you're gonna lay the blame on Kushida-chan any further, we are definitely gonna need some proof."

From the sounds of it, he apparently had intense feelings for Kushida.

"You're right," I said. "It's true that it's probably pointless for me to keep going on about this without presenting anything. So, right now, I'm going to tell you the reason Kushida trusted me."

I didn't hurry. I took my time, letting everything I said sink in as everyone listened.

"This happened a long time ago. After Kushida threatened me, I made a contract with her that I would give her half of my Private Points every month in exchange for her not trying to get me expelled."

Even the faction that supported Kushida looked slightly shocked when they heard this story, a story that no one could have possibly imagined.

"Isn't that right, Kushida?" I asked.

"Huh...?"

Either she hadn't expected this to come up or she just hadn't decided how to respond to it if it did, even though it was already floating around in the back of her mind. At any rate, Kushida was at a loss for words. She couldn't honestly admit that she's been getting additional Private Points, but on the other hand, it would also be difficult for her to deny that she had been receiving them.

Even if she could manage to fool everyone else into thinking that she wasn't getting points from me, the truth would come out if someone asked to confirm it later. That was because there were records in her account history that someone had been transferring points to her, and how many were transferred.

"So, what do you have to say? Can you say with absolute certainty that you haven't received a single point from me?"

"That's—"

I wasn't going to let her take her time. Just as I was about to shoot a look over to Chabashira, Kushida gave me her answer, her lips quivering.

"Y-yes, it's true that...I have been getting Private Points from Ayanokouji-kun every month..."

Kushida had denied most everything that I had said up until that point, but she had no choice but to admit it this time. If I were to turn and check with Chabashira right here and the teacher confirmed that she could see points had been changing hands, then there'd be no avoiding the fact. It would make the situation get much, much worse for Kushida in an instant. It was doubtful whether Chabashira, as a teacher, knew exactly how many points were changing hands between individuals at any given moment or if she would divulge personal information like that, but Kushida still couldn't bet against that risk.

"B-but...it's for a completely different reason! It's because Ayanokouji-kun came to me. He said that he wanted me to hold onto the points for him... I haven't even used a single one of those points, of course. You see?"

She was receiving half of my Private Points each month, and there were one or two ways at most that she could try to justify or explain that away. She could either say that she had been asked to hold onto them, as she did just now, or she could claim that they were freely given to her. Those were the only reasons she could give. If she had claimed the latter, that they were freely given to her, then she would have to supplement that claim. So, in a situation like this, someone would almost always say that they had been asked to hold onto the points in a situation like that.

"I didn't give them to you to hold onto," I replied. "I was paying the price you had set so you wouldn't get me expelled."

"That's a lie..."

The deal we made was that I would give her half of my Private Points. I was sure that Kushida remembered that quite well. She even carefully recorded our conversation, preserving the memory of that day. However, I could shut her down, preventing her from using it, depending on how this situation unfolded. If anything, that recording could end up doing the opposite of what she intended. I could turn it into a deadly weapon that would end up piercing her instead.

"A lie, huh?" I said. "But Kushida, you told me that you recorded our conversation, for insurance purposes back when we made our agreement. Did you not? If we get that recording from your phone or whatever device you used, you won't be able to talk your way out of this."

"R-recording? I-I don't know anything about that..."

Though she was being pressured, she continued to deny it for now. She probably saved the recording somewhere, but apparently it wasn't on her phone. I guess she probably didn't walk around carrying risky recorded data around with her. Well, this would have gone much more quickly if she did have it, but that didn't matter.

"Even if you hid the recording somewhere we don't know about, it's all the same in the end, Kushida. We formed a contract earlier this year, in February. I also recorded the details of the conversation we had at that time. That way, if anything went wrong, I could use it as a weapon."

Kushida looked at me and her eyes went wide. She probably didn't think I'd do that.

"I listened to the recording over and over and have it memorized, word for word. 'I'll give you half. Half of all of the Private Points I get moving forward.' I believe that's what I started with when I made the offer."

"You're lying," Kushida protested. "I've never heard you say that."

"You responded by saying, 'It's certainly not a bad offer, I suppose. But unfortunately, I'm not really hurting for Private Points. It's certainly better to have more money than none, but I'm fine where I am now.'"

"...I don't know what you're talking about," she insisted.

"If you prefer, I can go ahead and ask Chabashira-sensei to bring me my cell phone right now?" I asked.

"I don't really mind," said Kushida. "But you can't do that, can you? We're in the middle of a special exam right now."

"I mean, of course they confiscated our phones since students could cheat if they had them," I agreed. "But

I can ask Chabashira-sensei to use my phone and play back the recording for us. That way, there wouldn't be any concern over me using my phone to cheat."

Of course, I didn't expect that I'd be granted any exceptions to the rules during a special exam. Still, Kushida, overcome with anxiety, couldn't help but direct her gaze to Chabashira at the front of the classroom.

"If she takes out my phone, then you're going to be in trouble. All the hard work you've put in so far to desperately fool everyone will go up in smoke. But you already know that I'm not going to stop there, don't you?"

Kushida was talking less and less. I had to wonder what she was thinking right now. Her back was to me, and her eyes were fixed on the front of the room like she had been frozen in place. Kushida remembered what happened that day, of course. And, being the cautious person that she was, I was sure that she must have checked the audio file herself to make sure that she had a clear recording. She too had listened to it repeatedly.

Since I had come out and uttered parts of our conversation word for word, I was sure that at least some of what I had said must have matched the audio that she saved that day.

"'You might have more than enough points to use for spending money, it's never a bad thing to have more tucked away for an emergency,'" I said, quoting another part of our conversation.

A tremendous change was unmistakably happening in Kushida right now. She was playing the victim up until this point, but she had reached the point where it was no longer possible for her to continue to pose like she was an angel in this class.

"God... Just shut up already..." she huffed.

Our classmates gulped. They just heard a voice that they couldn't understand, making them wonder just who that was. The only way for her to stop me from talking more was to reveal her true nature. But if she showed her true nature, then everything would fall apart.

"'Chabashira-sensei said as much too, I believe. That Private Points may become necessary in order to protect yourself,'" I said, reciting the other part of what I said.

"Shut up, shut up, shut up..."

I continued speaking, without paying any care to Kushida's attempts to reject what I was saying or to stop me.

"'No matter how I look at this proposal of yours, it looks like you're putting yourself at a disadvantage, Ayanokouji-kun. If you said that you were in danger of being expelled from school, then I could understand, I suppose.' That was what you said before we made our deal. I'm sure that if I can have the rest of the class listen to the audio, right here, right now, that'll settle the matter once and for all."

Whether I actually had the recording wasn't really all that important. It was more the fact that what I was saying now matched what we had said in our conversation before was both necessary and important.

"Enough already!!!" Kushida screamed. And then she fell silent again.

I knew she must've been feverishly going back over what happened back then. As for why we formed a contract, it happened because I wanted to know some first-year students' weaknesses, their embarrassing secrets. Since I figured Kushida would have known any number of our classmates' secrets, I went to her, and we formed a contract. When she asked me about quid pro quo, I offered to give her half of my Private Points in exchange for helping me.

I had no doubts whatsoever that the part of our conversation before I made the proposal, when Kushida expressed her wish for Horikita and me to be expelled, would be in the recording. Kushida likely thought that the audio would be a convenient card for her to play, but it was turning out to be a huge mistake. All she did was leave behind a trail of evidence that would end up strangling her.

"Please tell me specifically, right now, where in our conversation I suggested that I wanted you to hold onto my points for me," I said. "I want to make sure that everyone in class understands."

Kushida's friends were hoping that this was all some sort of mistake. They watched her anxiously.

"...I'm sorry." Kushida mumbled a brief apology.

"What are you saying sorry for, exactly?" I asked.

"Yes, it's true that I promised I wouldn't fight with Ayanokouji-kun in exchange for half of his Private Points," she confessed. "That's... That is true, which is why..."

She wasn't apologizing to me. She was apologizing to our classmates, admitting that she had been lying.

"B-but... I don't think that way anymore! I really do want to be friends with Horikita-san and Ayanokouji-kun. Truly. That's why I never voted in favor of..."

Just as Kushida was about to appeal to everyone, attempting to capitalize on the total anonymity of the exam, she suddenly stopped. Our classmates' eyes had changed drastically. The warm looks they had been giving her until now were gone. Even if she really wasn't the student who had originally voted in favor, it would no longer be possible for her to go about her daily life as she had been. Kushida seemed to understand that completely. But as she looked over at me and there was still life in her eyes.

"Isn't the truth here that...you were really the one voting in favor all this time, Ayanokouji-kun?" she said.

"What do you mean?" I asked.

"You wanted to get me expelled, Ayanokouji-kun. That's why you acted, to force things toward a unanimous decision in favor. After all, it's strange, isn't it? It's funny that you're always so quiet and unassertive, but now you're spontaneously working to get someone expelled..."

Kushida was, to many, almost certainly the true offender. However, she was now attempting to shift the blame away from her and onto me. *Sorry, Kushida, but I already counted on you to try and use that strategy.*

"Hey, Karuizawa-san." Kushida brushed back her hair as she turned her gaze to Kei.

"What," said Kei, tersely.

"It sounds like you and Ayanokouji-kun are going out. Did you know that when we started school here, Ayanokouji-kun desperately came on to me because he wanted to go out with me?"

"...What are you talking about?" said Kei. "What is this?"

Kei was able to see things more calmly and objectively than the average person, but even she had her weaknesses. Namely, when romantic feelings were involved, her uncontrollable emotions exploded. Even when I nominated myself as a candidate for expulsion earlier, Kei assertively spoke up in my defense, even though she knew the risks. Kushida must have spotted an exploitable weakness in Kei's heart then.

"I didn't want him to, but when we were in the dark, he even touched my breasts," Kushida went on. "Did you know that?"

"Wh... Y-your breasts?! Wh-what does she mean by that, Kiyotaka?!" shouted Kei.

"You really didn't know about that? He did such a horrible thing to me right after we started school here," said Kushida.

Starting with the guys who had taken a liking to her and then spreading to the girls in class, a wave of disgust toward me began to spread.

"I tried to stop him then. I gently admonished him... But I was so scared, I couldn't do anything..."

"I know this might sound self-serving, but the truth is I never touched your breasts," I cut in.

"S-see?!" Kei exclaimed. "That's what Kiyotaka says!"

"That's true, but that's all he can say in this situation," Kushida replied. "But Ayanokouji-kun really did touch my breasts."

"Kushida," I said. "I hate to say this, but isn't this kind of shameful for you to do?"

"It might not be like the recording we talked about earlier, but I have evidence of my own," she insisted. "I have the uniform with Ayanokouji-kun's fingerprints all over it. I kept it as it was back then. What would happen if I were to present it here? You know what I'm getting at, right?"

Just as I used the cell phone recording, she was trying to do something similar back to me. If her claims were later proven to be true, I would be the one in a tight spot.

"Explain to me what's going on," said Kei.

She was listening to this story objectively, and it made sense that she would want an explanation for this.

"There isn't a shred of truth to it," I told her. "At any rate, there's something else I wanted to comment on, before even getting to whether it's true or false. You mentioned having clothes with fingerprints on them, but how well-preserved are they? If this happened right after we started school, then that means a year and a half has already passed. It's not easy to pull fingerprints from clothes, and on top of that, if they aren't well-preserved, then of course you're not going to get anything from them. I find it highly unlikely that you would be able to get fingerprints from that uniform."

Even clothing has uneven surfaces due to the stitching, and that would make it difficult to see fingerprint marks. And considering other factors such as exposure to ultraviolet rays, humidity, dryness, etc., I could say that it would be 100 percent impossible to get prints off them.

"...Ngh."

Just like the recordings you have, none of the cards in your hand are viable. The same goes for whatever others you have, no matter how many there are. You can't just come up with any excuse and try to talk your way out of this. I won't allow it.

"Besides," I added, "if you really had been victimized like that in the first place, then you should have reported it immediately."

"Why... Why... Why... Why...?!"

Kushida came up next to me and grabbed me by the collar. Her glare was intense. She was furious, but I simply continued to talk to her in a matter-of-fact manner.

"And then there's one time you worked with Ryuuen to try and get Horikita and me expelled. What about that?"

I exposed Kushida's deeds to the class one after another, bringing them into the light of day. Even if I provided new information here that was partly wrong, it likely wouldn't make a noticeable impact.

"Why? *Why?!*" she screamed, gripping onto my uniform even more tightly. "Why are you betraying me?!?! Did you forget that you promised not to antagonize me?!"

"I never had any intention of antagonizing you, of course," I told her. "I wasn't even interested in the fact that you have a two-sided personality. That was why I wanted to come to a unanimous decision, *Against*, without my or Horikita's names coming out. But since someone must be expelled, I had no other choice. I'm doing this to protect my classmates."

With a few simple words, the false bonds that Kushida had created with her "friends" she had steadily accumulated over the past year and a half all came crashing down in an instant. No one could say anything.

Kushida relaxed, beginning to calm down. "Oh... Well... It's hopeless, then," she said. "It's over."

There was a look of resignation on her face, as if she understood everything now. Her face contorted in disgust at her shame. But then she quickly regained her composure, stifled a chuckle, and removed her hands from my collar.

She sighed. "Ugh... I guess this means I really was an idiot, after all. That deal was a huge mistake..." Kushida's anger dissipated in an instant and now she spoke in a calm, detached way. "I thought I understood that you were a formidable opponent, Ayanokouji-kun, but I still never imagined that you'd betray me here. It was just outside my expectations, I guess."

"Y-you're kidding, Kikyou-chan... Everything Ayanokouji-kun said just now was a lie...wasn't it?"

"A lie?" asked Kushida. "Unfortunately, no, it's all true."

"But... Why...?"

"Because some things must be protected at all costs, no matter the sacrifice. Don't you understand that? Forget it, there's no way you'd understand." Kushida sighed again. "Ugh... I'm done with all of it now."

She shrugged her shoulders and spoke confidently, like she couldn't feel her own predicament. "It's true. I couldn't *stand* Horikita-san and Ayanokouji-kun being around. I couldn't forgive them for knowing the secret I kept hidden. I've been trying to get them expelled for some time now."

"I was certainly surprised to see what this last issue was," I said, "but even so, you surely knew it wasn't going to be easy to get us removed, right? You knew what would happen if you tried to force things, didn't you?"

Even if she hated us, she still would have had plenty of time to pull back. She didn't have to rush here. But even so, Kushida continued to vote in favor of the issue, a repeated action that could have been described as crazed. To that point, I had this nagging feeling that this was rather out of character for her.

At that moment, Kushida's eyes darted around a bit,

and she seemed shaken. It quickly faded. Before the special exam, Kushida asked Horikita to be the leader of the class. It was almost as though she was anticipating that an issue like this was going to be on the exam, but...

"It didn't really matter... I just couldn't stand the situation. People kept finding out about my past," Kushida sighed. "I knew it was going to be extremely difficult to get Horikita-san expelled. But I couldn't resist the urge to try anyway."

Even the students who continued to stand up for Kushida could no longer find the words to speak. Still, her friends couldn't take too much blame over what happened, even if the truth was that Kushida really had been planning to get Horikita expelled. Kushida was still guilty of making the class take the route of expelling someone by continuously voting in favor of the issue. Even so, it was difficult to say whether that was enough to get the class to vote unanimously in favor of expelling her. To make sure that she absolutely was removed from the class, we would need her to cause even more damage.

"You can't get Horikita or I expelled," I told her. "Too bad."

"I guess that settles that. I'll be expelled in the next vote," she said. "So, by sacrificing me, you'll get Class Points, right? Good for you, everyone. I guess you'll be able to become Class B thanks to this."

She spoke to everyone in such a detached tone that it was impossible to imagine that she had been good friends with all of them just until this afternoon.

"There's no way you can turn the tables any longer," I replied.

"Ah ha ha, yeah, you're probably right about that. But..." Kushida paused there for a moment. Then she brought her face in close, approaching my neck, and whispered to me coldly. "...I can at least show a little resistance, can't I?"

Even though she spoke in a whisper, it was still loud enough for other students in the class to hear. It was safe to assume that Kushida was already emotionally prepared for this without the need for me to provoke her.

"It's pointless," I told her. "You don't have any friends who will vote against your expulsion anymore."

"You're right, I don't. But if I'm going to be expelled anyway... I just need to destroy everything on my way out."

Kushida's true nature, the thing which had caused her entire class to fall apart during her junior high school days, was emerging.

"...What are you saying?" I asked.

"Don't you understand? There are secrets in this class that only I know. And there's still time left in this interval. I figure I'll go ahead and tell everyone everything."

"You won't gain anything by doing that, though... right?" I asked.

"But I won't lose anything either," she argued. "I'm sure this is going to cause trouble for you too, Ayanokouji-kun, so I think I'll go ahead and get started."

Yes, that's good. Let out all the secrets and the stress that you have been holding onto and letting build up. I'm sure everyone will be shocked and terrified by how twisted you are. Only when any room for sympathy disappears will there be a possibility for a unanimous decision.

"Let's see, aside from Karuizawa-san, who I touched on earlier... Oh, that's right," Kushida said. "Shinohara-san, you talked to me about lots of different things, didn't you?"

The first person chosen to be the target of the countless slings and arrows that Kushida had ready to aim at most of the girls in class was none other than Shinohara Satsuki.

"Wh-wh-what?!" squawked Shinohara.

"Shinohara-san isn't particularly cute, huh. If anything, she's a little on the ugly side, don't you think? Maybe that's why only the unattractive guys like Ike-kun and Komiya-kun come on to her. Karuizawa-san, Matsushita-san, and

Mori-san, you all said those things. You found it *so* funny, and you were all laughing about it, weren't you?"

One attack instantly split into many, and student after student was targeted.

"S-stop it! I never said anything like that! Stop lying!" Mori denied it immediately, but Kushida had no intention of laying her arms down.

"Oh? You were the one laughing the hardest about it, though. You said that they were the perfect couple. But don't worry! Even though I had a forced smile and told you to stop saying those kinds of things, I felt the same way you did."

"Is... Is that true... Nene-chan...?" asked a hurt Shinohara.

"N-no, it's... I-I just, I..." stammered Mori.

"Oh, and Shinohara-san," Kushida said. "From the sounds of things, you decided to start going out with Ike-kun after he told you how he felt about you on the boat. But I have to say... Wow! You sure made your decision quickly, considering you were going back and forth between him and Komiya-kun just before that. Or perhaps you were just going out with Ike-kun on a trial basis, to see how it went? Then, you could go after Komiya-kun instead, since he was closer to your true love."

"H-hey, Satsuki, wha—?!" flailed Ike.

There were countless bits of and pieces of information

Kushida had that she could use to burn the whole class down. Once a fire began to spread in one place, she quickly jumped over to something new, letting her words loose.

"Oh, and speaking of love and relationships, Wang-san, you came to me for advice too, didn't you?" she said.

"P-please stop!" wailed Mii-chan.

"Stop? Stop what? You mean you don't want me to say that you love Hirata-kun like crazy, so much that you can't stand it?"

"Wh—?!"

Mii-chan was suddenly forced to hear the name of the object of her affections said aloud for all to hear in the classroom. Her face immediately went bright red, and she broke down in tears when she noticed Yousuke looking at her.

"Hmm, think I'll stop with the small ones," Kushida mused. "You realized I've just been sharing the *little* secrets, right? After all, not all the things I've heard are like that. Next, let's hear something a little juicier, shall we? Oh, I've got one... How about we go with someone like you for starters, Hasebe-san?"

"...Kyou-chan..."

"Oh, stop calling me that. It's not like we're close friends," Kushida sneered. "You can't even actually make real friends. You just call people by nicknames because it makes you *feel* like you're getting to be closer to them. Besides, I'm sure it's annoying to the people you address that way."

Kushida shifted her focus to Haruka. Shinohara, and Mori and the other girls, as well as Ike and other people, continued to shout back and forth, trying to refute things. "I didn't say that." "No, what I really said was…" Everyone was pressing each other about what was true and what was a lie. The interval period would be over soon, and a unanimous decision to expel Kushida was drawing near… but if we continued to carelessly draw this situation out, Kushida would only continue to expose more and more information.

8.1

AFTER LISTENING to Ayanokouji-kun speak for only a few minutes, people's opinions of Kushida's worth had done a complete 180. It even happened with her friends, who should have had as strong a sense of solidarity as Ayanokouji-kun's group of friends. For some reason, I couldn't help but see their relationship as having been terribly fragile before this. Ayanokouji-kun's narrative was so incredibly effective that even someone like me, who knew Kushida-san's past before anyone else did, could easily move to push her out if Ayanokouji-kun asked that I make Kushida Kikyou our target. I may have just caught a glimpse of Ayanokouji-kun's power before anyone else did.

Right now, our class was like a scene from hell. The vote for Kushida-san, who would likely get a majority of the votes once the interval was over, would soon begin. This special exam was likely almost over. Our class would get 100 points, despite our sacrifice. That would be a valuable asset to us in our efforts to get to Class A, but... Yes, I needed to sort out this situation I found myself in first.

I was most definitely in the same moment in time as the rest of them, and yet time was dilating for me, little by little. The passing of each second felt drawn out. The analog clock, which even didn't look like it belonged in this classroom, was slowing down, its second-hand ticking so slowly that it almost felt like it was coming to a stop. But on the contrary, it was my senses becoming more and more heightened.

What was my purpose? I answered that question myself: to graduate from Class A, of course. That was why Class Points were so important. That was obvious. In that case, how much was Kushida-san worth? It was difficult to assign a clear value to every individual student. But at the very least, if you were to ask me if she were equal to 100 Class Points, I would immediately answer no.

In that case, I'd try shifting my thinking. If we were to fail this special exam, we would end up losing 350 Class Points. If I could protect Kushida in exchange, could I calculate that she'd be enough of an asset to be able to make up for that loss?

I didn't think it would be impossible...but it would be difficult. That answer wasn't just limited to her either; the same was true for me. Allowing Kushida-san to be expelled because she wasn't worth 350 points was a normal way of thinking. In that case, what did I, Horikita Suzune, want to do? What did I want to do about the student named Kushida Kikyou?

Did I want to save her, without thinking too much about it? Did I want to abandon her? By concentrating, I transcended time, even eliminating superfluous concepts like sound. Could I just leave everything to Ayanokouji-kun as things were right now? No, there's no way I could. *Then, think.* What was right? What was wrong? Wasn't there anything that only I could do? *Acknowledge and respect Ayanokouji-kun's abilities and think again.*

A ray of light shined through the darkness, behind my eyelids.

...Yes. I see now. I had finally arrived at just one answer. Right now, Kushida-san was going to be expelled.

And that was not the correct choice.

At that moment, I was surely the only person who could save Kushida-san. Time had come to a stop before, but it was now beginning to unfreeze.

The second hand started ticking once again.

8.2

As one student after another started to agree with the idea of Kushida being expelled, one student stood up.

"Don't go any further, Kushida-san," said Horikita. "You won't be able to take it back." Horikita.

"Huh? It was finally starting to get interesting," Kushida pouted. "Don't butt in, Horikita-san."

"I can't let this go on," Horikita insisted. "I don't think I can listen to any more of this disgraceful ranting."

"Is the real me that disgraceful?"

Perhaps Kushida took Horikita's words as a compliment. Kushida looked at her with the liveliest expression that she had worn all day.

"Well, at the very least, I don't think that exposing people like this is particularly beautiful," said Horikita.

"But it's not just you that I think is disgraceful here. The same is true for the people who are clamoring for your expulsion now that you've revealed their secrets here."

That unexpected rebuke made her classmates cry out in protest.

"Why do you say *we* are?! We didn't do anything wrong!"

"You all told Kushida-san secrets that you didn't want other people to know. Why was that?" asked Horikita.

"W-well, that's because we thought we could trust Kushida-san! But she..."

"That's right. Kushida-san was the most highly trusted person in class. Normally, it's not easy to gain the trust of others, and there are probably only a few people in your life with whom you can share secrets that you can't tell anyone else. Of course, I can't praise Kushida-san for divulging those secrets...and it's understandable for you to be surprised that she has another side to her. But that being said, *everyone* has another side to them, whether it's big or small. Don't they?"

A person who lived truthfully without any lies or falsehoods at all would certainly be quite a rarity.

"B-but...isn't the fact that she kept voting in favor still a problem? We can't forgive her for that, can we?"

"You're right," Horikita agreed. "It was a very selfish choice on her part to try to get Ayanokouji-kun or me expelled. She has to feel the heavy responsibility for that. But instead of making her pay for that by having her expelled, we can have her make use of her skills for us many times in the days to come and pay us back that way."

That was when Horikita started to convey what she really wanted to say to her classmates.

"Are you saying that you're not going to expel Kushida-san?"

"That's right. I... I want to keep Kushida-san in this class."

"Huh? Hold on, what are you babbling about now, after you interrupted me?" The first person who argued against Horikita's position to not have Kushida expelled was none other than the person in question herself.

"Why are you defending me?" asked Kushida. "You don't have anyone else here that you're going to vote for, do you? What, do you just want to have fun torturing me to death? Wow, you have *such* good taste, really."

"Unfortunately, I don't really like to make jokes," Horikita replied. "I'm being serious,."

"Well, if you say you're being serious, then I'll go ahead and change your mind for you," Kushida said. "Let's re-open the gates of Hell, shall we?"

"From what I could see, that spectacle earlier didn't look at all like 'Hell' to me," remarked Horikita.

"...Heh. Okay then, what did it look like to you? Tell me that."

"It was idiotic, comical, and frankly disgraceful. Nothing more. You looked like nothing but a fool."

"Oh?" said Kushida.

"You certainly are more academically capable than the average person, but you are fundamentally stupid to an almost fatal degree." Horikita sighed, insulting Kushida unsparingly. "To begin with, your classmates found out about your true nature when you were in junior high, so... you revealed their secrets and destroyed the class. Then, you came to this school to reflect on what happened back then, but unfortunately for you, you were reunited with me, someone who attended the same junior high. And right after starting school here, Ayanokouji-kun also happened to witness your hidden self? That makes me laugh. Not only that, he wasn't even interested in your past, but you selfishly continued to insist on trying to get us expelled, all because you couldn't stand him being here. You even told us all about it. And to top it all off, you thought you made a deal with Ayanokouji-kun, thinking you were taking advantage of him, but in the end, he turned it around and used you. And *this* is where everything ended up? You were too obsessed with trying to get us expelled by voting *For*. Instead, you had the rug pulled out from under you."

Kushida's expression had changed. Before, she had worn a vicious smirk on her face, but before anyone realized it, the look on her face transformed into the demonic fury of a woman scorned.

"You're just selfishly spouting off whatever you want!!!" she screamed. "You don't know what I feel! I want to be the best! Even though I'm feeling stressed as hell, I just want to feel happy! What's wrong with trying to make you go away when you're in the way of that?!"

"I don't know what you feel?" Horikita repeated. "How *could* I know? You're always focused solely on listening to and hoarding other people's worries. You didn't look for anyone you could talk to, to let them know what you felt."

Kushida balled both of her hands into fists, clenching them so tightly that her veins were bulging out from her skin.

"You have some personality issues, sure, but so do I," Horikita went on. "And you are a much, much harder worker than I am."

"Don't lie, it just makes me want to laugh. You always seem to say things that get on my nerves."

"I'm not lying at all. I'm telling the truth, which you seem to love. I honestly admire and envy your effort and your talent, to be able to befriend so many people, both men and women. It's honestly incredible."

When the students who were upset by Kushida heard Horikita say that, they spoke up in disagreement.

"What's so great about her?" one of them shouted. "She's been insulting us!"

"Being kind with lies? Pretending to be nice? So, she's terrible because of that?" Horikita asked. "That's honestly just frivolous nonsense. Think again just how difficult it is to be kind. Do you have the talent to smile at others? To reach out and lend an ear to everyone?"

How much stress did Kushida have to deal with daily while reaching out to her friends? Many people wanted to be like Kushida but understood that they couldn't. Even if they just cut out the part about listening to other people talk about things that they didn't care about, an ordinary person wouldn't be able to go on doing what she did. Kushida had continued to do all that with a kind smile, continuing to stand behind a substantial number of students and supporting them from behind the scenes.

"Stop," spat Kushida. "Just stop already. I don't want to hear any more of this bull from you."

"Why? You're good at seeing into people's hearts so you know, don't you? You know that I'm not trying to tease you or insult you. I sincerely do appreciate you." Horikita then preemptively blocked the other students before they could refute her, as if she were trying to get ahead of them. "She has talents that no one else does. Expelling her would be a huge loss for our class."

"Knock it off!" Kushida shouted.

Horikita continued regardless. "That is why I cannot agree to Kushida-san's expulsion. I'm willing to bet on it. I am willing to try and do everything in my power to make use of her strengths. No, I definitely *will* make the most of her strengths."

"I told you to stop!!!" howled Kushida.

"There were things about you I didn't know," added Horikita. "But once I learned everything about you was when I started to take a great liking to you."

Thinking back on it, Kushida told me about the details of her past for some reason. She wasn't trying to hide it, even though she wanted to keep it locked away. Perhaps she had done that not because she was trying to get me expelled, but because deep down, she actually *wanted* to tell people things. In fact, perhaps she wanted to share things about herself with other people.

Huge tears streamed down Kushida's face. And then, like a child, she started to sob. She was no longer able to hide her frustration and regret, nor could she string words together in a sentence. She kept repeating "No, no, no, no," over and over without end.

Of course she felt that way. Anyone who knew Kushida's true nature would leave her. I stayed away from her myself. And yet, for some reason, Horikita—someone who had kept her distance from Kushida until now—had moved closer to her. There was no way Kushida could have expected something like that to happen.

Horikita, someone that Kushida couldn't help but hate, could very well be the first one to understand her. Whether she accepted that remained to be seen, but there was no denying that this had definitely brought about a change in her. I previously determined that it would have been impossible to win Kushida over, so I produced this strategy to get rid of her. Meanwhile, Horikita had decided not only not to get rid of her, but to protect her. However, if that was what Horikita was determined to do, another inevitable problem was going to emerge.

"We're still in the middle of this discussion, but the interval period is almost over. What do we do now?" asked one student.

What should we do? Well, obviously, someone would need to nominate themselves, or we would need to recommend someone to vote on.

"We're short on time," Horikita said. "All of you who recommend we vote for Kushida-san right now, change your votes to me instead. I'll explain later."

Horikita appealed to her classmates to change their recommendations to her. She couldn't nominate herself again since she already did it once before.

"S-stop fooling around!" Kushida yelled out. "I'm going to be expelled anyway! Just recommend me and vote me out!"

"I am not fooling around," Horikita insisted. "Let me be clear. You are the one who created this situation, and you will be held accountable for it in the end. However, I will not accept your expulsion as your punishment. If you are expelled, I will continue to make fun of you for the rest of your life. I will make you into an eternal laughingstock."

I was sure that some students were still unsure of who to recommend in the end, but that wasn't important at this moment.

"It's time," announced Chabashira. "We'll now begin the vote for Horikita as she holds the majority of recommendations."

Hypothetically, even if Kushida were chosen via recommendation, it would be meaningless as long as Horikita voted against her expulsion. Cheap provocation must have worked well enough for Kushida. Everyone finished entering their votes within sixty seconds.

Round 20 Voting Results: FOR: 1 Vote, AGAINST: 37 Votes

"Now that we're in another interval period, I will reiterate my stance," Horikita said. "I am opposed to Kushida-san's expulsion."

Kushida was ranting and raving incoherently, but Horikita was no longer paying any attention to her. That further wounded Kushida's pride and seemed to have the opposite effect, successfully silencing her. If Kushida had once again become a target for expulsion, she would have no more means to oppose Horikita.

But still, this was all rather unexpected. I had been planning to screw over my opponent, no matter who they were. I felt the inside of my head getting hotter. Horikita didn't simply decide that she wanted to protect Kushida on a whim, or as a joke. She even went as far as to declare with confidence that she would overcome Kushida's major weaknesses and make the most of her strengths.

Horikita had set foot on the next stage earlier than I had expected from the looks of it. Of course, that wasn't to say that there were no objections from the other students. There were many who wouldn't mind if Kushida were expelled, since she had been propped up as the bad guy. It wasn't like Horikita couldn't force things ahead, of course, but it was difficult to imagine that Horikita would get through this easily now that she had raised the issue.

I couldn't rule out the possibility that she might force the class to choose not to expel someone by purposefully letting time run out, depending on how the situation played out. *Sorry, Horikita, that would be unacceptable.*

"But Horikita-san, will protecting Kushida-san mean we're going to choose to let time run out?" Yousuke brought up a question that needed to be answered immediately.

"I understand that protecting Kushida-san isn't the end of this," Horikita replied. "I have my own answer to that."

Don't tell me, you... Actually, wait, so that's *what you're planning, huh, Horikita?*

"We must avoid failing this special exam. So, it's absolutely imperative that someone is expelled."

This meant that Horikita was not only determined to rescue Kushida, but she was also prepared to get rid of someone else. While I did certainly sense there was growth in Horikita, I acted before she could speak. There was no need for Horikita to take on the cruel role of being the one to declare who should be removed from class.

I forcefully cut her off before she could attempt to go on. "Wait a minute."

No matter how justified Horikita might've been, making a judgment right here and now would take an intense emotional toll. I could easily brush it off as a worthwhile experience for her, but it would be a heavy burden for Horikita right now. More importantly, if she made even a single mistake, she could very well end up running out of time even if she didn't mean to.

There was no one but me who could get the class to make a unanimous decision on who to expel. Wait...no. Horikita was also giving me a certain look. That's how I understood—it was obvious that Horikita and I were thinking of the same person.

"Kushida, the only person who kept voting *For* the whole time, is the person who deserves to be expelled," I said. "However, like Horikita said, she's also a capable student. So, in that case, we'll have to consider a different approach."

"W-wait, Ayanokouji, hold on," Ike protested. "We all voted in favor of the idea because we ain't traitors to our class, right? So now we're just gonna throw all that out the window and choose someone to expel?! I can't buy this, not for one second!"

"You're not the only person unhappy about this, Ike," I told him. "We all are. But even so, we must make a decision. We have no other choice but to move forward in a way that we can describe as the fairest."

"Fairest...? How could there even be a fair way of doing this?" asked another student.

"The option of expelling someone to gain Class Points, of course," I replied. "The expulsion part tends to give a negative impression, but if certain conditions are met, we could turn the situation into a positive, as would have been the case if we were to vote for the traitor who voted in favor of the issue. If the Class Points gained are worth more than the student to be expelled, then that would mean the choice would be worthwhile. In other words, the only students we should consider expelling are ones who are not needed by the class at this point in time. If so, then what are our criteria? Well, that would probably be overall ability. We can disregard those with particular academic ability, physical ability, or other abilities that do not fall into those two categories. Putting it simply, think of students with leadership abilities like Horikita. Or students with the ability to rally a group of people, like Yousuke and Kei. Those sorts of people can inevitably be excluded from our list. Of course, if you think that I'm showing favoritism here, you are free to argue with me on those points."

With time running out, our classmates remained silent. No one dared interrupt with needless commentary.

"It's better that we don't consider future prospects here, or how things *might* turn out," I added. "Determining exactly how much someone will develop is objectively difficult and requires speculation. So, if we're going to draw a final conclusion, OAA would be an impartial means of doing so."

OAA was the school's quantification of a student's abilities that showed how capable a student was. Feelings were completely out of the equation. As of September 1, the lowest score in our class was thirty-six points overall. Although many students checked their own rank and scores from time to time, not many students knew who was in last place at any given moment.

"Right now," I said, "the student with the lowest score in OAA at this point in time is...Sakura Airi."

I didn't look over at Airi as I spoke. Instead, I scanned the entire class.

"...Huh? What are you saying...? Don't play stupid jokes at a time like this!" shouted Haruka. She was furious. Haruka stood straight up and glared at me.

"I'm just expressing my objective opinion," I told her. "The class can decide whether or not they agree with it."

I planned to continue ahead and ignore things like personal opinions.

"Objective?" yelled Haruka. "What's objective about it?! Who even cares about OAA rankings? So, what? You're saying that makes it okay to expel Airi? But why would you... Why would you say that, Kiyopon?!"

"In that case, can you think of anyone who should be expelled?" I asked.

"Th-that's—!"

"Someone who isn't prepared to name a candidate outright isn't qualified to choose if it's acceptable, nor do they have any right to," I interrupted her.

"Wh-what about someone like Ike-kun?! His academic and physical ability scores aren't that different from Airi's, right?!" argued Haruka.

It was certainly true that he was in the running for last place with Airi in OAA. But right now, he had a total of thirty-seven points. Sure, his lead was only one point, but he was still ahead of her.

"In that case, I'll simply go ahead and ask everyone for a show of hands, right here and now. All those opposed to Airi being expelled, please raise your hand," I announced.

Haruka's hand immediately shot up. Akito's and Keisei's went up at almost the same time. Of course, being members of the Ayanokouji Group, it was obvious that would be the case.

"Three people, huh. Next, what about the students who oppose Ike being expelled?" I asked.

Several guys, including Sudou and his friends, raised their hands. Several girls did too, including Shinohara,

Mori, and other girls who felt obligated to help out Shinohara. In total, there were eleven people who opposed Ike's expulsion.

"Wh-why'd..." sputtered Haruka.

"Building friendships is also an admirable skill," I replied. "I'd have to say that means she is inferior to Ike in that respect as well."

"Could you look Airi in the eyes and say that?!" wailed Haruka.

"Is that what you really want me to do?" I asked in return.

I was about to meet Airi's frightened gaze when Haruka stopped me.

"N-no! Don't!" she shouted.

"We can have a show of hands for Hondou, Okiya, or another student. But they're not going to have fewer than the three that Airi did," I told her.

"What is... You have seriously got to be kidding me," said Haruka. "Okay, sure, we don't have that many friends in our group. But that doesn't mean we can just expel Airi like this because of that!"

If there were another choice, I would have taken it, but we were long past that point now.

"But, to be completely honest...losing 300 points would be fatal."

Those quiet words had come from someone from within the Ayanokouji Group—Airi's friend Keisei.

"Yukimuu, you're seriously saying that right now?!" said Haruka. "Don't tell me you *agree* with the idea of Airi getting expelled...?!"

"N-no! I'm not for it yet!" he flailed.

"Not 'yet'? So, what? You mean that you're going to change your mind and vote for it eventually?! Is that it? I can't believe you!"

"N-no, I'm just...!" sputtered Keisei.

Then, as if she now understood everything that was going on, Haruka bit her lip and made up her mind.

"Gross. I just can't even. Seriously, what's wrong with you? I thought we were friends?" she said coldly. That wasn't just to me, but to Keisei as well as he let his true thoughts slip.

"And the same goes for the rest of you too. No one wants to protect anyone. Yeah, I said it. You're all fine as long as you save yourselves, so you don't care what happens to Airi, the person you're not friends with anyway. So, what? You're gonna prioritize Kyou-chan just because you have a little use for her? And you'll abandon a girl trying her absolute hardest, who doesn't cause any trouble for the class? Oh yeah. This totally is just the *best* class ever. Wow," said Haruka sarcastically.

Keisei's unintentional comment proved to have been careless. It completely revulsed Haruka. No other student would make eye contact with her. They shrunk back in their seats as not to get involved.

"Well, whatever. I'm not letting Airi get expelled," Haruka declared. "If you insist on it sooo much, you can go ahead and vote for me instead. I'll happily let myself be expelled."

Unlike the strategy that Kushida had gone with, Haruka was trying to protect Airi by volunteering to be expelled herself. *I already took all of that into account though, Haruka. If anything, your words just now only served to put the noose around your own neck.*

"W-wait, Haruka-chan! I can't let you get expelled either though!" wailed Airi.

"It's fine, Airi. You need to stay here at this school. I never liked this class to begin with anyway. But still, after I got to be friends with you, and Kiyopon, and Yukimuu, and Miyacchi, every day got to be fun. Even though Yamauchi-kun got expelled, I never thought something like this would happen again. I thought we could make things work, if everyone was together, but..."

Haruka then looked over at Chabashira and made a formal declaration. "I'm nominating myself for expulsion. It's almost time, isn't it?" she said.

Just as I had anticipated, Haruka announced that she would take Airi's place and voluntarily marched up to the gallows.

"Listen up, Airi," she said. "You need to vote in favor for me. And I'm sure the rest of you aren't gonna have any complaints about this, right? You can protect yourselves this way anyway, so there's no reason for you to vote against it."

"But, that's... There's no way I could vote in favor of your expulsion!" shouted Airi, telling Haruka that she couldn't do it.

"It's all right. If I get expelled protecting you, then I won't have any regrets."

"But—!"

"That's enough talking amongst yourselves," said Chabashira. "We'll now begin the vote."

Because of Haruka's strong will, we were now voting on whether we were in favor or opposed to expelling her. The results were tallied and shown up on the monitor. And they showed...

Round 21 Voting Results: FOR: 35 Votes, AGAINST: 3 Votes

Though almost every student in class voted in favor, there were three votes against. I figured it was easy for Haruka to guess who those three people were.

"Airi!" she yelled in dismay.

Of course, one of those votes had obviously come from Airi herself, without a doubt.

"But I just couldn't do it! I just... I can't expel you, Haruka-chan!" wailed Airi.

"I'm doing this to protect *you* though!" said Haruka. "And Miyacchi, Yukimuu, what the hell?!"

Haruka had been prepared to be expelled, but apparently, there were some students who didn't want that.

"I don't want you to be expelled... I couldn't vote in favor of that." Despite the look of anguish on his face, Akito looked Haruka straight in the eyes as he answered her.

"So, what, does that mean it's fine if it's Airi?!" she replied.

"I wouldn't say that... But it's just, if I had to take one over the other, then...I..." stammered Akito.

"...I'm sorry!" shouted Keisei, suddenly interrupting their conversation.

He stood up and bowed.

"I... I voted in favor... Because at this rate, our class won't...we won't be able to make it to Class A..." Keisei spoke up to tell Haruka how he voted, even though no one would've known what he voted for if he stayed silent.

"Huh? Wait, so then who was the other person?! Who was the other person who voted against?!" shouted Haruka.

"That was me," I replied.

"Wh... Kiyopon, what...?! You know you don't need to defend me, right?!"

"I already told you. As part of my newly instituted policy, I should cut the least capable student in this class. I will not be changing this policy from here on out, no matter who comes forward, whether it's someone who wants to volunteer to be expelled themselves like you, or like Kushida, who tried to get someone else expelled. I won't change it."

If I took a step back right now, we wouldn't come to a unanimous decision in favor.

"Hasebe-san... It's a fact that Sakura-san has got the lowest scores in OAA, and besides... Cutting out the student who contributes to the class the least isn't such a terrible thing, is it...?" said Matsushita, who prepared herself to take the risk of speaking up in this situation.

"You've got to be joking. Think about if it were you. If your dear friend were expelled, would you be able to laugh happily afterward? I couldn't. There's no way I could!" countered Haruka.

"Airi is the one who should be expelled. There is no other choice at this point," I told her.

"No... No, Kiyopon! No matter who else is in favor of this, Kiyopon, you... Kiyopon, you and only you need to be on Airi's side! You *have* to!" protested Haruka.

I know that. It's precisely because I know that, that I'm saying this, Haruka.

"My thinking won't change. Haruka, if you continue to go on like this, unable to agree to Airi's expulsion, then this class will have no other choice but to end things right here," I told her.

"Then why don't you just go ahead and do whatever you want, huh? I'll continue to oppose Airi's expulsion until the very end!" shouted Haruka.

Just one person. If just one person continued to vote *Against* until time ran out, then no one would be expelled. The rule was absolute. And the most effective way to break that rule was...

"Thank you, Haruka-chan... It's okay," said Airi. She smiled despite her voice trembling. It seemed like she understood everything.

"Ai...ri...?" stammered Haruka.

"If there really is someone this class doesn't need, then... Then that someone probably would be me, I suppose... There's nothing wrong about what Kiyotaka-kun is saying at all, Haruka-chan."

"Airi!"

"Everything he said was exactly right. If someone must be expelled, then I, the biggest burden for our class, should be the one to disappear."

The most effective method would be for the person being expelled to make their supporter give up on voting opposed, directly.

"I can't!" Haruka insisted. "There's no way I could expel you, Airi! I just can't! I don't care if this class doesn't get to A!!! We'll all graduate with you, together, Airi!!!"

"No," said Airi. "Even if you could save me that way, I'm sure that I'd regret it so, so much. I think I would regret it for a long, long time if we didn't make it to Class A because of me."

"It's fine! You aren't doing anything wrong! This is just me being selfish, protecting you!" Haruka protested.

"Thank you... But I couldn't possibly put that kind of burden on your shoulders, Haruka-chan."

"What?! What do you... But that's not...!" sputtered Haruka.

Preventing a student from getting expelled was not necessarily in that student's own best interests. Now that things had reached this point, even if Haruka voted against her, it would cause Airi to suffer.

"Self-sacrifice sounds nice," I said. "It's got a nice ring to it. I'm sure that the people in this class would be deeply relieved to have someone like you in their lives, Haruka. Okay then, if it really does help make the class run smoothly, then maybe it would be a good idea for us to make a choice like that. So, hey, Sudou, are you willing to sacrifice yourself for the sake of the class?"

"W-well... I... Um..." he stammered.

"Satou, what about you?" I asked.

"M-me? Well, I, um, that's kind of..."

"Onodera, how about you?" I asked.

"I...probably couldn't..."

"Even if we ask others, their answers will be the same. Basically, no one is going to sacrifice themselves," I declared.

"Well, I truly am fine with getting expelled," said Haruka. "There shouldn't be any problem..."

"Suppose we rely on students who are willing to sacrifice themselves of their own volition," I said. "Once the class learns to do things that way, the easy way, we'll keep seeking people who will volunteer out of their own free will when we're placed in similar situations in the future. It would mean losing our last chance to make fair judgments."

"I don't care... I don't care about that kind of logic!" yelled Haruka. "I want to protect Airi! That's all!"

"Even if you protect Airi right here and stop her from getting expelled today, she could be expelled tomorrow, Haruka," I pointed out.

"Don't talk to me about an uncertain future!"

"There is no certain future anywhere. So, we have to choose the best option we can."

No matter how many arguments I strung together, Haruka wasn't hearing it, even if it seemed like she did. However, Airi *was*, and that was the important part.

"It'll be okay. It will all be okay, Airi. All right? I will keep voting opposed to your expulsion, definitely. No matter who else votes in favor, I'll—!"

"Everyone... Please...vote for me..."

Airi spoke so softly, it was like her voice would fade into the background, but it was loud enough that everyone could hear her.

Haruka grabbed both of Airi's arms, in a frantic display of resistance. "I hate this," she said. "I absolutely hate this... We were having so much fun together just until yesterday, and yet...! Even this morning was just a typical morning. I met up with Airi, and we came to school. We chatted about stupid stuff, talked about things like the cultural festival, and... And today, after class, we were going to call Kiyopon, and Airi was going to unveil her surprise! You're taking that away from me!"

We had less than ten minutes remaining in the exam. This was, essentially, the final vote. No one could easily vote *Against* this time, no matter who was going to be expelled. That was the weight this final voting session had.

Airi shook her head from side to side and did not grab hold of Haruka's outstretched hand. She was rejecting her friend's offer to save her.

"No! No, no, no!"

Haruka shouted and screamed, denying what was happening, rejecting it like a child. Every time Haruka protested, Airi tried to express her gratitude to her, but was still trying to persuade her to accept what was happening.

The situation could no longer be changed.

Haruka, understanding everything at last, sat on the ground as if she collapsed right on the spot.

"Someone who doesn't have any ability accepted the situation and came forward," I said. "We have an obligation to respond to her wishes. It would be easy for you to vote *Against* in the next vote, but even if you did that, Airi likely won't stay at this school anyway. She'd be torn apart by strong feelings of self-condemnation for having dragged her classmates into this situation, and would leave the school, unable to face forward. Haruka, the only way to save your best friend Airi is for you to vote *For* and make her face forward."

"I-I...!"

Airi hugged Haruka while she was still collapsed on the floor. "Thank you, Haruka-chan... Thank you for helping me so, so much, all this time. I couldn't give you anything in return, but... Please, listen to my final selfish request."

"I hate this, Airi... I can't..." muttered Haruka.

"Vote in favor for me."

Airi thanked Haruka, gently stroking her hair as Haruka sobbed. Then, she addressed Chabashira, speaking up loud and clear.

"I'm nominating myself. Please vote for me."

Then, after making Haruka get up and return to her seat, Airi returned to her own seat to accept everything that was about to happen. However, even after Chabashira had declared it was time, the vote didn't end as normal. Even sixty seconds, seventy seconds after the vote started, the period hadn't ended. Students had a total of ninety seconds of extra time after the sixty-second voting period. That meant that in over seventy seconds, Haruka's expulsion would be set in stone.

The thought, *if my best friend Airi is going to disappear, then I'll disappear too,* may have crossed her mind. If she chose that weak option here, then that would be that. Although the class would suffer from losing another person, we'd still come to a unanimous decision without any issues, because that would mean Haruka's vote would be eliminated. Now that 100 seconds had passed, Haruka had forty-something seconds remaining. Haruka just kept crying and showed no signs of reaching for her tablet.

"HARUKA-CHAN!!!"

There was anger in Airi's voice, something I had never heard from her before. It was also the loudest she had ever shouted.

Haruka quickly looked up in surprise, like someone had slapped her on the back. Airi looked at her crying face, smiled, and nodded. If Haruka didn't come to a decision and vote right now, then it would be denying everything Airi was doing.

"...Voting has finished," said Chabashira. "I will now show you the results."

Round 22 Voting Results: FOR: 38 Votes, AGAINST: 0 Votes

Chabashira, who had been watching the entire spectacle, forgot to report the voting results aloud. She simply stared at Airi and Haruka. Airi, with her expulsion now confirmed, just looked straight ahead as though she had accepted what had happened. On the other hand, Haruka was struggling desperately to hold back her tears. She couldn't protect her friend Airi. Despite her attempts, she couldn't hide her sobbing from the now speechless class.

"Um... Um, Chabashira-sensei," said the monitor. "*Ahem.* Please continue."

Even the monitor, who had been silent and composed throughout, only uttering the bare minimum necessary to give reminders and warnings, seemed to have forgotten to prompt Chabashira to signal to the students that it was the end of the special exam.

"Regarding the matter of the expulsion of Sakura Airi...the final issue is now complete with the class having come to a unanimous decision in favor," Chabashira said. "The decision has been validated and you will be awarded 100 Class Points. Just as a reminder, there is only one way for you to cancel her expulsion. If you had 20 million Private Points at this moment in time and you used them to..."

Chabashira was about to continue providing us with the explanation as she was obligated to do, but she suddenly stopped mid-sentence.

"Well, I suppose no further explanation is necessary," she admitted.

Hypothetically, even if we were to gather up all the Private Points everyone had, there was no way we'd come close to 20 million.

"The other three classes have already finished their special exams, so you will be heading back to the dormitories immediately. As for Sakura, you will remain in the classroom for now, but you will come with me to the faculty room afterward."

"I understand."

Although Airi responded to Chabashira quietly, unlike her shouts from earlier, she still answered without hesitation.

"That is all. Everyone, please get up from your seats and leave the room as instructed," said Chabashira.

After that announcement, we all got up from our seats, although not all at once. Airi, of course, remained where she was as instructed. Haruka couldn't seem to stand up. She struggled to get to her feet, but her knees shook, and she couldn't seem to find her balance well. Her breathing was labored, and she was starting to show symptoms of hyperventilation. Akito, unable to bear the sight, rushed over to her and helped her to her feet, forcing her to stand upright. Nothing good would have come from just leaving her here, after all.

I stepped out into the hallway right away, and my phone was immediately returned to me. Keisei came out after me and called out to me.

"Kiyotaka... I'm not going to tell you that you did the

wrong thing. It's just... Still, I... I don't know if I can say what *I* did was right, I guess. No, there's no point in me asking you this anyway... Just forget it."

Even though he still had plenty of things on his mind that he wanted to get out, Keisei turned his back to me and started walking down the hall. Even if I waited around for Haruka and Akito, it would likely be pointless. Things like justifiability were irrelevant. There was no way that they *wouldn't* feel something after I had gone ahead and thrown away a precious member of their friend group.

Kei approached me. I noticed that she seemed upset and on edge, so I stopped her with a glance. It would probably be better to have Kei settle down quietly right now as well since she was probably grieving over the loss too. There was no need for me to incur hate from others by doing something necessary.

If I remembered correctly, Chabashira mentioned wanting to meet with me after the special exam. I looked at my phone and saw that I had received a message, telling me that we were supposed to meet at six o'clock. That was a while off, so I decided that I should leave, figuring that it would be best if I didn't stick around for too long. Still, I knew if I headed straight for the entrance, I would likely bump into Keisei and other students... In any case, since I had an appointment with Chabashira, I supposed I'd just wander around the less-populated parts of campus.

I had known there was someone following me, but they didn't call out to me until there was no one else around.

"Ayanokouji-kun."

"What's up?" I asked. "I would've thought you'd be talking with Kushida."

"No, not really. I just urged her not to do anything desperate, that's all," she replied.

Kushida had many friends before the exam, but no one went to talk to her after it. It made sense—as people would've found her difficult to approach right after witnessing her intense true nature.

"I'm sorry." Horikita's hair was a little longer now than it used to be, and it swayed when she bowed deeply. "This special exam... I... I wasn't good enough..."

"Not good enough? You did the best you could though, didn't you?" I asked. "Besides, this year's exam was a much, much more difficult battle than last year's In-Class Vote."

"Still, no matter how difficult it was, you ended up with such a big burden on your shoulders... You took on all the responsibility, which should have been broken up and dispersed."

It was inevitable that someone would be expelled. That was precisely why Horikita wanted to illustrate her intentions.

"I was the one who told you to be quiet," I assured her. "It's fine."

"No, it's not fine. It left a huge scar on your treasured friend group. It's very... I can't imagine that it's ever going to recover."

"It's all right. If anything, there might come a day when they'll see this as a good thing."

If Horikita had gotten involved, then the blame certainly would have been divided equally between the two of us. I hadn't wanted that to happen.

"A good thing...? Whatever do you mean by that?" asked Horikita.

"Nothing, don't worry about it," I replied. "It's trivial."

Of course, I didn't expect Horikita to accept that and immediately change her mind about things, but I also didn't want this special exam to become something that would drag her down in the future.

"Think positively," I added. "We earned 100 precious Class Points, which will help us move up to Class A. We cannot foolishly dismiss those points."

"But...we lost Sakura-san," said Horikita.

"That's a positive, because it raised the average value of the class as a result. It was the perfect conclusion."

"Stop. You don't need to force it, trying to act cruel."

"Force it?"

I thought about denying it, but I ended up getting caught on one thing she said, deliberately repeating it back to her.

"That's right. Maybe you're trying to push away painful feelings," said Horikita.

"Kiyotaka-kun!" called a kind, familiar voice, from far down at the end of the hallway.

Horikita, startled by the voice, turned around. She was surprised to see who was approaching us.

"Wait... Sakura...-san?"

Airi, who had no stamina to speak of, was completely out of breath. She walked over to us.

"...I'll be going now..." said Horikita.

"Yeah, that's probably a good idea," I answered.

Just as Horikita walked past Airi, she tried to say something to her, but she hesitated, and ultimately said nothing. She probably couldn't think of the right words for when someone was about to leave.

"I really want to show you while I have this last chance, Kiyotaka-kun... What do you think?" said Airi.

Just before we took the final vote, Haruka mentioned that Airi wanted to unveil something. *This was it, huh?*

"You look completely different," I said. "No wonder Horikita didn't recognize you for a minute." "I guess... I was a little late in working up the courage to do it though... He he." Airi stood there with her glasses off and her hair done up in a fashionable style. She smiled shyly. "I know this probably isn't for me to say, but... Please take care of Haruka-chan."

"I understand," I answered.

"Bye-bye... Kiyotaka-kun." Airi showed me an extraordinary smile, the likes of which I had never seen before.

She then turned away from me and started to walk away. However, her steps gradually slowed town, and it seemed like she was about to come to a full stop. Even so, she desperately kept putting one foot in front of the other, pushing ahead without looking back. I could hear her wordless voice carrying down the hallway—the sounds of her sniffling and desperately fighting back tears.

The sight reminded me of something I often saw in the past. The failures would always look back on their miserable situation and be filled with regret, even though it was too late for them. It was just as true here in this school as it was in the White Room.

CLASSROOM OF
THE ELITE

9 ▶ FAREWELL TO THE PAST

T HE UNANIMOUS SPECIAL EXAM lasted for approximately five hours and was now over. Not long after, we heard that our class was the only one out of the four that chose to expel someone. It was likely that more than a few students would be strongly resentful over what happened. However, the fact that we had gained 150 Class Points from this special exam while the other three classes only got fifty was most certainly going to be a positive factor in the battles to come. If this didn't change by the time September was over, we would finally be moving up to Class B.

After school, I stood on the stairs leading up to the roof, waiting for the person I was scheduled to meet as promised. About ten minutes after our meetup time, the person in question showed up.

"Sorry to have kept you waiting," said Chabashira. "I had my hands full taking care of some things afterward. It was time-consuming."

"I don't mind. So, anyway, did you get the conclusion you wanted? Or was it the opposite?" I asked.

"Don't ask me such tough questions. Besides, there's no real correct answers in this exam... Or that's what I think, anyway. It's possible someone could see us here. Let's get moving."

"That would be wise."

The corners of her mouth raised slightly. Chabashira began to climb the stairs to the rooftop and took out a key with a simple blue nameplate on it.

"Every year, the school gets increasingly resistant to the idea of people using the rooftop," she said. "Perhaps even this school won't be an exception to the norm anymore, and it'll become difficult for anyone to come up here at all."

Even though there was a fence installed up here, there was still a danger of falling, after all. Besides, there were other issues with the rooftop as well; it could be used for nefarious purposes, like the way Ryuuen had used it before.

After quietly stepping out onto the roof, Chabashira leaned against the railing and exhaled deeply.

"Today was a long day... It really, really was."

Chabashira was simply expressing her feelings about the special exam as though she were thinking aloud.

"I mentioned this before during the exam, but...I took this same one when I was in my third year of high school."

"It sounded like it."

I wondered what she was looking at so intently. Chabashira was simply staring straight ahead at the open sky, tinged by the evening glow.

"If you don't mind...would you listen to my confession?" she asked.

"You're talking about the sacrament of penance and reconciliation, right? Well, I don't know very much about religion, but you can go ahead, if you want," I answered.

She had gone through the Unanimous Special Exam back when she was a student too. Though her class had the same issue posed to them, the look on her face suggested that what happened in her class was such a significant development that it changed her class for good.

"I remember that day like it was yesterday," she said. "We, Class 3-B, were finally on the verge of catching up to Class A. Our graduation exams were right around the corner. There was only a difference of seventy-three Class Points between us. Even though we couldn't surprise them with what little time we had left in school, we were in a position where we could have turned the tables on them with just one special exam."

An awfully close race indeed. I was sure that their Class A must not have thought they held the lead by that wide a margin either.

"Then came the Unanimous Special Exam. There were five issues in all. Just like with your class, we were able to forge ahead smoothly all the way until the fifth issue, even though there were some minor differences in opinion in the first four."

"And if I recall, you had said that your final issue was the same as ours," I said.

"That's right... That's right, I did. My memory of today's exam already seems to be a little fuzzy."

Perhaps the overlap with her past had thrown the sequence of events into disarray in her mind, confusing her on what she wanted to think and say.

"Of course, there were only a few votes in favor and many opposed in the first round," she continued. "But as the discussion went on, things started to change dramatically. If Class A voted unanimously in favor, the gap between our classes would've widened to 173 points."

"At that point, you didn't know what the graduation exam was going to be like, did you?" I asked.

"That's exactly right. You've probably already guessed as

much, but special exams don't always result in large Class Point gains, even if you win them. Even if our Class B took first place in the graduation exam, and Class A placed second, there might not have been that big a difference in the awarded Class Points."

Did that mean the difference in Class Point rewards for first and second was just 100, or maybe 150? Well, I supposed that it could have even been 200 or more, of course, but there was no guarantee of that.

"The debate heated up as time went on. There were some who argued that there was no way Class A was going to choose to expel someone and they were going to vote unanimously opposed to the issue. And if that was the case, they argued we should do the same and get through the exam by voting *Against*. After that, we should've strived to overtake Class A by beating them in the graduation exam. But there were others that enthusiastically argued that if Class A wasn't going to expel someone, that it meant it was our chance to turn things around. We discussed every possible angle."

Even if the text of the issue was the same, it ended up being completely different depending on the situation of the class. There were only two options, but the only way to arrive at one of those two was to navigate through many winding paths.

"We spent so much time on it and discussed so much, but even then we never found the right answer. Should we work on getting to Class A, no matter the sacrifice? Or should we choose our friends and throw ourselves into a difficult battle ahead...?"

She was probably remembering her past self at that very moment. When I stole a glance at Chabashira's side profile, her eyes seemed to be welling up with moisture from the rays of the setting sun.

"Eventually, little by little, our classmates' attitudes began to change. They started to feel that if we were trailing behind Class A by only a slight margin, then we should get those 100 points, no matter what the cost. As the discussion proceeded with more and more students operating on that assumption, students from the opposition camp started drifting over and joining the side *For* the issue, one by one."

"Even so, it wouldn't be that easy to come to a consensus in favor of the issue, would it?" I asked. "Considering that the result was that someone would be expelled... Students with a low level of ability or students with poor communication skills, for example, or students with one or two peculiar quirks, they would likely be the first choices for someone to expel. That much is unavoidable."

"Yes. Once you unanimously voted in favor of the issue, it was impossible to take it back. You're exactly right—no one was voting in favor so readily."

That meant that something happened to change the situation. Something like how I prompted people to vote in favor during our special exam by promising to only have the traitor expelled.

"There was a guy in my class," Chabashira said. "He was... Well, if I had to compare him to someone from your class, I suppose he was a combination of Hirata and Ike. I think that's probably the best way I could describe him."

"Yousuke and Ike, huh...I can kind of imagine it, I guess. But that's a personality that I can't quite picture all that well in my mind."

"He was earnest, but he could be kind of silly too. He was smart and was a good friend, but he couldn't read social situations all that well. He was something of a leader for our class, but at the same time, he was a class clown."

I see. From her description, that meant he was the sort of person who had both Yousuke's strengths and Ike's strengths—and downsides.

"He was struggling the entire time we dealt with that final issue. In the end, our class chose that we would vote in favor. And because of that, he took the leadership role on himself to decide who was going to be expelled."

Chabashira started gripping the railing even more tightly.

"And then...he arrived at his answer. After he brought us to settle on a unanimous decision in favor, he told us what he had decided. He said that he would nominate himself for expulsion. I guess it was probably because he decided that he couldn't just abandon his friends who he had been fighting alongside for three years by that point."

"The only exam left after that would be the final exam before graduation," I mused. "The absence of a leader would be painful, but even so, I suppose...it's not like that would be completely off the table, as an option."

Of course, you couldn't exactly call it a wise choice. But if all their classmates were close to being on even standing, it would've been extremely difficult to pick one person. It would have been possible to leave the decision up to chance, but few students would've accepted that.

"But even after that, we never came to a unanimous decision," said Chabashira.

"Why was that?" I asked. "It was agreed that the leader would be expelled though, right?"

"Well... It's because there was one student who kept voting *Against* over and over until the exam was done.

That one person never changed their vote. And eventually, they used up all their remaining time," Chabashira said. "And the person who continued to vote opposed was none other than myself."

Based on how this conversation had been going, I thought that might have been what happened, but... If that was true, then that meant...

"That means that to you, Chabashira-sensei, that student wasn't just the leader, was he?" I asked.

Chabashira closed her eyes and chuckled at herself in self-deprecation before slowly opening her eyes once again. She then looked up at the colorful sunset in the sky and confirmed what I had suspected.

"That's right... To me, he was...a leader, a friend... and...a lover. Someone more precious to me than anyone... Though we had only just started being involved at that point. There's the added irony that we had started seeing each other the day before the special exam was held."

The two of them had overcome many hardships and had come to understand one another. They were supposed to have a future where they would grab hold of the most amount of happiness that they could get in their remaining days at school while striving to end up as Class A. Chabashira couldn't let go of that.

"I knew that if I kept voting *Against*, my classmates would obviously be perplexed and angry. There were some who decided to come after me instead, making me their target. Well, that was to be expected."

"But you didn't get expelled either, Chabashira-sensei. Which means..."

"That's right," she said. "I protected him, and he protected me. We were locked in a stalemate and it dragged on and on. In the end, we were unable to finish the special exam in time, and our class was penalized by 300 points. On top of that, Class A *had* chosen to expel someone, and after the exam, that meant that there was a difference of 450 points between us. When added to their existing lead, that brought the total gap to 523 points. The distance between us and Class A had been within our reach before, but it became hopelessly vast in an instant."

That was a point difference that would be impossible to overcome, no matter how big a chance there was in the graduation exam.

"It might not be any consolation, but your boyfriend didn't get expelled, did he?" I asked.

"I don't know why I was protecting him," sighed Chabashira. "Our relationship ended right after the Unanimous Special Exam was over. It only lasted a day... No, actually, it didn't even last a full twenty-four hours...

After that, we ended up losing the final exam in a direct competition. Our three years ended with nothing."

"What happened to him after?" I asked.

"I haven't seen him since. I don't know where he is or what he's doing right now. When I was a high schooler, this school was everything to me, and he was everything to me too. Heh... Thinking back on it now, it's all so stupid. Overall, the three years you spend in high school is just a tiny part of your life. Even if we didn't make it to Class A, we should have fought until the end with no regrets."

This meant that Chabashira had been regretting the error of her choice for the past eleven years. Well, no, I supposed that in this case, it would be better to say that she continued to agonize over whether she made the correct choice or not rather than to call it an error.

"I didn't have what it took to graduate from Class A," she said. "But what was I supposed to do? Should I have aggressively persuaded him to have me expelled instead? Or should I have abandoned him after he told me that he nominated himself to be expelled...?"

"There were no real right answers in that special exam," I replied. "If you're voting purely from the heart, it would probably be impossible to come to a unanimous decision. Unless, of course, you have a student who is thoroughly incompetent and no one needs them. In that case, it'd be a different story..."

But even then, that wouldn't necessarily mean that person wouldn't have a way out.

"If I had to say anything, I think the reason your class failed was because he failed to see things through with his strategy," I said. "I think that there was only one way for your class to get to Class A, Chabashira-sensei."

"Because he failed to see things through...?" she repeated.

"When he convinced everyone else in class to give up on the idea of voting *Against*, he made the decision to be expelled himself for you to hold onto the possibility of getting to Class A. What he did was, he first brought the class to a unanimous decision in favor, and then he thought about what to do afterward."

Chabashira nodded, reflecting on what happened back then.

"So if I had let him go, then..."

"Was the graduation exam easy enough that you could've won, even without an exceptional leader?" I said, cutting her off. "Your class failed the Unanimous Special Exam even though you hadn't gotten anyone expelled, right?"

"That's right. If we had come together as one and performed flawlessly, we might've won, or we might've been evenly matched."

"Meaning that it's unthinkable that you would've chosen to be without your leader," I said. "Still, even if you were missing someone else aside from him, you still wouldn't have beaten Class A. With that in mind, the only option you could've chosen was to hold your ground between the two choices, to agree or disagree. You should have turned down all attempts, all temptation, to sway the vote to be in favor of the issue."

"But even if I had held my ground, the other students weren't in a position to be persuaded to vote against it. You admitted as much yourself, Ayanokouji."

"There wasn't any need to persuade them," I replied. "Opinions in your class were divided on how to win. If the vote wasn't united, then defeat would be inevitable once time ran out. So, when time was about to run out, those who were in favor would have absolutely changed their mind and voted *Against*. Even if they vocally resisted it, if there was just one minute remaining and it was the final vote, what do you think they would've done? If they voted in favor, there wouldn't have been time to expel anyone anyway. The interval times were fixed ten-minute periods, but the voting time was a maximum of sixty seconds. If you adjusted the timing by deliberately delaying voting periods, you could force everyone into a final vote with no wiggle room."

If those students voted *For*, the class would have failed and been penalized 300 points. But if they voted *Against*, they would pass and get fifty points. It would be impossible for anyone to choose the former in that situation.

"No matter how much those students lost their cool over it or how angry they got, there would be no way that they could look away from the reality of the situation," I went on. "Either they would run out of time and lose 300 points, or, even if it meant forgoing the additional 100 points, they could pass the exam for certain and gain fifty points and still be able to challenge Class A in the graduation exam. There would only be one conclusion to make. Of course, it still wouldn't be certain whether you could've made up for that 173-point difference though."

The students in her class were fixated on those 100 points dangling in front of them, unable to throw away their chance of winning. The leader had leveraged those students' states of mind and successfully guided the class to a decision in favor. However, that strategy in itself was a mistake. He had failed to see Chabashira's heart and her stubborn will, as the person of the other sex with whom he had a romantic entanglement.

"I... If we had a student like you around back then, then maybe..."

Chabashira was about to continue, but then stopped.

"No, it'd be pointless to say anything about it now. I can't go back to the past. But let me ask you something, Ayanokouji. Sakura must have been someone you were close with, as a member of your friend group. And moreover, she had special feelings for you."

"You're well informed," I replied.

"I'm your homeroom teacher. I can figure out lots of things just from the way my students look at me," she said. She didn't sound proud, but instead seemed somewhat exasperated. "Wasn't there a way you could've saved Sakura and sacrificed someone else?"

"I'm not so sure," I replied. "At the time, Horikita had this force about her that prevented me from saying if there was another choice or not. There wouldn't have been enough time to challenge her on it."

"You're being very businesslike about this. Didn't it... hurt, emotionally?"

"If I could've kept Airi from getting expelled, that would've been the best option, of course. As for me, personally, I tried to lead the class to a unanimous decision *Against* in every way possible, but Kushida wasn't letting me. Then, after we chose to expel someone, I decided that there wouldn't be any solution unless I cut off Kushida's every escape route and drove her into a corner. Still, while it's possible that this is just a conclusion based on hindsight, there might have been a possibility we could've come to a unanimous decision *Against*," I admitted. "At the time, Kushida's heart was in such disarray over Horikita's presence that she accepted the choice to remain at this school. I didn't foresee that at all. As it turns out, I'm not the only one who wants to help the students close to me. Anyway, I figured that since things had come to that, the only option I had left was to remove people. I had no other choice but to weigh the relative merits and flaws of my classmates. Were they academically capable or not? Athletic or not so much? Communication skills. Insights. Observational skills. All I could do was look at objective data, meaning their OAA rankings."

If you used the system the school had created, you would see who should be expelled, even if you didn't want to.

"Of course, there were a few students whose abilities aren't that much different from Airi's," I added. "However, if arguments broke out over those students, then those students' friends would naturally take their sides and defend them. But in Airi's case, the only major obstacle was Haruka. And even if Haruka nominated herself, we'd only lose ten minutes."

"Meaning that you intentionally chose one of your own friends..."

"Personality was one of the deciding factors. Taking Airi's into account, she wouldn't be good at pleading her case with people, telling them that she didn't want to quit school or appealing to them not to vote for her. That meant I could take any number of convenient measures to counter that. A good friend, in this case, Haruka, would never, ever vote in favor of Airi's expulsion. However, the exception to that rule would be if Airi herself came forward and made a statement, asking her friend to vote for her. There would be no way that Airi could choose to stay at this school after causing trouble and making the class sacrifice 300 Class Points."

"So, you even understood Sakura's mentality," said Chabashira.

"Her overall abilities, those people close to her, and her personality. And as one final push, for Airi to be told by someone precious to her that she was the person who should be expelled. If she were to hear that come from my mouth, then she'd have no choice but to understand," I said.

"Ayanokouji... You're..."

"People might call those who think like me monsters or fiends," I admitted. "No one wants to take on the role of the bad guy. Even so, I need to carry that out at times, without hesitation, when it's necessary. That'll be inevitable to protect the class, or in other words, the system."

"In this school, expulsion is always a looming threat, in every possible situation. As a teacher at this school, I'm prepared to accept that. Even so, I will never be able to make a decision like you did, without hesitation, for as long as I live," said Chabashira, admitting the weakness in her own heart. "I don't know you very well, but... how many people have you cut down without a second thought? How many people would you have to cut down to reach that level of... No, don't answer that. I'm sure that there's no way I'll ever understand."

How many people would I have to cut down, huh? I had never thought about that before. Just like you wouldn't remember the shape of every single little stone on the side of the road, both those you studied with and those who taught you would be removed and disappear if they were incompetent. That was artificial selection.

"Thank you for taking the time to meet with me today, Ayanokouji," Chabashira said. "I've been standing still for a long, long while now, regretting my past choices. But I understand now that I don't have the time to keep standing around. I will fulfill my role as a teacher and guide the students of my class so they can continue to fight without regret."

"It sounds like you've been able to bid farewell to your past through this special exam," I said.

When I saw Chabashira's face from the side as she spoke, she looked somewhat sunny, unlike moments earlier.

"Even now, it's not like I haven't been dreaming of reaching Class A," she said. "Even when I try not to think about it, I still end up hoping. I pray that I might be able to make my unfulfilled dream come true. And every time I think those things, I ridicule myself for being so stupid and erase it from my memory. I've been stuck doing that."

Then, Chabashira turned and smiled at me. It was something I had never seen her do until now.

"I've made my decision, Ayanokouji. I am going to get your class to graduate from A, no matter what it takes."

"It's all well and good to be enthusiastic, but please don't deviate from your position as a teacher," I replied.

"Hmph... Well, yes, I do understand my position, of course. There is only so much I can do, but what I mean is that I am prepared to do that much. I have to say though, every time you say something, it doesn't sound like something a student would say."

"Like what a student would say, huh? And what would have been the correct way for me to have answered you then?" I asked.

"I can't tell you that. I'm not a student," said Chabashira.

Ugh. She was such a ridiculous person.

"If we're done talking, I'm leaving," I told her.

"I understand," she said. "Sorry for taking up so much of your valuable time."

"No problem. Anyway, I'll be heading out now, Chabashira-*sensei*," I put deliberate emphasis on calling her that, even though I was already calling her as such lately.

I wondered if she thought I was just being impertinent. Chabashira-sensei smiled back at me and nodded. She'd probably be all right now. She had grown just as much as her students did through this special exam. Her heart had stopped when she was in her third year of high school, but all at once, it was beginning to catch up with her current age.

POSTSCRIPT

A S I WRITE THIS, we're already nearing the end of 2021. This is kind of a silly topic, but while I was cleaning up my house, I found my elementary school and junior high graduation yearbooks. I read through them again. In my elementary school book, I wrote that I wanted to become a game programmer, and I reflected deeply on the difficult industry I dreamed of entering. In my junior high book, I said that I wanted to write for a living, because I had no talent for drawing... (Well, that's what I *wanted* to say, but I was too embarrassed to be specific.) Anyway, I digress, but I cried when I saw that a girl I was good friends with wrote "being able to meet Kinugasa-kun" in the section about the best things that happened in junior high. I guess there are some things that are best left unnoticed, huh?

Jokes aside, the second semester of the second-year story arc has officially started. This semester is packed with major events, and the cultural festival and school trip in particular will be new kinds of stories as they were things that didn't happen in the first-year arc. I sincerely hope that you're looking forward to what's to come. Please sit tight!

Looking back on this fifth volume, almost none of the students from the other grade levels made an appearance this time. I was thinking it really *has* been a long time since there was a story like this, with just this group of characters. The stories of the first-years and third-years will continue to develop, but this volume served as a reminder that the focus of the story is on the students currently in their second year.

Moving on, I have a little announcement to make! To be honest, one of the things that I've been eagerly looking forward to for a long time but that I just couldn't seem to make a reality was a manga of the second-year arc. However, I'm pleased to announce that we've finally reached the stage where I can tell you all about it. The manga version of *Classroom of the Elite Year 2* by Xia Sasane-san will be serialized in Japan starting in the December 2021 issue of *Monthly Comic Alive*. Thank you so very much! Also, I would once again like to express my deepest thanks to Yuyu Ichino-san, who is continuing to draw the first-year arc manga. I would like to extend my gratitude to you all for turning what I couldn't do into a reality.

Lastly, there's something else that I've been keeping in the back of my mind for the past two years now, and I'm hoping I'll be able to touch upon it in the postscript for the next book, which will be volume six.

Well, the next time we meet, it will be the start of 2022! See you next year!